Dear Reader

Jilted at the altar!

An old phrase that still puts a dagger in our hearts—because we know that when it happens *someone* is suffering the most agonising pain.

In THE GREEK'S LONG-LOST SON, Stella Athas undergoes this life-changing experience. Then, just as she gets her life together and things are going well, the man who shattered her heart and her dreams makes a sudden dramatic appearance, informing her he's never going away again.

Her first instinct is to run from him—but where? It isn't that easy when neither of them wants to hurt the adorable six-year-old son they made together. How would *you*, the reader, have handled this situation? Find out what our heroine did.

Enjoy!

Rebecca Winters

Rebecca loves to hear from her readers. If you wish to e-mail her, please visit her website at: www.cleanromanccs.com

A very loyal fan who read one of my Greek romances, IF HE COULD SEE ME NOW, urged me to write Stella's story. Stella was a member of the powerful Athas Greek shipping family and a secondary character in the book. How lucky am I to have readers who get hooked on a novel and want to know more?

Stella's story, THE GREEK'S LONG-LOST SON is for you, BUFFER, with my gratitude!

CHAPTER ONE

AFTER a hard day's work negotiating prices with their overseas clients, Stella Athas left her office at the Athens headquarters a little after three o'clock in her new white Jaguar XK convertible, the first car she'd ever owned. Until she'd bought it with her own money two months ago, she'd used the old clunker estate car to get around.

Along with her new purchase, it seemed a different hairdo was necessary too. She'd always worn her dark hair long and straight, but all that had changed with the convertible, because the whole point of having the top down was to feel the sun and the breeze. It had only taken one day of whizzing around in it looking like the head of a mop for Stella to go to a beauty salon and get her hair cut in a trendy jaw-length style.

Everyone seemed to approve of her new look. Her colleagues said it emphasized the high cheekbones of her oval face. Her friends insisted it brought out the velvety texture of her midnight-brown eyes.

Her oldest brother, Stasio, teased her that she'd better watch out; she was a great beauty like their deceased mother. All the men, eligible or otherwise, had their eye on her now that she'd been seen around Athens in her flashy new sports car. When was she going to get serious over Keiko and take him for a ride in it? Didn't she know she was breaking his heart?

Stella knew that her brother was hoping she and Keiko Pappas would get together, but she'd been too burned by an experience in her past to get into an intimate relationship with another man. She preferred to remain friends with Keiko or any other guy hoping to get close to her for that matter.

As for today, she didn't want to think about anything but having fun because this marked the beginning of her three-week vacation from work. It was also the end of the school year for her six-year-old son, Ari.

Although she liked the family's town villa in

Athens well enough—after all, it had been home to the Athas clan for three generations— she was a beach girl at heart and always looked forward to their holidays on Andros with Stasio and his wife, Rachel.

When Stella had attended college in New York, she'd met an American girl named Rachel Maynard. They had become best friends at a time when Stella had been recovering from what she could only look back on now as a nervous breakdown. When Theo Pantheras had deserted her and their unborn child, she'd allowed it to almost destroy her. Of course, that had been six years ago. She'd long since recovered, but the experience had caused her to lose her faith in men.

Still, with a vacation looming, none of that mattered now. She was eager to join Rachel, who'd married Stasio and who now had two little daughters, Cassie and Zoe, who adored Ari and he them. Everyone was looking forward to being together at the family villa on Andros and at some point her brother Nikos would be arriving from Switzerland with his wife Renate to vacation with them, too.

Nikos's arrival was always a worry for

Stella, because he had a nasty temper and could make life difficult when he wanted to. Hopefully, this time he'd be on his best behavior, but she didn't know if it was possible.

Rather than be flown in Stasio's helicopter, Stella planned to drive her and Ari this visit. She wanted the new car at her disposal as she sped around the island and enjoyed the glorious summer. Tomorrow morning they'd leave early and take the ferry from Rafina. Ari loved ships of all kinds and adored being on the water. So did she and couldn't wait to get away from the city. It was starting to get overcrowded with tourists.

Once she'd pulled around the back of the house, she parked away from the trees and birds and hurried through the screened-in back porch where deliveries were left. When she entered the big kitchen, she saw the elderly house-keeper watering a plant at the sink.

"*Yiasas,* Iola. How was your day?"

She turned her gray head to look at Stella. "Busy."

"Cheer up. Ari and I will be leaving in the morning. With Stasio's family out of here, too, you'll have three weeks to take it easy and enjoy yourself." Stella gave her a kiss on the cheek. "I'm going upstairs to get packed."

"Everything has been washed and dried. You want me to bring up the luggage?"

"Thank you, but my suitcase is already in my closet. We don't need to take that much to the beach. Mine will hold both our things."

Grabbing an apple from the basket, she took a big bite and headed for the staircase at the front of the house. When they weren't on Andros, Stasio and Rachel lived at the villa on the third floor with the girls, she and Ari on the second. Nikos's suite was on the first floor next to the pool, but he was rarely here.

Once she entered her suite adjoining Ari's, she got to work. Ari had gone to spend the day with his school friend Dax, and Stella planned to pick him up at his friend's house around four-thirty. That gave her an hour.

While she started gathering tops, shorts and swimsuits for both of them, the house phone rang once. She picked up the receiver at her bedside table. "What is it, Iola?"

"You need to come downstairs. The postman has a registered letter for you that only you can sign."

Stella frowned. "Anything legal goes to Stasio's office, but you already know that."

"I told him, but he said this one is for you. He insists he has to deliver it into your hands, no one else's."

The postman could have done that while Stella had still been at the office. "I'll be right down."

What on earth was going on? Stella hung up the phone, eager to straighten out what was obviously a mistake so she could finish her packing. She hurried downstairs to the foyer and entered the front room.

"Yiasou."

The postman nodded. "You are Despinis Estrella Athas?"

"Yes." But no one ever addressed her by her birth name.

He thrust a clipboard at her. "Please sign the card on the bottom line to prove this was delivered to you personally."

"May I ask who sent it?"

"I have no idea."

Despite her irritation, Stella smiled while she wrote down her signature. "Don't shoot the messenger, right?" But her comment was wasted on the postman, who remained stoic.

He took the clipboard and handed her the letter. "I'll see myself out."

Iola followed him to the front door and shut it behind him. Stella wandered into the foyer, more bemused than anything else by the interruption. "Perhaps I got caught speeding in my new car by one of those traffic cameras. You think?" Stella quipped.

"Aren't you going to open it and find out?"

Stella had waited too long for her vacation to be bothered by anything now. "Maybe after I get back from our trip. After all, if this had been brought to the door tomorrow, I wouldn't have been here."

"But you signed for it today!"

"True. Why don't you open it and tell me what it says while I finish packing." She handed it to Iola before starting up the stairs to make inroads on her packing.

Stella fully expected the housekeeper to come rushing after her with the news, yet no such thing happened. In fact it was eerily quiet. After a few minutes Stella stepped out in the hall and walked to the head of the stairs.

"Iola?"

Total silence.

"Iola?" Stella called in a louder voice.

When nothing was forthcoming she raced down the stairs. No sign of her in the salon. "Iola?" She ran through the house to the kitchen, where she found her sitting on one of the kitchen chairs, her head in her hands. The letter lay open on the table.

As she started to reach for it, Iola grabbed it from her and pressed it to her ample bosom. "No! This is not for your eyes."

The loyal housekeeper had been with their family since Stella had been in elementary school. She knew everything that went on under their roof. Stella had no doubt Iola would defend her to the death if the situation warranted it.

"What's so terrible you don't want me to see it?" Her question was met with quiet sobs. Stella sat down on the chair next to her and put a loving arm around her heaving shoulders. "Iola? Please. Let me see it."

A minute passed before she handed Stella the one-page letter. Her eyes fell on the missive. It was handwritten in bold, decisive strokes that looked faintly familiar. Stella's heart skipped a beat.

Dear Stella:

It's been a long time since the last time we were together. After the letters I sent you came back unopened and I'd exhausted every possibility of finding you, I left for New York to work, but now I'm back in Athens for good.

I saw you walking near your villa with a boy who has Pantheras written all over him. He's my flesh and blood, too.

You and I need to meet.

I can be reached at the phone number on my office letterhead. I've also written my cell phone number here. I'll expect your call tomorrow before the day is out. Don't make me petition the court to secure my right to be with my son. That's the last thing I would want to do to either of you.

Theo.

Stella's cry reverberated against the walls of the kitchen.

As she read the letter again, Theo's name swam before her eyes. She started to get up from the chair, but her body began to feel icy. Nausea rendered her too weak to stand. There was a ringing in her ears. In the distance she heard Iola cry before she felt herself slump against the housekeeper.

When next she had any cognizance of her surroundings, she discovered she was lying on the kitchen floor. Iola was leaning over her whispering prayers while she patted Stella's cheeks with a cold, wet cloth. As the house-keeper fussed over her, a memory of the letter filled her mind.

After six years Theo Pantheras had reap-peared in her life, as if from the dead, wanting to talk to her? The very idea was so staggering Stella could hardly fathom it.

She'd known moments of anger in her life, but no amount of pain compared to the violence of her emotions against Ari's father, the man who'd come close to destroying her.

For him to think for one second she would pick up the phone and call him was too ludi-crous to comprehend. The night she'd told him she was pregnant, he'd acted thrilled and told her he would find a way to take care of her and their baby. They would get married immedi-ately despite their families being against it.

They had arranged to meet at the church, and

once Theo arrived they would get married in secret, but Theo never came and Stella never saw him again. It was as if he'd simply disappeared off the face of the earth. The pain and the shame of waiting for him pretty well shattered her. Without Stasio's love and support, and of course the love she had for her gorgeous Ari, she probably would have died.

"I'm all right, Iola," she assured her. Sheer negative adrenaline flowed through her body, driving her to get to her feet. She clung to the chair back while she waited for her head to stop reeling.

"Drink this." Iola handed her a glass of water.

It tasted good and she drank the whole thing. "Thank you."

"Theo Pantheras has obviously been stalking you. That is not good. You must call Stasio at once."

"No," she countered in a quiet voice. "That's the one thing I won't do. I have Ari to think about. This is something I intend to handle myself."

Since her parents' deaths, Stella had relied on her brother for everything. It had almost ruined his life in the process, but she wasn't a helpless teenager anymore. She'd grown into a twenty-four-year-old woman with a responsible position in the company, who'd been raising her son for the last six years.

Stasio had done more for her and her son than any human could expect of another. Her love for her brother bordered on worship. The only way to repay him in some small way was to leave him out of this. He had a wife and children he doted on, and Rachel was expecting for a third time. Stella wasn't about to impose her problems on him or his family. Never again.

She stared at Iola. "Not one word of this to anyone, especially not Nikos or Stasio. It will be our secret. You understand?"

The older woman nodded, but she said another prayer under her breath.

With no time to lose, Stella went upstairs for her purse. While there she phoned Dax's mother and told her she was coming to collect Ari. After telling Iola where she was going, she put the letter in her purse, then left the villa and drove to Dax's house.

As soon as Ari saw her, he ran down the steps of the front porch carrying his backpack and got into the car. She gave him a kiss on the cheek. "How was your last day of school?"

"Okay. We had to bring all our pictures and stuff home. Can we fly to Palaiopolis tonight?" It was the village on Andros where Stasio lived.

"No, honey. I'm planning to drive us tomorrow morning. I'd like my own car while we're on vacation."

"Hooray! I love our new car."

She chuckled. "So do I."

"Stasi says I'll be able to drive a car like this one day."

"Not for years yet, honey."

Whatever Stasio said, that was it. Long ago, when Stasio had told Stella he'd help her raise Ari, Nikos had warned Stella that Ari would always look to Stasio as his father. No other man could hope to compete. Nikos had told Stella that she should put her son up for adoption so he could have a normal life with a mother and father, but Stella wouldn't hear of it. Ari was her life! Since Theo had opted out of all responsibility, a boy could pray to have a surrogate father like Stasio.

While they waited for an old man to cross the street in front of them she glanced at her son. For six years she'd purposely concentrated on his Athas traits, but since receiving the letter from Theo, she was forced to take a second look at him.

Like Stasio, Ari was tall for his age with brown-black hair. He had Nikos's beautiful olive skin and her smile. But if she were honest with herself, his jet-black eyes, the musculature of his lean body, the shape of his hairline with its widow's peak belonged to Theo.

Pain stabbed her heart. Ari was the most adorable six-year-old in the entire world. Theo had no idea what he'd given up when he'd turned his back on the two of them. Why in heaven's name would he be interested in his child now? It didn't make sense.

She moved on. The breeze played with Ari's overly long hair. It had a tendency to curl at the tips, like Theo's…. Sometimes he held his head at an angle while he was looking at something with intensity, and again he reminded her of the man she'd once loved so completely she'd thought she couldn't live without him.

But that man who'd shown her so much love and had made her feel immortal had disappeared from her life. After realizing he was never coming back, she'd thought she was in the middle of a nightmare and would wake up. To her horror, she discovered she'd been awake the whole time. Welcome to the new reality of her life.

Remembered pain still had the power to shake her. She glanced at Ari. "Are you hungry?"

"No. Dax's mom fed us. Do you think Dax could come to Andros for part of our vacation?"

Any other time she would have said yes without thinking about it, but her entire world had been turned upside down this afternoon. She dreaded broaching the subject of his father with Ari, but if she put it off she would become more frantic than she already was. Then he'd know something was terribly wrong.

Ari had a very intuitive nature. Since she'd always been honest with him, she couldn't be any different now. When they pulled around the back of the villa, she didn't immediately get out of the car.

"Ari—before we go inside, there's something I have to tell you."

He looked upset. "Is it about Dax? You don't like him, huh."

She blinked. "Where did you ever get that idea? He's my favorite friend of yours."

"Because you wouldn't let him come with us to Andros last year, either."

Stella let out an anxious sigh. "That wasn't the reason. Dax's parents had other plans for him, remember? They took him to Disneyland. It was a surprise. That's why he couldn't come with us."

"Then how come you haven't said he can come with us this time?" He continued to look at her with those penetrating black eyes while he waited for an answer. Sometimes he could be very adult for his age. It always caught her off guard, probably because he reminded her of the Theo she had once known.

At sixteen Stella had been so shy and unsure of herself, yet he'd been tender and patient with her and he'd slowly built her confidence. When Nikos had been mean to her and made fun of her and her friends, Stella had turned to Theo, whose love and acceptance had made all the hurts go away.

Where had that man gone? After he'd disappeared from her life, she'd wanted to die.

Clearing her throat she turned to Ari and said, "Do you remember when you asked me if I knew where your father lived and I said no?"

All of a sudden she felt Ari go quiet. He nodded.

"It was the truth. I didn't know anything

about him. When I asked why you wanted to know, you said there was no reason, but I knew that wasn't true."

He didn't move a muscle.

"I...I'm afraid I haven't made it easy for you to talk about your father," she stammered.

"Stasi said he hurt you so much you got sick."

"He was right. You see, my mommy died before you were born. Then your father went away and I never saw him again. I was so sad I fell apart for a while."

To make the pain even more unbearable, Nikos had been cruel and impossible to live with back then, always siding with their father that Theo came from the wrong kind of people with no background or class and no money. A marriage between them was unthinkable. She should be thankful he was out of her life.

Sensing how traumatic the situation was, how fragile her feelings were, Stasio had taken Stella to New York to have her baby. Six months later their father had suffered a fatal heart attack. After his funeral she and Ari had stayed in New York for the next four years. With Stasio there doing business half of every month, it had worked out well for all of them, and Stella had been able to get her college degree.

Thankfully at the time, Nikos went back and forth from Athens to the family's condo in Chamonix where he skied. She rarely saw him. That was a plus.

"Because of your uncle Stasio's love and kindness, I got better. The point is, that was a long time ago and a lot has changed since then." She moistened her lips nervously. "I found out this afternoon that your father has been living in New York."

His eyes rounded. "Just like *we* did?"

"Yes." That had come as another shock. For four years they'd both lived in the same city and hadn't even known it. Incredible. "However, he's back in Athens now to stay. He…wants to see you."

A long silence ensued. She could see him digesting what she'd just told him, but before he could ask another question, she needed to tell him the rest.

"Because it's been six years and he's never come near us until now, I need to know how you feel about seeing him. You don't have to answer right now. Just think about it. If you decide you'd like to meet him, then we'll call him up, but if you don't feel comfortable, Ari, you just have to say so—okay?"

If he didn't want to meet his father, then Stella would phone him when Ari wasn't aware of it. How she would love to hear Theo's reason for wanting to be with his child after all this time!

She couldn't imagine what Theo could say that would absolve him of what he'd done to her—to them! Stella couldn't comprehend a man walking away like that with no conscience, but it happened to other women all the time.

There were a lot of amoral men in the world, but she didn't want this one to be anywhere near her son. To her horror, Theo had brought up the possibility of getting the court involved if she didn't cooperate. She couldn't bear the thought of it, so she didn't dare ignore his letter.

Ari lowered his head. "I don't want to go and live with my father. I want to stay home with you. But I'd like to see him." He reached for her.

Waves of intense love for her son swept over her. "If that's your decision, then we'll tell him together."

He squinted up at her. "Can he make me go

with him? Alex always has to go with his father to his new house and he doesn't like it."

Alex was one of Ari's friends. The situation in their home was very sad since his parents had divorced.

Her heart pounded with sickening intensity. The court could order visitation, but in the letter Theo had said he didn't want to go that route. Right now she was praying he meant it. "Let's not worry about that today."

In an abrupt motion Ari broke away from her and got out of the car with his backpack. "I'm going to call Stasi."

"No, Ari!"

That brought her son to a halt. He turned around, not quite believing her firmness. "Why can't I?"

"Because he's been forced to worry about us for too long as it is."

"But—"

"I said no." She cut him off before getting out of the car herself. "This isn't his business and doesn't involve anyone but you and me. Do you understand? After we go into the house we'll phone Dax's parents. Maybe they'll let him come to Andros with us for a few days. But whatever happens, when we get to the island, I don't want you to say a word about your father to anyone.

"Except for Iola, no one else knows he's back in Greece. You're not to tell the girls or Rachel or Stasio or Nikos. Can you promise me you'll keep quiet about it?"

"Yes." She'd thought the mention of Dax joining them might take the edge off this new worry in his life, but she was a fool to think that. After hearing his father wanted to see him, what little boy could think about anything else?

At this point Ari was horribly confused. So was she, and heartsick for him. His dark eyes filled with tears before he trudged toward the porch, leaving her devastated.

The resort Theo had built on St. Thomas in the Saronic Islands brought an influx of the elite from the major continents. The manager Theo hired said they were fast becoming the preferred vacation destination in all Greece and had the statistics to back it up.

That was always good news, but after leaving Athens to spend the night here, he'd had other things on his mind. He'd give Stella another hour to respond to his letter before phoning her. There was no telling where she was right now. Probably with her brothers while they planned a way to stop Theo cold. It would do them no good.

There was a reason for that and it lay in front of him. The velvety green of the golf course extending in two directions from the sprawling white hotel represented many lucrative investments that now ensured Theo's wealth. It took this kind of money to be on a par with the Athas dynasty.

Theo had never been a mercenary man. He still wasn't. That was why the medium-size villa he'd had built on Salamis was comfortable without overwhelming Theo's own parents and siblings with a lifestyle foreign to them.

Needing an outlet for his energy, he walked around the resort to the marina. Most of the motorboats and small sailboats were out enjoying the beautiful late afternoon. One morning soon he'd take his boy out on the calm water.

He didn't doubt his son had been exposed to every water sport imaginable, but he'd only been taught by the Athas family. There was a whole side to him he didn't know about yet that only Theo could show him because he was his father.

After chatting with a few of the employees,

he entered the hotel and headed for the manager's office. The other man had arranged for Theo to meet the new head chef and go over the various menus for Theo's approval.

Once their business was concluded, he had the office to himself. Boris, his bodyguard, stood outside the room while Theo walked over to the window that looked out on the blue sea. He pressed the digit for Stella's cell phone he'd programmed into his. Nestor Georgeles, his attorney, had his methods of obtaining information. Theo flicked on the device that blocked his caller ID.

When Stella picked up after four rings, she was still talking to someone else. He could hear another voice in the background.

"Hello?"

It was her voice. Yet it was different. It was the voice of a woman.

"*Kalispera*, Stella."

He heard her sudden intake of breath. "Theo—h-how did you—" She paused. "Never mind. I guess I shouldn't be surprised."

"I have to admit that when I drove past your villa for old-time's sake, *I* was surprised to discover you hadn't aborted our baby after all."

"Aborted?" she cried.

Just then Stella had sounded too aghast at his comment to have faked it. He clutched his phone tighter. Among Nikos Athas's many sins, he'd coldbloodedly lied to Theo about Stella getting rid of the baby.

Sickened by the possibility that she'd really gone through with it and couldn't face him with the truth, Theo had left for New York determined to start a new life and make the kind of money so his family would never know poverty again.

However, now that he was back home and had discovered he had a son, no power was going to keep Theo from him. If Nikos interfered again and tried to do his worst, it wouldn't get him or her brother Stasio anywhere. Theo was more than prepared to fight fire with fire because he intended to be a full-time father to his child.

All these years he'd accused her in his heart of doing the worst thing a mother could do. He should have known she wouldn't have done away with their child. It wasn't in her nature. But for her to keep all knowledge of their son from him wounded him so deeply, he could hardly talk. His eyes smarted.

"What did you name him?"

There was a period of silence before she said,

"I...I'm surprised you didn't find that out since you seem to know everything else." After another pause while he waited, she added, "He was christened Ari."

He sucked in his breath. "Is that an Athas family name?"

"No. I just liked it," she murmured.

Now that he knew that, he liked it, too. Very much, in fact. For the moment she was sounding like the old Stella.

In the past they'd been forced to speak quietly over the phone so her family wouldn't know she was making plans with him. She hadn't been allowed to start dating until she was eighteen, but she'd caught his eye before her seventeenth birthday. The thrill of falling in love had made both of them careless.

They'd slipped out at different times to be together. Theo had paid an old fisherman on a regular basis for the use of his wooden rowboat. There had been a protected cove on Salamis and he had always taken her there. They'd swim and then lie on a quilt spread on the sand. Theo knew he shouldn't touch her, but he couldn't help it, not when she begged him to make love to her.

She had been so giving, so utterly sweet and

passionate while at the same time being so innocent, he had told her that if they waited until she turned eighteen, they'd get married and have a real church wedding. Though they'd tried to wait, there came a day when neither of them could stand it any longer. Once they'd made love, there was no going back.

He cleared his throat, intent on learning everything about his son. There were six years to catch up on. "If you could tell me the most important thing about him, what would it be?"

"I couldn't pick just one thing." Her voice shook. "He's sweet, loving. I think he's the smartest, kindest little boy in the world."

That described the woman he'd once loved. She'd spoken like a mother who adored her son. Ari sounded the antithesis of his uncle Nikos who years before had caught up to Theo with his first volley of threats. "Stay away from my sister or you'll live to regret it."

Nikos had been watching them at church, following them while they went for walks. When his threats didn't work, he had tried to bribe Theo with money. Theo had thrown it back in his face.

A week later there had been a small fire at his parents' taverna. The police had said it was arson, but they never found the perpetrator. Someone working for Nikos had phoned with more threats, and Theo had been warned there was more to come if he didn't leave Stella alone.

When Theo's brother Spiro had been injured on his motor scooter by a luxury car driving way too fast for that time of night, Theo realized Nikos was in dead earnest.

The last time he ever saw Stella, she had told him she was pregnant. The news had over-joyed him and suddenly everything made sense. She'd been impregnated by a Pantheras. It was no wonder Nikos had behaved like a madman—Theo had violated his sister and there'd be hell to pay.

That night Theo had told her he wanted to marry her as soon as possible. They would go away and he'd get a good job to support her and the baby. They'd planned everything out and had decided to meet at the church in secret. But on the night in question, Nikos had been waiting for him in the church parking lot. He had told Theo that Stella wouldn't be coming now or ever, that she had aborted their baby and wanted to forget all about Theo.

In shock Theo had lunged for him, but he had

been beaten up by hired thugs and left for dead on the island of Salamis. After he had recovered from his injuries he'd looked everywhere for Stella, but no one had seen her. She didn't answer his calls or letters. She'd simply vanished.

Eventually he came to the conclusion that she really didn't want to see him again. It was evident her family had talked her into getting rid of the baby. *His* baby.

He shifted his weight. "I've been waiting all day for your call so we could discuss Ari. When I didn't hear from you, I decided to phone you. Where and how would you like my first meeting with him to take place?"

"I'd rather it never happened in this lifetime or the next."

A nerve throbbed at the corner of his mouth. "Then you're saying you want this handled through the court?"

"No," she blurted in agony. For a moment she reminded him of the vulnerable girl he had once known. "I have to know what you plan to do. Ari keeps a lot of things to himself. Naturally he's frightened about things."

"So am I," his voice grated. "Do you have a sense of how he truly feels?"

A groan escaped her throat. "I wish I could tell you he despises the idea of you and would prefer you didn't exist, but the truth is, I have no idea how he feels deep inside."

In other words, Ari knew his mother hated Theo.

"Today he was probably reacting the way he did to please me. He always tries to please," she explained. "Maybe more than is healthy at times."

He had little doubt that Ari hated the man who'd fathered him and then had promptly rejected him even before he was born. A six-year-old could hate just as vehemently as a fifty- or an eighty year-old. Theo was under no illusion that this would be easy. In this case the hatred would be worse because Ari would have been indoctrinated by his uncles who'd wished Theo dead long ago.

He realized he needed to be prepared for hostility from Ari that might last a lifetime. A lot of factors would enter in, beginning with the atmosphere in which Ari had been raised, the amount of hate built up against Theo on the part of Stella's family. Her parents had been against him from the beginning.

Taking into account that the Athas brothers

considered Theo the underbelly of Greek society and had done everything short of killing him to keep him away from Stella, Theo was starting off with an enormous minus handicap.

"Thank you for that much honesty, Stella." He hadn't expected it. "Since I already love him more than life itself and know you do, too, let's meet somewhere this evening to discuss him. A public place or not, whatever you prefer. Can you arrange for someone to watch him while we're together?"

"Of course, but it's not possible. I'm on Andros right now."

In other words, she assumed he was in Athens and that any plans he had for tonight were out of the question. He had news for her. "I can be there in an hour. Just tell me where you'll be exactly."

He counted a full minute while she was forced to realize he had a helicopter at his disposal. That put him in the same league with the way her family moved around. "There's a paddleboat concession on the beach in Batsi. I'll wait for you there in the parking lot at seven-thirty."

She clicked off before he could say thank you, but it didn't matter. Progress had been made. The gods had been with him today.

He checked his watch. It was six-thirty. After phoning the pilot to give him their next destination, he rang the manager to say goodbye, then headed for the helipad with Boris.

Theo had never been to Andros, but Stella had told him so much about it, he felt like he knew its special places by heart. Certainly his son, young as he was, could probably show Theo around and know what he was talking about.

Andros was the home of the legendary Stasio Athas, where some of the most elite Greek families lived. To the people in Theo's family it represented lala land. A smile broke one corner of his mouth. This Pantheras member was about to trespass on ground not meant for untouchables.

Stella's elite family viewed other families like Theo's, who lived close to the poverty line, at the bottom of the food chain. When Theo had refused the money Nikos had thrust at him to stay away from Stella, Nikos had snarled words like *scum* and *untouchable* among the many insults hurled at him. Nice people, Stella's family.

He looked out the window. Summer had come to the Cyclades. As Andros came into view, his breath caught at the lush green island dotted with flowers. No wonder Stella loved it here. St. Thomas was idyllic, but it didn't compare in the same way.

After the helicopter had dropped down over the little port of Batsi, his gaze swerved to a white convertible sports car driving along the road at a clip toward the water. The sight intrigued him. Once the chopper touched ground, he jumped down and started across the wooded area to the car park where it had just pulled to a stop.

To his surprise he saw a well-endowed brunette woman climb out and walk around the area with confidence, as if she were searching for someone. Closer now, he noticed she bore a superficial resemblance to the lovely long-haired teen of Theo's youth.

Stella.

CHAPTER TWO

THE years had turned the only Athas daughter into a gorgeous female, whose classic white dress was cinched with a wide belt, highlighting curves above and below her slender waist. She'd always been beautiful to Theo, but having the baby had caused her to blossom.

Her high cheekbones, combined with the lovely contours of her face and glossy hair made her so striking, he couldn't look anywhere else.

He'd wondered how much she might have changed. What he hadn't expected was to feel his senses ignite by simply looking at her again. That wasn't supposed to happen, not when she'd kept all knowledge of their child from him.

Another step and their eyes met. Those velvety brown eyes he remembered so well stared at him with a mixture of shock and anxiety. After what she'd done, she ought to be terrified of him. She seemed to weave for a minute before she wandered back to her car and held on to the frame as if needing support.

He strolled up to the other side of the car. Deciding they were too much of a target for any observers, he climbed in the passenger side and shut the door. She hesitated before following suit.

The second she sat behind the wheel, her fragrance reached out to him. Again he was stunned because it was the scent he would always associate with her. It took him back to the last time they were together. Everywhere he'd kissed her, she'd tasted delightful, like fresh flowers on a warm spring morning.

Right now it was the last thing he wanted to be reminded of, but trying to blot out certain intimate thoughts was like attempting to hold back a tidal wave.

He turned to her, sliding his arm across part of the seat. She'd averted her eyes. If he wasn't mistaken, she was trembling. On some level it pleased him she wasn't in total control.

"Thank you for meeting me, Stella."

"You didn't leave me a choice." Her words came out jerkily.

"Actually, I did."

"You're talking about court. I can't imagine anything more terrifying for Ari," she cried, sounding desperate.

"Believe it or not, it frightens me even more. Too much time has been lost as it is." It surprised him how much he wanted to reach out and touch her, to see if she was real. "You were always lovely before, but you've turned into a startlingly beautiful woman."

If anything, her features hardened at the compliment.

His gaze drifted beyond her face. "Strange how this little secluded stretch of beach reminds me of—"

"Don't." Her profile looked chiseled. Apparently she'd had the same impression and didn't want to travel down that road of remembered ecstasy. "I agreed to meet you so we could talk about the best way to help Ari deal with this situation."

A situation that had been put in play six years ago and was never of his choosing, but he didn't voice his thoughts. For the moment Theo was walking on eggshells. "Do you think he'd be more comfortable meeting in Athens than here?"

She kneaded her hands, drawing his attention to her beautifully manicured nails. He grimaced to realize every part of her body looked quite perfect to him. It was impossible to eye her dispassionately. "Ari won't be comfortable anywhere with you, but since we're staying on Andros for a while, it should probably take place here."

"What have you told him about me?"

She sucked in her breath. "Very little."

"Even so, could you spell that out for me?"

Suddenly she jerked her head in his direction. Those gorgeous brown eyes pierced his with laserlike intensity. "You mean the way you spelled it out for me?" she cried. Her hands had gripped the steering wheel with enough force he imagined she could bend it. "I told him the truth, that you didn't love me after all, so we never saw each other again. That was all I knew to tell him. It's all he knows."

Theo studied her features. "Yet you left out half the story. It's time he heard that *you* stopped loving me. I'm sure he has no idea that you never intended to come to the church and go away with me so we could be married and have our baby in peace."

The blood seemed to drain out of her face. "I was there, waiting inside the back of the nave. I waited for hours," her voice throbbed.

Theo was incredulous. "That's an interesting fairy tale. I was attacked before I could make it inside and was told that you got rid of our baby because you didn't want anything to do with me." For now he didn't want to mention Nikos's name and give her something else to fight him about.

"You're lying!" she lashed out. "No one would believe such a monstrous story."

"In the beginning I didn't, either, not until you never, ever tried to make contact with me again. Obviously, this is a case of your word against mine, except I have the scars to prove it."

"What scars?"

"The ones you're looking at. While we've been talking, I've felt your eyes on me. They're traveling over the small cuts, noticing the dents where my face got smashed in and my nose had to be rebuilt. These are nothing compared to what my X-rays show below the neck."

Stella quickly concealed her glance, but not

before he glimpsed confusion in those dark brown depths. That was something, at least.

"Whatever happened to you," she finally said in a less-than-assured voice, "don't you think it's stretching it just a little to take six years before showing up?"

"Under ordinary circumstances, yes, but after you were nowhere to be found and all my mail to you came back unopened, I realized I would have to return to Greece and hire a PI to locate you. Unfortunately, I didn't have that luxury at the time, not when I was building a business I couldn't leave."

Her head whipped around. "I don't know what mail you're talking about."

Theo reached in his trouser pocket for the first letter he'd sent to her after he'd gotten out of the hospital. He'd addressed it to Stella at the Athens villa. It had the canceled stamp and date. Across the bottom the words "Addressee Unknown" had been scrawled.

"Take a look." He handed it to her. "If you're ever curious enough to read what's on the inside of the envelope, then you'll know my state of mind at the time. In the meantime, I'm here to claim what's mine—Ari."

She glanced at the front of it before tossing the letter back at him. "Ari's not yours," she said in an icy voice he didn't recognize.

He put the letter back in his pocket. "Let me phrase that a better way. He's both of ours."

She threw her head back, causing those glistening dark strands to splay across her jaw. Combined with her golden skin, she was a miracle of womanhood. "You gave him life, but that's all you did."

"That was all I was allowed to do," he countered. "Since you clearly don't believe me, let's not talk about the past. It's over and done with. I much prefer to discuss Ari's future. Perhaps you could bring him here tomorrow so we can get acquainted. We'll let him choose what he'd like, or not like, to do. How does that sound?"

Her body stirred in agitation. "You can't expect too much, if anything, Theo."

As if he didn't know. "I'm aware of that. What time shall I meet you both?"

She started the car. "Tomorrow's Sunday. We have plans." She was stalling, but he had to be patient if he hoped to get anywhere with her. "The day after would be best. One o'clock."

"I'll be here. Stella, I swear I'll treat him with the greatest consideration possible. I'm not unaware he wouldn't be the marvelous boy he is if you weren't his mother. You were meant to be a mother, Stella. Every child should be so lucky."

Though they weren't touching, he could feel her trembling. "Y-you can have two hours with him if he's willing," she stammered.

"That's more than I'd hoped for. The Stella I once knew was a giver. Remember that little heart I gave you?" It had been a cheap trinket he'd bought her in the Plaka because it had been all he could afford, but the sentiment had described her. "Love the giver."

She revved the engine, obviously not liking being reminded of anything to do with their past. "Please get out of the car. Ari's waiting for me."

There was a time when she would have begged him not to leave. Of course, back then he wouldn't have gone anywhere because he'd needed one more kiss, one more embrace before wrenching his mouth from hers. Damn if he didn't need her mouth so badly right now he was ready to explode.

Forcing himself to act, he got out of the front seat. "I love your car by the way. With its classic lines, it looks like you. In case you didn't know, that white dress was made for you."

For an answer she backed out and drove off.

Stella only made it two kilometers before she had to stop the car for a minute. She buried her face in her hands. How was it possible Theo could get under her skin like this after the pain she'd undergone at his hands?

Inside of half an hour he'd pushed every button until she'd wanted to scream. But what truly haunted her was the change in his facial features.

As far as the gradation of male beauty was concerned, Theo had been a beautiful man before. If she were honest with herself, he still was. However, one scar pulled at the corner of his mouth a little. His right eyelid didn't open as wide as the other. At some angles it gave him a slightly sinister look. His nose was still noble, but there were several bumps.

Theo hadn't lied about the damage done to him. As he got out of the car, she'd seen the scar below his left earlobe. A thin white line ran down his bronzed neck into the collar of his dark blue shirt.

The rest of his tall body covered by his

elegant clothes revealed he'd grown into a powerfully built man. She didn't want to think about
the damage beneath the surface he'd referred to,
the kind an X-ray could detect.

He had an aura about him that hadn't been
obvious six years ago, but that was because
he'd needed time to mature. Other men would
be intimidated by him now. She bit her lip
because she recognized that women would be
irresistibly drawn to him.

While deep in torturous thought, she heard
his helicopter pass overhead. Embarrassed that
he might think she'd had to pull over because
of her reaction to him, she started driving
through the cobblestone streets of Batsi toward
Stasio's villa in Palaiopolis.

En route she picked up some toiletries in the
village, proof of the reason she'd had to go out
for a little while. She'd left the boys swimming
in the pool with Rachel and the girls.

Unless Ari had let something slip to the
family by mistake, she felt relatively confident they could keep Theo's presence a secret
so they could get through this holiday without
anyone being the wiser. On Monday she would
tell the family she was going to drive the boys

around the island as Dax hadn't been to Andros before.

Stasio worked so hard. Now that he'd taken three weeks off work to enjoy his wife and children, she didn't want her problems to mar their families' precious time together. Hopefully when Nikos arrived, he wouldn't cause trouble.

He'd been wildly against her keeping Ari. In his opinion it wasn't fair to their parents' wishes, nor to Stella, who didn't have a husband and who couldn't give Ari what adoptive parents could. He'd been furious at Stasio for helping her, telling him he should have kept out of things.

She knew Nikos didn't like Ari. Her son knew it, too, thus the reason he clung to Stasio who openly adored him. That Nikos couldn't show Ari affection caused Stella perpetual sadness and made it hard for her to be around him. A long time ago she had decided he didn't have the capacity to be happy, especially after their parents died.

Perhaps it was wicked of her, but a part of her hoped he might decide not to come this holiday. With the advent of Theo in their lives, Ari had enough going on without worrying about Nikos. But maybe she was getting way ahead of herself. It all had to do with Theo, who was well and truly back in Athens, demanding to spend time with her son.

His son, too, her conscience nagged.

No matter what terrible things had happened to Theo, surely it was too late for him to start up a relationship with Ari that should have begun at his birth?

Hot tears rolled down her cheeks. The agony of his rejection and the desolate years that followed could send her over the brink if she allowed herself to dwell on that night-mare. No more.

All she wanted was to be able to provide a wonderful life for Ari. She wasn't about to let Theo suddenly show up and turn their lives into chaos. Did he really think she would believe that the letter he'd shown her was authentic? She wiped the moisture from her cheeks before entering the gate that led up the drive to Stasio's villa.

Apparently she'd arrived in time to join everyone for a motorboat ride followed by dinner further up the coast. It was probably Stasio's idea because he knew Ari liked to steer part of the time, with Stasio's guidance of course. Undoubtedly Dax would get a turn, too. An evening out on the water sounded heavenly to her.

Stasio helped her into the boat with a hug. Her handsome brother looked so happy, she knew her secret was safe for the moment.

Theo flew to Andros on Monday at noon. He'd brought a backpack filled with treats and a few other essential items. Not sure what Ari would like to do, Theo had opted to wear casual trousers with a navy T-shirt and hiking boots. Today he would let Ari make all the decisions.

After grabbing a sandwich and a drink at a nearby taverna with Boris, he strolled over to the concession area to watch for Stella's car. It hardly seemed possible this day had come. He'd been dreaming of it for too long. This morning he'd awakened wired, unable to concentrate on his work.

The beach had filled up with tourists. He would have preferred not to be around a lot of people, but he had to follow Stella's lead if he wanted to gain a modicum of trust. While he tried to imagine his son's thoughts, his heart picked up speed as he spied Stella's car.

Riding with her were two boys of the same age sharing the passenger seat. One dark, the other blond, they pulled into the parking area. Stella had sprung a surprise on him. If she felt there was strength in numbers, that was all right with him. He'd deal with it.

Adjusting his pack to his shoulders, he approached the car. "Hello, Ari," he said, smiling at his son, who had on khaki shorts and a soccer jersey. He was on the lean side with black-brown hair; the kind of handsome child every man dreamed of fathering. The sight of him and his mother caused Theo's breath to catch in his throat.

He studied his son. The only thing that was going to guarantee any success at all was the purity of Ari's spirit and Theo's unqualified love for the child who was part him, part Stella. If their boy had inherited her sweetness, her loving nature, then maybe Theo had a prayer of getting through to him. But he knew it would have to be on Ari's timetable.

"Hi," he responded without enthusiasm, refusing to look at him.

"Who's your friend?"

"Dax."

"Hi, Dax. I'm glad you came. I want to get to know Ari's friends. I think there's a character on the *Star Trek* television series with your name? He has special powers."

Dax blinked. "I already know that. How did *you* know?"

"I love science fiction. Especially UFO stories."

"Me, too. My dad thinks they're stupid though."

"Well, I don't."

"Rachel knows some real ones," Ari said, drawn into their conversation in spite of himself.

"Who's Rachel?"

"My aunt. Her daddy was a pilot in the air force."

Theo's eyes took in Dax, who wore jeans and a tank top. Stella had put on trousers and a white blouse that her figure did wonders for. Considering everyone's attire to be appropriate, he made a decision.

"Your mother told me we would only have two hours today, Ari, but I think it's long enough to go for a hike. What do you say we all go?"

"That sounds cool," Dax responded enthusiastically.

Ari stared at Theo in surprise.

"You mean Mom, too?"

"She and I spent all our time outdoors. We must have walked all over Salamis Island. There's no one I'd rather trudge up a mountain with. In fact, I'd like to see if she can still keep up with me."

Theo moved around the other side of the car and opened the door for Stella, who looked at a total loss for words.

"I...I didn't plan to come with you." Her voice faltered.

"Please, Mom?" Apparently this idea pleased their son. With his mother along, he wouldn't be so afraid. Theo couldn't ask for more than that. She would have trouble refusing.

"I second the motion," Theo murmured. "You know all the secret places around here. I remember you telling me about the deserted lookout on the mountain behind us where you once found an eagle's nest."

Again Ari looked surprised. He stared at Stella. "I've never seen it."

"That's because I've never taken you hiking up there, honey."

Good. This would be a new experience for the

four of them. "Let's find out if it's still there, shall we? I've brought enough goodies for all of us."

Everyone was looking at her. She could hardly say no. Stella would walk through fire to protect their son. "Well, all right."

While the boys got out, Theo assisted her. The sight of those long, elegant legs covered in khaki raised his blood pressure. When their arms brushed by accident, it sent a rush of desire through his body so intense he was staggered. To his chagrin, everything about her appealed to him more than ever.

"Ari? I bet you know how to put the top up on the car for your mother." The boy nodded, but Theo could tell Ari hadn't thought of it until it was mentioned. "That's good. We want it to be safe while we're gone. This car's a beauty," he said, eyeing Stella. She looked away.

"Will you let me do it, Mom?"

"I'll help," Dax volunteered.

"Yes. Of course." She'd been outvoted and outmaneuvered. Nothing could have pleased Theo more. He helped the boys and made easy work of it.

Once she'd locked the car with her remote, Theo opened his pack. "Give me your purse."

Though he sensed she was fighting him every step of the way, she had to be careful in front of Ari. After she'd handed it to him, he zipped the compartment and eased it onto his shoulders a second time.

"If everyone's ready, there's a footpath beyond that copse of trees running up the side of the valley. Last one to the lookout is a girlie man."

Both boys laughed. Dax asked, "What's that?"

"A phrase I picked up while I was living in New York. It means wimp!"

Ari's smile faded. He stared hard at him as they walked. "Mom and I used to live in New York."

That was where she'd gone? Where she'd been for so long?

It was an astounding piece of news, despite the fact that he knew Stasio did business there on a regular basis. To think Ari had been living in the same city where Theo had worked... So close? It slayed him. "Did you like it?"

"Yes, but I like Greece better."

"So do I."

"Come on, everyone," Stella urged. "At this pace we'll never get there." Theo wondered what had made her so nervous that she'd been a little short with Ari just now. A tight band constricted his breathing. By the end of their hike he intended to find out.

"I've never been to New York," Dax muttered.

"It's an exciting city."

"I thought you lived in Greece."

"I did until my twenties, Dax, then I moved to New York to earn my living. Now I have an office in Athens and am back to stay." Stella walked ahead of him with Ari, but he suspected she was listening to make sure the conversation didn't touch on things she wanted kept quiet.

"What do you do?"

"I deal in stocks and investments. Some real estate. What does your father do?"

"He owns a bank."

Of course. Dax belonged to the approved sector of Greek society. "Does your mother have a job, too?"

"No. She stays home with my brother and sister and me."

"You're very lucky. Do you know my mother still helps my father run their taverna on Salamis? I can't ever remember when they weren't working. Sometimes I wished my mother could stay home with me and my brothers, but we were too poor. She had to work."

"Is she a cook?"

Theo smiled. "She's a lot of things. The other day I told her she and papa didn't have to work anymore because I planned to take care of them from now on. Do you know what she said?"

Dax looked up at him. "What?"

"'I've worked all my life, Theo Pantheras. If I didn't have work, I wouldn't know what to do with myself.'"

Ari slowed down and turned around. "Do they know about me?" Stella looked back. The pain in her eyes as she reached for their son tore him apart.

"They know all about you and hope the day will come when you might like to meet them."

To ease the moment, Theo pulled off his pack and opened a compartment. "Let's see. I've got water, oranges, peanuts, hard candy. Who wants what before we race the rest of the way?" The relief on Stella's face needed no explanation.

Once they'd refreshed themselves, Theo stood next to a pine tree. "I'm going to count to twenty while you two guys head up the trail first. Take my binoculars, Ari. If you see something exciting, shout."

The second he started counting in a loud

voice, they took off on a run. It was steeper in this section and the trail zigzagged up through the forest. "Twenty!" he called out at last, then eyed Stella. "Are you ready to try catching up to them?"

"Just a minute, Theo."

"What's the matter? Are you about to tell me I've done everything wrong?"

Her chest heaved with the strength of her emotions. "Don't pretend you don't know you've done everything right," her voice shook. "Inviting Dax along made Ari feel comfortable."

"I thought that was why you brought him with Ari."

"No. I was going to take Dax on a little tour of the island while we waited for you, but your idea was much better." She wouldn't make eye contact with him.

"Then you're angry because I got you involved in the hike. When I saw Ari's face stripped of animation, I made an impulsive decision hoping it would help our son."

She wiped the palms of her hands against her womanly hips in a gesture of nervousness he'd seen many times years ago. He would always be touched by her vulnerability.

"Your instincts were dead on," she admitted. "I didn't expect him to have a good time today. Instead I…I have the feeling he won't be averse to seeing you again," she stammered. "That's what I need to talk to you about."

He chewed on some more peanuts. "Go on."

She cleared her throat. "We're here on vacation for two and a half more weeks." After a pause she leveled a guarded brown gaze with its hint of pleading on him. "Before you ask to see him again, would you wait until we're back in Athens?"

Two and half weeks sounded like a lifetime. "Of course I will," he answered in a husky tone without hesitation, "provided you tell me why you're so frightened for any more visits to take place here."

"I'm not frightened." Yet her whole trembling demeanor told him otherwise.

"Yes, you are." Without conscious thought he grasped her cold hands. "I take it your family is here and you haven't told them about me yet." Stella tried to pull away, but he drew her closer. "They're going to find out through Ari or Dax. You can't keep something of this magnitude a secret."

"Maybe not, but I'm hoping to deal with everything after we're back home in the city."

He grimaced. "It's like déjà vu, the two of us sneaking around to see each other without your family knowing what's going on. Nothing's changed has it."

"Please let me go." She tried to get away, but he still had questions.

"It wouldn't be because you're afraid to see me again, would it?"

"Theo—"

"Do my scars repel you so much?"

"Your scars have nothing to do with anything!" Her anger sounded genuine enough to satisfy him on that score.

"Then stay here with me for a little while."

"I can't!"

"That isn't what you used to say to me."

"You mean until you left me waiting at the church?"

"We've already been over this, Stella. I told you I came for you, but I was accosted. When I was able to search for you, you'd disappeared on *me*."

A strange cry escaped her throat.

His hands slid up her arms where he could

feel the warmth of her skin through the thin material of her blouse, seducing him. He gave her a gentle shake. "Do you honestly believe I wouldn't have come to the church unless a life-and-death situation had prevented me? You and I talked marriage long before I found out I'd made you pregnant."

Her eyes filled with tears. "I don't want to talk about it. The boys might see us."

"They're at least a kilometer away by now. We *have* to discuss this at some point." He slowly relinquished his hold on her.

She shook her head, backing away from him as if the contact had been too much for her. "I don't know what to believe about anything. If you'll please give me my purse, I'm going back to the car while you join the boys."

He took several deep breaths to calm down while he got it out for her. The fact that she needed to run away from him meant it was possible his logic was getting through to her. His heart leaped. "Will you be all right going back alone?"

"That's an odd question to ask when you haven't been around in years. Please go and catch up to the boys. This is unfamiliar territory to them."

"I'll bring them back safely."

She darted away like a gazelle, leaving him bereft. He watched until he couldn't see her anymore, then he hurried up the mountain filled with new energy.

The Stella he'd loved to distraction was still there beneath her defenses, breathing life back into his psyche. He'd forgotten he could feel like this. In time he would get answers to why she never tried to get in touch with him again. She wasn't going anywhere now. Neither was he.

Before long he discovered the boys at the outlook. Dax had the binoculars trained on something. When he saw Theo, he pointed to an area along the ridge, then handed them over. Theo raised them to his eyes.

"You have a sharp eye, Dax. That's an Elenora falcon having fun with a friend."

They weren't thirty meters away. He handed the field glasses back. "Just like you and Ari."

Dax laughed, but there wasn't a glimmer of a smile from Ari's lips. Theo hadn't expected much positive reaction from his son yet and he wasn't getting it. To make progress he was going to have to practice infinite patience if he hoped Ari would let him into his life, let alone show him love.

Stella had received his promise that he wouldn't try to see Ari again until they were back in Athens. He had to honor it, but he didn't have to like it.

"I hate to break this up, but your mother is waiting for us." He opened his pack. "Finish off whatever's left and we'll go."

The boys needed no urging to eat the snacks. Theo packed the binoculars and they took off down the mountain.

Stella had already put the top back down. She looked as composed and untouched as before. Much to his satisfaction Theo could see the little nerve throbbing madly at the base of her throat, giving him irrefutable proof to the contrary.

When they reached the car, he checked his watch. The outing had taken three hours. More time with his son than he'd expected. He studied Stella's profile while he fastened the boys' seat belts and shut the door. "You guys were great sports today. I had one of the best times I've ever had. Maybe we can do it again some time."

Dax high-fived him. "It was awesome."

Ari squinted at him. "Is that your helicopter over there?"

His son didn't miss much. "Yes."

"Who's that man walking around?"

"My bodyguard. His name is Boris."

A short silence ensued. "Stasi has one, too." And his own hit men who included Nikos, but Ari wouldn't know that. "Are you going back to Athens now?"

Theo thought about his question. Ari probably couldn't wait to get rid of him. But fool that Theo was, he'd dared hope he detected a forlorn tone in his son's question. Then again it was possible Ari was just being curious. Hell— Theo didn't know what to think.

Ari was his son, a boy he'd only known for three hours. The horror story of the past shouldn't have happened. His pain was starting all over again in a brand new way. "Actually I'm flying to my home on Salamis Island."

"Do you live with your mama and papa?" Ari asked quietly.

They are your grandparents, Ari. "No. They live in Paloukia, upstairs above the taverna." Ari wouldn't know what that would be like to live with so many bodies thrown together in a small space. So little privacy. The walls thin. Hand-me-down clothes. The smells from the kitchen permeating everything. "My house is on the beach about ten minutes away from them."

"Oh."

"Thank you for a fun hike, guys."

"It was cool!" Dax cried with enthusiasm. Nothing from Ari of course. Stella had averted her eyes.

Theo wheeled away from them and strode toward the helicopter. He didn't dare look back or he wouldn't want to leave.

CHAPTER THREE

FOR one crazy minute a sense of loss swept over Stella, the kind she used to feel every time she had to leave Theo and hurry home.

No— This couldn't be starting all over again. She wouldn't allow it.

Like the other day she found herself speeding toward the villa while Theo's helicopter flew overhead. But there was one difference. This time she didn't stop to give in to her emotions or relive feeling Theo's hands on her again. Today he'd caught her off guard. Never again.

"When we get back and anyone asks, remember that we drove around, got some treats and stopped at Batsi to do some paddle boating. Do you guys think you can handle that?"

Dax nodded. Ari didn't say anything, but she knew he'd keep quiet. She wasn't surprised he was in a state of shock. A full dose of Theo Pantheras for three hours would awe any child, especially when the bigger-than-life man was his own father.

Once they reached the villa and the boys hurried to Ari's room to change into their swimsuits, Stella went straight to hers to call Dax's mom and assure her all was going well. This was the boy's first trip away from his parents with her and Ari. It was an experiment of sorts. So far Dax seemed perfectly happy. Theo had made the outing so exciting she doubted the boy had given home a thought.

She sat down on the side of her bed to phone her. As soon as they talked, maybe she'd be able to enjoy the holiday she'd been looking forward to before Theo had burst on the scene like one of those UFOs they'd talked about earlier.

That particular conversation had been a natural icebreaker in ways Theo couldn't possibly have imagined. For his age Ari showed an interest in science fiction on an adult level. After the talks with his aunt Rachel, he was determined to be an astronomer when he grew up and search for new galaxies with life on them.

All this time Stella had thought he'd picked

up this passion from his aunt, but now she was convinced he'd come by it through his Pantheras genes. Ari had several of the *Star Trek* series on DVD. Who could have guessed Theo was a *Star Trek* junkie too? It only showed Stella how little she knew about Theo.

"Stella?"

"Hi, Elani."

"How's it going with my boy?"

"They're having a terrific time. We just got back from a hike, and now they're going to swim."

"No problems yet?"

She smiled. "Not one." For the next few minutes she told her everything they'd been doing, only leaving out the details that Theo had been along. After Stella got back to Athens, she would confide in Elani about him. For now the episode on the mountainside when she'd been alone with Theo would be her secret. That was a mistake she wouldn't be making another time.

"Promise to let me know if there's any trouble with him and we'll come for him."

"So far so good, my friend. I'll make certain he calls you tonight before he goes to bed. I'm sure he'll want to."

"You're an angel, Stella. Talk to you later."

They both hung up.

Stella sat there in a daze, her thoughts on Theo. Though he might have killed her love long ago, the way he'd treated their son today convinced her he didn't want to make any mistakes with Ari.

She went over the day's events in her mind. He hadn't tried to influence Ari unduly or put fear in him with underlying threats of any kind. The truth was, he hadn't done one thing wrong. Not in front of their son.

The other part had been her fault for not telling Ari to go hiking alone with his father. Instead she'd let his apprehension persuade her to join all of them for the hike.

Except that wasn't the whole truth, and this was the part she hated admitting to herself. When Theo conned her into going with them, it hadn't been Ari she was thinking about.

Her curiosity over the man he'd become had been her Achilles' heel. In that moment of weakness she had given in and it had almost cost her her soul all over again. Would she never learn her lesson when it came to Theo?

She jumped up and hurried into the bathroom to put on her bathing suit. Amazing that on the way to meet Theo in Batsi, she'd imagined the outing would end in disaster, but nothing could have been further from the truth.

Stella was in shock. A new Theo had risen from the ashes, yet in all the ways that counted, she found him to be remarkably similar to the younger man. That Theo had stolen her heart before hurling it into the void where it could never be recovered.

Now he was back with a different explanation of what had happened the night she'd waited for him at the church. Wherever the truth lay, it had happened too long ago to do anything about now. The damage had been too pervasive for too many people. You couldn't go back and pick up the pieces. It wasn't possible.

"Mom?" Ari came running into her room.

"I'm in the bathroom changing!" Mortified that Theo was still on her mind, heat stormed her cheeks. "I'll be right there! I had to phone Dax's mother first."

"Aunt Rachel wants to know if you're coming out to the pool."

"Of course!"

"She says Stasi's starving and wants to eat outside now."

When her brother got hungry, it was wise to

feed him. "Tell her I'll be right there," she called from the doorway. A second later she walked in the room with her towel and discovered Ari still standing there. Dax had to be downstairs. If Ari didn't want to talk, he would have run back to the pool.

"What is it, honey?"

He stared at her with the most somber expression. "Does my father want to see me again?"

Naturally it was about Theo. "You know he does. That's why he went to all the trouble to take you on a hike today."

"But he didn't say anything before he left in his helicopter, so does that mean he changed his mind about me?"

Was it fear or hope she heard in his question? "Ari, come here." She sat on the end of the bed. He walked over to her. "While we were alone, I told him our family is on vacation right now and asked him if he would wait to plan another visit until we get back to Athens. I hope that eases your mind a little."

By his frown, it appeared her answer didn't satisfy him. She began to realize there was nothing she could say to help him right now.

"Will I have to go with him?"

She sucked in her breath. "I tell you what. If you don't want to be alone with him, I'll go with you again next time." She searched his eyes. "He was nice to you today, wasn't he?" Her son didn't say anything. Stella couldn't tell what was going on in his mind.

Ari stared at his feet. She recognized that look of uncertainty. "Did your father frighten you today in some way I don't know about? You have to be honest and help me understand."

He shook his head. "No."

"But he did upset you, didn't he."

"Yes."

He dashed out of the room leaving her totally desolate. She hurried through the myriad of corridors and down some steps to catch up to him. When she reached the patio he was just jumping in the pool.

"Oh, good!" Rachel called to her. "Stasio! Come on out! We're ready to eat."

Stella found Dax and made sure he filled his plate. She fixed herself some food too and sat on the swing next to him because Ari was still swimming.

Speaking in a hushed tone she said, "Did you really have a good time today?"

He nodded. "It was great!"

"Then could you tell me what Ari's father did that seemed to upset Ari? Do you know anything?"

"No, but he got mad at me."

She frowned. "Mr. Pantheras got mad at you?"

"No. Ari."

"He did? When?"

"When we got back to the house he wouldn't talk to me and started playing with the girls."

That didn't sound like Ari. "I'm sorry, honey. His behavior doesn't have anything to do with you."

"He told me I should go home."

Stella hated hearing that. "He didn't mean it, Dax. Of course your feelings got hurt, but he'll get over what's wrong and apologize. After dinner I'll have a talk with him." *Another one.* "I bet he tells you he's sorry before we finish eating."

Except that Ari didn't do anything typical for him. He stayed in the pool, refused to eat and teased Cassie until she got out of the water and ran to her mother in tears. Even Stasio was aware something was wrong and got in the pool to talk to him.

But Ari wasn't having any of it and left the patio on a run. Stasio sent her a questioning glance. This wasn't good.

"Excuse me for a minute, Dax. I'll be back."

With a pounding heart she chased after her son. When she caught up to him, he was on the verge of locking his bedroom door.

"Ari—" She crushed him in her arms, refusing to let him go.

It didn't take long before the sobs came. In his whole life she'd never seen him convulsed like this.

"Tell me what you're feeling, darling. Let me help," she begged. "I know you're upset over your father."

"I don't want to talk about him."

"Then we won't."

"I'm glad I don't have to see him until after our vacation." He wiped his eyes. "I'm going to go back downstairs now."

"To talk to Stasio?"

"No."

"Then what?"

"Nothing."

"Please wait—" He was about to leave. "Dax said you got mad at him. How come?"

"Because he made me mad while we were hiking."

"I see." Except that she didn't. Dax was a darling boy. They'd always gotten along perfectly. "That happens with friends. You've had a lot of togetherness today. When you go back downstairs, do me a favor and make up with him? He's out on the patio feeling bad. If the shoe were on the other foot, you'd be feeling pretty awful about now."

"I don't want to make up."

"That doesn't sound like you." Stella didn't see her son act this way very often. "You still have to apologize because he's our guest. And while you're at it, how about telling Cassie you're sorry for keeping her beach ball away from her in the pool? She's only four, honey. When a big boy like you takes her stuff, she can't defend herself."

"Sorry."

"Tell *her* that. Okay?"

He nodded, then disappeared.

By the time she reached the patio, Ari had found Dax and had started to eat a lamb shish-kabob with him while they talked privately. Pretty soon the boys got in the pool and played nicely with Cassie, letting her have the ball when it was her turn. Stasio flashed her a smile, glad all was well again.

Stella slipped in the deep end and did the backstroke, trying to unwind after a day she'd never forget. Ari might be acting normally right now, but she knew that deep inside, his emotions were in turmoil. So were hers.

Maybe she was wrong to ask Ari not to say anything to Stasio yet, but she wanted to believe they could handle this situation on their own. Stella hated to think she had such a weak character she always turned to her brother for help. How would Ari ever stand on his own two feet if he ran to Stasio every time there was a crisis? It had to stop.

The next day Stella walked into Ari's bedroom with some ice water for him. They'd just come back from a day's sailing. He'd picked up a little too much sun and complained he didn't feel very well. While the rest of the family and Dax played in the pool before dinner, she excused herself to see about him.

He lay on his back on top of the covers with his suntanned arm covering his eyes.

She sat down next to him and felt his forehead.

"You're hot. Drink this, honey. I'm going to get my phone and call the doctor."

She raced to her room, then hurried back to him. Relieved to see him drink part of it, she phoned information and got connected to the doctor's office. His receptionist said he was busy. After leaving a message for him to call, she hung up and took the glass from Ari.

"I don't want to see the doctor. I'll be okay."

"Let's let him be the judge of that."

"I wish Dax could go home, but I know he can't."

Dax again.

"Of course he can. All I have to do is call Elani and she'll come for him." She studied him with an aching heart. He hadn't been the same since the hike with Theo yesterday. "Did you two have trouble again today?"

"Yes."

"Want to tell me about it?"

"No." He turned over so he wouldn't have to look at her.

"We have to talk, honey. Something's very wrong. Don't you know how much I love you?"

"Yes."

On impulse she said, "If you need to talk to

your uncle about your father, then I'll ask him to come up here after he's through eating."

"I don't want Stasi." That had to be a first. He rolled off the bed so fast, she knew she'd touched a live wire.

"Why aren't you getting along with Dax?"

"Because he wants to talk about stuff I don't want to talk about."

"You mean like personal things?"

He nodded.

On a burst of inspiration she said, "Has he been asking questions about your father?"

"Yes."

"Like what?"

"He thinks my daddy is cool."

"I take it Dax got along well with him."

"They talked all the time."

She knew she was getting closer to some kind of answer. "Dax's father is an older man and fairly quiet. Dax probably liked Theo's attention."

"He keeps asking me about when I'm going to see him again so we can all do stuff together." His eyes filled with tears. "He's not Dax's daddy!"

"What do you mean?"

He blinked back the tears to keep them from falling. "My daddy liked Dax better than me."

"What?"

"I thought he wanted to be with me, but he was nicer to Dax. I hate both of them."

"Oh, darling!" Stella reached for him and hugged him harder while she tried to comprehend that far from feeling hostility toward his father, Ari was jealous of the attention Theo had paid to his best friend.

In order to feel jealous, it meant you had to care.

This meant Ari had nursed a longing for his birth father all his cognitive life, but it had lain dormant until put to the first test.

Before yesterday she'd assumed Theo would see that it was too late to bond with Ari. She'd been positive her son would never be able to warm up to him. Ari already had a surrogate father in Stasio, the best man in the world. He didn't need or want another one. In the end Theo would find out it was no use, but the surprise had been on Stella.

She had to do something immediately to help Ari, but what? Only one person had the power to make this right. For once it was beyond Stasio's ability to fix, which was a revelation in itself.

While she rocked her son back and forth, her cell phone rang. The last thing she wanted to do was answer it, but it was probably the doctor.

"Let me see who it is." She let go of him long enough to reach for her phone on the dresser.

She recognized the blank caller ID. It was Theo! She almost bit her lip all the way through before answering it. "Hello?"

"Stella?" The sound of his deep voice permeated through her body to the soles of her feet. "I promised you I wouldn't try to see Ari until after your vacation, but I need to see you tonight. Alone," he added, sending a shock wave through her body. "I'm here in Palaiopolis at a small bistro called Yanni's. I'm seated at a table on the terrace overlooking the water and will wait an hour for you to come."

Stella's pulse sped up. She'd been there once with Rachel, but it was a romantic spot meant for couples so she had never gone to that particular restaurant again. "I-is there something wrong?" she stammered.

"Yes. I'll tell you when you get here."

She shifted her weight nervously. "I don't know if I can come without arousing suspicion."

"It's important." After a slight pause, "While

you're thinking about it, I'd like to talk to Ari for a minute and tell him how much our outing meant to me yesterday. With Dax around I couldn't say all the things I wanted to. Do you think he'd be willing to come to the phone or call me back? If he doesn't want to do either, then I'll leave it alone."

Stella couldn't believe the timing of his call or the reasons for it. But she heard something in his voice that sounded like he was anxious. "Just a minute and I'll check."

She put it down on the dresser and walked over to Ari. "It's your father on the phone. He'd like to talk to you for a minute."

That brought Ari's head around. "What does he want?"

Her poor boy had been suffering all last night and today. She'd known it, but she hadn't known about the jealousy.

"He said there are things he wanted to tell you but couldn't because Dax was there. You don't have to talk to him now. He said you could call him anytime or not at all. It's your choice, honey."

He took a long time making up his mind before he walked over to pick it up.

She held her breath as he said a tentative hello.

At first it was a very one-sided conversation with Theo doing most of the talking. She thought it would end fast, but like every assumption she'd made since he'd come back into her life, he surprised her with the unexpected.

In a minute Ari grew more animated. He actually laughed at one point. Before the phone call, she hadn't thought it possible. The call went on another five minutes.

All of a sudden he said, "Mom?"

"Yes?"

"Do I have to wait till our vacation is over to see my father again?"

How utterly incredible! She'd died and come back to life several times since Theo had returned to Athens. "What about Dax?"

"Dad says I can ask him to come with us if I want. It's up to me."

Amazing. Theo had taken the sword out of their son's hand without knowing it. "Then it's fine."

Stella couldn't believe she'd just said that, but after Ari had been honest with her just now, she was thankful tonight's crisis had been abated by the only person who could help their son.

The fact that Theo was the cause of all the trouble in the first place hadn't escaped her, but none of that mattered in light of Ari's pain which seemed to have vanished at the sound of his father's voice. She would call the doctor back and tell him everything was okay after all.

"Mom? Do we have anything planned for tomorrow?"

That soon?

"Nothing special."

More conversation ensued before he walked over with her phone still in his hand. She waited for him to say something.

"Did you make plans?"

He made an affirmative sound in an offhand manner like it was no big deal, but the light in his brown eyes told her it was a very big deal.

"Mind filling me in first?"

"Dad's going to fly us to Meteora at four o'clock. He says that's where the monasteries are. We're going to hike around until it gets dark. He'll bring his telescope so we can look at the stars. Maybe we'll see some UFOs."

Stella could only marvel.

"It's a good thing your aunt Rachel won't know about this or she'd want to go with you."

"Don't worry. He said no women allowed this

trip." This trip? Theo was doing everything right. She could find no fault. "I've got to tell Dax."

"Not yet," she cautioned him. "You and I still need to talk for a minute first. Stay here."

"Okay. Dad wants to speak to you again." He handed her the phone.

"Theo?" she asked too breathlessly for her own ears.

"Ari's response was more than I'd hoped for. It's yours I'm counting on now. This time, however, I'm the one waiting for *you* to show up. Let's pray no dark forces will prevent you from arriving."

Before she could say anything, Stella heard the click. It echoed the thud of her heart.

"Mom? Do you think Aunt Rachel would let me borrow her photos of Mars some time? I want him to see them."

"I'm sure she will."

"When do you think I could ask her?"

"Honey? I was hoping we'd keep this from the family until after we go back to Athens. You know, until we've got things a little more settled."

"Okay."

"Ari? Listen to me. Your father's here on Andros."

His eyes lit up. "He is?"

"Yes. He says he has to talk to me about something very important before he flies back to Salamis. I...I told him I would try to meet him, but I need your help because I don't want anyone else to know about it."

"I won't tell."

"I know that, so what I'd like you to do is stay here in your room and get ready for bed. I'll send Dax up to keep you company and you can tell him what your father has planned for tomorrow. In the meantime I'll tell Rachel I need to do an errand and will be right back."

"I wish I could go."

"Not this time, honey. Your father and I have things we need to discuss alone. Can you understand that?" He nodded. "You'll be seeing him tomorrow, right?"

His lips broke into a smile. "Yeah."

Stella kissed him and hurried to her room for her purse. She didn't dare change out of her pants and top she'd worn sailing. It might give her away.

"Rachel?" she said a minute later. Everyone was out by the pool eating. "Ari's resting. I think he got too hot, but he's feeling better now. Anyway, I'm running into town for some things he wants. I'll be back shortly." She turned to Dax. "When you're through eating, Ari hopes you'll come up."

"I'm all finished," he declared before darting away.

Glad everyone was preoccupied with the girls, Stella hurried out to her car and headed into town. On the way she phoned the doctor and told his receptionist that Ari was doing much better so the doctor didn't need to call back.

Due to the tourists, she had to park a street away from Yanni's. It was getting crowded. By the end of the evening, the night life would take over.

She hurried inside the bistro and told the hostess she was meeting someone out on the terrace. There was no sign of Boris, but that didn't mean he wasn't there.

The other woman showed her to Theo's candlelit table on the terrace. With every step, she wished she'd been able to wear an evening dress at least. Especially when she saw him get to his feet wearing an expensive black silk shirt and gray trousers. He stood out from the other males, drawing feminine attention from every direction including that of the sultry hostess.

His black gaze swept over Stella with that old

intimacy. When he helped her to be seated, she felt his hands caress her shoulders lightly, as if he couldn't help himself. It took her back to another time when they hadn't been able to keep their hands off each other.

"You picked up a lot of sun today," he whispered against her ear. "Your beauty radiates like a torch. Every man out here envies me."

She tried not to react, but inside she was a quivering mass of emotions. Theo always did have that effect on her. Right now she was in danger of forgetting the chasm of pain separating them.

Once he was seated he said, "Since I knew you couldn't be gone long from the villa, I took the liberty of ordering for us."

Stella could hardly breathe for the way he was devouring her with his eyes. "You're very sure of me, aren't you."

His gaze narrowed on her features. "I'm sure of what we felt for each other before we were tragically prevented from getting married. Nothing since that time has changed for me. I'm operating on the belief that deep down you still have feelings for me."

She looked away while the waiter served them baked shrimp with garlic and onions.

Theo remembered. It was one of their favorite dishes, accompanied by bread and a glass of house wine.

After their server had gone, she began to eat, realizing she was hungry. "This is delicious."

"Like the shrimp we used to eat at the Blue Lagoon during our walks on Salamis."

She reached quickly for the wine, wishing he wouldn't remind her. "We don't have much time. Why don't you tell me what's so important you had to see me tonight."

He broke his bread apart. "I asked you here to let you know I want a relationship with you, not just Ari."

The world reeled for a moment.

Theo had always been frank and direct. In that regard he hadn't changed, but life had changed the situation. She had to keep her head. "If you'll take a look around, Theo, there are any number of females who'd like to accommodate you given half a chance."

A sly smile broke one corner of his compelling mouth. "What females? I only see Stella Athas, the girl who ruined all other women for me."

"Theo..." her voice throbbed.

"You did, you know." He cocked his head. "I

saw a lot of women in New York and found every single one wanting. I'd hoped to meet someone who would make me forget you, but it never happened. Believe me, if it had, I would have married her and stayed in the States."

His words sent a shiver through her body. After seeing him again, after knowing what he already meant to Ari, the thought of him married to anyone else brought a fierce new pain to her heart.

"How many men have you known since me?" His deep voice had taken on a territorial quality.

"That's none of your business."

"How many, Stella? They must be legion."

She stared at him through veiled eyes. "If you're asking what I think you're asking, the answer is none."

"But not for want of trying?" He lifted the last of the wine to his lips.

"I've been too busy raising Ari."

His jet-black gaze seemed to gleam in the flickering light. "You've done a superb job."

"Thank you." She couldn't handle this conversation any longer. After putting her napkin down, she got up from the table. He didn't make a move to stop her. "I have to buy a few items in town before I return to the villa. If I'm gone any longer, the family will wonder why."

"We can't have that, can we," he drawled.

Theo knew she was worried about her family's reaction to him being in her life again. It made her unable to sustain his glance. "I'll have the boys waiting at four."

"Come with us tomorrow."

"No," she blurted. She was in too deep already. Any more time spent in his company would confuse her even more. "Ari's looking forward to being alone with you. Good night, Theo."

After a few purchases she headed back to Stasio's. On her way, she needed to figure out an excuse why she and the boys would be gone from the villa tomorrow. She couldn't say they'd be going on a drive around the island again.

By afternoon of the next day Stella had finally come up with a plan. She told the family they'd decided to take a long hike in the mountains. Afterward they'd get a big dinner at one of the restaurants in Batsi and see a film, thus the reason they'd be home late.

At four, when she drove into the paddleboat parking area with the boys, Theo was waiting for them in thigh-molding jeans and a creamy cotton crew neck sweater. He looked so striking her pulse ticked right off the charts.

He put his hands on the door frame next to her. She felt his gaze wander over her, missing nothing. The smell of the soap he used had a familiar tang, causing her to tremble. "We'll be back at ten. Will you plan to join us for a light dinner afterward?"

"I don't think so." She looked at Ari who was still sitting next to her. "This is your night with your father."

"But I want you to come, Mom." He leaned closer and gave her a kiss on the cheek. On that note he got out of the car with Dax.

"You may be too tired to eat a meal that late. Why don't we see what happens."

"I'll take that as a yes" came Theo's low, smooth rejoinder before he put an arm around Ari's shoulders.

Stella didn't know her son, who laughed freely before the three of them hurried toward the waiting helicopter. She stared after them. Was that Theo's first physical gesture of affection toward their son? If so, Ari appeared to welcome it.

The two of them seemed to be bonding before

her very eyes. If things continued like this, then she had to face the truth. Theo planned to be Ari's father in every sense of the word, something Ari obviously wanted. That meant Stella needed to grow another skin to survive.

Last night he'd told her he wanted them to have a relationship, but she was terrified. Right now the lines were blurred because she had an undeniable fatal attraction to him. Stella feared that given more time, she'd be right back where she'd started—madly in love with Theo.

On a groan, she walked toward the little town of Batsi where she would while away the hours until their return. She heard the helicopter pass overhead. The sound caused her to quicken her pace so she wouldn't think about the excitement she was missing by not being with them.

CHAPTER FOUR

THAT night Theo took the hostess aside and slipped her a tip. "Can you put us in front where the boys can watch the dancing up close?" He'd picked a taverna in Batsi that was tourist friendly regardless of ages.

"If you and your wife will follow me, I'll seat you."

"Thank you."

Stella had to have heard what the other woman said, but she pretended not to notice. Ushering the boys forward they moved through the crowded terrace to a table overlooking the bay. How many years had he dreamed of being with Stella like this, knowing he could take care of her and his own....

Several couples were already on the dance floor moving to the live band. He was aching to get her out there. Once he got the boys started on some snacks, he planned to steal her away where they could keep an eye on them while he held her as close as decency allowed.

Once a waiter came for their orders and the boys had told Stella about their outing, he asked to be excused before grasping her hand.

"Dance with me?"

"Do it, Mommy. I've never seen you dance before."

"She's an expert," Theo murmured. Without waiting for a yes or a no, he drew her out of the chair onto the floor.

Her body was stiff. "I haven't danced in years."

"Neither have I. The last time was at a church dance with you. Do you remember it was in the basement? Everyone was afraid with all the adults watching. I stepped on your foot."

"No, you didn't. I was the one who stepped on yours several times. I was so embarrassed I wanted to die."

He caught her close, pressing his cheek against the hotness of hers. "All I remember was that I was in heaven because Stella Athas, the most desirable girl in the world, had agreed to dance with me. I was the envy of all my friends who laid bets you wouldn't let me get near enough to touch you."

"Was I that impossible?"

"I thought that at first, but soon discovered you were just painfully shy. You presented a challenge I couldn't resist. My biggest fear was that once you found out I was a Pantheras, you would run from me and go to a different church where I couldn't find you."

"When I was a teenager, the last thing I thought about was money."

"I know that now, but everyone whispered you were an Athas who couldn't see the urchins at your feet."

She pulled back, staring at him through wounded eyes. "How awful that people felt that way."

"Not everyone, Stella." Obeying an insatiable need, he brushed his mouth against hers before winding his fingers into the back of her hair. She was so beautiful. She could have no idea how much he'd missed feeling her next to him.

Her eyes closed tightly. "Please keep your distance. We're on a dance floor with the children watching."

Theo couldn't help smiling. "Everyone else is dancing close." He was fast losing control.

"We're not everyone."

"No, we're not, thank heaven. There's only one Stella." He kissed her hair at the temple. "There are things we have to talk about. Expect a call from me before you go to bed tonight." Theo swung her toward their table and held the chair for her to sit down.

"How's the food, guys?"

"Good," Ari said. "The waiter brought us more drinks."

Dax nodded. "He said we could have as many as we wanted."

Feeling euphoric, he eyed his son. "Have you ever danced with your mother before?" He shook his dark head. "Now's your chance."

"I don't know how."

"I do. My mom taught me." Dax got up and went over to Stella.

She smiled. "I'm honored." Without hesitation she took him for a whirl around the floor.

Theo grinned at Ari. "You see? There's nothing to it."

He could tell his son was girding up his courage. A minute later they came back to the table. To Theo's delight, Ari got up and took his turn with Stella. Nothing like a little healthy competition.

Good for him. He had a shy side like his mother. With a little confidence, he was going to grow up to be an outstanding man. Whatever he chose to do, be it astronomy or otherwise, he had the intelligence and perseverance to succeed. Theo wanted to be his father on a twenty-four-hour basis. The way to do that depended on getting through to Stella.

As if she knew what he was thinking, the minute she came back with Ari, she checked her watch. "It's really late. I'm afraid we have to be going."

Theo put some bills on the table and helped Stella to her feet. The four of them left the restaurant and walked out into the warm Greek night. He accompanied them to the car, knowing better than to hug her too tight.

This time he high-fived his son first. "I had one of the best times of my life today."

"Me, too."

"You can call me anytime. When you're back in Athens, check with your mother and we'll make more plans."

Ari's head whipped around to Stella. "Can't we decide now?"

She looked tormented. "We'll talk about this later."

"Your mother's right. It's been a long day." He tousled both boys' hair, then flicked her a glance. "Drive home safely. Your car holds precious cargo."

Their eyes held for an instant before a look of determination to leave altered her features and she started the car. Ari looked back while they drove away and waved.

He raised his hand. Keep it up, Ari. Keep it up.

No sooner did the three of them walk into the villa than Stella heard a voice that always made her uneasy call to her. It was terrible to feel that way about her own brother, but there'd been too much history in the past to pretend his presence didn't affect her.

"Well, well." He scrutinized the three of them. "Who would have imagined you keeping such late hours."

"Hi, Uncle Nikos."

She paused in the entrance hall to give him a kiss on the cheek. He looked lean and dashing in his swim trunks. Her brother was the personification of the Olympic silver medallist who'd won one of the few medals for Greece in the downhill and giant slalom. He was an icon in his own right.

"Hello, Nikos. It's good to see you. Where's Renate?"

"Upstairs unpacking." His glance alighted on Dax. "Who's this?"

"My friend, Dax."

"Haven't seen you around here before."

"Ari invited me."

Knowing Ari felt uncomfortable, Stella put a hand on their shoulders. "Hurry on upstairs and get ready for bed. Don't forget to brush your teeth. I'll be up in a few minutes to say good night."

She gave them each a kiss before sending them off. Without the boys around, it was easier to deal with Nikos. "Is Stasio still up?"

"They're out on the patio. Are you joining us?"

"Not tonight. To be honest, I'm exhausted. Tell Renate I'll see her in the morning."

"How come you let Ari bring someone? This is our family time."

Stella bristled. "I can't believe you just said

that. He's not going to be here the whole time, but even if he were, what difference does it make to you? You'll come and go as the mood suits you. As for the girls, they're two and four, hardly company for a six year-old all the time."

He looked taken back. She couldn't remember the last time that had happened.

"Since when did you become so prickly? I hardly know you like this."

"I didn't pick this fight, Nikos. You did by being offensive, not only to me but the boys." Theo had shown more loving kindness to Dax than Nikos had ever shown to Ari.

"Stella?" he called her back, his dark eyes angry. "What's gotten into you?"

"I'm still the same person. I've just decided to speak my mind the way you do. Sometimes it's not pleasant is it? Good night."

She walked up the stairs without looking back. It had felt good to be honest with him. However, there was no deluding herself. For as long as he stayed on Andros with his Austrian skier wife, also an Olympian, Nikos would make her and Ari pay the price.

That was still on her mind when she reached her room and discovered her son waiting on the top of her bed in his pajamas. Somehow it didn't surprise her.

"Hey, honey…why the long face after such a wonderful outing?"

"Mom? Do we have to stay here for our whole vacation?"

Thank you, Nikos!

"It's what we'd planned."

"But I want to be with my daddy. He has all these fun things we can do at his house."

She'd thought this was about Nikos, but it clearly wasn't. Stella took a steadying breath. "Haven't you been enjoying it here?"

He averted his eyes. "Yes."

"But?"

"I like being with him. He's awesome. Dax says so, too."

"I noticed. Is it like being with Uncle Stasio?" He was Ari's hero.

"Kind of, but he's my papa," he said quietly. His papa…

"I wish we could go home tomorrow."

Knowing he already felt this strongly about his father, she had no doubt this was going to be a permanent situation from now on. But she needed to know a lot more about Theo's agenda. He wouldn't always have this much free time to spend with Ari. Her greatest desire was to protect their son from being hurt.

The fear of history repeating itself was uppermost in her mind, especially when things were moving so fast. Their lives were changing in ways she hadn't thought possible a week ago. Certainly Ari's world had undergone a total transformation.

"Tell you what. Your father will be calling me in a little while and we'll talk. I'll let you know what we decide in the morning."

His crestfallen look spoke volumes. He wanted answers now, but she couldn't give him one. "Okay." He slid off the bed and darted out of her room.

Her mind on Theo, she went into the bathroom to brush her teeth. If he'd flown straight to Paloukia, then he was probably home by now. She decided to get ready for bed first. Maybe by then he would phone her.

Ten minutes later she slid under the covers, still waiting for his call. Deciding to take the initiative, she reached in her purse for his letter and dialed his cell phone number. He picked up on the second ring.

"Ari?" The tender excitement in his voice was a revelation in and of itself.

"No. It's Stella. Is it a bad time for you to talk?"

"It's a perfect time. I just walked into the house and was about to call you."

She'd thought she could do this, but now she wasn't so sure. Too nervous to lie there, she got out of bed and began pacing.

"This is about Ari."

"I presumed as much, but I live in hope the day will come when you and I can have a conversation about the future. Our future."

Her breath caught. "We don't have time to talk about that right now."

"Why not? Did Ari get sick on all those hors d'oeuvres they ate while we were dancing?"

"No." She wished it were that simple. "Since he's been with you, he's a different boy."

"So am I. That's what happens when a father and son get together."

"That's my concern." She crushed the phone in her hand. "For how long?"

"Forever."

Her body started to shake. "Lots of relationships start out on a forever basis, but deteriorate with time."

"Our love didn't die, Stella," he declared in his deep male voice. "We were ambushed by a force neither of us had the power to stop at the time."

"You keep saying that!" she cried.

"Because it's true. If I thought you would take me at my word that I was torn from you, I'd never tell you another thing because I don't want you and Ari to go through any more hurt."

"What hurt? After what happened, how could there possibly be any more? Look, Theo—for Ari's sake I want to believe you because he wants to be with you, but I'm afraid my ability to trust died years ago."

"So, what are you saying?" His voice sounded bleak.

"Th-that I'm going to go on sheer faith and give you free access to him." Tears rolled down her cheeks. "You've got Ari's heart in your hands. If you do anything to disappoint him…" She couldn't talk for a minute.

"I'm here to stay, Stella. My life is totally tied up in him."

This was hard. So hard when those were the things she'd wanted him to say to her years ago.

"I pray you're telling the truth, because

tonight he asked if we could cut our vacation short and go back to Athens in the morning. He wants to be available to you."

"What did you tell him?"

"That we'd talk about it in the morning."

"I'm sure that's the last thing you want to do when you love being with your family. They still don't know I've been seeing Ari?"

"No. It's my business. I've preferred keeping things private. They'll find out soon enough. I'll be driving back home in the morning with the boys."

"In that case I'd like to come to see him tomorrow afternoon. The three of us can talk over plans then."

"He'll be thrilled," she murmured.

"Even with all our history, it'll be the first time for me to make it inside your home, Stella."

She realized that. Years ago they'd had to be careful when he brought her back from an outing on his brother's motor scooter. He'd leave her a block away, then wait for her call when he got back home to make sure she was all right. Theo had never failed her. That's why his unprecedented behavior on that horrific night had been too much for her psyche to handle.

"Ari will be overjoyed." But nothing else has been resolved.

"No more than I. Thank you. This means more than you will ever know." His voice sounded thick-toned.

Get off the phone, Stella. "Good night."

"Good night. Drive home safely." She heard the concern in his tone before hanging up. The rest of the night she tossed and turned, hoping she'd made the right decision.

The second Ari came in the next morning, she told him they were leaving. He whooped it up before running to tell Dax to get his stuff together.

Stella packed quickly before going down to Stasio's study. He usually checked in with his secretary in the early mornings, even when he was on vacation. Like Theo, he was tall with arresting male features. There wasn't a mean bone in his body.

"Knock, knock."

"Stella? We missed you last night. Come on in."

"I'm just peeking in to say goodbye for now. Let's hope Rachel's morning sickness improves."

He frowned. "Bad as it is, I'm more concerned about you at the moment. Tell me what's wrong."

"Nothing specific." She hated lying to him,

but she wasn't ready to talk about Theo yet. "Ari and Dax are restless. At home they have more friends their own age to do things with."

He studied her through veiled eyes. "You're not telling the truth, but that's your privilege. I've seen a marked difference in both of you since you arrived. Just remember, I'm here if you need me."

Her brother had radar. "I've always known that and I love you for it. Tell Rachel I'll call her later today after I'm back at the house. Say goodbye to Nikos and Renate for me, too."

Stasio came around his desk and gave her a big hug. "I'll walk you to the car."

The boys were already strapped in. It was so unusual for Ari not to seek his uncle out first, Stasio had to know something of great significance was going on.

"See you later, Uncle Stasi. Thanks for a great time."

"I had fun, too. Thanks a lot," Dax said.

"You come again, anytime you like." He gave Ari a hug.

Stella started the car and they took off for the port of Gavrion to catch the ferry.

No sooner had they driven onboard and

walked to the promenade deck than a steward approached Stella.

"You are Despinis Athas?"

"Yes?"

"Your room is ready for you."

She blinked. "I didn't reserve one." Depending on weather and wind conditions to Rafina, the cruise only took two to three hours.

He gave her a knowing smile. "Someone else did. This way please."

"Come on, boys. Someone has planned a surprise for us." The blood hammered in her ears. She could only think of one person.

They followed the steward down to the next deck. He led them around a passageway to a row of cabins and opened the third one for her. Stella gasped when she walked in and saw two dozen long-stemmed red roses in a vase on the nightstand between two double beds.

To one side was a table and chairs. She spied a bowl of fruit, another filled with candy and cookies, and half a dozen cans of various juices.

"Are these for *us?*" Ari cried in delight.

"Who else would they be for?" sounded a deep, familiar male voice.

Stella spun around. "Theo—"

"Papa!" Ari ran to hug him. "We didn't know you were coming with us!"

Theo's black eyes found Stella's. They were so alive she could feel his energy. "Work can wait. I decided I wanted to join in the fun."

"Goody!" their son cried while Dax beamed and began loading up on candy.

Stella was happier to see him than she'd thought possible. "The flowers are gorgeous."

He came all the way inside and shut the door before leaning against it with his arms folded. In a tan sport shirt and white shorts, he looked incredible. "Remember the time we took a ferry to Poros? It was so crowded we had to stand the whole way against the railing at the back? I only had one red rose to offer you. In those days I was so poor, I could only afford to give you token presents."

Stella cherished any little thing he ever did for her. "I still have it," she half whispered. "It's pressed in the big dictionary I keep on my bookshelf at home."

"I've seen that," Ari commented. "I didn't know Daddy gave it to you."

Theo's white smile turned her heart over.

"Your mother and I liked to give each other little gifts. I still have the bracelet she once bought me."

Ari munched on a cookie. "Where is it now?"

"Right here." Theo lifted his leg. They all stared at the tiny gold chain around his ankle.

"You still wear it?" Stella was in shock.

"I told you that night I would never take it off."

Her face went hot. Before they'd gone swimming, she'd given it to him and he'd made her put it on him. She remembered him crushing her in his arms, telling her they were now joined forever.

"I want to get one."

"Me, too!" Dax chimed in.

Stella laughed. "Maybe when you two are older."

"Speaking of you two…" Theo walked over to the closet and pulled out a couple of junior life preservers. "I want you to put these on and wear them the whole time." He helped them get them on.

"How come?"

He finished tying them. "Because you never know when something could happen and I want you to be safe."

She could see Ari wasn't too happy about it, but she loved Theo for insisting.

"I bet nobody else is wearing one."

"Maybe not, but I want you to do this for me because I love you so much."

"I love you, too, Papa. Now you have to put yours on."

Both Stella and Theo burst into laughter. He pulled two adult jackets from the closet. "What's good for the goose, eh?" He started toward her with a wicked glint in those fabulous black eyes.

Stella would have put it on herself, but Theo insisted on doing the honors. His touch sent curls of delicious warmth through her body. With his back toward the boys, his eyes ignited as he took his time tying the ends near her throat. She wanted him to kiss her so badly she felt pain to the palms of her hands.

Needing something to do before she acted on her desire, she took the other life jacket and helped him put it on. Had he always been so broad-shouldered and powerful? When her hand touched his chest, she heard his sharp intake of breath.

"Can we go play shuffleboard?"

"Yes," Theo answered while she was still fastening his tie. "We'll come up and join you in a minute."

"Okay. Let's go, Dax!" They grabbed some candy and left the cabin.

When the door closed, Theo pulled her closer to him. "Our son just did us a favor. Without this body armor, you wouldn't be safe from me right now. Let's try it out, in case I'm wrong."

Before she knew what had happened, she was engulfed in his arms, unable to move. "I'm going to kiss you whether you want me to or not."

She thought he would start with her mouth, but he began an exploration of her face, slowly inching his way around until she thought she would die if he didn't satisfy the craving building inside her.

A moan escaped her throat, her body's way of begging him to stop torturing her and really kiss her. When it came, she almost fainted from ecstasy.

Somehow, she didn't really know how, they ended up on the bed in a kiss that seemed to have no beginning or end. She lost complete track of time. It was just the two of them communicating in a wine-dark rapture of need escalating out of control.

Suddenly the door opened. "Hey, Mom? Papa? Aren't you going to play with us?"

Theo recovered first. He bit her earlobe gently, then rolled off the bed. "I'm coming up now. Your mom will join us in a few minutes. You guys want some drinks?"

"Yeah. Thanks."

After they left, Stella sat up, but her head was so woozy from being kissed senseless she had to maneuver carefully so she wouldn't fall over when she stood up. The life preserver made it difficult.

One look in the mirror over the dresser spoke a thousand words and needed no translation. It took her back to her teenage years. After being with Theo, her lips were always swollen, her face flushed and the hair he loved to play with was in disarray.

She buried her face in one of the roses. Their scent filled the room. Whenever she smelled roses in the future, she would remember this day and treasure it. Once again Theo had worked his magic.

After brushing her hair and putting on fresh

lipstick, she phoned Elani and told her they were coming home but were still going to keep Dax if it was okay. With that accomplished, she went up on deck to find the guys.

They all played shuffleboard, then walked around to watch the water traffic. Theo entertained the boys. She mostly listened. Eventually they went back to their cabin for more treats. While the boys stretched out on one of the beds, Theo lay on his side behind Stella who sat on the edge of the bed to talk to them.

He did it on purpose, knowing it would be pure torture for her not to be able to lie down next to him. Ten minutes to port her cell phone rang. She checked the caller ID. It was Rachel. She had to answer and said hello.

"Stella—I had no idea you were going to leave today. Stasi let me sleep in. I just woke up and found out you'd gone. Cassie's so upset."

She got up and went outside the cabin so she could talk in private. "I'm sorry, Rachel. It's just that with school out, Ari and Dax want to do some things with their friends."

"I understand, but I have to admit I'm disappointed."

"Forgive us."

"Of course."

"We'll be back again after Dax goes home in a few days."

"I'm counting on it. Take care."

"You, too. I want you to get over your morning sickness."

"It'll pass. Talk to you later."

Stella hung up feeling horrible, but she couldn't change plans now. It was very evident Theo and Ari loved each other and wanted to be together. This was a vital time for them. She couldn't allow anything else to interfere.

Theo seemed to know instinctively how to handle Ari. Suddenly their son was acting more confident and excited about life. Stella had to admit it was wonderful to think Ari had his own real father in his life like his other friends had theirs. She would never have imagined it, but when she saw them together, it was like they'd never been apart.

At one point she would have to let Stasio and Rachel know. The best time to tell them would be when their vacation was over. He already knew something was going on. When he learned the truth, he'd be thrilled for Ari, even with all the bad history.

A boy needed his father. If Theo wanted to fill that role now, Stella had no desire to prevent it. As long as he made Ari happy, then she'd be happy. She was a fool, of course. It was her middle name, otherwise she wouldn't be living for later this afternoon when Theo said he'd be coming to the villa.

After she clicked off, she went back in the cabin.

Theo flicked her a penetrating glance. "Everything all right?"

"Yes. It was Rachel. She was still asleep when we left, so she called to say goodbye."

"We're docking now," Theo murmured. "It's time to walk to the car. Everybody off with their life jackets." Soon they were all put away in the closet.

Ari looked at his father. "Are you going to come with us?"

"I'd like to, but I have a little work to do at the office. The helicopter will fly me into Athens from here and I'll come to the villa later."

"What time?"

"Around four."

Stella walked over to the flowers. "I want to take these with us."

Theo reached for the vase. "I'll empty the water and carry them to the car. Is everybody ready?"

The boys nodded and trooped out first. Stella reached for her purse while Theo brought up the rear. They walked down the passage to the stairs and went below to the next deck. When they reached the car, Theo put the roses in the trunk.

"Looks like you're all set." He came around to Stella's side and squeezed her shoulder. The contact spread fire through every atom of her body. "Drive carefully."

"See you later, Papa."

"See you, Mr. Pantheras."

Stella started the motor and put the car in gear. It was a wrench having to drive away from him. From the sideview mirror she watched him until they'd driven off the ferry.

"Can Dax play at our house when we get home?"

"I've already checked with his mother and it's okay."

"Hooray."

Forty-five minutes later they reached the house. "Aiyee," Iola cried when she saw them enter the kitchen.

Stella was carrying the roses which she took

over to the sink. They needed to be put in water again. "We decided to cut our vacation short. Don't worry. Tell the staff I plan to do the cooking and the cleaning around here. You go on doing exactly what you intended to do. We'll try to stay out of your way."

Iola crossed herself. "What's going on?"

Ari gave her a hug. "My papa's coming over this afternoon."

If the housekeeper's eyes grew any bigger, they'd pop. "Your papa?"

"Yup. He's awesome! Come on, Dax. Let's take our stuff upstairs. Do you want me to take up your suitcase, Mom?"

Since when. "Yes. I'd love you to." Wanting to copy his father was a good thing.

"Okay."

Once they disappeared, Stella turned to Iola. "I know what you're thinking. How could I let this happen after that man nearly ruined my life. But this isn't about me."

They walked through the villa to the salon where she set the roses on the coffee table. "Ari has spent quite a bit of time with him and wants to be with him all the time. That's why we're back in Athens so soon."

Iola's hands went to her own cheeks. "I hope you know what you're doing."

"So do I, but you saw Ari just now. There's a new light in his eyes."

"We'll see how long it lasts."

The housekeeper had been through it all with her. Of course she was fearful. In time she would see what Stella could see right now.

"It's still a secret," she warned her. "No one knows but you and Dax."

"Not Stasio?" She sounded scandalized.

"Not yet. Rachel's nausea has him preoccupied." Though it was true, she knew her brother hadn't been deceived.

Iola shook her head. "He worries over her the way Ari's father should have worried over you!"

"That's in the past, Iola. Ari's happy. I want him to stay that way."

Iola crossed herself again.

CHAPTER FIVE

IT WAS a novel experience for Theo to be allowed onto Athas property. The guard at the gate let his limo pass through to the front of the square, three-story villa. Built along neoclassic lines, it gave the impression of a temple. In ways it was like a sanctuary, one he'd been forbidden to enter.

But not today. It meant her brothers still didn't know what was going on. He would enjoy his entrée into her world until everything hit the fan. Then he would sit back and watch the spectacle.

At quarter after four he alighted from the limo and bounded up the steps, almost breathless to see Stella. After kissing her on the ferry, he was on fire, and nothing would ever put it out because that was the effect she had on him.

He'd barely rung the doorbell when he heard voices and it opened to reveal his son. They smiled at each other. Dax stood behind him. "Hi, Papa…come on in."

Papa… The most wonderful word he'd ever heard.

"Thanks. Who's your friend?"

The boys laughed.

"Hi."

"Hi, yourself, Dax."

"Mom said to bring you into the salon."

He squeezed Ari's shoulder. "Lead the way."

The elegant interior was what he'd expected of a family of their status, but the only thing that mattered was being with the two people he loved.

"Stella." She looked so gorgeous, the air caught in his lungs. "I like you in yellow." Earlier today she'd been in pink.

A flush swept over her as she looked up from a tray of sodas and snacks she'd just put on the table. The sleeveless top with a matching skirt was sensational on her. "Thank you. Why don't you sit down and we'll talk. Dax, if you'll go to the kitchen, Iola has a snack ready for you. Our meeting won't take long."

"Okay."

Once the three of them were alone, she subsided into a chair facing the couch. Theo guided Ari to it and they sat down together. His son made sure he was supplied something to eat and drink.

"Umm. This baklava is excellent. Thank you. I'm always my hungriest about this time every day."

"Me, too," Ari agreed with him. "We always eat dinner early, huh, Mom."

She nodded. "I thought we ought to talk about plans for the rest of the summer."

"If you don't mind my going first, this might make it easier for you," Theo stated.

"Go ahead."

"As you know," he said, eyeing both of them, "I'm back in Greece with only one agenda, to spend as much time as possible with you."

Ari smiled.

"I want to do what every father wants to do—take you to lessons, the dentist, the doctor, meet your teachers for school this coming fall, plan minivacations, play soccer with you and your friends, shop, go to movies, hang out at my house, just be with you."

"Me, too. Can you stay here and watch *Star Trek* with me tonight?"

"I'd love it. Maybe we could get some takeout for dinner and bring it back while we all watch, but before we plan anything, I want to know what's on your mother's mind. Are you working full-time this summer?"

She put down her soda. "Yes, but I still have two weeks of vacation. Once it's over, I've made an arrangement with Keiko. He'll work from nine to five. I'll plan to go in at six-thirty every day so I can be home by two-thirty. I've planned for Ari to do some reading and math at the next session of summer school in the mornings."

"But I don't want to go to school."

"It's a good idea, Ari," Theo backed her up. "You need to keep your mind active. I was thinking we could get ourselves enrolled in a young astronomers program, too."

"What's that?" He jumped off the couch too excited to sit still.

"I'm sure some of the colleges have them. You look through a telescope and they teach you about the stars."

"Could I do that, Mom?"

"Of course."

"If you would bring me your telephone book, we could call around and see what's being offered."

"I'll get it."

After he dashed out of the room Theo sat forward. "Stella? Look at me for a minute." She lifted her head. "I hope you know I'm not trying to usurp your place. I want to help ease the burden of all you have to do. Look on me as your support system, a permanent one. I'll do whatever you'd like. If I'm overwhelming you, tell me."

She got to her feet. "You're not. It's what Ari wants. I can't deny that Ari is a changed boy already. That's all because of you."

"Thank you for saying that."

She held on to the back of the chair. "All his life he's been surrounded by other children who live with a father and mother. However, I didn't think he noticed that much or cared, not with Stasio, who has been won-derful to him."

Only because he and Nikos had stolen Ari from him. The bile rose in Theo's throat.

"You have no conception of how changed he

is. Otherwise he would never have begged to leave Andros where he could have Stasio's constant attention. He didn't even say goodbye to his uncle, the man he has always depended on."

Theo liked hearing it, but when Stasio found out what was going on, there was going to be a showdown. This time Theo was ready for whatever the Athas family had to throw at him.

"His need to be with you supercedes all else," Stella confessed. "There's a new confidence about him. That's because he knows his real father loves him. I have to admit I can't be sorry about that. In truth I've always had to help Ari work on his confidence."

Puzzled, Theo got to his feet. "What are you talking about?"

She rubbed her hands together, a sure sign of nervousness. "It's a long story. You need to hear everything so you'll understand Ari's psyche. I'll tell you after he goes to bed tonight."

He had a feeling that whatever she had to say to him was going to turn his guts inside out all over again. Though he wanted to press her, he could hear the boys coming.

"Here's the directory, Papa." Dax came in with him.

"Terrific. Let me make a few calls and we'll see what's available."

Ari eyed him expectantly while he made inquiries. Eventually he hung up and said, "We're in luck. There's a star gazing program that started this week, but we can join in on Friday evening, so I have an idea.

"Why don't we visit the college in the morning. After we've registered for the session, we'll fly to St. Thomas for the day."

"Hey," Dax piped up. "My parents went there a couple of weeks ago. My dad loves golf. He said the resort has the best golf course he ever played on."

That was nice to hear. "Have either of you ever played?"

Both boys shook their heads.

"How about you, Stella?"

"No."

"Then we'll make up a foursome and do nine holes. How does that sound?"

"Cool." Ari high-fived his friend.

Stella's mouth lifted at the corners. "Ari? Why don't you show your father to the family room upstairs to watch your DVD."

"Okay. Come on, Papa."

His gaze held hers. "Before we do anything, I'll go pick up some food for us. You guys can come if you want to help me choose."

"That's not necessary, Theo. We have plenty of food here. Ari and Dax can carry it up when you get hungry."

"Then bring on the starship *Enterprise*," he said before tearing his eyes from hers.

The five-hour marathon with the boys entertained him no end. Stella slipped in and out with sandwiches and salad, but he was glad when she finally insisted the boys go to bed. Until she explained what she'd meant earlier, he would have no peace.

As soon as she joined him in the salon, he said, "What's this about Ari not having confidence?"

Once again she sat down opposite him. "Let me give you some background. After what happened at the church, my grief made me ill. There was too much tension in the house. My father was upset that I'd gotten involved with you, and Nikos's attitude made everything so much worse. Stasio had to leave for New York on business and took me with him.

"I lived in his apartment both before and after I had the baby. He hired a Greek couple to help me when he couldn't be home. He also made it possible for me to attend college and get my business degree there."

Nothing she'd just told him added up to what he'd been thinking about Stasio. Had Theo been wrong about him?

"You're an amazing woman." He was proud of what she'd accomplished, but he could hardly hold on to his rage over events he'd been helpless to prevent at the time.

She shook her head. "No. Thousands of women do the same thing every day. Once I'd graduated, I told Stasio I wanted to go back to Greece and get a job. Ari was old enough to attend kindergarten and I could work out my schedule with Iola's help.

"Everything went well except that in returning to Athens, it brought us back into Nikos's orbit. He never accepted Ari and it showed. The last couple of years have been hard on our son.

"Though Ari doesn't understand why, he's aware of the way Nikos feels and goes to great lengths not to antagonize him for fear of being mocked or ridiculed. As a result, he doesn't always show a lot of confidence. That's what I wanted you to understand." Tears prickled against her eyelids. "For him to finally have his own father who champions him is making all the difference."

He got to his feet. "None of this should have happened," he muttered. More and more he was beginning to think the cruelty was all on Nikos's part. "Though there's nothing we can do about the past, I swear to you I'll never let any harm or hurt come to you or Ari again."

"Theo," she cried in abject frustration. "If you want me to believe you, you have to confide in me completely about the past. No lies."

"If you'll do me one favor first, then I promise to tell you details."

When she closed her eyes, tears squeezed out. "What favor?" she whispered.

"Tell your brothers I've returned to Greece and have been seeing you and Ari." There was going to be an explosion, one Stella needed to experience to understand.

A stillness surrounded her before she got up from the chair. "I don't want them to know yet because this is a very precarious time for you and Ari. I've been waiting to see how things would go. Naturally, I plan to tell them."

"But you're afraid to tell them. I can see it

in your eyes. I don't blame you. We always had to hide our love from your family, but we were young then. Now we're two mature adults with a six-year-old son. There's nothing to be afraid of. I'm here to protect you. Does Ari know how you and I used to have to sneak around to be together?"

"No. As I told you before, he knows nothing about my turmoil."

"I'm indebted to you for that. It's the reason he and I have been able to bond so fast. For that very reason he'll think it's strange if you're not straightforward with your family."

"You're right. It's just that—"

"What?" he broke in. "Are you afraid they're going to object?"

She bit her lower lip, the one he wanted to kiss. "You hurt me. I was their younger sister."

"But we were torn from each other in the most cruel way possible. Surely that would make a difference to any sane, rational person." What she couldn't know was that he didn't put Nikos in that category.

"I'm not ready to say anything quite yet. In a couple of weeks Stasio will be back from vacation. Then I'll tell him." She shook her head, causing her dark hair to swish. "I have to tell him at the right time."

Theo realized she was terrified because he would always be a Pantheras in their eyes and she knew her family would never approve. She had every reason to want to put it off.

"Tell them soon, Stella," he urged, afraid it fell on deaf ears. "We don't want Ari hurt by this if he doesn't have to be. I'm leaving now. My limo's waiting. I'll be by for you at ten tomorrow."

He strode out of the house without looking back. She was too much of a temptation for him to be alone with her in the same room any longer.

The next morning Stella ate breakfast with the boys, aware of an excitement building inside her she couldn't control. After going back and forth, she chose to wear white cargo pants and a sleeveless lime-green top that tied at the shoulders. There was no use pretending she didn't care what Theo thought. She had her pride and wanted to look beautiful for him.

While she was putting on lipstick, her phone rang. Theo? Her heart thudded as she reached for her cell. It turned out to be Dax's mom. She'd be by at dinnertime to pick him up.

They chatted for a minute before Stella hung up to brush her hair. She had an idea Dax wasn't ready to go home yet. He'd been enjoying Theo's company too much. Ari on the other hand would be thrilled to finally get his daddy to himself.

Twenty minutes later he appeared at the villa. Stella stepped outside and got in the limo next to him. She could feel him studying her. While the boys chattered, she and Theo made desultory conversation. After visiting the campus, they headed for Theo's office.

Once they rode the elevator to the roof, they got in the helicopter. Boris was already onboard and everyone got acquainted. Soon they were airborne. She smiled at Ari. "Are you excited about your star-gazing class?"

"Yup. It's going to be awesome."

Awesome was a word that covered everything fun or wonderful. The class started at nine o'clock and went three times a week for two more weeks.

"I'm sure it will be fascinating."

Theo sat in the copilot's seat looking at home there with headgear on. "As soon as we land, are you guys ready for golf or do you want to play on the water slide first?"

"I didn't know it had one of those." Dax sounded euphoric.

"It's guaranteed to curl your hair."

Everyone laughed. Even Stella. She could trust Theo, couldn't she? Ari did, wholeheartedly. For the rest of the day she was determined to put all doubts behind her and just enjoy the moment.

As soon as she made that decision, her body started to relax, enabling her to entertain feelings she'd been forced to suppress since she'd first seen him at the paddleboat concession.

He had the kind of hard-muscled body that looked good in anything. Today he'd worn a magenta sport shirt and cream-colored trousers that rode low on his hips. Theo was unaware of his masculine charisma. She, on the other hand, had trouble keeping her eyes off him.

Years ago every girl at church had woven a fantasy about him. Stella hadn't been able to believe it when he'd sit behind her in Sunday school and whisper things to her while the priest gave a lesson. When they went into mass, he'd sit in the same row and lean forward so he could smile at her.

Whatever activity, he came and made certain they were together in some capacity. Her friends thought he was sexy and told her how lucky she was. Stella knew it, but with her family looking on, she had to be careful they didn't find out what was happening.

When the church had put on a festival to raise money, he had chosen her as his partner to perform a folk dance. There were practices and they had to wear costumes. The thrill of those moments while they got ready for the big night still set her pulse racing. He'd dance too close and kiss her hair. Theo drove her crazy with all his attention. She loved him with a passion that broke down her inhibitions.

Their son, Ari, sitting next to her was proof that she'd loved Theo body and soul. She hadn't been able to hold back her desire. That period had been filled with the greatest ecstasy imaginable. Then it had ended so abruptly in one night, something in her had died.

She realized she'd been dead for years. Now suddenly he was back. Despite the things she didn't know, something inside her had leaped to life again, portending something bigger and brighter than before. Yesterday in the cabin on the ferry, she'd forgotten everything in the sheer joy of being in his arms again.

"Stella?" The voice infiltrating her body jerked her from her intimate thoughts.

"What is it?"

"We've landed." So they had. "The boys have run ahead to set up our golf game." She noticed that the pilot and Boris had already exited, too. "Do you need help?"

He looked as if he was going to come back and start removing the straps one kiss at a time. Her cheeks grew warm at the direction of her thoughts. If someone saw them… "No, thank you. I can manage."

After unstrapping herself, she moved to the entrance where he swung her to the ground. He did it slowly, causing her body to slide down his, creating delicious heat between them. Yesterday they'd had the life jackets between them, but no longer. She quickly hurried ahead of him, but her legs felt like mush.

As they got closer, she saw the boys come out the doors of the clubhouse with two bags of clubs, but they weren't alone. A shudder rocked her body. To her shock it was Nikos with his longtime Swiss ski buddy Fritz walking behind them. Her secret was out now to the one person she hadn't wanted to know anything!

Who would have thought she'd bump into her brother here? Except that it wasn't a complete surprise. Nikos loved golf when he wasn't skiing. He said the mental game kept him sharp. Was Renate with him, or had he left her on Andros for the day?

She watched him take Ari aside and engage him in conversation. Even as far apart as they still were, she could tell her son was being vetted. Dax stood by Fritz. She'd have given anything if things hadn't happened this way, but there was no help for it now.

Fritz came forward and gave her a kiss on both cheeks. "Stella Athas. It's been a few years. Nikos didn't tell me you'd grown into such a raving beauty."

She'd never cared for his brash manner and didn't like the way he was checking her out. "How are you, Fritz? Let me introduce you to Ari's father, Theo Pantheras. Theo? Fritz here took the bronze for Switzerland in the slalom a few years ago."

"Hello." Theo shook his hand without saying anything else. Most people fawned over Fritz and Nikos, but she knew Theo wasn't as easily impressed.

Ari walked over to stand next to Theo who put his arms around him and hugged him close in a protective gesture. It thrilled Stella. Her son now had his own dad, thank heaven. Nikos couldn't say or do anything about it.

Her brother trained his eyes on her and came closer. They glittered in that icy way they did when his anger was truly kindled. "Well, well, well. A day of golf for my little sister."

Nikos didn't even pretend to acknowledge Theo. Six years had done nothing to teach her brother a thing about human decency. His behavior now reminded her of one time in New York when he'd humiliated Rachel so thoroughly, Stella had thought she'd lost her best friend for good. He'd called her a fat, orange-haired, American military brat in her hearing. Stella had never forgiven him for hurting her friend.

"Who would have imagined finding you on the world's newest and most celebrated golf course?"

"I was about to say the same thing," she said, daring to speak her mind again. It was cathartic to be able to. "Where's Renate?"

"With Rachel," he muttered. "Since you left Andros so fast, I think it's time you and I had a little talk to catch up. If the rest of you will excuse us for a few minutes."

"Maybe another time," Theo interjected smoothly. "We don't want to be late for our tee-off time."

Nothing would have enraged Nikos more than to be snubbed in front of Fritz like that, by Theo no less. She could feel her brother seething. Theo on the other hand seemed to care less.

He put his other arm around Stella's shoulders. "Come on, everyone—Dax—" he urged the boy hauling the other golf bag. Together the four of them headed for the first tee.

"Stella? I'm waiting." Nikos said coldly.

In order to prevent a contretemps, she decided to talk to him, but Theo stopped her from moving. "I'm afraid you'll be waiting a long time. It appears the two of you will have to have one of your family chats another time. She and the boys are with me and we're busy."

Her brother came closer. "I could have you thrown off this resort for talking to me that way," he snarled at Theo. "One word to the owner from me and that's that."

"Stop it, Nikos," Stella muttered, mortified and infuriated by his behavior. He was out of control. Even with the boys around, he didn't care what they thought of him.

"I will, after we've had our talk." He wouldn't let this go. It was unbelievable.

She felt Theo remove his arm and pull out his cell phone. Whatever he said was short and to the point. Almost immediately she saw Theo's bodyguard and another man coming toward them from the clubhouse at full speed.

"Boris? If you would see that these two gentlemen leave the course, we'd be grateful."

Nikos was a skier, not a body builder. The two men could take care of him with no problem. Part of her was thrilled to see him thwarted, but another part grieved for him. He was her brother and she loved him, but it had been years since she'd liked him. She had to search back in her memory when he was a preteen to remember anything good.

"Who in the hell do you think you are?" Nikos demanded.

"Nikos," Stella cried, "what's the matter with you?"

"It's all right," Theo assured her. "He's just surprised to see me with you again after all these years, aren't you, Nikos. Better get used to it since the blood of our two families runs through Ari's veins.

"If you can learn to behave yourself, you're welcome to golf here again another time when you've cooled down. My treat. I'm the owner. Now we really have to get cracking, don't we Ari."

Her son smiled. "Yes. See ya, Uncle Nikos." When they'd walked a little distance, Ari looked up at him. "I didn't know you owned this place."

"There's a lot you don't know about me, or me you. That's why it's so great we're planning to spend as much time together as possible, don't you think?"

"Yes." He was beaming. "Mom? I've never seen Uncle Nikos so mad."

She was still shivering. It was truth time. "Unfortunately I've seen him worse, honey. We'll just stay away from him for a while until he apologizes."

"He doesn't like me."

That was the first time Ari had admitted it aloud. All because of his father, who'd given him new confidence.

"It's *me* he doesn't like, Ari," Theo said softly.

"How come?"

"I come from a very poor family. Your uncle didn't like me being with your mother or having anything to do with her."

"That's stupid."

"I agree, but a lot of wealthy people like your uncle feel that way."

"Uncle Nikos isn't wealthy. Uncle Stasi has to give him money when he runs out."

A gasp escaped Stella's lips. Ari knew too much for his own good.

"Well, let's forget it and have ourselves a fun game. Who wants to go first?"

"I do," Stella volunteered. After the awful scene with Nikos, she needed to do something physical to channel all that negative energy in a different direction.

"This is going to be an adventure," Theo whispered against her neck. All her anxiety flew out the window as other sensations took over.

He'd already put his arms around her to demonstrate how to do a golf swing. The weight of his hard body cocooning hers caused her to forget what she was doing. She felt him nibble her sun-warmed shoulder where the tie had slipped a little. It made her breathless.

"How soon is it going to be our turn?" Ari stood next to Dax, resigned it might be a long wait.

He'd asked it so seriously, she and Theo burst out laughing at the same time. It suddenly occurred to her she hadn't been this happy in years. He'd brought joy to his son's life. He'd slain a dragon for her today. A week ago she couldn't have imagined any of it.

Please, God. Don't let the darkness come again. Make this happiness last.

CHAPTER SIX

AT SIX that evening, Stella walked Dax out to his parents' car. Ari and Theo followed with his suitcase and the games and stuff he'd brought with him. Everyone hugged. Dax gave Theo a super-duper hug.

In front of Dax's parents, Theo invited Ari's friend to come to Salamis Island in a couple of weekends for a sleepover. The other man nodded his agreement of the idea. They chatted about the golf course for a few minutes.

"I love you guys," Dax said to Stella before giving her a hug. "I had an awesome time."

"It was a treat for us, too, honey," she told him. With Theo around it couldn't have been anything else.

Elani stared at Theo before flashing Stella a private message. She could hear her friend asking where *he'd* come from. Not even Elani was immune. Dax would fill her in on some of the details. The rest would have to wait until Stella phoned her friend and confided in her.

When the three of them went back into the house, Ari turned to her. "Now that Dax has gone home, can papa sleep in my room tonight? Please?"

Stella should have seen it coming, but the thought of Theo staying over made her heart skip a couple of beats.

"What do you say, Stella?" Theo teased gently.

He probably sensed how much she wanted him to stay. Maybe it would be a good thing. Maybe they could really talk after Ari went to bed. She was finally in a mood to listen. "It's all right with me, but only if you don't tell UFO stories and keep each other awake all night."

Ari launched himself at her. "Thanks, Mom." His eyes looked suspiciously bright in the foyer light. "I love you."

"I love you, too, honey."

"This was the best day of my life!"

He said that every time he'd been with Theo. She believed it.

His father grabbed him. "And it's not over yet!"

"Come on upstairs, Papa."

Stella nodded to him. "I'll be up in a minute to bring you a few things." While she was at it she'd find one of Stasio's robes for Theo to wear. He was a tall, powerfully built man like Theo. They'd be hanging in Stasio's closet.

"Hurry," he whispered with urgency in his voice before racing Ari up the stairs two at a time. They whooped it up like two kids. Their laughter floated down and followed her to the kitchen.

Iola came rushing in. "What's going on? I thought Dax went home."

She gathered some fruit and chips for them. "He did, but now we have another guest."

"Who?"

"Ari's father."

She crossed herself. "Aiyee—"

Stella chuckled. "It's all right. I'm glad they're together. A boy should be with his father."

"That isn't what you thought last week."

"A lot has changed since then. He's come back to stay, Iola."

"You have forgiven him?'

She sucked in her breath. "Yes." Until I know differently.

"What if he disappears again?"

"He won't." She knew that in her heart even if she didn't know all of it. Theo had convinced her that Ari meant everything to him. She had to believe him. She would go on believing it.

"How long is he going to stay here?"

"I don't really know yet. He and Ari have a lot of stuff to catch up on."

"And you, too?"

"Maybe."

"Just don't get hurt again."

If it was going to happen, the advice had come too late. "Don't fuss about anything, Iola. We'll just be lazing around here for a few days." Ari needed a taste of what it was like to be around his father all the time.

"But what if your brothers come home for some reason?"

"It doesn't matter." Now that Nikos had seen them together, it wouldn't be long before he told Stasio. In a way it was just as well. With the word out, both brothers would have time to get used to the idea. Once she told Stasio how happy Ari was, he'd be his loving, understanding self.

She had this dream that one day Theo and Stasio would become good friends in their own right, and not just because of Ari, whom they both adored. Though the two men were almost ten years apart, they had the strongest work ethic she'd ever seen. Best of all, they were both intrinsically kind and loved Ari.

"Good night, Iola."

Stella darted off to her room. She was pretty sure there was an extra toothbrush in the bathroom cupboard. She also had some throwaway razors Theo could have if he wanted.

Once she'd found everything and made a detour to Stasio's room, she hurried to Ari's room.

"Hi, Mom. I'm showing papa my scrapbooks so he can see what I looked like when I was a baby." They sat on the bed side by side, poring over everything.

She laid things down on the end of the other queen-size bed. "Those are precious photos."

"Amen." Theo's voice grated with deep emotion. She knew why. He hadn't been there for any of it. He patted the side of the bed next to him so she'd join them. "Ari's been telling me about the couple who lived with you in New York. I want to meet them."

"They're marvelous people."

"They were really nice, Papa."

"And lucky," Theo added. "They got to hold

you all the time, change your diapers, tell you stories and kiss you when you cried. I'm jealous."

It wrenched Stella's heart that Theo had missed out on all of it. She felt his hand slide around her waist and squeeze her hip. "I'll be eternally grateful to them for helping your mom when I couldn't. One day we'll fly to New York so I can meet them."

"Could we?" Ari cried.

"We'll do a lot of things."

Stella was curious to know what kinds of things he had in mind, but she would have to ask him later. "I think it's time you got ready for bed," she reminded Ari.

"Okay."

"Theo, I brought you a robe and a couple of other items. You can use Ari's bathroom to change."

"Thank you." His eyes captured hers. "This is what I call living!" He got up from the bed and disappeared into the bathroom.

Ari slipped on his pajamas in record time. "Mom? Can Papa stay with us all the time?"

"I'm afraid not, honey."

"How come?"

Floundering, she said, "Because he has his

own house. Like you, I'm getting used to having him in my life again."

His eyes shone. "But you like him."

"You know I do."

"I love him."

"I kind of figured that out."

"I'm so glad he came back."

"I'm glad, too," she admitted. Her son was a different person. "Good night, honey."

She kissed his forehead, then rushed to her own room to get ready for bed. Stella couldn't imagine how she would get to sleep knowing Theo was next door. The knowledge that they'd be spending tomorrow together made her even more excited.

After slipping on a nightgown, she went into the bathroom to brush her teeth. Once she'd turned off the light, she had every intention of going to bed. However, she heard their voices carry because she shared a bathroom with Ari. Though she hated herself for eavesdropping, she couldn't resist listening at the door for a second.

"…because I felt inferior to my brother. Hektor was the oldest in my family and had a calling for the priesthood. My parents loved him so much, I thought they didn't love me."

"Did it make you cry?"

"A lot when I was really young."

"I love you, Papa."

"I know you do. I love you, too. More than anything on earth."

"Did your other brothers feel bad, too?"

"I think so, but I never talked to them about it. When he left our house for good, it was very hard on me. I'd lost my big brother. About that time I made plans to go away with your mother and marry her, but the night we were going to meet at the church, some mean guys beat me up."

"How come, Papa?" he cried in a tear-filled voice. "Why did they do that?"

"Because they didn't like me and wanted to keep me and your mother apart. They got their wish."

Stella felt bile rise in her throat. Who was responsible for such a crime? Who would have cared to that degree?

"When I got better, I looked everywhere for your mother. My friends and family helped me. I made phone calls and sent her letters, but no one had seen her and I realized I'd really lost her."

"She went to New York with Stasi."

"I know that now, but at the time it was like

she'd never existed. Suffice it to say that when I lost her, I lost my very best friend."

Tears gushed down her cheeks. *You were mine, too, Theo.*

"And because I lost her, I lost you."

"I'm here now, Papa."

"Don't I know it. Unfortunately back then, I was in a very bad way. That's when I decided to leave home and start working on a career, but it was the most painful time in my life. I never thought I'd see her again, but then I drove by your house last week and saw both of you walking. I couldn't believe it! It made me so happy, I wrote your mother a letter and asked her to call me."

"But Mommy thought you didn't love her anymore."

"I realize that now, but it wasn't true. I loved your mommy so much I would have done anything for her. But I had to make money so I could pay someone to help me find her."

"Because you were poor, huh."

"Yes, because I'm a Pantheras from the poor part of Salamis and Stella was an Athas from the best part of Athens."

"I'm a Pantheras, too!" Ari declared.

"Yes you are, half me, half your mom, and none of it matters as long as we're all together."

She couldn't take any more and went back to her room. Theo had told her there were things she still didn't know that could hurt her and Ari. Had her father been so against her marrying Theo, *he* was the one behind the attack?

Stella's father had been a very stern man who'd risen to prominence in the Greek government. He was very proper, old-fashioned. His pride had always made it difficult for her to approach him about her personal life.

When she thought about it, he had many influential friends in high places. Had he arranged things behind the scenes, never expecting Theo to come back and fight for his son? Deep down, had he been a corrupt man?

If so, and Nikos knew about it, then it would explain why her brother had been so obnoxious at the golf course. It was almost as if he were carrying on where her father had left off, but he was blatantly open about it. Stasio would have been kept in the dark. She knew for a fact he would never have sanctioned anything cruel or criminal. It wasn't in his nature.

Was that why Theo was afraid to tell her, because he didn't want her to hate her father?

For the rest of the night her mind ran in circles, driving her crazy with more questions until she knew no more. By morning she was worn out. When Ari came to her room and begged her to let his daddy stay at their house through the weekend, she couldn't say no. They were all on vacation and her brothers were on Andros.

Every day Ari spent with his father in their house, she could see that he was becoming more secure. Between walks around Athens and their star-gazing class, there was plenty to do that was all new to him. Theo had opened up a different world for him, and her son was having the time of his life.

Before bed on Saturday night, Stella sought out Iola. "Tell cook we'll be wanting a big breakfast in the morning before we go to church."

Stella dashed upstairs and discovered Ari and his father watching a DVD about the day the earth stood still. A smile broke out on her face. "Hi, guys. Considering our plans for tomorrow, you'd better get to bed soon. In the meantime, I need to check and make sure your suit is ready for church, Ari."

She went to his room and walked inside his closet. The pants of his navy three-piece could use a pressing. She pulled them out. The jacket looked fine. After an inspection she discovered both dress shirts had been washed and ironed.

"I like the blue-and-white stripe the best," Theo murmured right behind her. A little cry of surprise broke from her throat. Except for the day he'd helped her with her golf swing, he hadn't made any kind of overture toward her. When he slid his arms around her, bringing her back up tight against his chest, it took her totally by surprise. He'd already changed into his robe.

For quite a while now she'd been so aware of him physically, it had become painful to be near him. With a sense of wonder she felt him kiss her nape, sending little fingers of delight inching their way through her body. She grew weak with those old, breathtaking feelings of desire.

"What a wonderful place to find you," he whispered in a husky voice. In the next instant he'd turned her around so their faces were mere centimeters apart. "I don't know about you, but if I can't have this right now, I'm not going to survive the night."

His dark head descended, covering her mouth with his own. Surrounded by clothes that muffled sounds, he kissed her with a hunger that brought a moan to her throat.

Back and forth they returned each other's kisses, setting off waves of desire. He smelled wonderfully male, intoxicating her. As her hands slid up his chest, she came in contact with a smattering of black hair.

The feel of his skin electrified her, bringing back memories she couldn't afford to entertain with Ari just outside the door. This was crazy. Insane. She wrenched her lips from his. "We can't do this."

His deep chuckle thrilled her. "It appears we are." He kissed her again, long and deep until she was a throbbing mass of needs. He undid one of the ties to kiss her shoulder. Rapture exploded inside her, but she knew where this was leading and finally backed out of the closet, gasping for air.

"Did you forget these?" He dangled Ari's pants in front of her while she retied her blouse on top of her shoulder. His wolfish grin was the last straw. She took the pants and threw them at him. Ari roared with laughter.

Theo ducked, then swiped them from the floor. "You better watch out, little girl. You're playing with a big boy now."

She screamed and ran away from him. Ari was jumping on top of the bed with a huge smile while he watched them. Stella backed up against the wall. Theo came closer, twirling the pants in the air. He looked dark and dangerous and capable of doing anything.

"Wh-what are you going to do?" She stumbled over the words.

His eyes narrowed. "What you'd like me to do."

"Get her and tickle her, Papa. She hates to be tickled."

"Traitor!"

"Thanks for the tip, son." Except that Theo already knew about her ticklish side.

"No, Theo… Please."

He came at her anyway with a frightening growl. While she tried to dodge him, Iola came to the door with an anxious look. "Is everything all right?"

"No." Stella grinned. "I'm getting tickled to death."

The housekeeper's frown actually turned into

a smile. Stella couldn't remember the last time she'd seen one of those from her.

"Good night, but keep the noise down so people around here can sleep!"

"Sorry, Iola," Theo called out. Ari echoed him.

Stella turned to the men. "I'll say good night, too."

"Don't go yet," Theo whispered, but she didn't dare linger. Quick as lightning she grabbed the pants before closing the door. Tomorrow she'd press them.

After giving Iola a hug, she went to her room but couldn't imagine how she would get to sleep after being thoroughly kissed in Theo's arms. The knowledge that they'd be spending tomorrow together caused her body to ache with longing. And trepidation, too.

They were going to church tomorrow to meet Theo's family, and the only reason she was going to be introduced to them after all these years was because of Ari. His parents had never approved of his association with Stella. Knowing that, Theo had never taken her home to meet them. It was all very sad.

She could only hope they would learn to tolerate her for Ari's sake. No matter what Theo might have told them, Stella was the reason Theo had left Greece in the first place. That wouldn't exactly have endeared her to them, but Ari would win them over.

When Theo had returned to Greece, he'd received a blessing from his oldest brother, who was one of the priests at the church in the Plaka near the cathedral. To Theos mind, Hektor had never looked more impressive than in his vestments.

Their reunion had been a heartwarming one. They had spent part of the day together catching up on each other's lives. There was laughter and weeping followed by a serious talk about Stella and Ari. Theo promised his brother that when and if he could, he would bring them both to the church to meet him.

That day had come.

Following the mass, his brother had invited Theo's family into his private study in the old house next to the church. He shared it with two other priests who had apartments there.

"Come in here."

Theo was the last to enter the room with Stella and Ari. He was proud to be able to introduce them. Like his son, he'd dressed in a navy suit that went with the sobriety of the occasion. Stella looked a vision in a summery two-piece hyacinth suit, elegantly tailored. Her coloring added to the picture of classy femininity.

He ushered them over to the couch where the family had congregated. Theo's parents couldn't take their eyes off Stella and Ari. His brothers and their families were equally dazzled.

"As you can all see, I brought a surprise today," Theo began. "Stella? Ari? I'd like you to meet my family starting with my mother, Ariadne, and my father, Gregory."

His mother beamed at both of them. "I've wanted to meet you for a long time."

"I have, too," Stella responded quietly.

Her gaze rested on her grandson. "You and I have the same name."

"I know." Ari smiled as he moved around the room with Stella to shake everyone's hand.

Theo's father studied him. "You look so much like my Theo, I think I'm seeing things."

"We have the same peak," Ari said, pointing to his hair. Everyone laughed.

"This is my brother Dymas, his wife Lina and their children, Calli, Dori and Spiro."

Ari eyed his older cousins. "Hi."

"Hi," they all said in turn.

"This is my brother Spiro, his wife, Minta, and their children Phyllis, Roxane and Leandros."

Ari looked at Theo before he said, "He's the one my age, huh."

"Right. You're both six going on a hundred."

Everyone laughed again.

"Last but not least, my oldest brother Hektor, Father Matthias."

Ari walked up to him and shook his hand. "Papa said he misses you a lot."

Hektor seemed moved. "I'm not supposed to admit it, but I miss all of my family, too."

"Do you like being a priest?"

He smiled. "Very much. I'm so happy you and your father have been united. He didn't know he had a son. What a wonderful present to come home to. He loves you very much."

"I love him, too!"

"If you don't mind, I'd like to give you a blessing. Is that all right with you?"

Ari nodded.

It was a short blessing, sweet and it brought a lump to Theo's throat. He eyed Stella out of the corner of his eye. Her head was bowed. He could tell the words had touched her, too.

After a few more minutes they all said goodbye and climbed into two limos Theo had provided for the family. He and Stella rode with his parents and Ari. They headed to Salamis. During the drive everyone got a little better acquainted. His father laughed more than he'd heard him in a long time.

By the time they ate dinner at the *taverna*, spirits were high. Theo could tell Stella and Ari were enjoying themselves. His son went off with Leandros for a little while, breaking the ice even more.

Stella chatted with his sisters-in-law about their children. The subject was something they could all relate to. As far as he could tell, there were no uncomfortable moments.

"It was a good beginning, don't you think?" Theo asked Stella during their trip back to Athens via the linking road from Perama to the mainland. She was seated across from him next to Ari.

"We had a wonderful time." With Ari along, she couldn't ask Theo how his parents really felt.

"Yeah, but I wish I didn't have to wear this suit all day long."

Theo threw his head back and laughed. "You're

so much like me it hurts. I promise you won't have to wear one until we go to church again."

He eyed Theo soberly. "Do you like church?"

Stella glanced at him, waiting to hear his answer.

"Honestly?"

Ari nodded.

"I don't exactly like it, but I always feel better after I've gone."

"Is that how you feel, too, Mom?"

Now the shoe was on the other foot. He grinned while she decided what to say.

"Yes."

"But how did you feel when you were my age?"

She chuckled. "I didn't like it all that much."

"You see why I loved your mother so much, Ari? We think alike."

"I bet you wouldn't tell Hektor that."

"He knew how I felt when I was little because I squirmed all the time. I didn't have to say anything."

"He was nice. So are my grandparents."

"I'm glad you feel that way because they're crazy about you."

"They want me to come and see them next

week. Grandma said I could help them in the kitchen."

"Would you like that?"

"I'd love it!"

"Then we'll definitely go over. While your mom and I have dinner, you can serve us before we have to leave for our class."

"That would be awesome. Leandros wishes he could come with us."

"Maybe sometime we can arrange it. We'll have to check with the staff at the college. Does he like UFO stuff?"

"Yeah. He's pretty cool."

High praise. Theo's cup was running over tonight.

"Can you sleep at our house again tonight, Papa?" They'd just driven up in front of the villa.

Without looking at Stella he said, "I have a much better idea. Since your mother still has ten days of vacation left, why don't the three of us take our own vacation on St. Thomas? I haven't been on a real one in years. I can promise you we'll never run out of things to do."

Ari looked like he was going to burst with joy. "Could we, Mom?"

Theo could tell he'd surprised Stella with his

suggestion, but knowing she would have to think about it, he would give her the time because it had been a perfect day and he refused to ruin it.

"Tell you what, Ari. I have some business to do and will probably work at my office until I pick you up for our class tomorrow. Afterward, we'll fly to St. Thomas, that is if your mother approves."

"Can we, Mom? Please?"

"I...I think that sounds exciting," her voice faltered.

Until she'd said the words, Theo hadn't realized he'd been holding his breath. "While you guys pack, I'll get my work out of the way so I can concentrate on you for the next ten days."

"I can't wait, but I wish I could come to your office and see what you do."

"Another time and you can. We've got the rest of our lives, Ari."

"Your father's right," Stella interjected. "He's a busy man and you have to respect that."

"What are you going to do tomorrow, Mom?"

"Lots of errands to get ready for our trip."

"I'd rather go with you in our new car."

As she laughed, her eyes happened to meet Theo's. For the first time he felt they were communicating like they once did, sharing the same joy. It was a moment he wanted to freeze.

If he weren't afraid of losing the ground he'd gained, he would take her and Ari to St. Thomas in the morning, but he didn't want to push Stella. Though his work could wait, he pretended otherwise and kept silent, endeavoring to avoid Ari's pleading look. Nothing would please him more than to keep Ari at his office with him, but again, Stella needed time to get used to Theo being in her life again.

Once he'd undone his seat belt, he got out to help them to the front door. "Good night, son." He gave Ari a bear hug.

"Sleep well, Stella." He darted her a penetrating glance before getting back in the limo. After the day they'd spent together, he didn't dare touch her.

CHAPTER SEVEN

WHILE Stella got ready for bed, her mind was on Theo. Today had been a great highlight for her meeting his family, going to church with them. But when he'd brought her and Ari home, she'd sensed a certain reticence on his part to linger. It was impossible to know what was going on inside him. She was afraid, but didn't know of what exactly.

Yes she did. Deep down she knew he didn't want to tell her about her father. Theo was afraid that when he shared that with her, it would devastate her. Maybe it would when confronted with the irrefutable proof, but her austere father had passed on. What was important was Ari's relationship with Theo. No one could hurt that now.

Before she slipped under the covers, she

reached for her phone to check any messages. Afraid it would ring while they were in church, she'd turned it off and had forgotten about it. When she looked now, she noticed three from Rachel. Each one begged her to call immediately, no matter how late.

Fearing this had to do with her pregnancy, Stella phoned. Rachel answered right away. "Thank you for calling!" she cried anxiously.

She clutched the phone tighter. "Is there something wrong with the baby?"

"No. Stella—why didn't you tell us about Theo while you were here? When Nikos flew back from St. Thomas the other night, it was all he could talk about."

A band constricted her lungs. "It's exactly for that reason I didn't want anyone to know anything."

"Know what?"

Rachel was Stella's oldest, closest friend. She trusted her with her life. Without preamble she told her everything. When she'd finished, the silence on the other end was deafening.

"Rachel? Are you still there?"

"Yes. Oh, Stella—"

"I know what you're thinking, but…I trust

him. He was beaten up. You can see the damage. I think my father had something to do with it."

"You're kidding—"

"No. I've had time to think it all out. At the right moment, I'll get the truth from Theo. In the meantime, don't tell Stasio my suspicions. He revered father so much, it could really hurt him." In fact, the truth would hurt him a lot more than it was hurting Stella right now.

"You honestly believe Theo, don't you."

"Yes, Rachel. You'd have to see him with Ari to understand."

"Well if it's good enough for you, then it is for me, too."

Tears welled up. "Thank you, dear friend. You couldn't possibly know what that means to me."

"Your happiness is everything. Stasio feels the same way. Unfortunately, Nikos keeps talking about your parents and how upset they would be if they knew you'd been seeing him again. He blames your father's heart attack on your association with Theo. Maybe Nikos was in your father's confidence."

"I'm thinking the same thing," she whispered. "The point is, it happened a long time ago. With father gone, this is no longer any of

Nikos's business. Not that it ever was, but if father told Nikos how he felt about Theo, then it makes a sick kind of sense."

"I agree. Is it true Theo owns that new resort on St. Thomas?"

"Yes."

"You might as well hear the rest, then. Nikos told Stasio he believes Theo is tied to underworld crime, otherwise he couldn't possibly have made that kind of money, not when he didn't have a drachma to his name."

Outraged, Stella cried, "Where did he come up with such a ludicrous accusation?"

"I don't know."

Stella rubbed her temple where she felt an ache. "Theo has been out of the country for six years working his head off to build a successful career. Nikos is only making wild accusations because his own business plans didn't turn out to be successful."

"I'm sure jealousy enters into it. Stasio's been trying to reason with him, but Nikos insists he's going to have Theo investigated."

"What? That's crazy."

"You're right. Poor Renate has no influence over him right now. She wants to go back to

Switzerland, but he won't hear of it. He won't even talk to me, but then he never did like me so that's no news."

Nikos had never approved of Rachel, though he'd had to pretend to get along with her because she was Stasio's wife. At this point Stella feared the worst. "Nikos isn't behaving rationally right now. You should have seen him. He didn't care that Ari and Dax were watching."

"How awful. Listen…when Stasio comes up to bed, I'll tell him you're waiting for his call. He'll be relieved you're available to talk."

"Okay. Love you, Rachel. Take care of yourself."

"Ditto."

They hung up before she realized she hadn't even asked her sister-in-law about her nausea. She eased herself down under the covers and waited for Stasio's call, but he didn't phone for another half hour. It was after midnight when she finally said hello to him.

"I'm so sorry you had to find out about Theo through Nikos. I wanted to handle this myself before I told you."

"I understand. My whole concern is for you."

"I know that. The point is, Theo is back in Greece and he wants to be a father to Ari. He's not asking for anything else. I have to tell you he's done nothing but be wonderful to Ari and me. As I told Rachel, he said he'd been accosted before he could meet me at the church that night, and then he could never find me again.

"He sent me a letter that was sent back to him saying addressee unknown. I saw it with my own eyes. According to him someone tried to destroy our love. I...I believe him, Stasio, even though he hasn't told me everything."

"Did you read what the letter said?"

She shivered. "No. I was too angry at the time, but while I'm on St. Thomas, I'll ask him to let me see it."

"When are you going there again?"

"Tomorrow. I'll stay in touch with you while we're gone. As for Nikos, please don't tell him where I am." Stella had made a decision. "After our vacation I'm going to find a new place to live. As long as Nikos continues to stay at the villa when he comes to Athens, it's not a place I want to be."

After they got back from their vacation, if her brother ever came near her or Ari or Theo again with threats of any kind, then she'd call Costas, their family attorney, and have a restraining order put on him.

"Stella…you have every right to be upset. Before things go any further, let's meet in the morning on Andros to talk."

"You mean with Nikos?"

"Yes. It can't hurt anything. If you include him, he'll see you've forgiven him for his outburst on St. Thomas. When he learns that Theo wants to be a father to his son, he'll settle down enough to be more reasonable."

"No he won't, Stasio. He's never fully accepted Ari. Knowing Theo is back in Ari's life is only going to make him more unpleasant to be around. I won't let him hurt my son."

"I'll try to reason with him one more time."

"Thank you for that. I love you, Stasio."

"I love you, too. If Theo is all the things you believe he is and he can make Ari happy, then I couldn't ask more for you. When you never developed an interest in another man, I prayed Theo might come back to you."

Her eyes smarted. The kisses they'd exchanged over the last few days might have rocked her to the foundations, but these were still early days in their tentative relationship. "I…I'm not sure about that, but I do know he wants to father Ari from now on."

"Six years is a long time to be out of his life," Stasio murmured, "but it's never too late. A boy needs his own father if he's lucky enough to have him."

Stasio was talking about their father of course. Her brother was a saint. To have his blessing was all that mattered to Stella. Now that he knew everything, she felt free and couldn't wait to see Theo tomorrow.

"Kyrie Pantheras?"

Theo was on an overseas call. "What is it?" he asked his secretary.

"There's a courier from the court here with a summons. You have to sign for it."

He'd been expecting it. Nikos Athas hadn't wasted any time. "Send him in."

Theo made his excuses to the other man on the phone and hung up. In a minute the courier entered his office. Theo walked over to him. "I understand you have a summons for me?"

"Yes. If you'll sign and date it, please."

After he'd written his signature, he was given

the envelope. Theo closed the door and walked over to the window to open the document.

Pantheras *vs* Athas.

Now that Nikos was back in the picture, Theo had tripled the security on himself, his family, not to mention Stella and Ari. Nikos had tried to destroy them once before. It could happen again. He wouldn't put anything past him and wasn't about to take any chances.

Plaintiff Nikos Athas seeks a restraining order against Defendant Theo Pantheras who has proved to be a threat to Plaintiff's sister, Stella Athas, and her son, Ari. You are hereby summoned to appear before the court at nine a.m., Wednesday, June 15, to answer to charges of manipulation and coercion with intent to harm. Failure to comply will result in your arrest.

Nikos must have been born with a twisted mind.

This summons was what the six years of hard work, sacrifice and preparation had all been about. Theo was more than ready to take on Stella's brother. Since being with her again, heaven knew he hadn't wanted it to come to this, but after bumping into Nikos on St. Thomas, their chance meeting had escalated the situation to a white-hot point.

Theo tapped the paper against his cheek. Stasio Athas's name wasn't on the suit. At this point he began to think he'd been totally wrong about Stella's oldest brother. Stasio had been the one to take her to New York and look after her. He'd been the one to come to Ari's rescue when he and Rachel had been kidnapped. Stella loved Stasio.

He moved over to his desk and phoned Nestor. "I just received a summons from Nikos Athas out of Costas Paulos's office. Who is he?"

"The Athas family attorney. Read me what it says."

After Theo complied, Nestor grunted. "I'll answer it and be in touch with you."

"Thank you. As you know, I don't want a court fight. Do everything you can to prevent it."

"That may not be possible. Costas is one of the best there is and could hold sway over the judge."

"When I made inquiries, I was told you were one of the best, but whatever happens, keep me posted. I'll be on vacation for the next ten days."

"Enjoy yourself. You deserve it."

"Thanks, Nestor."

With that out of the way, Theo couldn't wait to leave the office. He had plans for the three of them, plans he was praying would change his entire life.

The resort's swimming pool resembled an aqua-blue lake. At one end was the giant slide Theo had told the boys about. Ari had been going down it all afternoon. Stella had taken quite a few turns herself and was worn-out. The hike to the top of the slide provided a work out all its own.

Theo never seemed to tire. He and Ari had thought up a dozen different ways to descend. Her boy was in heaven. If she didn't miss her guess, Theo was, too.

Ari ran over to the stairs. "I'm coming down on my stomach next time, Papa!"

Theo grinned. "Be sure and keep your head up. I'm waiting for you!"

"This is the last one for today, honey," Stella called to him from the sun lounger. "You and your father have your star-gazing class tonight. You need to eat dinner before you go."

"Oh, yeah. I forgot."

As he scrambled up the steps, Stella's gaze drifted to Theo who stood at the bottom of the serpentine slide to watch for him. Every female in the vicinity had their eyes on him, but Theo appeared oblivious. He and Ari were having too much fun.

Stella had brought out a book to read, but she kept looking at the same page over and over again because all she'd done was stare at the dark-haired male no other man compared to. One day Ari would grow up to be every bit as gorgeous and arresting. It gave her a thrill to know she was with Theo, that Ari was their son.

Several females cast her an envious glance. One woman who'd walked over to this part of the pool in a minuscule bikini made a play for him, engaging him in conversation. Stella felt so territorial she wanted to push her into the water, but of course she didn't do it. For one thing, Theo would know without a doubt her attraction to him had reached a dangerously strong level.

Close your eyes, Stella. Don't look at him.

Ari's life had become complete with the advent of his father's vital presence. His un-qualified show of love for their son should be enough for Stella. Theo's private life was something else again.

They'd been here four days already. Once this vacation was over, she would get an apartment in the same neighborhood and life would get back to a new kind of normalcy. She'd go back to her work. So would he. Theo had talked about wanting a relationship with her, but they needed to go slowly.

In the meantime she had to put up with other women eyeing him. His kind of charisma brought the females running, just like the one with the tanned body and flowing blond hair still talking to him while he watched for Ari.

Since Theo seemed to be enjoying the attention, Stella decided she'd watched the spectacle long enough. After putting the book in her bag, she slipped on her beach coverup and headed inside the hotel where she wouldn't have to undergo more torture.

Certain things had changed since six years ago when Theo had never done anything to make her jealous. But that was when they'd been young lovers hiding from their families in order to be together. Everything was different now.

As she let herself in the room adjoining

Theo's penthouse suite, a shaft of pain robbed her of breath because a part of her didn't want things to be different. In her heart of hearts she longed to be in his arms again. She ached for that fulfillment he'd brought to her life while they'd shut out the rest of the world.

But you could never go back. She didn't want to revisit all the pain that followed after he'd disappeared. Somehow she had to learn to survive with him back in Ari's life, but maybe not hers! Much to Ari's chagrin this special time with him on St. Thomas wouldn't last much longer, but it would be the very best antidote for the illness slowly killing her.

With tears threatening, she hurried into her room with the intention of showering, but all of a sudden Theo burst in through the adjoining door. Ari ran in behind him and disappeared into the bathroom.

"How come you didn't wait for us?" was the first question out of his mouth.

Stella was surprised he'd even noticed. "You two were having such a great time, I didn't know how long you'd be."

She heard him curse before he said, "You and I need to talk." He sounded angry.

"What's wrong?"

"How would you have felt if you'd turned around and discovered I was missing."

"It's not the same thing, Theo. You were talking to that woman. I didn't know if it was about business or not so I decided not to disturb you."

"That woman was a total stranger to me. When she invited me to a party, I told her I was married and my wife was right over there. Except that you weren't anywhere in sight."

"I'm sorry. I don't know what else to say."

"It upset Ari, too."

By now her heart was thundering unmercifully. "I had no idea."

"Next time give me a thought before you bolt." In the next breath he was gone.

"Mom?"

She swung around to see Ari with a towel wrapped around him. "Yes?"

"I thought you liked daddy."

Stella reeled. "You *know* I do. I've already told you that."

"But you don't love him like you used to, huh?"

His question trapped her. No matter how she answered it, Ari would internalize it and eventually tell Theo. "For now, why don't we concentrate on you and your father."

"I wish we could stay here forever."

Unable to resist, she kissed his cheek. "I've never seen you have so much fun before."

His dark eyes shone. "I love him."

"He loves you."

"I know. He's going to take us sailing tomorrow. We're going to stay out overnight and the next day we're going to fish."

"That'll be exciting for you."

"But you'll be with us."

"I don't think so, honey. Your father wants some private time with you. Think of all the years you've both missed."

His cute face crumpled. "Daddy says we won't go if you don't come."

Was Theo worried that Ari might get frightened without her there? If he could have heard his son just now, he'd know the bond between them was so strong, he had nothing to fear in that regard. After they came back from class she would ask Theo about it and reassure him if necessary.

"I'll talk to him later."

"We're going to eat dinner in his room. Come on. You can talk to him right now."

"Not yet. I have to shower first."

A few minutes later Stella rushed back into the bedroom and dressed in a pair of tan slacks and a print top in various shades of earth tones. She'd picked up a darker tan over the past few days. The new lipstick she'd purchased accentuated it. For the first time in years she felt as if she was on a real vacation with nothing to do but eat, sleep and play. She never wanted it to end.

In the past they'd always had to hide from everyone. Yet even after he'd disappeared, she'd never felt free. There was a gloom Nikos brought with him that had always darkened her world, but with Theo she felt free to be herself and Ari was a totally different child.

The more she thought about it, the more she was determined that as soon as they returned to Athens, she would start looking for another place to live. Stasio and his family preferred living on Andros. That left Nikos who could take over the family villa where he'd grown up. It would make him feel in charge. Maybe that's what he needed.

When she walked into Theo's suite, he captured her gaze. They both studied each other. "You look beautiful."

"Thank you."

"In truth you're the most beautiful woman at this resort. I can't believe how lucky I am."

She tried to stifle her gasp of surprise, but she couldn't suppress the surge of pleasure that curled through her body. Since it was Theo, he'd already noticed the signs, like the fact that right now her breathing had grown shallow just being this close to him.

He could read all the little clues that meant she was so aware of him, she was jittery. Of course she wasn't fooling anyone, especially not him, but it was a game she had to play for self-preservation.

"I'm lucky to be with two such handsome men."

"Am I handsome?" Ari wanted to know.

"Yes, just like your father," she blurted before realizing what she'd just said. Theo simply smiled at her.

Stella looked away. "Um, this looks good." She sat down next to Ari where Theo served them a light dinner from the cart sent up from the kitchen. So far they'd been eating all their meals in his room. She loved the intimacy, like they were a real family.

Theo eyed her for a long moment, seeming to assess her until she felt exposed. Her heart did a little kick she couldn't control. "Did Ari tell you my plans for the next few days?"

"Yes. We were just talking about it." If they all went sailing overnight, they'd be away from her brother's long reach a little longer. Without hesitation she said, "I can't think of anything I'd rather do."

"Hooray!" Ari cried.

There was a look in Theo's dark eyes that told her he was pleasantly surprised. "In that case I'd like to leave early in the morning."

"We'll be ready. While you're at class, I'll pack."

"I'll see the galley is stocked with food. That was a luxury I couldn't provide when we used to go rowing. Remember?"

"I didn't know you went rowing with Daddy."

Stella almost choked on the lamb she was eating. "Sometimes we did." Ari had been conceived on one of those outings.

"Was it fun?"

Theo's jet-black gaze shot to hers. "How would *you* describe it?" he asked her in his deep voice.

She couldn't meet his eyes. "As I recall, it was a lot of hard work."

"But the end justified the means every time."

Theo...

Unable to sit there any longer, she got up from the table. "I think I'll get started on that packing. Enjoy your class and come back safely."

Stella couldn't get out of his room fast enough.

Two nights later Stella stood at the bow of the sailboat, gazing at the view.

"That's a sunset you don't see very often." Theo had come up behind her.

"It's glorious." She'd been marveling over a golden orange sky slowly fading into pink. He ran his hands up her arms, kissing the side of her neck. "Wh-where's Ari?" When Theo came up on her like that, she couldn't even talk clearly.

"In the galley finishing his ice cream. Why do you think I stole up here for a moment?" His hands caressed her shoulders.

"No, Theo," she cried, "this isn't the time—" But he wasn't listening to her.

"You're wrong. It's the perfect time. Before I went away, you were my whole life." He turned her around to face him. "Since I've been back,

I've discovered you still are. *Agape mou,*" he whispered, finding her mouth, avidly kissing her lips apart. "I need to taste your sweetness again."

His hunger for her made her forget everything else. All she knew was that his mouth set her on fire and she couldn't stop what was happening. As his passion grew, she was engulfed in his arms, craving his touch. There was no one in the world who could make her feel the way Theo did. Her need to merge with him was overpowering.

He finally lifted his head enough to look into her eyes. "I can't believe that when I flew to New York, you were there, too, having our baby. I should have been there for you." She heard tears in his voice. "We were robbed of our lives for a long time. Now that we're back together, I need this more than ever. Tell me you feel the same way…."

For a dizzying moment she felt their bodies meld. The chemistry between them had always been volatile. Right now it was as if they'd never been apart. "Obviously I'm not immune to you, Theo," she confessed on a little moan of surrender, "but having told you that, it changes nothing. We're not young kids anymore."

"No. We're a man and woman who've never been able to stay away from each other."

She searched his eyes. "There are things we have to talk about."

"I agree, but let's enjoy the rest of our trip first. This is heaven for me. I want to make it last as long as possible. Don't you?"

"Of course," she admitted, "but—"

"Do you trust me?"

She felt him probing deep into her soul. "Yes. Otherwise I wouldn't be here."

"That's all I needed to hear."

Once again his mouth fused with hers. This was ecstasy. His lips roved over her face, capturing each feature. As she sought his mouth helplessly, she heard a sound behind them.

"What kind of fish do you think we'll catch tomorrow?"

While she tore her lips away and eased out of Theo's arms, he turned to Ari. "Probably some sea bass. It's very tasty. If they're not biting, then we'll do some snorkeling."

"Will we see a lot of things?"

"I'll take us to a spot where the water's so clean and pure, you won't believe what's swimming underneath."

"Will it be scary?"

"Not where we're going. Besides, your mom and I will be right there with you."

"Yeah."

"Now that we've dropped anchor for the night, come on and help me put the boat to bed."

"A boat doesn't go to bed, Papa."

"Sure it does. It's tired after working hard all day." Ari giggled. No one was more exciting to be with than Theo. "We have to clean up any messes, fasten down anything loose, turn out lights. There's a lot of stuff."

"Will we be able to fish as soon as we wake up?"

"Yes, but it'll be foggy so we'll throw out our lines and see what we can catch until the sun burns it off."

"How did you learn to fish?"

"My father taught me and my brothers. We had to go out very early to catch enough for my mother to cook."

"You mean for breakfast?"

"No. She used fish to make the food we sold at the taverna."

"But what if you didn't catch any?"

"That happened a lot."

"Then what did you do?"

"We had to go to the meat shops and wait for them to sell us the meat parts for a cheap price nobody wanted."

"You mean like brains and liver and stuff?"

"That's right."

"Did we eat brains at the taverna the other day?"

Theo roared with laughter. "No. For you she prepared the very best food."

"It was yummy."

Stella's heart swelled with emotion as she gathered Ari's damp towels and sandals and listened to them talk. For one six-year-old boy, he left a lot of items around, but she didn't care. Theo was telling her son things she hadn't known, not during all the time she'd spent with him.

"Papa? I'd like to live on this sailboat."

She chuckled along with Theo. Ari loved everything they did because he was with his father.

"Shall we do it? Shall we just sail off to wherever we want?"

"Could we?"

"Yes, but I think you'd start to miss your friends and school."

"Did you like school?"

"For the most part."

"I like recess the best."

"So did I. You must be my son."

"I am!" At that remark, Theo threw back his head and laughed that deep, rich laugh Stella loved to hear. "I wish Mom and I could live with you."

"I'd love it," Theo answered without hesitation. His narrowed gaze captured hers. "How about *you, Stella?*"

Her heart thudded in her chest. He didn't play fair asking her a loaded question like that in front of their son. "Are you being serious?" She'd decided it was his turn to be put on the spot.

There was a strange tension between them. He finally said, "So serious that I'd like to discuss it further after we turn in."

Staggered by his response, Stella left the deck and hurried below. She needed to gather her wits and headed straight to the galley to finish cleaning up. The two of them followed a few minutes later.

There were two bedrooms, one with a double bed and another with two bunk beds. She would have slept with Ari, but Theo insisted she have the big bed because the men were on an adventure.

After kissing Ari good-night, Stella brushed her teeth and changed into a pair of navy-blue tailored pajamas. Turning on the reading lamp, she sat up in bed and pulled out the book she'd tried to read at the pool. It was a spy novel written by an author she liked.

To her dismay she couldn't get into it tonight, either. When Theo entered the room dressed in a pair of sweats and a T-shirt, her heart thumped so hard, it hurt. In the semidarkness his striking masculine features stood out. Disturbed at the appealing sight of him, she pretended to keep reading.

In the next instant he came to sit down beside her and plucked it out of her hands. Then he got on the bed and stretched out next to her with one elbow propped. She felt his eyes study her with toe-curling intimacy. "You could have no comprehension of how gorgeous you look tonight."

She could hardly swallow. "Thank you."

"After I went to New York, there were nights when I thought I'd die if I couldn't have you. I couldn't fathom that you'd stopped loving me."

Stella averted her eyes. "Then you have some comprehension of how I felt. It took raising Ari to help me deal with the pain."

He took a shuddering breath. "I threw myself

into work. I had three jobs, one with a well-to-do Greek café owner who was a boyhood friend of my grandfather's. He told me that if I wanted to make real money, I should study the real estate listings. There were properties I could buy without a down payment. The trick was to fix one up and then sell it for as much as I could.

"I thought he was crazy, but I took his advice. You wouldn't believe how fast I started making money. He told me where to put it. Some of it went to high-risk investments that paid off. I sent money home and started planning my return. One of my goals was to find you and make you tell me face-to-face what happened."

She stirred restlessly on the bed before flicking him a glance. "I was the opposite. It was such a nightmare, I hoped I'd never see you again."

Theo grimaced. "My letter must have come as a shock."

"I fainted, but Iola caught me so I didn't crack my head open on the floor." The compassion in his eyes was too much. She looked away again.

"I'm sorry, Stella. After driving past the villa and seeing you, I didn't know how else to make contact."

She moistened her lips. "No matter how it was done, it was like finding out you'd come back from the dead."

"I was told you'd gotten rid of our child."

"Theo—"

"To see Ari skipping along with you almost sent me into cardiac arrest. To think the whole time in New York, I believed—"

"That I'd ended my pregnancy?" she cut in on him. "How you must have despised me."

His body stiffened with remembered pain. "I was riddled with rage until I saw Ari. Then I was plunged into another kind of fury because you'd kept him from me."

After taking a deep breath she said, "Who did this to us?"

"It doesn't matter anymore." He leaned over her. "In the beginning I tried to despise you, but I couldn't. I fell in love with you a long time ago, Stella. That's never going to change. Marry me, sweetheart. I can't go on without you."

She let out a little moan as he began kissing her, sweeping her away. "I never stopped loving you, either. You're my whole life!"

"Did you just say yes?"

"You *know* I did," she cried. "I love you, I

love you, Theo. I want to be your wife as soon as possible."

"Stella—" came his exultant cry. "Let me love you tonight. Really love you."

The feel of his mouth brought her such rapture, she'd become a trembling mass of need. Over and over she cried out his name. His powerful legs entwined with hers, reminding her of those other times when they'd given in to their desire.

"Papa?"

They both groaned.

"When are you coming back to bed?"

"Don't tell him yet," she whispered. "Let's wait until we know all our plans."

"Agreed." Theo kissed her throat before rolling away from her. "I thought you were asleep, sport."

"I had a nightmare."

"Oh, honey," Stella said. "Come on up here." Ari scrambled on the bed between them. "What was it about?"

"A shark. It was trying to catch me."

"Well, you stay right here with us. We'll keep you safe."

She felt Theo's fingers creep into her hair,

tantalizing her. He'd expected her to urge Ari back to bed so they could take up where they'd left off, but it wouldn't be a good idea for several reasons. The main one was snuggled up against them happy as a new puppy, his nightmare forgotten.

"Good night, everyone."

"Good night, Mom. Good night, Papa."

Theo squeezed her shoulder. "Good night, Mom. Good night, son."

"Mommy's not your mom."

More deep laughter reverberated in the room. It was the last thing she remembered before falling asleep.

By the time their vacation was over, Stella felt like they were a family. She could have stayed there forever playing with and loving the two men she adored. The thought of going back to work made her groan. That was how transported she'd been.

"What was that sigh all about?" Theo was so tuned in to her feelings, they could read each other's minds.

"How much I don't want this to be over." The three of them were carrying their bags to the helicopter.

He caught her around the waist. "It's not going to be. You and I need more time together. Hire a temp to help Keiko for another week. Someone in the office will want the opportunity."

Another week with Theo? She almost stumbled in her excitement. "I'll see what I can arrange."

Before long they flew back to civilization. When the helicopter landed on top of his office building, Stella rebelled. For a moment she had the premonition that now he'd asked her to marry him, this fragile new world they'd been building was going to explode by an unseen force and they'd never be able to pick up the pieces.

As Theo helped her out of the helicopter she whispered, "Do you still have that letter? I'm ready to read it."

His black eyes ignited like hot coals. He pressed a hungry kiss to her mouth. "It's in my office."

"Will you get it for me before you drive me and Ari home?"

"I'll do it right now and join you at the limo." He ruffled Ari's hair. "See you in a minute."

CHAPTER EIGHT

THEO made a detour to his suite. There was a message waiting for him. Nestor had talked to the judge, but there was no budging him. The show-cause hearing was going ahead as planned for the day after tomorrow.

He closed his eyes tightly, imagining Stella's reaction. After asking her to marry him, he'd do anything to protect her from being hurt, but it was all going to come out, and he was terrified what it would do to her.

The letter was in his drawer. He put it in his pocket and left his office, catching up to them out in front of the building. The second he climbed in the back next to Stella, Ari said, "I wish we didn't have to go home. I love fishing."

"So do I, son. After our astronomy class has ended, we'll do it again. I know a place in the mountains where we can camp out and fish the stream. Leandros and his papa love to fish, too. Maybe the four of us could go. Would you like that?"

"I'd love it."

That was one of the things he loved most about Ari. His constant enthusiasm. Stella had been right. Their son was the brightest, sweetest boy in the world. They were both his life!

Too soon the limo drove up in front of the villa, bringing their trip to an end.

"See you tomorrow, Papa." Ari gave him a big kiss and climbed out first. Taking advantage of the moment, Theo drew the letter from his pocket and put it in her purse lying next to her on the seat.

He reached for her hand and kissed the palm. "Call Keiko and make those arrangements. I have more plans for us."

She nodded. "I'll let you know tomorrow."

"Stella—" He cupped her face to kiss her one more time. It wasn't long enough or deep enough.

"Come on, Mom."

Theo reluctantly let her go.

"Good night." She got out of the car, leaving him with an ache that was never going to go away.

He watched her rush up the steps to join Ari. Once they were safely inside, he told the chauffeur to take him back to the office. Theo knew he wouldn't be able to sleep, so he might as well get some work done.

A time bomb was ticking. Before long it was going to go off. There had to be a way to help Stella when the time came, but his greatest fear was that she would go into shock. When he thought about one of his own brothers having the capacity to betray him to that degree, he couldn't imagine it.

One thing and one thing only was helping him to hold on to his sanity tonight. To his everlasting gratitude, he had Ari, his greatest ally and link to Stella. Ari always pulled through for him.

What a wonderful son. His joy. That's because he had a mother like Stella. On this trip Theo found out he needed them like he needed air to breathe. If the crisis that was coming was too much for her, he might never be able to reach her again in the same way.

This trip had drawn them so close together, the thought of anything destroying what they had now was killing him. He buried his face in his hands.

* * *

Iola took one look at Ari and threw up her hands. "You've turned into a lobster!"

"Lobster..." Ari roared with laughter. "Guess what? I caught two sea bass!"

"How big were they?"

"This long." He demonstrated.

"Good for you! Did you eat them?"

"Yes. Papa's the best cook just like my grandma. The fish was yummy, wasn't it, Mommy."

"Delicious." On their trip she'd discovered Theo had many hidden skills.

"Are you hungry now?"

"No. We're ready for bed," Stella declared. "If he's going to play with Dax in the morning, he needs his sleep. Run on up, honey, and get your bath. I'll be there in a minute to tuck you in."

"Okay."

As he darted up the stairs, she turned to Iola. "How are you?"

"I'm fine now that you've come home so happy. You're in love again."

Stella nodded. "Theo's even more wonderful than he was before."

"He's a man."

"Yes. He's my life and Ari's." She kissed Iola's cheek. "See you in the morning."

Once in her room, she couldn't wait to read the letter. Her hands trembled as she got it out of her purse. When he'd given it to her on Andros, she'd thrown it back at him. At the time, her state of mind wouldn't allow him inside her head. Now he filled her whole heart and soul.

She sank down on the side of her bed, dying to find out what he'd written. Taking as much care as possible, she opened the sealed envelope and pulled out the short, one-page letter.

Agape Mou,
Something terrible has happened to me. That's why I couldn't come inside the church to get you. I'm in Salamis Hospital, room 434W. Spiro is writing this letter for me because I can't use my hands yet.

Find a way to leave the villa and come to me as fast as you can, sweetheart. My family's going to let you stay with us until I'm better, then we'll get married and find a place of our own.

I love you, Stella. I love our baby.

Come soon. I need you.
Theo.

Stella moaned.

"Kyrie Pantheras?"

"Yes?"

"Stella Athas is here to see you."

Excitement charged his body. "Tell her to come in." He threw down his pen and hurried around the desk to greet her. This morning she was wearing a stunning cocoa-colored silk blouse with pleated pants in a café-au-lait tone.

She looked good enough to eat. Her velvety brown eyes sought his with a new eagerness. She must have read his letter or she wouldn't have that expectant look on her face.

"Am I disturbing you?"

"Yes," he whispered in a husky tone and reached for her, sliding his hands up and down her arms. "In all the ways only you can do." He could tell she was out of breath. "Did you work things out with Keiko?"

She nodded.

"Anything else you want to tell me?"

"Yes. It's about us. Weeks ago you asked me

to accept you on faith. Last night on the boat you asked me to marry you. It's what I want, what Ari wants. That's what I've come here to say and I want us to tell Ari today."

"Stella," he cried. "I prayed that was why you'd come. Now that you're here, I don't intend to waste another second."

He lowered his mouth to the lush moistness of hers, leaving her no escape. They began devouring each other with a fervency that transported both of them back in time to halcyon days when nothing mattered but to be together communicating like this.

His body trembled with desire while they clung in such a tight embrace, there was no space between them. He couldn't believe it. She was giving him everything. It was as if a light had been turned on. Theo couldn't get enough of her as their kisses grew more breathless and sensual.

"I'm in love with you, Stella," he cried into her hair.

Her gasp of ecstasy thrilled him. She burrowed her face in his neck. "I'll love you forever, Theo. I couldn't get through life without you now."

To hear those words caused the blood to sing in his ears. "Do you think I could?" His euphoria made him forget everything except the wonder of holding and kissing her until he was delirious with longings that needed assuagement soon. They were already in deep trouble.

"Kyrie Pantheras? You asked me to buzz you when it was ten to twelve."

Stella's moan of protest was as loud as his.

"Thank you."

He drank from her mouth one more time before putting her away from. Her eyes were glazed from desire. She swayed in place.

"Only Ari could force me to let you go at a time like this."

She kissed his hands. "Let's go pick him up together. I can't wait to tell him our news. He'll be so happy." Her gaze played over him with so much love he felt like he was drowning.

Theo pressed his lips to her palms. "Neither of you could want it as much as I do. After we get him, I'm taking you both to my house on Salamis. While we have lunch there, we'll tell him it will be our home. I want to marry you right away. Will you mind living on the island?"

Her brows formed a delicate frown line. "How can you ask me that?"

"Because you've lived in the heart of Athens all your life."

"As long as I'm with you, I don't care where I live. We used to talk about the house we would have right on the beach one day. It was my dream. Have you forgotten?"

He caught her face between his hands. "There isn't one second of our lives I haven't lived over and over until it has driven me mad. I'm hardly going to forget the plans we made." After kissing her with refined savagery, he wheeled away from her to gather his suit jacket and the phone.

Together they rode the private elevator to the car park where his limo was waiting. En route to Dax's house he held her on his lap and kissed her senseless. For a little while he felt like a teenager again, crazy in love with Stella Athas, the most gorgeous girl in the world.

"We've got to stop doing this before we get there, Theo. Ari's going to know what we've been up to."

He chuckled. "Our son knows exactly what's been going on with us from day one." She slid off his lap and sat across from him to brush her hair. "I love the taste of your lipstick by the way. You can lay it on me anytime."

"Behave, Theo."

"I don't want to. Besides, you don't want me to."

"That's beside the point," she said while she applied a fresh coat to her lips.

"Are you as happy as I am?"

She shot him a glance that enveloped him in love. "I'm so happy I'm in pain. The kind that's never going to go away."

"We can be married in three weeks, Stella. I'll arrange it with Hektor."

Three weeks without being married sounded like an eternity. While Stella was wondering how she would last until then, the limo turned into Dax's driveway. The boys were out in front throwing a ball. Ari waved goodbye to his friend and ran toward them.

"Mom!" He climbed inside next to Theo. "I didn't know you were coming with Papa. This is great!"

"Your mother and I have a plan. I'll tell the driver to run us to your house. Both of you grab some clothes for a sleepover and we'll spend the night at my house. Though you've seen it, your mother hasn't."

"Goody! Will we go to class from there?"

Theo nodded. "Tell me what you and Dax did this morning."

Stella scarcely listened. Too much excitement over the news they had to tell Ari made her restless. Not only that, she couldn't wait to see Theo's house.

While they were at class, she had a wedding to plan. Rachel would help her. She'd include Elani, too. In fact she'd call them both tonight. It would be a joyous time for all of them.

"Stella?" Theo whispered. "What's going on inside that lovely head of yours?" She blinked to realize they were in front of the villa.

"Ari's gone in to get his things."

"I need to get mine, too."

"Just a minute." He pressed a deep kiss to her mouth. "Tell me you're not having second thoughts. I couldn't handle it."

"Hush, Theo." She kissed him back passionately. "Actually I was thinking of Rachel and how excited she'll be to help me plan our wedding."

"I'm looking forward to meeting her."

"You'll love her."

He kissed her temple. "Do you want me to come in while you get your things?"

"No. It'll only take me a minute."

"Hurry!"

"I promise."

He helped her out. She passed Ari in the foyer with his backpack. "I'll be right out, honey." All she needed were some toiletries, a change of clothes and a nightgown.

While she was putting everything in her overnight bag, Iola came in her bedroom. "Where are you going?"

She closed the lid. "To Theo's. I'm not sure when we'll be home. It might be a few days."

"Are you sure you know what you're doing?"

"Absolutely. Iola, you might as well know first. We're back together for good. In fact we're getting married in three weeks."

Her eyes filled with tears before she broke down with happy sobs. Stella gave her a hug. "You'll have to help me with the wedding plans."

Iola finally pulled herself together. "Before I forget, Rachel wants you to call her right away. She says it's an emergency."

"Thanks for telling me. I'll phone her."

"Good."

After she walked out, Stella reached for her

phone. She'd purposely turned off the ringer while she'd gone to Theo's office. Much as she'd like to put off this call, she couldn't, but with Ari and Theo outside waiting for her, she'd make this fast.

It barely started to ring when Rachel answered. "Stella?"

"Hi. What's wrong?"

"If you have to ask me that question, then you don't know."

Her heart picked up speed. "Know what?"

After a silence. "I hope you're sitting down."

Stella stood there unable to move. "If this is about Theo, I don't want to hear it."

"You have to hear it, Stella." She heard tears in Rachel's voice.

"Then tell me."

"Nikos has brought a full-blown lawsuit against Theo for misrepresenting who he is and taking advantage of you. The case is set for tomorrow morning. He expects the family to be there for support. I told him I wouldn't have anything to do with it. Stasio's in shock that Nikos has carried it this far."

"I am, too," she murmured. It meant Theo had been aware of the court date for some time now, but he'd never let on.

"Stella?"

"I have to go now."

"Are you all right?" Rachel sounded frantic.

"No. I have to talk to Theo. Tell Stasio I'll call him later."

She hung up feeling so ill she didn't know if she'd survive another second. For her brother to do this at the height of her happiness made him sound unbalanced. In a panic, she rushed downstairs and out the front entrance to the car.

Theo opened the limo door and gave her a squeeze around the waist. "We thought you were never coming."

Avoiding his eyes she said, "I had a phone call that detained me. Before we go anywhere, I need to talk to you alone."

She lowered her head to look at Ari. "Honey? There's something I have to discuss with your father in private. It will only take a minute. Would you mind running inside the house? I'll let you know when we're finished."

He could tell she was serious. His happy expression faded. "Okay." He slid out of the limo leaving his pack behind and raced up the porch steps into the house.

Stella climbed inside and sat opposite Theo. He sat back, studying her features. She saw nothing but love in those dark eyes.

"Rachel just phoned me. I've been told Nikos has brought a lawsuit against you and you have to appear in court tomorrow. Is it true?"

She thought he paled. "Yes."

"Why didn't you tell me?"

"Because I wanted to put the past behind us."

"I don't understand my brother. There's something really wrong with him."

"Let me worry about it."

"How can you be so calm? Were you planning to go to court without me?"

"Yes. I don't want you there."

"I've just told you I'll marry you. You think I'd let you walk into a courtroom alone after what we've been through in the last six years?"

"You can't come, Stella. I won't let you. The court session shouldn't take long. I'll be back soon enough."

Stella decided not to argue with him. After he left for court, she'd take Ari to Dax's house and slip into the courtroom. Theo wouldn't be able to do anything about it then.

"All right."

He kissed her hard on the mouth. "I'll go in and get Ari now."

"Third district court is now in session. The Most Honorable Judge Antonias Christopheles presiding."

"You may be seated," the judge said, looking out at the crowd assembled.

Besides Theo's entire family, including Hecktor, half of the closed-session courtroom was filled with witnesses Nestor had lined up. The other half of the room was conspicuously empty. Nikos sat at the table with his attorney, but just as the judge began to speak, Stella slipped inside the back and sat down next to Stasio.

Theo hadn't wanted her anywhere near here, but there wasn't anything he could do about it now.

"There are several charges laid before the court this Wednesday, the eighteenth of June by Nikos Athas against Theo Pantheras for unduly manipulating and coercing Stella Athas against her will. Mr. Pantheras, in turn, has laid countercharges against Nikos Athas.

"The first is to ascertain if Nikos Athas

intended to murder Theo Pantheras on July 6, six years ago.

"The second is to discover if he set fire to the Pantheras Taverna in Paloukia on the night of July 1.

"The third is to discover if he caused an accident to Spiro Pantheras while he was riding his motor scooter the night of June 27.

"The fourth is to learn if he threatened the lives of the Pantheras family on repeated occasions by telephone calls from June 2 until July 6."

"The fifth is to learn if he tried to bribe Theo Pantheras with ten thousand dollars to leave his sister alone."

With each count, Theo watched Stella's head drop a little lower. He'd warned her not to come. This part was going to devastate her.

"Mr. Paulos, if you'll make your opening statement, please."

Theo watched the burly-looking attorney take the floor. "Thank you, Your Honor. My client has been forced to respond to these totally false allegations without having been given adequate preparation time."

"I'm aware of that. However, may I remind you this is only a show-cause hearing to determine if this case warrants a full jury trial. Please go ahead."

"Thank you." He cleared his throat. "Athas Shipping Lines is one of Greece's greatest resources. I don't need to tell the court of Nikos Athas's extraordinary talents as one of our Olympians. Their father filled one of the highest positions in our government.

"To think Nikos could perpetrate such crimes is beyond the imagination of this counsel and I dare say this country. I consider it a crime to waste this court's time, Your Honor. If opposing counsel can produce one shred of evidence to the contrary, then let him speak."

The judge nodded. "Mr. Georgeles? If you'll approach the bench."

Nestor patted Theo's arm before getting to his feet. "If Your Honor will look at Exhibit A, I'll ask the physician, Dr. Vlasius, who attended Mr. Pantheras in the E.R. at Salamis Hospital on the night of July 6 to explain. He's on the board there now."

"Step forward, Doctor, and be sworn in."

Once that was accomplished, Nestor began. "Dr. Vlasius, would you tell us about these X-rays, please."

"Certainly. These show the injuries to Mr. Theo Pantheras, the nineteen-year-old man brought in by his friends. When he was beaten up on his way home and left for dead, it revealed that the bones in his lower legs, arms and hands had been broken by a pipe. The type of weapon used has been corroborated by the police. His face was smashed in. He resided in the hospital six weeks while his bones healed and reconstructive surgery was done on his face and nose."

A feminine cry came from across the aisle. Stella's.

"Thank you, Dr. Vlasius. If you'd be seated, I'd like to call on Damon Arabos, Theo's closest friend who brought him in to the hospital."

Again Theo could tell Stella was stunned to see him walk to the bench. He'd been Theo's sidekick through high school. He was a tease who'd made everyone laugh.

As soon as he was sworn in, Nestor began. "Did you witness this attack on him?"

"Only at the end."

"Did you recognize who did it?"

"There were five men bent over him. I got some of our friends and we started to attack them. They ran away and got in a van. One of our friends took down the license plate. The police traced it to a man who works at the docks for Athas Shipping Lines named Yanni Souvalis, but he suddenly didn't show up for work anymore."

"Thank you, Mr. Arabos. You may be seated. Now I'd like to call Alena Callas to the bench to be sworn in. She works at the telephone company in their records department and has gathered some evidence useful to this case which I've submitted under Exhibit B."

This was the part Theo had been waiting for. It was the paper trails that would bring Nikos down.

"Mrs. Callas, would you tell the court the nature of Exhibit B."

"Yes. These represent the phone logs of the dates between June 2 and July 6. Nine phone calls in all. They originated from the private phone of Mr. Nikos Athas. All calls were made to the Pantheras Taverna on Salamis Island."

"Were they long phone calls?"

"Each one was different, but none of them were longer than forty-five seconds."

"Thank you. You can be seated. I'd like to call Mr. Bion as my next witness."

"I object, Your Honor!" Mr. Paulos blurted.

"Objection overruled. I'm here to listen to the evidence. Please make it short, Mr. Georgeles."

"Yes, Your Honor."

Theo couldn't see Nikos's face. He was huddled behind the desk with his attorney.

"Mr. Bion? Please tell the court who you are."

"I'm the battalion commander for the Paloukia Fire Department."

"Were you witness to a fire at the Pantheras Taverna on the night of July 1?"

"Yes, sir. Of course, then I had just joined the department."

"Tell us what you discovered at the fire?"

"It was an arson case. A chemical was used that the police traced to Athas Shipping Lines. Only a few companies use it."

"So it could have come from another shipping line?"

"Not at that time, no."

"Thank you. You can be seated. I'd now like to call Mr. Spiro Pantheras to the stand."

Spiro winked at Theo on his way to the bench.

"Tell the court who you are, please."

"I'm Spiro Pantheras, Theo's older brother."

"I understand you met with an accident on your motor scooter on the night of June 27 near the taverna."

"That's correct."

"Can you tell us what happened."

"I was on my way home from the store when I heard a car rev behind me. I moved to the right to get out of the way, but it followed me and sideswiped me, knocking me off my scooter."

"Did you see the car?"

"Only the tail end of it before it rounded the corner. It was the latest model black Ferrari with local license plates."

"Were you hospitalized?"

"No, but because of the threatening phone calls to my parents at the *taverna,* I called the police to report it. You have a copy of the police case."

"Did anything happen as a result?"

"No."

"Thank you very much. You may step down." Nestor turned to the judge. "Your Honor? If you'll look at Exhibit C, I've provided a list of every new Ferrari sold within that twelve-month period in Athens. Two could be accounted for. One belonged to the deputy prime minister, the other to Nikos Athas. For my final witness today, I call Theo Pantheras to the stand."

This was it, but Theo felt no joy having to expose her brother this way in front of her.

After he was sworn in, Nestor said, "Mr. Pantheras, please tell the court in your own words the happenings during that month leading to your hospitalization."

He took a deep breath and leveled his gaze on Stella. "I committed the crime of falling in love with Stella Athas when she was sixteen and I, eighteen. Her family didn't approve of me and we both knew it, so we had to be creative how we could be together.

"I knew Nikos Athas didn't like me, but I didn't realize he'd go so far as to harass me and my family so I'd stay away from her. One night he followed me home from church. On the way he offered me ten thousand dollars to get out of Stella's life and stay out.

"I told him what he could do with his money and took off. Later that week we received threatening phone calls from him, then the *taverna* was set on fire. After Spiro's accident I realized Nikos was serious. On the last phone call I received from him, he said that if I didn't break up with Stella, he would injure my parents until I didn't recognize them.

"I had to believe him, so I called Stella and told her we were getting married. I'd meet her at the church, but I was beaten up outside in the car park. It was clear Nikos wasn't about to let the Pantheras family merge with his on any level, not even to letting me claim my rights as a father.

"After I got out of the hospital, I left for New York to begin carving out a career for myself. Since then I've returned to Greece and have been with Stella and my son Ari."

Nestor smiled at Theo. "Thank you, Mr. Pantheras. You may step down." Theo went back to his seat behind the desk. "Your Honor, I turn the time back over to Mr. Paulos."

"Mr. Paulos?" the judge asked. "Do you wish to cross-examine?"

"Not at this time, Your Honor."

"What can he say?" Nestor whispered to Theo. "There is no rebuttal to the case we just presented. His case has fallen apart."

Theo agreed. Nikos had already hung himself.

"After hearing the proceedings of this case, I plan for this to go to a full jury trial which is set for September 13. Bail on Nikos Athas is set at ten million dollars. You will not be allowed to leave the country."

Nikos exploded. "You can't keep me here! I live in Switzerland!"

"One more outburst, Mr. Athas, and I'll have the sergeant-at-arms restrain you. This session is dismissed until September 13 at 9:00 a.m." He pounded his gavel and left the courtroom.

The family swarmed around Theo. This was a day they'd needed for closure. Everyone wept. When Theo eventually stood up to find Stella, he discovered she had gone. The emptiness in his heart threatened to swallow him whole. Charging her brother with attempted murder wasn't something easy to forgive. He would treasure the memories of the last few weeks with her and Ari, but they might be all he'd ever have.

CHAPTER NINE

STELLA left the courtroom and raced to the villa ahead of everyone. "Iola?" she cried out the second she entered the house.

"I'm here." The housekeeper came running. "What's wrong?"

"Wait right here." She dashed up the stairs to get the letter Theo had sent her. When she came down again she said, "I'm going to show you something. I want you to think back very hard to the time when Theo didn't come to the church for me."

The older woman frowned. "I'll never forget it as long as I live."

No one would forget. "I want you to take a look at this envelope. Read everything on the front. The date is from six years ago." She handed it to her.

Iola studied it for an overly long moment without lifting her eyes.

Pure revelation flowed through Stella. "You recognize it, don't you."

Still no response.

"Is that your handwriting at the bottom that says addressee unknown?"

She shook her head violently.

"Do you know whose it is? This is important, Iola. I have to know the truth."

"I can't tell you."

"Why?"

"Because I will lose my job."

"What? That's impossible! You're a part of this family." Stella reached out and hugged her. "This is your home. Who told you that?"

She kept her head bowed. "Please don't make me tell you. I'm afraid."

"I can see that."

Stella put a hand over her own mouth, absolutely devastated to think Nikos had blackmailed her into keeping quiet about this. "Did more letters like this come to the house I don't know about?"

"I don't know," she muttered. In the next breath she handed Stella the letter before running down the hall toward the back of the villa.

Stella slowly walked into the salon and waited for the rest of the family to arrive. She'd arranged for Ari to stay with Dax until she came for him.

In a minute she heard footsteps in the foyer. Stasio's pained expression left nothing to the imagination as he entered the salon with Nikos, who'd gone somewhere mentally where she couldn't reach him.

His year-round tan had turned a sickly white. He'd been Stella's nemesis for years. Every truly unhappy moment in her life she could lay at his feet. Her own brother.

Poor Stasio. He'd been just as wounded by him, maybe more, because he was the big brother Nikos hated to love and loved to hate.

On impulse she reached for Nikos's hand. "I have something important to tell you, Nikos. Despite what you've done, I know in my heart Theo doesn't want to send you to prison. That wasn't his focus.

"When he came back to Greece and discovered he had a son, all he wanted was to fight for him and ultimately for me." Never had a woman had more evidence of a man's love.

She squeezed Nikos's hand to get a reaction

from him. "Listen to me—I know he'll drop all the charges against you provided you do something for me."

He looked at her in torment.

"If he still wants me after this, we're going to be married. All he would like is peace from my family. He would like to be able to come and go with me and Ari and be treated kindly and fairly. That's all."

Stasio's eyes glistened with tears.

"But that's not all I want. Once upon a time you were a sweet boy, but something happened when you grew up. You'll have to promise me and Stasio that you'll get psychiatric help. You've needed it for years. It'll save your marriage. Renate really loves you, but she can't do it alone."

"It's too late for me," Nikos whispered in a tortured breath.

"No." Stasio sat forward. "It's never to late to change."

Stella patted his hand. "Look at Theo. He's back after six years ready to take up where we left off. He didn't think it was too late."

He shook his head. "I told the guys to rough him up, not kill him."

"I believe you. So does he."

"He has every right to hate my guts forever."

"Theo's not like that." Her voice trembled. "He has so much goodness in him you can't imagine."

The sobs started coming. Suddenly he got up from the couch and left the room. They could hear his anguish all the way to his suite down the hall.

Stasio moved over to sit by her. He put his big arms around her and rocked her against him. "Stella…" She heard every ounce of pain and love in his heart. They'd been through it all together. "When you and Theo work everything out, I want to have a long talk with him. He's a man like few others. No wonder no other guy ever measured up."

"I love him so terribly."

"I know. He's a lucky man to be loved by you. Go to him and put him out of his misery. He deserves every bit of happiness you can find together."

Since returning from court, Theo's family had sequestered him above the taverna. The women got food ready while he sat at the dining room table with his father and brothers. They'd closed the taverna for the day. It was like a holiday with the kids milling around, but the last thing he felt like doing was celebrating.

He kept reliving the court scene in his mind. With each damaging piece of evidence, Stella seemed to have shrunken inside herself a little more. No matter how he went over it in his mind, there hadn't been another way to do it.

If he'd called her on the phone after returning to Athens, and told her the truth right off, she would have hung up on him. There wouldn't have been a discussion. He would never have been able to meet Ari.

"Theo?" Dymas poured him a little wine. "She's going to forgive you."

Spiro nodded. "Give it time. You said she's always had to be careful around Nikos. When it sinks in and she realizes there wasn't any other way for you to handle things, she'll get in touch with you."

He sat back in the chair with his arms crossed. "I'd like to believe you, but I saw anguish on her face today. She has loved her family a lot longer than she has loved me. You know what they say. Blood is thicker than water." His gaze flicked to his family.

"Thank you all for being there for me today."

"As if we'd have been anywhere else." His father patted his arm. "You've suffered long enough. Today we saw justice done. I'm very proud of the great man you've become."

For his father to tell Theo that was something. He'd never said those words to him before. "Thank you, Papa, but I don't feel great. To destroy the woman I love in order to be with her and my son has brought me no joy."

"Nikos Athas destroyed himself without anyone's help, my boy."

"It's too bad the jury trial can't be sooner so this can all be over with."

"There isn't going to be one, Spiro." Theo shoved himself away from the table and got to his feet.

All three of them stared at him, waiting for an explanation.

"Tomorrow I'll tell Nestor I'm dropping the charges."

Dymas looked shocked. "After all you've done to get ready for it?"

"Yes. It's over."

"Nikos could still be dangerous."

"I've thought about that, Dymas. Nevertheless, today's court session is as far as I go. He's been exposed. Enough damage was done for Stella to know the true reason for what happened."

His father got to his feet and walked over to him. "How much does Ari know about any of this?"

"As far as I know, nothing. But today everything exploded. No doubt he'll learn all about it and totally despise me."

"No, Theo. You've won his love. He'll figure it out. Like Spiro said, give this time."

"You mean like another six years? Maybe then my son will be mature enough to acknowledge me again?" Theo was dying inside. "Papa? Will you tell Mama I couldn't stay. I have to leave."

He patted Theo's shoulder. "I understand. Where are you going to go?"

"I don't know. I need to be alone."

"Do you want to take a drive with me?"

"No, thank you, Papa. I have to be on my own." He felt like running until he dropped and the pain went away.

They walked to the top of the stairs. "I love you, Theo."

"I love you, too, Papa." He kissed his cheek before descending the steps leading to the restaurant below. He let himself out of the back of the *taverna* and locked the door before he started running in the direction of the beach.

Stella showered and changed into the white dress with the wide belt Theo seemed to like so much. Wherever he was, when she caught up to him she wanted to look her most beautiful for him.

After talking to Ari on the phone at Dax's house, she found out he hadn't heard from his father all day. It was after four right now. This had to be the first time Theo hadn't checked in with their son.

She grew even more apprehensive because they had their star-gazing class tonight. Theo could have gone anywhere after court. She wanted to believe he was with his family, but after what he'd lived through today, he was probably out of his mind in pain. Somehow she had to get through this and find him without alarming Ari.

Once she was ready, she said good-night to Stasio and slipped out the back door to her car. She'd told Ari to be waiting for her. When she eventually drove up to Dax's house, he came flying out the front door and jumped in the car.

"Where's Papa?"

She smothered the moan rising in her throat. "I think he's at the taverna with his family. I thought we'd drive there for dinner before you guys leave for class."

"He'll be glad. Papa's afraid you don't like his family."

Stella glanced at her son. "That's not true. I like them very much."

"He talks about you all the time and told me what you were like when he first met you. He said you were really shy. What does that mean?"

"That I didn't speak up and kind of hung back."

"Papa said that was his favorite thing about you. All the other girls…well, you know. They wanted to be with him, but he said that once he met you, that was it."

She was certain there'd been other women while he'd been in New York. He was too attractive and had too much drive to live like a monk, but he'd come back for her. It proved that whatever had gone on in his past, it hadn't kept him in the States. That was all that mattered to her.

"It's nice to hear."

"He wanted to know if you'd had boyfriends."

"What did you tell him?"

"That there'd been some, but you never let

any of them come up to the family room or sleep over. Papa was pretty happy to hear that."

In spite of her fear that they wouldn't be able to find him, she chuckled. "I'm afraid when I met him, I never really looked at another man again."

"You love him like crazy, huh."

Her throat practically closed up with emotion. "Yes. How can you tell?"

"Because you're always smiling now."

"So are you. Let's go find him right now and surprise him."

They'd crossed over to Salamis Island. The traffic was horrendous with tourists and people driving home from work.

Be there, Theo, she cried. But when they came in sight of the taverna, she couldn't see his car. That didn't necessarily have to mean anything, but it still made her stomach clench.

She pulled up in front. Ari jumped right out. "I'll get him, Mom."

It was just as well he went inside alone. She didn't feel up to facing his family, not after what they'd all been through this morning in court.

Stella's brother had been the cause of all the pain their family had suffered. Nothing she could ever say or do would make up for what they'd had to endure. Whenever her mind remembered what the doctor had said in court about Theo's injuries, her heart broke all over again.

When Ari came back out, she had to dash the moisture off her cheeks so he wouldn't suspect anything was wrong.

"Grandpa said he was there earlier, but he left to go home."

"Then, that's where we'll go. Do you know where his house is from here? I've never seen it."

"Yeah. I'll show you how to get there. Take that road over there and follow it to the coast road."

Once they reached the other road, everything started to look familiar to her. With each kilometer she realized Ari was directing her toward a favorite area she hadn't seen in six years.

Before long Ari told her to turn into the driveway around the next curve. A gasp of surprise escaped her lips to see a lovely white villa on the stretch of beach where Theo used to take her in the rowboat.

"*This* is your father's house?"

"Yeah. It's so cool. It has a gym and an indoor pool. I can walk right out on the beach from my bedroom. We've set up the telescope on the porch and look at the stars. Dax wishes he lived here."

"I'll bet he does," her voice trembled.

They both got out of the car and walked past the flowering shrubs to the front entrance. "Papa gave me a key. Come on." He opened the door for them. She stepped inside a new, modern world of white with splashes of color on the walls and floors. So much light from the arched windows thrilled her to death.

"Papa?" he called out. "Mom and I are here! Where are you?" He raced around the house but couldn't find him. "He's probably gone for a walk. Let's go find him."

If he wasn't here, Stella didn't know what she would do. "That's a great idea. I'll take my shoes off."

"Me, too."

They left them inside the sliding doors off the family room. She followed him outside. Steps led down from the deck to the sand. The evening air felt like velvet. Her eyes took in the ocean not thirty feet away.

The pristine beach was just as she remembered it from years ago. "Come on, Mom. This is the way Papa took me for a walk."

She ran to catch up to him. "There aren't any people around."

"This is his private beach. He said that when he was growing up, their family lived like sardines in a can." She laughed at the metaphor. "He decided that if he ever made enough money, he'd build a place where he could walk around and be by himself."

Her eyes smarted. "Well he certainly accomplished that here."

"Yeah. I love it. Our house in Athens is old and full of people all the time, too."

Stella hadn't ever thought about it before, but he was right. Rich or poor, both her family and Theo's had been through a lot of togetherness.

As they rounded a small headland, her feet came to a stop. This was the little cove where Theo always brought her in the rowboat. This was where they'd made passionate love for the first time. Ari had been conceived here.

She lifted wet eyes to capture the scene. In the distance she saw the man she loved hunkered down on the sand in shorts and a T-shirt, watching the ocean. This part of the coast was protected, making the water as calm as a lake.

"Papa!"

He turned his head. By the way he slowly got to his feet she could tell he was shocked to see her with Ari.

Her heart pounded so hard, it seemed to give her wings as she started running toward him. Suddenly he was galvanized into action and raced toward her as if he could outrun the wind. They met halfway and clung in euphoric rapture while he swung her around.

"Darling," she cried breathlessly.

Theo didn't speak words she could hear. He did it with his mouth, covering hers hungrily, letting her know how he felt while they communicated in the way they used to when they found this special spot to be together.

"Thank God you came," he whispered at last. "I swear I—"

"Shh." She pressed her lips to his. "We're never going to talk about this again. We're never going to think about the past again. Don't look now, but I think we've embarrassed our son."

When Theo lifted his dark head, the last rays of the sun gilded his features. They were more striking to her now than ever before. His black eyes devoured her before shifting to their son, who stood a little ways off watching a sailboat in the distance.

"Ari? You'll have to forgive your mother and me. She just told me she'd marry me."

"You did?" He shrieked for joy.

She nodded.

"That's so awesome, Mom!" He leaped in the air, shouting like a maniac. His whole face was wet from happy tears. Her heart thrilled to see the smile that transformed him.

"'So awesome' is right," Theo murmured, kissing her again. "I kind of lost control for a minute."

Ari laughed and ran over to them. They all hugged for a long time.

"How soon is the wedding?"

"Three weeks," they both said at the same time. He smiled into her eyes. "That should give us enough time."

"Why do you have to wait so long?"

She slid her arm around their son. "The wedding banns."

"What are those?"

"An announcement that we're getting married," Theo explained. "It gives anyone time to object if they know a reason why we shouldn't be married."

"That's crazy! Who wouldn't want you two to get married?"

Stella's eyes sought Theo's. The moment was bittersweet until he said, "Nobody I know, and you're absolutely right. It *is* crazy, but it's tradition. Come on. Let's go back to the house and plan the wedding."

"Are you going to ask Hektor to marry you?"

"Who else?" Theo teased.

"Are you guys going to go on a honeymoon?"

That forlorn little tone had sneaked into his voice. Theo smiled at her before he said, "We're thinking either Disneyland or Disney World. We'll let you make the decision."

"Disneyland!" he cried out. "Dax said it's awesome!"

CHAPTER TEN

Eleven Months Later

"RACHEL? Would you do me a favor?" She and Stella were lying by the pool at the villa on Andros looking at baby magazines.

"What is it?"

"Don't look now but Theo's staring at me from the other end of the patio. My due date isn't for another three days, but you'd think I was on the verge of giving birth right now. Tell Stasio to take him somewhere for the day. I swear if he hovers around me one more minute, I'm going to scream."

"I know exactly how you feel. Stasio drove me crazy for the last couple of weeks before Anna was born."

"I'm getting there fast."

"He's in the house changing her diaper. As soon as he comes out, I'll ask him."

"Thank you."

"Uh-oh."

"What?"

"Theo's coming over here."

Stella lifted the magazine higher, pretending not to see him.

"You've been in the sun long enough, Stella. Let's get you inside for a little while. Too much heat isn't good for you."

"I haven't been out here that long."

"I disagree." In the next breath he picked her up off the lounge with those strong arms and carried her in the house to their bedroom.

Once he'd placed her carefully on top of the bed, he lay down next to her and smoothed the hair off her forehead. The anxious concern in his eyes baffled her.

"Darling, I'm as healthy as a horse. You don't need to worry about me. When I was carrying Ari, I never had any trouble. There's no reason to believe I'll have it this time."

"But I wasn't there to take care of you. Now that we can enjoy this spring break with the family, I want to wait on you."

"I know, and I love you for it, but watching me all the time is like waiting for water to boil."

His lips twitched. "Not quite. You're much more interesting." His hand slid over the mound, sending delicious chills through her body. "Is she kicking right now?"

"Not at the moment. I'll let you know the second she does. Come on. Close your eyes and take a little nap with me."

"That's kind of hard when I want to do more than that with you."

"I think you've done quite enough for one year, Kyrie Pantheras."

He chuckled deep in his throat and bit gently on her earlobe. "You're a fertile little thing."

"So I've found out. We're going to have to be careful after she's born."

His dark brows furrowed. "Is that your way of telling me the honeymoon's over?"

"No." She grabbed his hand and kissed his fingertips. "It's my way of telling you we could probably have a baby every year for the next ten years without a problem."

"I like the idea in theory."

"You would. You're not the one who feels like a walrus."

He grinned. "Yesterday it was a hippo. A very sexy one, I might add."

"Oh, Theo." She cupped his cheeks. "I love you too much."

Their mouths fused for a long time. "Now you know how I feel all the time."

"Pretty soon this baby will be born and you can stop worrying."

She heard his sharp intake of breath. "If anything happened to you—"

"It's not going to," she said.

"Have I told you Ari's latest idea for a name?"

"No. What is it?"

"We were looking at the Andromeda constellation the other night and he said, 'Papa? Can we name the baby Andrea?'"

"That's a beautiful name."

"I like it, too."

"Then let's do it. Ari will be thrilled."

"We'll tell him later. Right now I have other plans for us. Roll over on your side and I'll give you a back rub."

"That sounds heavenly." She'd had a low backache all week. It was the pressure of the baby since it had dropped.

The second Theo began touching her, her

body quickened. Slowly his caresses sent sparks of desire through her, making her breathless. His mouth played havoc with hers. Stella wanted him with a need so powerful it turned into literal pain. She must have let out a little cry.

"What's wrong?"

"Nothing that a night of making love without our baby separating us won't cure."

"I probably shouldn't be touching you at all."

"If you didn't, I don't know how I'd go on living." She pressed her mouth to his and clung. All of a sudden she felt another pain that came all the way around to her stomach.

She grabbed Theo's hand and put it there. "Feel how hard that is?"

"Like a rock."

"I'm in labor, darling."

"You're kidding!" His voice shook.

"No. This is how it started before. We'd better call the doctor."

His face drained of color, Theo rolled off the bed and pulled out his cell phone. "His number's there on the bed stand."

The next few minutes were a blur while she timed her contractions. "They're coming every five minutes."

She didn't hear what Theo was saying, but after he got off the phone he told her they were leaving for the hospital. "The doctor says the baby could come fast because this isn't your first. Come on. We'll take Stasio's car."

"That's right," she quipped. "This beached whale couldn't get inside my sports car right now."

The joke was lost on Theo, who looked absolutely terrified. He helped her down the hall and the steps, calling to Stasio, who came running. By now the whole family had gathered around the car.

Rachel leaned inside the window. "I'll take care of the boys. Theo will take care of you. Don't worry about a thing."

It didn't take long to reach the hospital in Palaiopolis. She hadn't planned to have her baby there, but then you never knew what a baby was going to do. Andrea wanted to be born now.

Two and a half hours later she heard a gurgling sound and the attending doctor lifted up their little girl who was crying her lungs out. Knowing they were working and healthy meant everything.

"You've got a strong, beautiful daughter here, Kyrie Pantheras. Here—you cut the cord."

Theo, who'd put on a hospital gown and gloves, let out a cry of happiness. He'd lived through every second of the last few hours with her. Stella's tears ran down the sides of her cheeks. He hadn't been a part of any of this before. She was so thankful he had the opportunity now, she couldn't contain her joy.

A minute later the doctor laid the baby across her stomach so she could see her. "She's got a little widow's peak just like yours, darling!"

"She's got your hair and mouth."

"Oh, she's so sweet."

Theo buried his face in Stella's neck. "My two girls." She could tell he was overcome with emotion. She was, too, but so exhausted from the birth and filled with love for her new family, she could feel herself drifting off.

When next Stella came awake, she was in a private room. Theo stood at the side of the bed holding their daughter, who was all cleaned up and bundled. Her father had a five-o'clock shadow and his black hair was disheveled. Theo made a gorgeous sight!

Their gazes collided.

"You're awake!"

She smiled. "Yes. What do you think of our little girl?"

"Words don't cover it," his voice trembled.

"I know."

He lowered Andrea into her arms, then sat on a stool next to her. Together they examined their baby. "I've already checked everything. She's perfect."

Stella broke down laughing. "She is."

Theo covered Stella's face with kisses. "How are you feeling?"

"Good. Like I'm floating."

"You women are the stronger sex. I know that now." His eyes were pleading with her. "You've given me the world. What can I give you?"

"Just go on loving me. I need you desperately. I always will."

The baby started fussing. "She's hungry."

"She sure is," the nurse's voice boomed. "You'll have to leave for about a half hour while I help your wife start to nurse, Kyrie Pantheras."

He lowered his mouth to hers once more. "I'll be back."

"We'll be here waiting."

* * *

Theo drove back to the villa in record time. Ari and Leandros were waiting for him. "You have a new sister. We decided to name her Andrea."

He grinned. "Hooray. Can I go see her?"

"As soon as I've showered and shaved."

"Can I go, too, Uncle Theo?"

"Of course. Anyone who wants to."

"We'll all go." Stasio brought up the rear.

Ten minutes later they all piled in the car and left for the hospital. When they reached Stella's room, she was lying there propped up in the bed with the baby asleep on her shoulder. For a woman who'd given birth such a short time ago, Theo found his wife utterly breathtaking.

While everyone had a chance to hold the baby, he moved over to her side. "You must be exhausted, yet you've never looked more alive."

"That's because you were with me. We're the luckiest people in the world to be given a second chance at life. Oh, Theo…it was worth the six-year wait."

Theo had a hard time swallowing. "I can say that, now that you're alive and safe, but I wouldn't recommend it for everyone."

"No."

Unable to resist, he kissed her thoroughly. "I

know there's a part of you that wishes Nikos could be here. One day let's hope he can find our kind of happiness and come around again."

Her eyes filled with liquid. "You can say that after everything he did to you?"

"I've forgotten it. It's true what they say. Love really does heal all wounds."

"Theo…"

"Hey, Mom? She kind of looks like Cassie except she doesn't have red hair."

"Do you know something, Ari, honey? Every day you look at her, you're going to see someone else in the family she looks like. It's part of being a baby."

"She's cute."

"Of course she is," said Theo. "I'm her father!"

Ari laughed. "Did you hear that, Mom?"

"I heard it."

Theo had come back to Greece not expecting to claim her or their son. Instead he had both and their adorable Andrea. That was her joy and her blessing.

THE BRIDESMAID'S BABY

BY
BARBARA HANNAY

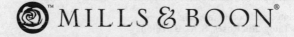

MILLS & BOON®

All the characters in this book have no existence outside the imagination of the author, and have no relation whatsoever to anyone bearing the same name or names. They are not even distantly inspired by any individual known or unknown to the author, and all the incidents are pure invention.

First published in Great Britain 2009
Harlequin Mills & Boon Limited,
Eton House, 18-24 Paradise Road, Richmond, Surrey TW9 1SR

© Barbara Hannay 2009

ISBN: 978 0 263 86971 2

Set in Times Roman 13 on 15½ pt
02-1009-44537

Harlequin Mills & Boon policy is to use papers that are natural, renewable and recyclable products and made from wood grown in sustainable forests. The logging and manufacturing process conform to the legal environmental regulations of the country of origin.

Printed and bound in Spain
by Litografia Rosés, S.A., Barcelona

Barbara Hannay was born in Sydney, educated in Brisbane, and has spent most of her adult life living in tropical North Queensland, where she and her husband have raised four children. While she has enjoyed many happy times camping and canoeing in the bush, she also delights in an urban lifestyle—chamber music, contemporary dance, movies and dining out. An English teacher, she has always loved writing, and now, by having her stories published, she is living her most cherished fantasy.

Visit www.barbarahannay.com

Dear Reader

Just as I finished writing THE BRIDESMAID'S BABY my son's wife gave birth to not one but two darling girls, Milla and Sophie, identical twins. They are the sweetest little heroines, and their safe arrival was a wonderful thrill for all of our family. For me it was also the perfect way to end my project *Baby Steps to Marriage…*

It's been a huge pleasure for me to write two linked books, and I've had such fun making the dream of a much-wanted baby come true in two quite different stories.

In THE BRIDESMAID'S BABY, which is Lucy and Will's story, I had the extra pleasure of sharing Mattie and Jake's wedding with you. It was lovely to revisit the heroine and hero from EXPECTING MIRACLE TWINS, and to let you see that the babies, Jasper and Mia, are thriving.

In Lucy and Will's story I was also able to explore one of my favourite romantic themes—friends to lovers—and to set their romance in the idyllic country town of Willowbank, where Lucy and Will, Mattie, Gina and Tom had all grown up.

As you can imagine, Willowbank and these characters are now incredibly special to me, as are the dear little babies. I can already imagine a new generation…and who knows where that will lead?

I hope you enjoy Lucy and Will's journey to marriage and parenthood.

Warmest wishes

Barbara

PROLOGUE

A PARTY was in full swing at Tambaroora.

The homestead was ablaze with lights and brightly coloured Chinese lanterns glowed in the gardens. Laughter and the happy voices of young people joined the loud music that spilled out across the dark paddocks where sheep quietly grazed.

Will Carruthers was going away, setting out to travel the world, and his family and friends were sending him off in style.

'Have you seen Lucy?' Mattie Carey asked him as he topped up her wine glass.

'I'm sure I have,' Will replied, letting his gaze drift around the room, seeking Lucy's bright blonde hair. 'She was here a minute ago.'

Mattie frowned. 'I've been looking for her everywhere.'

'I'll keep an eye out,' Will said with a shrug. 'If I see her, I'll let her know you're looking for her.' He moved on to top up other guests' glasses.

But by the time he'd completed a circuit of the big living room and the brightly lit front and side verandas, Will still hadn't seen Lucy McKenty and he felt a vague stirring of unease. Surely she wouldn't leave the party without saying goodbye. She was, in many ways, his best friend.

He went to the front steps and looked out across the garden, saw a couple, suspiciously like his sister Gina and Tom Hutchins, kissing beneath a jacaranda, but there was still no sign of Lucy.

She wasn't in the kitchen either. Will stood in the middle of the room, scratching his head and staring morosely at the stacks of empty bottles and demolished food platters. Where was she?

His brother Josh came in to grab another bottle of bubbly from the fridge.

'Seen Lucy?' Will asked.

Josh merely shook his head and hurried away to his latest female conquest.

A movement outside on the back veranda caught Will's attention. It was dark out there and he went to the kitchen doorway to scan the veranda's length, saw a slim figure in a pale dress, leaning against a veranda post, staring out into the dark night.

'Lucy?'

She jumped at the sound of his voice.

'I've been looking for you everywhere,' he said, surprised by the relief flowing through him like wine. 'Are you OK?'

'I had a headache.' She spoke in a small, shaky voice. 'So I came outside for a bit of quiet and fresh air.'

'Has it helped?'

'Yes, thanks. I feel much better.'

Will moved beside her and rested his arms on the railing, looking out, as she was, across the dark, limitless stretch of the sheep paddocks.

For the past four years the two of them had been away at Sydney University, two friends from the tiny country town of Willowbank, adrift in a sea of thousands of strangers. Their friendship had deepened during the ups and downs of student life, but now those years were behind them.

Lucy had come home to start work as a country vet, while Will, who'd studied geology, was heading as far away as possible, hurrying overseas, hungry for adventure and new experiences.

'You're not going to miss this place, are you?' she said.

Will laughed. 'I doubt it.' His brother Josh would be here to help their father run Tambaroora. It was the life Josh, as the eldest son, was born to, what he wanted. For Will, escape had never beckoned more sweetly, had never seemed more reasonable. 'I wish you were coming too.'

Lucy made a soft groaning sound. 'Don't start that again, Will.'

'Sorry.' He knew this was a sore point. 'I just can't understand why you don't want to escape, too.'

'And play gooseberry to you and Cara? How much fun would that be?'

The little catch in Lucy's voice alarmed Will.

'But we're sure to meet up with other travellers, and you'd make lots of friends. Just like you always have.'

Lucy had arrived in Willowbank during their last year at high school and she'd quickly fitted into Will's close circle but, because they'd shared a mutual interest in science, she and Will had become particularly good friends, really good friends.

He looked at her now, standing on the veranda in the moonlight, beautiful in an elfin, tomboyish way, with sparkly blue eyes and short blonde hair and soft pale skin. A strange lump of hot metal burned in his throat.

Lucy lifted her face to him and he saw a tear tremble on the end of her lashes and run down her cheek.

'Hey, Goose.' He used her nickname and forced a shaky laugh. 'Don't tell me you're going to miss me.'

'Of course I won't miss you,' she cried, whirling away so he couldn't see her face.

Shocked, Will reached out to her. She was wearing a strapless dress and his hands closed over her bare shoulders. Her skin was silky beneath his hands and, as he drew her back against him, she was small and soft in his arms. She smelled clean like rain. He dipped his head and her hair held the fragrance of flowers.

Without warning he began to tremble with the force of unexpected emotion.

'Lucy,' he whispered but, as he turned her around to face him, anything else that he might have said was choked off by the sight of her tears.

His heart behaved very strangely as he traced

the tears' wet tracks with his fingertips. He felt the heated softness of her skin and when he reached the dainty curve of her tear-dampened lips, he knew that he had to kiss her.

He couldn't resist gathering her close and tasting the delicate saltiness of her tears and the sweetness of her skin and, finally, the softness of her mouth. Oh, God.

With the urgency of a wild bee discovering the world's most tempting honey, Will pulled her closer and took the kiss deeper. Lucy wound her arms around his neck and he could feel her breasts pressed against his chest. His body caught fire.

How could this be happening?

Where on earth had Lucy learned to kiss? Like this?

She was so sweet and wild and passionate—turning him on like nothing he'd ever known.

Was this really Lucy McKenty in his arms? His heart was bursting inside his chest.

'Lucy?' Mattie's voice called suddenly. 'Is that you out there, Lucy?'

Light flooded them. Will and Lucy sprang apart and Mattie stared at them, shocked.

They stared at each other, equally shocked.

'I'm sorry,' Mattie said, turning bright red.

'No, it's OK,' they both protested in unison.

'We were just—' Will began.

'Saying goodbye,' Lucy finished and then she laughed. It was a rather wild, strange little laugh, but it did the trick.

Everyone relaxed. Mattie stopped blushing. 'Josh thought you might like to make a speech soon,' she told him.

'A speech?' Will sounded as dazed as he felt.

'A farewell speech.'

'Oh, yes. I'd better say something now before everyone gets too sloshed.'

They went back inside and, with the speed of a dream that faded upon waking, the moment on the veranda evaporated.

The spell was broken.

Everyone gathered around Will and, as he looked out at the sea of faces and prepared to speak, he thought guiltily of Cara, his girlfriend, waiting for him to join her in Sydney. Then he glanced at Lucy and saw no sign of tears. She was smiling and looking like her happy old self and he told himself everything was OK.

Already he was sure he'd imagined the special magic in that kiss.

CHAPTER ONE

THERE were days when Lucy McKenty knew she was in the wrong job. A woman in her thirties with a loudly ticking biological clock should not devote huge chunks of her time to delivering gorgeous babies.

Admittedly, the babies Lucy delivered usually had four legs and a tail, but that didn't stop them from being impossibly cute, and it certainly didn't stop her from longing for a baby. Just one baby of her own to hold and to love.

The longing swept through her now as she knelt in the straw beside the calf she'd just delivered. The birthing had been difficult, needing ropes and a great deal of Lucy's perspiration, but now, as she shifted the newborn closer to his exhausted mother's head, she felt an all too familiar wrench on her heartstrings.

The cow opened her eyes and began to lick her calf, slowly, methodically, and Lucy smiled as the newborn nuzzled closer. She never tired of this miracle.

Within minutes, the little calf was wobbling to his feet, butting at his mother's side, already urging her to join him in a game.

Nothing could beat the joy of new life.

Except...this idyllic scene was an uncomfortable reminder that Lucy had very little chance of becoming a mother. She'd already suffered one miscarriage and now there was a failed IVF treatment behind her. She was sure she was running out of time. The women in her family had a track record of early menopause and she lived with an ever growing sense of her biological clock counting off the months, days, hours, minutes.

Tick, tock, tick, tock.

Swallowing a sigh, Lucy stood slowly and stretched muscles that had been strained as she'd hauled the calf into the world. She glanced through the barn doorway and saw that the shadows had lengthened across the golden grass of the home paddock.

'What's the time?' she asked Jock Evans,

the farmer who'd called her in a panic several hours earlier.

Instead of checking his wrist, Jock turned slowly and squinted at the mellowing daylight outside. 'Just gone five, I reckon.'

'Already?' Lucy hurried to the corner of the barn where she'd left her things, including her watch. She checked it. Jock was dead right. 'I'm supposed to be at a wedding rehearsal by half past five.'

Jock's eyes widened with surprise. 'Don't tell me you're getting married, Lucy?'

'Me? Heavens, no.' Peeling off sterile gloves, she manufactured a gaiety she didn't feel. 'Mattie Carey's the lucky girl getting married. I'm just a bridesmaid.'

Again, she added silently.

The farmer didn't try to hide his relief. 'I'm glad you haven't been snapped up. The Willow Creek district can't afford to have you whisked away from us.'

'Well, there's not much chance.'

'Most folks around here reckon you're the best vet we've ever had.'

'Thanks, Jock.' Lucy sent him a grateful smile, but as she went through to the adjoining room to clean up, her smile wavered and then collapsed.

She really, really loved her job, and she'd worked hard for many years before the local farmers finally placed their trust in a mere 'slip of a girl'. Now she'd finally earned their loyalty and admiration and she knew she should be satisfied, but lately this job hadn't felt like enough.

She certainly didn't want to be married to it!

For Will Carruthers, coming home to Willowbank always felt like stepping back in time. In ten years the sleepy country town had barely changed.

The wide main street was still filled with the same old fashioned flower beds. The bank, the council chambers, the post office and the barber shop all looked exactly as they had when Will first left home.

Today, as he climbed out of his father's battered old truck, the familiar landmarks took on a dreamlike quality. But when he pushed open the gate that led to the white wooden church, where tomorrow his best mate would marry one of his oldest friends, he couldn't help thinking that this sense of time standing still was a mere illusion.

The buildings and the landscape might have stayed the same, but the people who lived here had changed. Oh, yeah. Every person who mattered in Will's life had changed a great deal.

And here was the funny thing. Will had left sleepy old Willowbank, eager to shake its dust from his heels and to make his mark on the world. He'd traversed the globe more times than he cared to count, but now, in so many ways, he felt like the guy who'd been left behind.

From inside the church the wailing cries of a baby sounded, a clear signal of the changes that had taken place. Will's sister Gina appeared at the church door, jiggling a howling ginger-headed infant on her hip.

When she saw her brother, her face broke into a huge smile.

'Will, I'm so glad you made it. Gosh, it's lovely to see you.' Reaching out, she beckoned him closer, gave him a one armed hug. 'Heavens, big brother, have I shrunk or have you grown even taller?'

'Maybe the weight of motherhood is wearing

you down.' Will stooped to kiss her, then smiled as he studied her face. 'I take that back, Gina. I don't think you've ever looked happier.'

'I know,' she said beaming. 'It's amazing, isn't it? I seem to have discovered my inner Earth Mother.'

He grinned and patted her baby's chubby arm. 'This must be Jasper. He's certainly a chip off the old block.' The baby was a dead ringer for his father, Tom, right down to his red hair. 'G'day, little guy.'

Jasper stopped crying and stared at Will with big blue eyes, shiny with tears.

'Gosh, that shut him up.' Gina grinned and winked. 'You must have the knack, Will. I knew you'd be perfect uncle material.'

Will chuckled to cover an abrupt slug of emotion that had caught him by surprise. Gina's baby was incredibly cute. His skin was soft and perfectly smooth, his eyes bright and clear. There were dimples on his chubby hands and, crikey, dimples on his knees. And, even though he was only four months old, he was unmistakably sturdy and masculine.

'What a great little guy,' he said, his voice rough around the edges.

Gina was watching him shrewdly. 'Ever thought of having a little boy of your own, Will?'

He covered his sigh with a lopsided grin. 'We both know I've been too much of a gypsy.'

Reluctant to meet his sister's searching gaze, Will studied a stained glass window and found himself remembering a church in Canada, where, only days ago, he'd attended the funeral of a work colleague. He could still see the earnest face of his friend's ten-year-old son, could see the pride in the boy's eyes as he'd bravely faced the congregation and told them how much he'd loved his dad.

Hell, if he let himself think about that father and son relationship now, he'd be a mess in no time.

Hunting for a distraction, Will slid a curious glance towards the chattering group at the front of the church. 'I hope I'm not late. The rehearsal hasn't started, has it?'

'No, don't fret. Hey, everyone!' Gina raised her voice. 'Will's here.'

The chatter stopped. Heads turned and faces broke into smiles. A distinct lump formed in Will's throat.

How good it was to see them all again. Tom, Gina's stolid farmer husband, was grinning like a Cheshire cat as he held baby Mia, Jasper's twin sister.

Mattie, the bride-to-be, looked incredibly happy as she stood with her bridegroom's arm about her shoulders.

Mattie was marrying Jake Devlin and Will still couldn't get over the changes in Jake. The two men had worked together on a mine site in Mongolia and they'd quickly become great mates, but Will could have sworn that Jake was not the marrying kind.

No one had been more stunned when Jake, chief breaker of feminine hearts, had fallen like a ton of bricks for Mattie Carey.

One look at Jake's face now, however, and Will couldn't doubt the truth of it. Crikey, his mate had never looked so relaxed and happy—at peace with himself and eager to take on the world.

As for Mattie…Will had known her all his life…but now she looked…well, there was only one word…

Mattie looked *transformed*.

Radiant and beautiful only went part way to describing her.

He couldn't detect any sign that she'd recently given birth to twins—to Gina and

Tom's babies, in fact, in a wonderful surrogacy arrangement that had brought untold blessings to everyone involved. Mattie was not only slim once again, but she'd acquired a new confidence that blazed in her eyes, in her glowing smile, in the way she moved.

All this Will noticed as everyone gathered around him, offering kisses, handshakes and backslaps.

'So glad you could make it,' Jake said, pumping his hand.

'Try to keep me away, mate. I'd pay good money to see you take the plunge tomorrow.'

'We're just waiting for the minister and his wife,' Mattie said. 'And for Lucy.'

Lucy.

It was ages since Will had seen Lucy, and he'd never been happy about the way they'd drifted apart, although it had seemed necessary at the time. 'Is Lucy coming to the wedding rehearsal?'

'Of course,' Mattie said. 'Didn't you know? Lucy's a bridesmaid.'

'I thought Gina was the bridesmaid.'

Gina laughed. 'You haven't been paying attention, Will. Technically, I'm the matron of honour because I'm an old married woman.

Lucy's the bridesmaid, you're the best man and
Tom's stepping in as a groomsman because
Jake's cousin can't get away.'

'I see. Of course.'

It made sense. If Will had given any proper
thought to the make-up of the wedding party,
he should have known that Mattie would ask
Lucy to be a bridesmaid. She was a vital
member of their old 'gang'.

And he was totally cool about seeing her again,
even though their relationship had been complicated since his brother's death eight years ago.

He was surprised, that was all, by the unexpected catch in his breath at the thought of
seeing her again.

Lucy glanced in the rear-view mirror as her ute
bounced down the rough country road towards
town. *Cringe.* Her hair was limp and in dire
need of a shampoo and she knew she looked decidedly scruffy.

She'd cleaned up carefully after delivering
the calf, but she couldn't be sure that her hair
and clothes were completely free of mud or
straw. Steering one-handed, she tried to finger-
comb loose strands into some kind of tidiness.

She wasn't wearing any make-up, and she was already in danger of arriving late for Mattie's wedding rehearsal, so she didn't have time to duck home for damage control. Not that it really mattered; tomorrow was the big day, after all. Not today.

But Will Carruthers would be at the rehearsal.

He was going to be best man at this wedding.

And why, after all this time, should that matter? Her crush on Will was ancient history. Water under the bridge. He was simply an old friend she'd almost lost touch with.

At least that was what she'd told herself for the past three months, ever since Mattie had announced her engagement and wedding plans. But, as she reached the outskirts of town, Lucy's body, to her annoyance, decided otherwise.

One glimpse of the little white church and the Carruthers family's elderly truck parked among the other vehicles on the green verge outside and Lucy's chest squeezed painfully. She felt as if she was breathing through cotton wool and her hands slipped on the steering wheel.

Her heart thumped.

Good grief, this was crazy. She'd known for twelve weeks now that Will would be a member of the wedding party. Why had she waited until the last moment to fall apart?

She parked the ute, dragged in a deep breath and closed her eyes, gave herself a stern lecture. She could do this. She was going to walk inside that little church with an easy stride and a smile on her face. She couldn't do much about her external appearance, but at least no one need guess she was a mess inside.

She would rather die than let on that she was jealous of Mattie for snaring and marrying a heart-throb like Jake. And she wouldn't turn the slightest hint of green when she cuddled Gina and Tom's darling babies.

More importantly, she would greet Will serenely.

She might even drop a light kiss on his cheek. After all, if her plans to marry Will's brother Josh hadn't been cruelly shattered, she would have been his sister-in-law.

OK.

She was only a few minutes late so she took a moment to check that her blouse was neatly tucked into her khaki jeans. Her boots were a bit dusty so she hastily wiped them with a tissue. There were no visible signs of the barn yard, thank heavens.

Feeling rather like a soldier going over the top of a trench, she didn't wait for second thoughts. She dived through the church doorway, cheery smile pinned in place, apologies for her lateness at the ready.

Thud. Will was standing at the end of the aisle, in front of the chancel steps, chatting to Jake.

Surreptitiously, Lucy devoured familiar details—the nut brown sheen of his hair, the outdoor glow on his skin and the creases at the corners of his eyes and mouth, his long legs in faded blue jeans.

As if these weren't enough to raise her temperature, she saw baby Mia, in a froth of pink, curled sleepily into the crook of Will's arm.

Heavens, had there ever been a sweeter place for a baby to sleep?

The tiny girl and the big man together made an image that she'd guiltily pictured in her most secret dreams and the sight of them now sucked vital air from her lungs.

Somehow she managed to walk down the aisle.

'Lucy!' Mattie called. 'I was just about to ring you.'

'I'm sorry I'm late. I was held up with a tricky calving.' She was surprised she could speak normally when her attention was riveted by Will, not just by how amazing he looked with that tiny pink bundle in his arms, but by the way his head swung abruptly at the sound of her voice and the way he went still and his eyes blazed suddenly.

Lucy felt as if the entire world had stopped, except for the frantic beating of her heart.

Thank heavens no one else seemed to notice.

'Don't worry,' Mattie was telling her calmly. 'We haven't been here long. I've just been going over the music with the organist.'

Everything was so suddenly normal and relaxed that Lucy was sure she'd misjudged Will's reaction. He certainly looked mega-cool and calm now as he greeted her. His light touch on her shoulder as he bent to kiss her and the merest brush of his lips on her cheek scalded her, but Will's grey eyes were perfectly calm.

He even looked mildly amused when he greeted her. 'Good to see you again, Lucy.'

In a matter of moments the babies were handed over to the minister's wife and daughter, who cooed and fussed over them in the front pew, while the members of the wedding party were taken through their paces.

Will, as the best man, would partner Gina. Lucy would process with Tom. So that was a relief. At least she didn't have to link arms and walk down the aisle with Will at the end of tomorrow's ceremony.

Lucy had been a bridesmaid twice before so she knew the ropes, but the minister wanted to explain every step of the service, and the rehearsal seemed to drag on and on.

On the plus side, she had time to calm down. This wedding was going to be a cinch. Nothing to get in a twist about.

Anyway, it was the height of self-indulgence to keep thinking about herself. Tomorrow was going to be Mattie's big day. Lucy, along with the entire population of Willowbank, loved warm-hearted, generous Mattie Carey and the whole township would probably turn out to watch her marry the hunky man of her dreams.

Lucy didn't want a single event or unhappy thought to mar this wedding's perfection.

Will who?

By the time the rehearsal was over, it was already dark outside, with a fragile fingernail moon hanging above the post office clock. The group dispersed quickly. Gina and Tom wanted to hurry home to get their babies settled. Mattie and Jake had to dash away to a special dinner Mattie's parents were hosting for assorted members of both families.

And Lucy wanted to hurry home to her 'boys', as she affectionately called her dogs. The Irish setter and the border collie enjoyed each other's company but, if she was away for any length of time, they were always frantic to see her.

She was fishing in her pocket for her car keys when she felt a tap on her elbow. She swung around to find herself trapped by Will Carruthers's smile, like a startled animal caught in a car's headlights.

'I haven't had a proper chance to say hello,' he said easily. 'I wanted to know how you are.'

Lucy gulped. 'I…I'm fine.' She was grateful that the darkness disguised the flush in her face, but it took a moment to remember to add, 'Thanks.' And, a frantic breath later, 'How about you, Will?'

'Not bad.' He gave her another smile and the skin around his eyes crinkled, then he shoved his hands into his jeans' pockets and stood in front of her with his long legs comfortably apart, shoulders wide. So tall and big he made her shiver.

She managed to ask, 'Are you still working in Mongolia?'

'Actually, no.' There was a slight pause and the tiniest hint of an edgy chuckle. 'I was there long enough. Decided it's time for a change, so I'm going to look around for somewhere new.'

The news didn't surprise Lucy but, after so many years, she'd finally got used to Will's absence. When he was safely overseas she could almost forget about him. Almost.

Without quite meeting her gaze, Will said, 'Gina tells me you've bought a house.'

Lucy nodded. 'I bought the old Finnegan place at the end of Wicker Lane.' She shot him a rueful smile. 'It's a renovator's delight.'

'Sounds like a challenge.'

'A huge one.'

He lifted his gaze to meet hers and a glimmer of amusement lingered in his eyes. 'You were always one for a challenge.'

Lucy wasn't quite sure what Will meant by this. He might have been referring to the way she'd worked hard at her studies during their long ago friendship at university. Or it could have been a direct reference to the fact that she'd once been engaged to his chick-magnet older brother.

She tried to sound nonchalant. 'I haven't managed many renovations on the house yet. But at least there's plenty of room for my surgery and a nice big yard for the dogs.'

'How many dogs do you have now?'

She blinked with surprise at his unexpected question. 'Just the two still.'

'Seamus and Harry.'

'That's right.'

A small silence ticked by and Lucy felt awkward. She knew that if she'd met any other old friend from her schooldays she would have offered an invitation to come back to her place. They could have shared a simple meal—probably pasta and a salad—eating in the kitchen, which she had at least partially renovated.

They could open a bottle of wine, catch up on old times, gossip about everything that had happened in the intervening years.

But her history with this man was too complicated. To start with, she'd never been able to completely snuff out the torch she carried for him, but that wasn't her only worry. Eight years ago, she'd made the terrible mistake of getting involved with his brother.

This was not the time, however, on the eve of Mattie and Jake's wedding, to rehash that sad episode.

From the darkness in the tree-lined creek behind the church a curlew's mournful cry drifted across the night and, almost as if it was a signal, Will took a step back. 'Well, I guess I'll see you tomorrow.'

'I dare say you won't be able to avoid it.'

Heavens, why had she said that? It sounded churlish. To make up for the gaffe, Lucy said quickly before he could leave, 'I'm so happy for Mattie. Jake seems like a really nice guy.'

'He's terrific,' Will agreed. 'And I'll have to hand it to Mattie. She succeeded in winning him when many others have failed.'

'Jake obviously adores her.'

'Oh, yeah, he's totally smitten.' Will looked suddenly uncomfortable and his shoulders lifted in an awkward shrug.

Lucy suspected this conversation was getting sticky for both of them.

'It's getting late,' she said gently. 'You'd better go. Your mother will have dinner waiting.'

He chuckled. 'That sounds like something from the dim dark ages when we were at high school.'

'Sorry,' she said, but he had already turned and was walking towards the truck.

He opened the squeaky door, then turned again and they both exchanged a brief wave before they climbed into their respective vehicles.

Lucy heard the elderly truck's motor rise in a harsh rev, then die down into a throaty lumbering growl. Will backed out of the parking spot and drove down the street and as she turned the key in her ute's ignition, she watched the truck's twin red tail lights growing smaller.

She remembered the times she'd driven with Will in that old truck of his father's, bumping over paddocks or down rough country lanes. Together they'd gone fossicking for sapphires, hunting for specks of gold down in the creek. At other times she'd urged him to help her to search for a new sub-species of fish.

They'd been great mates back then, but those days when Lucy had first moved to Willowbank with her dad after her parents' messy divorce felt like so very long ago now.

She had been sixteen and it was a horrible time, when she was angry with everyone. She'd been angry with her mother for falling in love with her boss, angry with her dad for somehow allowing it to happen, and angry with both of them for letting their marriage disintegrate in a heartbeat.

Most of all Lucy had been angry that she'd had to move away from Sydney to Willowbank. She'd hated leaving her old school and her friends to vegetate in a docile country town.

But then she'd met Will, along with Gina, Tom and Mattie and she'd soon been absorbed into a happy circle of friends who'd proved that life in the country could be every bit as good as life in the city.

OK, maybe her love of Willowbank had a lot to do with her feelings for Will, but at least she'd never let on how much she'd adored him. Instead, she'd waited patiently for him to realise that he loved her. When he took too long she'd taken matters into her own hands and it had all gone horribly wrong.

But it was so, so unhelpful to be thinking about that now.

Even so, Lucy was fighting tears as she reversed the ute. And, as she drove out of town, she was bombarded by bittersweet, lonely memories.

CHAPTER TWO

THE impact of the explosion sent Will flying, tossed him like a child's rag toy and dumped him hard. He woke with his heart thudding, his nerves screaming as he gripped at the bed sheets.

Bed sheets?

At first he couldn't think how he'd arrived back in the bedroom of his schooldays, but then he slowly made sense of his surroundings.

He was no longer in Mongolia.

He was safe.

He wished it had all been a nightmare, but it was unfortunately true. He'd been conducting a prospecting inspection of an old abandoned mine when it had blown without warning. By some kind of miracle he'd escaped serious injury, but his two good friends were dead.

That was the savage reality. He'd been to the funerals of both Barney and Keith—one in Brisbane and the other in Ottawa.

He'd been to hell and back sitting in those separate chapels, listening to heartbreaking eulogies and wondering why he'd been spared when his friends had so not deserved to die.

And yet here he was, home at Tambaroora…

Where nothing had changed…

Squinting in the shuttered moonlight, Will could see the bookshelf that still held his old school textbooks. His swimming trophies lined the shelf above the bed, and he knew without looking that the first geological specimens he'd collected were in a small glass case on the desk beneath the window.

Even the photo of him with his brother, Josh, was still there on the dresser. It showed Will squashed onto a pathetic little tricycle that he was clearly too big for, while Josh looked tall and grown-up on his first two-wheeler bike.

Will rolled over so he couldn't see the image. He didn't want to be reminded that his brother had beaten him to just about everything that was important in his life. It hadn't been enough for Josh Carruthers to monopolise their father's affection, he'd laid first claim on Tambaroora and he'd won the heart of Will's best friend.

That might have been OK if Josh had taken good care of Lucy.

An involuntary sigh whispered from Will's lips. *Lucy.*

Seeing her again tonight had unsettled him on all kinds of levels.

When he closed his eyes he could see the silvery-white gleam of moonlight on her hair as they'd stood outside the church. He could hear the familiar soft lilt in her voice.

Damn it. He'd wanted to tell her about the accident. He needed to talk about it.

He hadn't told his family because he knew it would upset his mother. Jessie Carruthers had already lost one son and she didn't need the news of her surviving son's brush with death.

Will could have talked to Jake, of course. They'd worked together in Mongolia and Jake would have understood how upset he was, but he hadn't wanted to throw a wet blanket on the eve of his mate's wedding.

No, Lucy was the one person he would have liked to talk to. In the past, they'd often talked long into the night. As students they'd loved deep and meaningful discussions.

Yes, he could have told Lucy what he'd learned at those funerals.

But it was probably foolish to think he could resurrect the closeness they'd enjoyed as students.

After all this time, they'd both changed.

Hell, was it really eight years? He could still feel the shock of that December day when he'd been skiing in Norway and he'd received the news that Lucy and his brother were engaged to be married. He'd jumped on the first plane home.

With a groan, Will flung aside the sheet and swung out of bed, desperate to throw off the memories and the sickening guilt and anger that always accompanied his thoughts of that terrible summer.

But, with the benefit of hindsight, Will knew he'd been unreasonably angry with Josh for moving in on his best friend while his back was turned. He'd had no claim on Lucy. She'd never been his girlfriend. He'd gone overseas with Cara Howard and, although their relationship hadn't lasted, he'd allowed himself to be distracted by new sights, new people, new adventures.

He'd let life take him by the hand, happy to go with the flow, finding it easier than settling down.

The news that Josh was going to marry Lucy shouldn't have upset him, but perhaps he might have coped more easily if Lucy had chosen to marry a stranger. As it was, he'd never been able to shake off the feeling that Josh had moved in on her just to prove to his little brother that he could have whatever he desired.

Unfortunately, Will had chosen the very worst time to have it out with Josh.

He would never, to the end of his days, forget the early morning argument at the airfield, or Josh's stubbornness, or the sight of that tiny plane tumbling out of the sky like an autumn leaf.

If only that had been the worst of it, but it was Gina who'd told him that the shock of Josh's death had caused Lucy to have a miscarriage.

A miscarriage?

Will had been plagued by endless questions—questions he'd had no right to ask. Which had come first—the engagement or the pregnancy? Had Josh truly loved Lucy?

A week after the funeral he'd tried to speak to

her, but Dr McKenty had been fiercely protective of his daughter and he'd turned Will away.

So the only certainties that he'd been left with were Josh's death and Lucy's loss, and he'd found it pitifully easy to take the blame for both.

To make amends, he'd actually tried to stay on at Tambaroora after Josh's death. But he couldn't replace Josh in his father's eyes and he'd soon known that he didn't fit in any more. He was a piece from a flashy foreign jigsaw trying to fit into a homemade puzzle.

For Will, it had made sense to leave again and to stay away longer. In time, he'd trained himself to stop dwelling on the worst of it. But of course he couldn't stay away from his home and family for ever and there were always going to be times, like now, when everything came back to haunt him.

Lucy dreamed about Will.

In her dream they were back at Sydney University and they'd met in the refectory for coffee and to compare notes after a chemistry practical.

It was an incredibly simple but companionable scene. She and Will had always enjoyed hanging out together, and in her dream they were sitting at one of the little tables overlooking the courtyard, chatting and smiling and discussing the results of their latest experiments.

When it was time to leave for separate lectures, Lucy announced calmly, as if it was a normal extension of their everyday conversation, 'Oh, by the way, Will, I'm pregnant.'

Will's face broke into a beautiful smile and he drew her into his arms and hugged her, and Lucy knew that her pregnancy was the perfect and natural expression of their love.

She felt the special protection of his arms about her and she was filled with a sense of perfect happiness, of well-being, of everything being right in her world.

When she woke, she lay very still with her eyes closed, lingering for as long as she could in the happy afterglow of the dream, clinging to the impossible fantasy that she was pregnant.

Better than that, she was pregnant with Will's baby. Not his brother's...

The dream began to fade and she could no longer ignore the fact that morning sunlight was pulsing on the other side of her closed eyelids.

Reality reared its unwelcome head.

Damn.

Not that dream again. How stupid.

Actually, it was more like a recurring nightmare, so far divorced from Lucy's real life that she always felt sick when she woke. She hated to think that her subconscious could still, after all this time, play such cruel tricks on her.

In truth, she'd never been brave enough to let her friendship with Will progress into anything deeper. At university, she'd seen all the other girls who'd fallen for him. She'd watched Will date them for a while and then move on, and she'd decided it was safer to simply be his buddy. His friend.

As his girlfriend she'd risk losing him and she couldn't have coped with that. If they remained good friends, she could keep him for ever.

Or so she'd thought.

The plan had serious flaws, of course, which was no doubt why she was still plagued far too often by the dream.

But now, as Lucy opened her eyes, she knew it was time to wake up to more important realities. This wasn't just any morning. It was Mattie's wedding day.

This was a day for hair appointments and

manicures, helping Mattie to dress and smiling for photographs. This was to be her friend's perfect day.

Get over it, Lucy.

Get over yourself.

Stifling a lingering twinge of longing for the dream, she threw off the bedclothes, went to the window and looked out. It was a beautiful day, cloudless and filled with sunshine. She smiled.

No more useless longings. No more doleful thoughts.

Surely clear blue skies were a very promising omen?

In Willowbank everyone was abuzz.

With the help of friends and relatives from around the district, Mattie's mum had grown masses of white petunias in pots and tubs and even in wheelbarrows.

Lucy happily helped a team of women to unload containers of flowers from their cars and place them strategically in the church and the grounds, as well as the marquee where the reception was to be held in an allotment next to the church hall. The instant floral effect was spectacular.

After that, the morning passed in a happy whirl, much to Lucy's relief. First, she met up with Mattie and Gina at the hairdresser's, then they popped into the salon next door for matching manicures, and finally they dashed back to Mattie's for a delicious light lunch prepared by one of her doting aunts.

During lunch the phone seemed never to stop ringing and all kinds of messages flew back and forth. Gina's mum, who was babysitting the twins, reported that they'd been fed and burped and were sleeping beautifully. Nurses from the Sydney hospital where the babies had been born rang to wish Mattie and Jake all the best for married life. The caterer had a question about the positioning of the wedding cake on the main table.

Lucy had to admire the way Mattie seemed to float through it all. She was the most serene bride ever. Nothing bothered her or was too much trouble. Mattie had always been sweet and easy-going, but she'd never been as blissfully relaxed and happy and confident as she was today.

It must be love, Lucy thought, and she wished it was contagious.

Shortly after lunch, the excitement really

began. Refrigerated boxes arrived from the florist, filled with truly gorgeous bouquets. Then it was time for the girls to put on their make-up, laughing as they took turns in front of Mattie's bedroom mirror, the same mirror where years ago they had first experimented with mascara and eyeliner while they'd gossiped about boys.

Back then, Lucy, being older and from the city, had been considered to be wiser and worldlier. The other girls had looked up to her with undisguised respect and considerable awe.

How the tables had turned. Now Gina was married and a mother, and Mattie was about to marry Jake, while Lucy was…

No! She wasn't going to tolerate a single negative thought today.

When they'd achieved their best with make-up, Gina and Lucy slipped into their bridesmaid's dresses, which were simply divine. The palest pink duchess satin looked equally pretty on Gina with her dark hair and olive complexion as it did on Lucy, who was blonde and fair-skinned.

Then it was time to fuss over Mattie, to fasten the dozens of tiny satin-covered buttons down her back, to help to secure her veil and then to gasp in sheer astonishment when they saw the completed picture of their best friend in her wedding gown.

'You look absolutely breathtaking,' Lucy whispered.

Gina was emotional. 'You're so beautiful Jake's going to cry when he sees you.'

'Please don't say that.' Mattie laughed nervously. 'You'll make *me* cry.'

'And me,' moaned Lucy.

Already, at the mere thought of an emotional bridegroom, she could feel mascara-threatening tears about to spill.

Oh, help. Weddings were such poignant affairs. And today Will was going to be there, looking dashing as the best man. How on earth was she going to get through the next few hours?

Dressed in matching dark formal suits with silver ties and orange blossoms in their lapels, Jake, Will and Tom were ushered into the minuscule vestry and instructed to wait till it was time to take their places at the front of the church.

Will anxiously patted a pocket in his suit jacket. 'The rings are still safe.'

Jake grinned and laid a reassuring hand on his friend's shoulder. 'That's the third time you've checked the rings in the past five minutes. Relax, man, they're not going to grow legs and run away.'

'Jake's the guy who's supposed to be nervous,' added Tom with a grin.

Will nodded and tried to smile. 'Sorry. Don't know what's got into me.' He shot Jake a questioning glance. 'Aren't you even a little nervous?'

'Why should I be nervous?'

'You're getting married.' Will wished his voice wasn't so hoarse. His sleepless night was really getting to him. 'It's par for the course for a bridegroom to have the jitters,' he said.

'But I'm marrying Mattie,' Jake responded simply, as if that explained everything. And his glowing smile made it patently clear that he knew, without doubt, he was the luckiest man alive.

Will wished he felt a fraction of his mate's happiness.

'So where are you heading for your honeymoon?' he asked. 'Or is that a state secret?'

Jake grinned. 'The exact location is a surprise for Mattie, but I'll tell you two.' He lowered his voice. 'I'm taking her to Italy. She's never been overseas, so we're going to Venice, Lake Como and the Amalfi Coast.'

'Wow!' Tom's jaw dropped. 'That's so over the top it's fabulous. You'll have an amazing time.'

Jake nodded happily but, before he could say anything else, the minister appeared at the vestry door and sent them a smiling wink. 'Could you come this way now please, gentlemen?'

A chill ran down Will's spine. For crying out loud, what was the matter with him today? Anyone would think he was the one getting married, or that they were criminals being led to the dock.

'All the best, mate,' he whispered gruffly to Jake.

'Thanks.'

The two friends shook hands, then headed through the little doorway that led into the church, where an incredible transformation had occurred.

Not only was the place packed to the rafters with people dressed in their best finery, but there were flowers and white ribbons every-where—dangling from the ends of pews, wound around columns, adorning windowsills and filling vases, large and small.

And there was organ music, billowing and

rippling like the background music in a sentimental movie. Will tried to swallow the lump in his throat. Why was it that weddings were designed to zero straight in on unsuspecting emotions?

He glanced at Jake and saw his Adam's apple jerk.

'You OK?' he whispered out of the side of his mouth.

'I'll be fine once Mattie gets here.'

'She won't be late,' Will reassured him and again he nervously patted the rings in his pocket.

There was a flurry in the little porch at the back of the church and, as if everyone had been choreographed, the congregation turned. Will felt fine hairs lift on the back of his neck. His stomach tightened.

The girls appeared in a misty mirage of white and pink. Will blinked. Lucy, Gina and Mattie looked incredibly out-of-this-world beautiful in long feminine dresses and glamorous hairstyles, and with their arms filled with flowers.

He heard Jake catch his breath, felt goosebumps lift on his arms.

The organist struck a dramatic chord.

Lucy and Gina, apparently satisfied with

their arrangement of Mattie's dress and veil, took their places in front of her, Lucy first.

Will couldn't be sure that he wasn't trembling.

Lucy stood, shoulders back, looking straight ahead, with her blonde head high, her blue eyes smiling. To Will she looked vulnerable and yet resolute and his heart began to thunder loudly.

It was so weird.

He'd seen countless weddings and endless processions of bridesmaids, but none of them had made him feel the way he felt now as the organist began to play and Lucy began to walk down the aisle with her smile carefully in place.

She'd always tried to pretend she was a tomboy, keeping her hair short and wispy and preferring to live in T-shirts and jeans, but today nothing could hide her femininity.

Her pastel off-the-shoulders dress and the soft pink lilies in her arms highlighted the paleness of her hair, the honey-gold tints in her skin, the pink lushness of her lips. She had never looked lovelier.

Except perhaps…that one night on a shadowy veranda, when she'd turned to him with tears in her eyes…

He willed her to look at him. Just one glance

would do. For old friendship's sake. He wanted eye contact, needed to send her one smile, longed for one tiny link with her.

Come on, look this way, Lucy.

She smiled at the people in the congregation, at her particular friends, at Jake, but her gaze didn't flicker any further to the right. It was clear she did not want to see Will.

Or, perhaps, she simply felt no need.

CHAPTER THREE

LUCY'S eyes were distinctly misty as she watched Mattie and Jake dance the bridal waltz. They looked so happy together and so deeply in love. She was sure everyone watching them felt misty-cyed too.

It had been an utterly perfect wedding.

The beautiful ceremony had been followed by a happy procession across Willowbank's main street to the marquee where the reception was held. Champagne flowed, a string quartet played glorious music and the guests were served delectable food.

Jake's speech had been heartfelt and touching and Will's toast was appropriately witty, although he went embarrassingly over the top with his praise for the bridesmaids. Lucy had felt her face flame when curious eyes had swung in her direction and the cutting of the cake had been a welcome distraction.

Everyone had broken into spontaneous cheering for Mattie and Jake, and Lucy was thrilled. The wedding couldn't have been happier.

She was relieved that she'd survived without making a fool of herself. Which mostly meant avoiding Will—a tall order given that her eyes had developed a habit of sneaking in his direction whenever she thought he wasn't looking. She'd tried so hard to ignore him, but she'd always thought he was the best-looking guy ever.

She could still remember the day she'd first met him as a schoolboy down by Willow Creek, crouched at the edge of the water.

Even viewing him from behind, he'd been beautiful.

He'd taken his shirt off and he'd been squatting, reaching down, panning for gold in the water. Sunlight breaking through overhead trees had lent an extra sheen to his dark brown hair and to the smooth golden-brown skin on his back.

Lucy hadn't been able to help staring. His shoulders were wide, his hips narrow, his limbs long—the build of a swimmer.

Now, so many years later, he was even more

irresistible in his dark formal attire. Lucy kept finding things she needed to check out—the manly jut of his jaw above the crisp collar, the neat line of his dark hair across the back of his neck, the stunning breadth of his shoulders in the stylish suit jacket...

Sigh...

Despite the wedding's perfection, the evening had been a huge strain and she was worn out.

She'd kicked off her high heeled shoes and they were now stowed under the table. She was thinking rather fondly about the end of the night when she could head for home. It would be so nice to greet her dogs, then curl up in bed with a glass of water and a headache tablet.

Tom leaned towards her. 'Lucy, it's our turn to dance.'

She winced. 'Is it really?'

Tom was already on his feet. 'Come on. Gina and Will are already up. You know the wedding party is expected to take a twirl on the dance floor.'

Bother. She'd forgotten about that. She suppressed a sigh as she fished beneath the table for her shoes. *Ouch.* They pinched as she squeezed back into them.

She looked over at the dance floor and saw that Tom was right. Gina was already dancing with Will and, for no reason that made sense, her silly heart began to trip and stumble.

'Lead the way,' she told Tom resolutely, slipping her arm through his. Thank heavens he was a reliable old friend. At least she could dance with Tom till the cows came home without being attacked by dangerous palpitations.

Unfortunately, Tom didn't seem to be quite so enamoured with her as his dancing partner. At the end of the bracket, other couples joined them on the dance floor and Tom leaned close to her ear. 'Would you mind if I asked Gina for a dance?'

'Of course I don't mind.' She took a step back to prove it. 'Please, go ahead. You must dance with your wife.'

Tom happily tapped Will on the back and Lucy retreated to the edge of the timber dance floor. Over her shoulder, she watched the men's brief smiling exchange. She saw Will's nod and her heart began to race as she guessed what might happen next.

It was logical—a common courtesy for Will to ask *her* to dance—but there were times when logic and courtesy flew out of the window. Times like now, when her out of date, unhelpful feelings for Will made simple things complicated.

On the surface, one quick dance with an old friend should have been a piece of cake. But on a super-romantic night like tonight, Lucy was trembling at the very thought of dancing publicly in Will Carruthers's arms.

She couldn't help thinking about that kiss all those years ago, when she'd made a fool of herself at Will's farewell party. She turned, planning to hurry back to her place at the table.

'Lucy!'

Will's voice sounded close behind her and she froze.

'I won't let you escape that easily.' His tone held a thread of humour, but there was also a note of command that was hard to ignore.

His hand brushed her wrist and the touch was like a firebrand. Lucy was helpless as his fingers enclosed around her, as he pulled her gently but decisively towards him. 'Come on,' he urged. 'We've got to have one dance.'

He made it sound easy, but when she looked into his cool grey eyes she was surprised to see a cautious edge to his smile, as if he wasn't quite as confident as he sounded. Which didn't help her to relax.

A number of wedding guests were watching them, however, and the last thing she wanted was a scene.

'One dance?' Lucy forced lightness into her voice. 'Why not?' She managed a smile. No way did she want to give the impression she was trying to dodge Will. One dance was no problem at all. She would dance with him till her feet fell off.

Will led her back onto the dance floor.

Gulp.

As soon as he placed one hand at her back and took her other hand in his, she knew this wasn't going to be any version of easy. She drew a jagged breath.

'Smile,' Will murmured as he pulled her closer. 'This is a wedding, not a funeral.'

He took the lead and Lucy obediently pinned on a smile.

She'd only danced with Will a handful of times, long ago. Even so, she could remember every single detail—his habit of enfolding her fingers inside his, the way he smelled of midnight, and the way her head was exactly level with his jaw.

Tonight, every familiar memory felt like a pulled thread, unravelling her poorly stitched self control. Being this close to Will played havoc with her heartbeats, with her sense of rhythm. She kept stumbling and bumping into him and then apologising profusely.

After the third apology, he steered her to the edge of the floor and he leaned back a little, and he smiled as he looked into her face.

Will said something, but Lucy couldn't hear him above the music and she shook her head, lifted her shoulders to show she had no idea.

Leaning closer, she felt her skin vibrate as he spoke into her ear. 'Are you OK? Would you like a break?'

That would be sensible, wouldn't it?

She nodded. 'Yes, please.'

A reprieve.

Maybe not. Will stayed close beside her as she returned to the table and, before she could resume her seat, he said, 'There are chairs outside. Why don't we go out there where it's cooler and quieter, away from the music?'

Lucy's heart stumbled again. Going outside where it was quieter suggested that Will wanted to talk.

Part of her yearned to talk with him, but she wasn't sure it was wise. What could they talk about now? They'd covered the basics last night after the rehearsal, and Will had been away for so long that they'd lost their old sense of camaraderie.

Besides, further conversation would surely lead to uncomfortable topics like her relationship with Josh. Wouldn't it be wiser to simply keep their distance now?

But the look in Will's eyes as he watched her sent a fine shiver rushing over her skin and she knew that wisdom would lose this particular battle and curiosity would win. She secretly longed to hear what Will wanted to talk about.

'I'm sure a little fresh air is a good idea,' she said and she went with him through a doorway in the side of the marquee into the moon silvered night.

They found two chairs abandoned by smokers and, as soon as Lucy sat down, she slipped off her shoes and rubbed at her aching feet.

Will chuckled softly.

'I'm not used to wearing such high heels,' she said defensively. 'You should try them. They're sheer torture.'

'I don't doubt that for a moment, but they look sensational.' He released a button on his jacket, letting it fall open. His shirt gleamed whitely in the moonlight and he stretched his long legs in front of him.

After a small pause, he said, 'I meant what I said in my speech. You look lovely tonight, Lucy.'

Her cheeks grew warm again. 'Thanks. Mattie chose our dresses. She has very feminine tastes.'

He let her self-effacing comment pass.

'It's been a perfect wedding,' she said to make amends, but then she was ambushed by an involuntary yawn. 'But it seems to have worn me out.'

'You've probably been working too hard.'

She shook her head. 'My work doesn't very often make me tired. Weddings, on the other hand…'

'Can be very draining.'

'Yes.'

He was watching her with a lopsided smile. 'It's not always easy to watch your friends tie the knot.'

'I…' Her mouth was suddenly dry and her tongue stuck to its roof. She shot Will a sharp glance, uncertain where this conversation was heading. She tried again. 'I'm really happy for Mattie, aren't you?'

'Absolutely,' he said. 'Marriage couldn't have happened to a nicer girl.'

Lucy nodded. A small silence limped by. 'I suppose weddings are tiring because they involve lots of people.' Hunting for a way to disguise the fact that Will's presence at this wedding was her major problem, she made a sweeping gesture towards the crowded marquee. 'I'm more used to animals these days. They're so much quieter than humans.'

'And I'm used to rocks.'

Lucy laughed. 'I dare say they're quieter too.'

'Silence is one of their better attributes.' Will chuckled again. 'Sounds like we've turned into a pair of old loners.'

'Maybe,' she said softly, but she knew it was hazardous for her to talk of such things with this man.

Quietly, he said, 'It's happening all around us, Goose.'

Goose…her old nickname.

Only her father and Will had ever called her Goose, or Lucy Goose…and hearing the name now made her dangerously nostalgic.

She tried to shake that feeling aside. 'What's happening all around us?'

'Friends getting married. Starting families.'

Lucy stiffened. Why did he have to bring up *that* subject? 'It's hardly surprising, given our friends' ages.'

'Yes, and we're older than all of them.'

Tick tock, tick tock, tick tock...

Lucy closed her eyes as the familiar breathless panic gripped her. *No.* She wasn't going to think about *that* worry tonight. She'd declared a moratorium on all thoughts that involved babies, having babies, wanting babies, losing babies. She couldn't imagine why Will had raised such a sensitive topic.

Or perhaps he didn't know about her miscarriage. After his brother's death, she'd barely spoken to Will at the funeral and then he'd moved as far away from Willowbank as was humanly possible. Since then, if they'd run into each other, it had been by accident, or because their friends had invited them to the same Christmas party.

Will had always been polite but he'd kept his distance and Lucy had always been busily proving to him that she was managing damn fine splendid on her own.

So why this?

Why now?

Lucy knew her sudden breathless fear would not be helped by a continued discussion of marriage and babies with Will Carruthers.

'Is there a point to this conversation, Will?' She thrust her feet back into her shoes and grimaced as they pinched. 'Because I don't enjoy being reminded of how old I'm getting.'

She jumped to her feet, only to discover she was shaking violently. Her knees had no strength whatsoever and she had no choice but to sink down again.

She was too embarrassed to look at Will.

In a heartbeat, he was bending over her solicitously. 'I'm sorry. I thought I was stating the obvious. Marriages, births, christenings all around us. Are you all right? Can I get you a drink?'

'I'm fine,' she lied, dragging in oxygen. 'But I...I should go back inside. Mattie might need me.'

'Are you sure you're OK?'

She gulped another deep breath. 'I'm certain.'

Will's hand was at her elbow, supporting her

as she got to her feet again, and she hoped he couldn't feel the way her body trembled.

With her first step she swayed against him. He put his arm around her and it felt amazingly fabulous to have his solid shoulder to lean on. 'I swear I haven't had too much to drink,' she said.

'I know that. You're just tired.'

She supposed he was right. What else could it be?

'As soon as this reception is over, I'll drive you home,' Will said.

'There's no need.'

'No arguments, Lucy. You don't have your car here, do you?'

'No,' she admitted. 'I left it at Mattie's place.'

'My vehicle's here. If you're tired, you need a lift.'

By now they'd reached the doorway to the marquee and Lucy could see Gina handing around a platter of wedding cake in pink and silver parcels.

'Oh, heavens,' she cried, slipping from Will's hold. 'I should be helping with the cake.'

'Are you sure you're up to it?'

'Of course.'

And, as she hurried to help, she knew that

it was true. She was perfectly fine when she was safely away from Will.

That went well, Will thought wryly as he watched Lucy hand around platters of wedding cake.

Already she was smiling and chatting and looking a hundred times happier than she had a few minutes ago when he'd crassly reminded her that life was passing them by.

Watching her with a thoughtful frown, he recalled the countless conversations they'd enjoyed when they were friends. They'd shared a mutual interest in science, and so they'd been totally in tune about many things. It was only later, when they'd talked about life after university, that their friendship had run into trouble.

Lucy was adventurous and as curious about the world as he was, but unlike him, she hadn't been keen to get away. She'd apparently wanted nothing more than to get straight back to Willowbank, to settle down in a veterinary practice.

Her father was a doctor and she'd claimed that she was anxious to follow his example. She'd worked hard to get her degree and she looked on travel as a waste of time. Why work at menial jobs simply to earn enough money to move on to the next travel spot, when she could stay in Willowbank and build her career?

At the time, when Will had left on his big adventure with Cara in tow, he'd had a vague idea that he might eventually return and find work closer to home.

The news of his brother's engagement to Lucy McKenty had come out of the blue and he'd been shocked by how much it had worried him, by the urge that had hit him to hurry home. Not that he could blame Lucy for falling in love with Josh.

Everyone in the entire Willow Creek district had loved his outgoing, confident brother—and Josh Carruthers had a habit of getting what he wanted, especially when it came to women.

Will could easily imagine how his brother had flirted with Lucy. Hell, yeah. Josh would have charmed and courted her so expertly she wouldn't have known what had hit her. And Josh would have offered her the exact life she wanted—marriage and a family, with a sheep station thrown in as the icing on the cake.

But had Josh really, deeply cared for Lucy? Had he wanted to make her happy?

It surprised Will that he still let these questions bother him after all this time.

'You look down in the mouth.' Jake's voice sounded at Will's elbow. 'Everything OK?'

Will turned guiltily and forced a grin. 'It's been a fabulous night,' he said, hoping to avoid answering Jake's question. 'Ace wedding, mate.'

'Glad you've had a good time.' Jake nodded his head in Lucy's direction. 'She's a lovely girl.'

It was pointless to pretend he didn't know who Jake meant. Will nodded. 'Yeah.' He shoved his hands deep in his pockets, as if the action could somehow comfort him.

'Mattie told me you two used to be really close.'

'Close friends,' Will corrected and he did his best to dismiss this with a shrug, but Jake was watching him in a way that made his neck burn hotly.

Jake smiled. 'You look as miserable as I felt four months ago, before I sorted everything out with Mattie.'

'This is totally different. More like a mystery than history,' Will muttered glumly.

'Perhaps. But, in the end, it all comes down to the same thing.'

Will glared at his friend. 'I didn't realise that a marriage ceremony turned a man into an instant relationship guru.'

Jake's smile faded. 'Sorry. Was I sounding smug?'

'You were.' Will gave another shrug. 'But I'd probably be smug too, if I was in your shoes.'

'Except that you're right,' Jake said, looking more serious now. 'I know nothing about you and Lucy.'

A heavy sigh escaped Will and he realised that, despite his fierce reaction, he'd actually been hoping that his friend could reveal some kind of magic insight that would help him to clear the air with Lucy. Anything to be rid of this gnawing guilt he still carried.

'I think we're heading off soon,' Jake said. 'I guess I'd better find my wife and finish our farewells.'

They shook hands and Will wished his mate all the best and it wasn't much later before the guests started gathering on the footpath to wave the happy couple off.

In the light of a street lamp, Will could see Lucy's golden hair shimmering palely as she kissed Mattie and Jake, before she drifted back to watch their departure from the edge of the crowd.

Mattie was laughing as she stood at the car's open door and lifted her bouquet of white roses. Will saw Lucy backing even further away, almost trying to hide.

Then the roses were sailing through the air in a high arc. There were girlish squeals of laughter and hands rose to try to grab the flowers, but Mattie's aim was sure. The bouquet landed square on Lucy's nose and she had no choice but to catch it.

A cheer went up and Lucy gave a bashful smile and held the bouquet high, no doubt knowing that all of Willowbank would love to see their favourite vet married.

But she was probably grateful that everyone's attention quickly returned to the bride and groom. Jake was already helping Mattie into the car.

Over the heads of the crowd he sent Will a flashing grin and Will answered with a thumbs-up.

The car's exhaust roared as they took off and the rear window was covered in 'just married' signs written in toothpaste, which only served to prove how old-fashioned this town really was.

Will, however, was watching Lucy. She stood in the shadows at the back of the throng, clutching the wedding bouquet in one hand while she used the other hand to swipe at her tears.

CHAPTER FOUR

LUCY wished the ground would open up and swallow her. It was bad enough that everyone knew the bride had deliberately thrown the bouquet to her. To cry about it was beyond pathetic, but to do so in front of Will Carruthers was more embarrassing than she could bear.

Turning her back on him, she gave one final swipe and an unladylike sniff and she willed her eyes to stay dry. It wasn't a moment too soon.

Will's voice sounded close behind her. 'We can leave whenever you like,' he said.

She drew a deep slow breath and turned to him with a smile on her face. Any number of people would have given her a lift, but she was determined to show Will that his comments about the two of them being a pair of old loners had not upset her.

'Could you give me just a moment?' she said. 'I'd like to say goodbye to a few people.'

'By all means. I've said my farewells. Let me know when you're ready.'

'I shouldn't be long, unless Mrs Carey needs my help with anything else. Shall I meet you at the truck?'

'Sure.'

It was crazy the way her stomach tightened as she crossed the road to Will's parked truck. Crazier still the way her heart thrashed when she saw his tall figure waiting in the shadows beside the vehicle. He stepped forward when he saw her and the white shirt beneath his jacket glowed in the moonlight. Fire flashed in his light grey eyes.

'Let me help you up,' he said as he opened the truck's passenger door.

'I can manage.' Lucy was anxious to avoid his gallantry. If Will touched her now, she might self-combust.

But managing alone wasn't easy. With her arms filled with her bridesmaid's bouquet as well as the bride's white roses and with the added complication of her long straight skirt and precarious high heels, the whole business of clambering up into the truck was fraught with difficulties.

Will was full of apologies. 'I forgot how hard it is to climb into this damned thing.'

'If you hold the bouquets, I'm sure I can swing myself up.'

Without waiting for his reply, Lucy thrust the flowers into his arms. Then, grateful for the darkness, she yanked her skirt with one hand and took a firm grip of the door handle with the other. She stepped high and hauled herself up, and everything would have been fine if one of her high heels hadn't caught on the step.

In mid-flight she lost her balance and then lost her grip on the handle and, before she could recover, she was slipping backwards.

Into Will's arms.

She was crushed against his chest, along with several dozen blooms.

'I've got you.'

Lucy wasn't sure if the pounding of Will's heart and his sharp intake of breath were caused by shock or the exertion of catching her.

Desperately, she tried to ignore how wonderfully safe she felt in his arms, how beyond fabulous it was to be cradled against his splendidly muscular chest. The wool of his expensive suit was cool and fine beneath her cheek. She could have stayed there...

'I'm sorry,' she spluttered. 'Anyone would think I was drunk.'

'The thought never crossed my mind.'

'You can put me down, Will. I'm quite all right.'

'I think it might be better if we do this my way.'

His face was in darkness so Lucy couldn't see his expression, but his voice was deep and warm, like a comforting blanket around her, and he hoisted her up onto the front seat of the truck with astonishing ease.

'Put your seat belt on,' he said, as if she was a child. 'And then I'll pass you what's left of the bouquets.'

Chastened, Lucy thanked him.

The glorious scent of crushed rose petals filled the truck's cabin as Will climbed behind the wheel and pulled the driver's door shut. But the fragrance couldn't disguise the smell of ancient leather and it couldn't block Lucy's memories.

This was the first time in ten years that she'd been alone in the dark with Will, and stupidly she remembered that embarrassing kiss on the shadowy veranda at Tambaroora.

She could remember exactly how he'd tasted and the warm pressure of his lips, the sexy slide of his tongue…

He turned to her. 'Are you OK now?'

'Perfectly,' she said in a choked whisper.

'Are you sure?' he asked, frowning at her, watching her intently.

She pressed a hand against her heart in a bid to calm its wicked thudding. 'I was hobbled by this jolly dress and I slipped in the stupid heels.' She sounded more astringent than she'd meant to. 'After tonight, these shoes are going straight to the Country Women's second-hand store.'

Will chuckled softly, then started the truck and soon they were rumbling down the street. Lucy buried her nose in the roses, glad that he didn't try to talk all the way home.

But, in the silence, her thoughts turned back to their earlier conversation. Will had shocked her when he'd raised the subject of marriage and babies, but perhaps she shouldn't have been so surprised. It was, as he'd said, happening all around them. Gina and Tom had their twins. Mattie was married.

She had been so busy trying to back away from the topic, so scared Will would discover how hung up she was about these very things, that she'd cut the conversation short.

Now she was left to wonder. Had he actually been leading up to something he wanted to discuss? She'd always been hurt by Will's silence after Josh's death and the miscarriage. He'd never given her the chance to confess why she'd become involved with his brother.

Of course, it would be dreadfully difficult to tell him the truth, but she'd always felt guilty and she wanted to come clean. Perhaps then she would be able to put it behind her at last. She might, at last, stop dreaming about Will.

As the truck rumbled down country lanes, past darkened farmhouses and quiet paddocks, a number of questions bumped around in her head and by the time Will pulled up in front of her house, Lucy couldn't hold back. 'Will, what was the point you wanted to make?'

In the glow of the dashboard's lights, she could see his frown. 'I'm sorry, Lucy, you've lost me.'

'When we were talking at the wedding, you were carrying on about how old we are now and I got in a huff, but were you actually trying to make a point?'

He turned to face her, one hand draped

loosely over the steering wheel. 'Nothing in particular.' He smiled shyly. 'I simply wanted to talk to you—the way we used to.'

A ghost of a smile trickled across his face. Then he looked out through the windscreen and tapped his fingers on the steering wheel. 'We have a lot to catch up on, but it's late. Why don't I give you a call some time?'

How could such a simple question send her insides into turmoil? It was so silly to be incredibly excited simply because Will Carruthers planned to talk to her again.

With difficulty, Lucy overcame her desperate curiosity to know what he wanted to talk about. She managed to speak calmly.

'I'll wait to hear from you, then,' she said as she pushed the door open.

'Don't move,' Will ordered, shoving his door open too. 'I'll help you out. I don't want you falling again. You're an accident waiting to happen tonight.'

A hasty glance at the huge step down to the road showed Lucy the wisdom of accepting his offer, but her heart skipped several beats as he rounded the truck and helped her down.

'Thank you,' she said demurely. 'My elderly

bones couldn't have taken another stumble this evening.'

His soft laugh held the hint of a growl. 'Get to bed, Grandma.'

To her astonishment, Will's lips feathered the merest brush of a kiss against her temple. Her knees almost gave way.

'Perhaps I should escort you to the door,' he said.

'I think I'm still capable of tottering up my own front path.'

'I'll wait here till you're safely inside.'

After years of being fiercely independent, Lucy had to admit it was rather pleasant to have a lordly male watching out for her. With the bouquets bundled in one arm, she lifted her skirt elegantly and took careful dainty steps as she made her way up the uneven brick path.

She'd left her car and her other set of keys at Mattie's parents' house, but there was a spare key under the flowerpot on the porch. Tonight, however, there was more than a flowerpot on the porch. A hessian bag had been left on the doorstep.

Lucy saw it and sighed. Caring for wildlife wasn't part of her veterinary responsibilities, but people knew she had a soft heart and they were always bringing her injured bush creatures. Animals hit by cars were the most common and this was sure to be another one— a wounded sugar glider, an orphaned kangaroo, or perhaps an injured possum.

She was dead tired tonight, but now, before she could crawl into bed, she would have to attend to this.

She found the key, opened the front door and reached inside to turn on the porch light. Behind her, Will was waiting at the front gate and she sent him a friendly wave. 'Thanks for the lift,' she called.

He returned her wave and she watched as he headed back to the truck, then, with the flowers in one arm, she picked up the sack. The animal inside wriggled, which was a good sign. Maybe it wasn't too badly hurt and she wouldn't lose too much sleep tonight.

She heard her dogs scratching at the back door, but they would have to wait a bit longer for her attention. She took the sack through to the surgery, put the roses and lilies in one of the huge metal sinks and set the bag down gently on the metal examining table.

First things first, she kicked off her shoes. That was *so-o-o-o* much better. Yawning widely, she unknotted the string around the neck of the bag.

A snake's head shot out.

Lucy screamed.

Panic flooded her!

A snake was the last thing she'd expected. The worst thing. She loved animals. She loved all animals. But she still couldn't help being terrified of snakes.

Her heart leapt in a rush of instinctive primeval terror. She couldn't deal with this.

Not now. Not alone in the middle of the night.

Paralysed by fear, she thought of Will driving off in his truck and seriously considered chasing after him, yelling for help. She whimpered his name and was ready to scream again when footsteps thundered up the path and Will appeared at the surgery doorway.

'Lucy, what's the matter?'

'A s-snake!' With a shaking hand she pointed to the sack.

'Let me deal with it.' He spoke calmly and, just like that, he crossed the floor to the wriggling hessian bag.

Lucy watched, one hand clamped over her mouth to hold back another scream, as Will carefully pulled the top of the sack apart, then, with commendable cool, gripped the snake firmly, just behind its head.

'It's a carpet python,' he told her smoothly as he lifted it out and took hold of the tail, while the snake thrashed wildly. 'And it's wounded.'

A carpet python.

Right. Lucy drew a deep breath. Her racing heartbeats subsided. Carpet pythons weren't poisonous. Actually, now that she was calming down, she could see the distinctive brown and cream markings on the snake's back.

'I'm afraid I panicked,' she said. 'Someone left the bag on my porch and I was expecting a small motherless furry creature.'

'Instead you have an angry snake with a nasty gash on its back.' The expression in Will's grey eyes was both tender and amused.

No longer trembling, Lucy came closer and saw the wound halfway down the snake's length. 'I'm afraid snakes are the one species of the animal kingdom I find hard to love. But this fellow's actually quite beautiful, isn't he?'

'As snakes go—he's extremely handsome,'

Will said dryly. 'What do you want to do with him? Would you try to treat a wound like this?'

'I can at least clean it up. Maybe give it a few stitches.'

'Can you leave it till tomorrow? Shall I put it in a cage for you?'

She bit back a sigh and shook her head. 'The biggest threat for him is infection, so I really should see to the wound straight away.' Shooting Will an apologetic glance, she said, 'It won't take long, but I'm afraid I couldn't possibly manage without an assistant.'

He chuckled. 'No problem. I'm all yours.'

The sparkle in his eyes sent heat flaming in her cheeks. Tightly, she said, 'Thank you. If you'll keep holding him right there, I'll get organised. First, I'm going to have to feed oxygen and anaesthetic down his trachea.'

'You're going to knock him out just to clean up a wound?'

'It's the only way to keep a snake still. They're actually very sensitive to pain.'

As Lucy set up the gas cylinders, her mind raced ahead, planning each step of the procedure. She would place a wooden board between the python and the metal table to keep him that little bit warmer. And she needed something to hold the wounded section steady while she worked on it. Masking tape would do the least damage to the python's sensitive skin.

Quickly she assembled everything she needed—scissors, scalpels, tweezers, swabs, needles—and then she donned sterile gloves. 'OK, let's get this gas into him.'

Will held the snake's head steady while she fed the tube down its mouth, and she was amazed that she wasn't scared any more.

'How many pythons' lives have you saved?' Will asked as they waited for the anaesthetic to take effect.

'This is the first.'

He smiled. 'I can remember your very first patient.'

She frowned at him, puzzled. 'You were in Argentina when I started to work as a vet.'

'Before that. Don't you remember the chicken you brought to school in a woolly sock?'

'Oh, yes.' She grinned. 'The poor little thing hatched on a very cold winter's morning and I was worried that it wouldn't make it through the day.'

'You kept it hidden under the desk.'

'Until Mr Sanderson discovered it during biology and turned it into a lecture on imprinting.'

Their eyes met and they smiled and for a heady moment, Lucy was sixteen again and Will Carruthers was…

No, for heaven's sake.

Shocked by how easily she was distracted by him, she centred her thoughts on cleaning the outside of the python's wound with alcohol wipes and foaming solution. Then, when her patient was completely under, she began to debride the damaged tissue.

All the time she worked, Will was silent, watching her with a curious smile that she tried very hard to ignore.

'I guess this isn't quite how you expected to spend your evening,' she said as she finally began to suture the delicate skin together.

'Wouldn't have missed this for the world.' He chuckled softly. 'You have to admit, it's a unique experience. How many guys have watched a barefoot bridesmaid stitch up a python at midnight?'

Lucy couldn't help smiling. 'You make it sound like some kind of medieval witches' ritual.'

'The rites of spring?'

'Maybe, but then again, how many vets have been assisted by a hun—a guy in best man's clobber?'

Lucy thanked heavens she'd retracted the word *hunk*. For heaven's sake. It was the dinner suit factor. Stick the plainest man in a tuxedo and his looks were improved two hundred per cent. Will in a tuxedo was downright dangerous.

But she was grateful for his help. Working side by side with him again, she'd felt good in a weirdly unsettled-yet-comfortable way. They'd always worked well together.

'You're a tough cookie,' Will told her. 'You were white as a ghost and shaking when I came in and yet you morphed into a steady-handed snake surgeon.'

'It's my job,' she said, trying not to look too pleased.

She dropped the suture needles into the tray and snapped off her sterile gloves, removed the paper apron and rolled up the disposable sheet she'd used to drape over the wound.

'So where will we put this fellow while he sleeps off his ordeal?' Will asked.

'He'll have to go in one of the cages out the

back.' Carefully, she peeled away the masking tape that had kept the snake straight.

'Shall I do the honours?'

'Thanks, Will. There's a cage in the far corner, away from the other patients. If you give me a minute, I'll line it with thick newspaper to keep him warm and dry.'

By the time the python was safely in its cage it was long past midnight but, to Lucy's surprise, she didn't feel tired any more. She tried to tell herself that she'd found working on a completely new species exhilarating, but she knew very well it had everything to do with Will's presence.

She'd felt relaxed and focused and it had been like stepping back in time to their student days. But, dear heaven, it was such a long time ago and they couldn't really go back, could they?

'Let's go through to the kitchen,' she said once they'd cleaned up.

She snapped the kitchen light on and the room leapt to life. She was rather proud of the renovations she'd made to this room, painting the walls a soft buttercup and adding hand painted tiles to the splashback over the sink. And she'd spent ages hunting for the right kind of cupboards and shelving in country-style second-hand shops.

'I'd better let the boys in.'

As soon as Lucy opened the back door, Seamus and Harry bounded inside, greeting her with doggy kisses and fiercely wagging tails, as if she'd been away for six months.

At last the dogs calmed down and she turned to Will. 'I think you've earned a drink.'

'I believe I have,' he agreed and he immediately began to remove his jacket and tie.

Lucy drew a sharp breath, already doubting the soundness of this idea. But she couldn't send Will packing after he'd been so helpful. Surely two old friends could have a drink together?

'What are you in the mood for?' *Oh, cringe. What a question.* 'Alcohol or coffee?' she added quickly.

She opened the fridge. 'If you'd like alcohol, I'm afraid there's only beer or white wine.'

Will chose beer and Lucy poured a glass of wine for herself. She found a wedge of Parmesan cheese and freshly shelled walnuts and set them on a platter with crackers and slices of apple.

'Come on through to the lounge room,' she

said. 'It's pretty shabby, though. I started renovating the kitchen and then ran out of enthusiasm.'

Tonight, however, Lucy was surprised. She hadn't drawn the curtains and the lounge room, now flooded by moonlight, had taken on a strangely ethereal beauty. The shabbiness had all but disappeared and the garish colours of the cotton throws she'd used to cover the tattered upholstery had taken on a subtle glow.

'I might leave the lights off,' she said. 'This room is definitely improved by moonlight.'

'Everything's improved by moonlight.'

She studiously ignored this comment in the same way that she avoided the sofa and flopped into a deep, comfy single chair instead.

With a be-my-guest gesture she directed Will to the other chair. Then, as the dogs settled on the floor, heads on paws, niggles of disquiet returned to haunt her. It was such a long time since she and Will had been alone like this.

'Try some Parmesan and apple,' she said, diving for safety by offering him the plate. 'Have you tried them together? It's a nice combination.'

Will obliged and made appropriately, appreciative noises.

Lucy took a sip of wine. In many ways this was one of her favourite fantasies—talking to Will late into the night. But in the fantasies there'd been no awkwardness. They had been as comfortable and relaxed as they were ten years ago, before they'd drifted apart.

Lucy wondered what they would discuss now. Will had hinted that he had specific things he wanted to talk about. Would he raise them now? She wasn't sure she was ready to hear his thoughts on marriage and babies and being over the hill.

Perhaps he still felt that tonight wasn't the night to be deep and meaningful. She searched for a safe topic that didn't include weddings, or honeymoons, or babies.

'So, have you started hunting for a new job?' she asked.

'I haven't put in any applications yet.' Will settled more comfortably into his chair, crossed an ankle over a knee. 'But I've found a few positions I might apply for. There's even one in Armidale, at the university.'

'In Armidale?' So close? To cover her surprise, Lucy said, 'I have trouble picturing you as an academic behind a desk.'

He shrugged. 'I thought it would make a nice

change, after years of hiking over deserts and mountains looking for rocks.'

'There's that, I guess.' She couldn't resist adding facetiously, 'I suppose geology is a young man's job.'

Will smiled into his glass, took a swig, then set it down.

'I imagine your parents would like you to take up farming,' she suggested.

'They've never mentioned it.' He sighed. 'They're actually talking about selling up.'

'Really?' Lucy stared at him, horrified.

'My mother's been bitten by the travel bug.'

'She must have caught it from you.'

Will smiled crookedly. 'Perhaps.'

'But your family's been farming Tambaroora for five generations.'

'And now they've come to the end of the line,' Will said dryly.

Nervous now, Lucy chewed at her lower lip. Already they were treading on sensitive ground. Everyone in the district had always known that Will's older brother, Josh, was expected to take over the family farm.

Josh's death had changed everything.

She closed her eyes, as if to brace herself for

the slam of pain that she always felt when she thought about that time.

'We've never talked about it, Lucy.'

She didn't have to ask what Will meant. The fact that they had never really talked since Josh's death had been like an unhealed wound inside her. 'There wasn't any chance to talk,' she said defensively. 'You went away straight after the funeral.'

'There were lots of good reasons for me not to stay. Your father didn't help.'

'My father?'

'After Josh's funeral, I tried to phone. I turned up on your doorstep, but your father wouldn't let me near you.'

Lucy stared at Will, stunned. 'I didn't know that.' Her eyes stung and she blinked back tears. If she'd known Will had called, what would she have done? What might have been different?

Will's shoulders lifted in a shrug. 'Your father was probably right to protect you. I…I can't imagine that I would have been much help at the time.'

Lucy swallowed to ease the aching lump in her throat. She'd been in a terrible state after the funeral and the miscarriage. The really awful thing was that everyone thought she was grieving, and she was, of course, but a huge part of her distress had been caused by her over-powering feelings of guilt. 'Did you know… about the baby?'

'Gina told me at the time,' Will said quietly. And then, after a beat, 'I'm really sorry, Lucy.'

He sounded almost too apologetic, as if somehow he felt responsible. But that didn't make sense.

Lucy willed her hand to stop trembling as she held out the plate to him and he made a selection. For some time they sat in silence, nibbling walnuts in the silvered half-light, and then Will changed the subject.

'You've done so well here,' he said. 'I'm hearing from everyone that you're a fabulous vet.'

'I love my job.'

Will nodded, then he asked carefully, 'So you're happy, Lucy?'

From force of habit, a lie leapt to her lips. 'Of course.' She reached down and patted Harry's silky black and white head. 'I'm perfectly happy. I love this district. I love my work.'

'But is it enough?'

Oh, help. Lucy covered her dismay with a snappy reply. 'What kind of question is that?'

'An important one.'

'You answer it then.' She knew she sounded tense, but she couldn't help it. Will's question unnerved her. It was too searching, too close to a truth she didn't want to reveal. 'Are you happy, Will? Is your work enough?'

'Not any more.'

It wasn't the answer she'd expected and she took a moment to digest it. 'I suppose that's why you're looking for something different?'

'I suppose it is.' He circled the rim of his glass with his finger. 'I've had a bit of a wake up call.'

A swift flare of shock ripped through Lucy like a sniper's gunshot. 'Will, you're not sick, are you?'

'No, thank God, but I've had a close shave. I haven't told my family this. I didn't want to upset them, but there was an explosion in an old mine we were surveying.'

'In Mongolia?'

'Yes.' His face was suddenly tight and strained. 'The two men with me were both killed. Right in front of me. I've no idea how I escaped with a few scratches and bruises.'

'Oh, God, Will, that's terrible.' Tears threatened again as Lucy tried not to think the unthinkable—that there had almost been a world where Will didn't exist.

'I went to their funerals,' Will said quietly. 'And they really opened my eyes.'

'In what way?'

In the moonlight, she could see the sober intensity in Will's face.

'Barney was a bachelor, you see. No ties. So his funeral was a simple gathering of family and friends. There were a few words to say he was a good bloke and then a rather boozy wake. But Keith was a family man, always talking about his wife and three kids. And at the funeral his son spoke.'

Will sighed and rubbed at his forehead. 'He was such a courageous little guy. He couldn't have been more than ten years old. And he stood up there in front of us, with these big brown eyes, shiny with tears. His voice was all squeaky and threatening to break, but he told us all how proud he was of his father and how he wanted to live his life in a way that would go on making his dad proud.'

Lucy's throat ached at the thought of that little boy. She could picture his mother, too. The poor woman would have been so proud, despite her grief.

'I can't stop thinking about that kid,' Will said. 'He was like this fantastic gift to the world that Keith had left behind.'

Lucy reached for the handkerchief she'd tucked into the bodice of her dress and dabbed at her eyes.

'I'm sorry,' Will said. 'I'm being maudlin, talking about funerals when we've just been to a wedding.'

'No, it's OK.' She sniffed and sent him a watery smile. 'It's just happened to you, so of course it's on your mind. Anyway, that's what life's all about, isn't it? Births, deaths and marriages.'

He smiled sadly. 'I guess I'm a slow learner. It wasn't till I was sitting in that church that I suddenly got it. I could finally understand why Gina went to so much trouble to have a family, and why Mattie was prepared to undergo something so amazingly challenging as a surrogate pregnancy.'

'Yes,' Lucy said, but the single word came out too loud and sounded more like a sob.

The dogs lifted their heads and made soft whining noises in her direction. With a cry of dismay, Will lurched to his feet.

'I'm so sorry,' he said. 'I should be more sensitive. I shouldn't be burdening you with this.'

He was referring to her miscarriage. Would he be shocked to hear that she still longed for a baby, that her need was bordering on obsession?

With an angry shake of his head, he went to the window, thrust his hands into his trouser pockets and looked out into the night.

Despite her tension, Lucy was mesmerised by the sight of him limned by moonlight. Her eyes feasted on his profile, on his intelligent forehead, on the decisive jut of his nose, his strong chin with its appealing cleft.

Without looking at her, he said, 'I'm surprised you haven't found someone else and settled down to start a family.'

Oh, help. Lucy stiffened. Again, Will had gone too far. Again, her chin lifted in defence and she hit back. 'I could say the same about you.'

'Ah.' He turned back from the window. His eyes shimmered and he said in a dry tone, 'But I'm the vagabond and you're the homebody.'

Too true.

However, Lucy couldn't help remembering how he'd come rushing back to Australia when she and Josh had announced their engagement.

She'd always wondered why.

But there was no way she could open up that discussion now. Not tonight.

She felt too vulnerable tonight and she was scared she might blurt out something she'd regret later. It would be too embarrassing and shameful to confess that she'd finally gone out with Will's brother, hoping that word would reach Will and spark a reaction.

If she told him that, she'd also have to confess that the plan had backfired when she'd become pregnant.

It was more than likely she would never be able to talk to Will about this.

Nevertheless, tonight's conversation felt like an important step. It was almost as if she and Will had picked up their friendship where they'd left off. He'd told her about the funeral, something he hadn't been able to share with his family.

It suddenly felt OK to say, 'I've actually become quite desperate to have a baby.'

Will spun around from the window and his chest rose and fell. Above his open white shirt, the muscles in his throat rippled. His eyes smouldered in the cool white light. 'You'd make a wonderful mother, Lucy.'

The compliment made her want to cry, but she gave him a shrugging smile. 'It's a terrible waste, isn't it?'

She hadn't expected to say more but, now that she'd started, it was surprisingly easy to keep going. 'To be honest, I worry constantly about the state of my ovaries and whether I can expect them to go on delivering, month after month.'

'The old biological clock?'

She nodded. 'Early menopause runs in my family. That's why I'm an only child.'

Will frowned. 'But I have it on good authority that you've turned down at least three proposals of marriage.'

Heat flooded Lucy's face. 'I suppose Gina told you that?'

He nodded.

'OK, so I'm fussy, but that's because I'm not so desperate that I'd settle for just any guy as a husband. Willowbank isn't exactly swarming with Mr Rights, you know. I'd rather be a single mother.'

Abruptly, Will came back to his chair and sank down into it, long legs stretching in front of him. 'Why would you want to be a single mother?'

'Because it's better than not being a mother at all.'

He looked surprised and thoughtful.

Lucy made herself comfortable with her legs curled and an elbow propped on the chair's arm, her cheek resting on her hand. 'I've been to a fertility clinic,' she told Will. 'And I've already tried one round of IVF.'

'IVF?' he repeated, sounding shocked.

'Why not?'

'Isn't that a bit…extreme?'

'It seemed logical to me. I've inseminated hundreds of animals and it worked beautifully for Mattie and Gina. But, unfortunately, it didn't work for me.'

Will made a soft sound, a kind of strangled gasp.

'I'm sorry. That's probably too much information,' she said.

But Will shook his head and, a moment later, a smile played around his lips. He tapped at the arm of his chair. 'It's a pity Mattie can't have a baby for you.'

Lucy knew he was joking and forced a weak laugh. Uncurling her legs, she sat straight in her chair. 'Don't worry, that thought's occurred to me but I imagine Mattie has other plans now she has a husband.'

'I'm sure she has.' With a thoughtful frown, Will scratched at his jaw. 'But it's a pity there isn't someone who could help you out.'

'Do you mean a good friend? Someone like you, Will?'

CHAPTER FIVE

LUCY could not believe she'd just said that.

What had she been thinking?

How on earth could she have boldly suggested that Will could help her to have a baby—out of friendship?

What must he think of her?

The only sound in the room came from Seamus, the Irish setter, snoring softly at Will's feet. Lucy stared at the sleeping dog while her heart beat crazily.

'You know that was a joke, don't you?' she said in a small voice.

To her dismay, Will didn't answer and she wished she could crawl away and hide with her tail between her legs, the way Seamus and Harry did when they were in big trouble.

If only she could press a rewind button and take those words back.

When the silence became unbearable she looked up and saw Will's serious expression and her heart juddered. 'Will, I didn't mean it. It was my warped sense of humour. You know I've never been very good at making jokes. They always come out wrong. I'm sorry. Honestly, I feel so embarrassed.'

He looked shaken. 'For a moment there, I thought you were serious.'

'I wasn't, Will. You can calm down.'

Suddenly a cloud covered the moon and the room was plunged in darkness. Lucy turned on the lamp beside her and the return of light seemed to clear the air.

Will rose abruptly and stood towering over her. 'Perhaps I'd better get going before I say something outrageous, too.'

As Lucy stood she prayed that her legs were steady enough to support her. 'Thanks for helping me with the python,' she remembered to say as they crossed the lounge room.

Will smiled. 'My pleasure. I hope he makes a good recovery, and thanks for the drink and the chat. It was like old times.'

No, Lucy thought. Blurting out her desire to have a baby was not remotely like old times.

They went through to the kitchen, where Will collected his jacket and tie, and then on to the front door. His hand touched Lucy's shoulder and she jumped.

'See you later, Goose.' He dropped a light kiss on her cheek and then he was gone.

Will felt as if he'd stepped off a roller coaster as he started up the truck and drove away, watching the lights of Lucy's house grow smaller and more distant in the rear-vision mirror.

What a crazy night! In a matter of hours, he'd gone from being best man at a wedding to standing in as a veterinary nurse to fielding a request for his services as a father for Lucy's baby.

Not that Lucy had been serious, of course.

But bloody hell. The thought gripped Will and frightened him beyond belief. His heart had almost raced out of control when Lucy made that offhand suggestion tonight.

He was still shaken now, even though the subject had been laid to rest. Problem was, he couldn't let it go.

He kept thinking about how badly she wanted a baby. If he hadn't seen the emotional pain that Gina had been through, or if he hadn't so recently attended Keith's funeral, he might not have caught the genuine longing in Lucy's voice. In her eyes.

He might not have understood, might have simply thought she was selfish, wanting it all, when she already had so much.

But now he got it, he really understood that the desire to have a child came from somewhere deep, so deep that it couldn't be properly explained. And it shouldn't be ignored.

But should he be involved? For Pete's sake, he'd seen the haunted loneliness in Lucy's eyes and he'd almost grabbed her suggestion and moulded it into a realistic option.

They'd been such good friends and he'd wanted to help her.

But father her baby?

That was even crazier than the way he'd felt when he'd danced with her tonight at the wedding. It was the kiss on the veranda revisited. He'd been caught out by unexpected emotions, by an inappropriate desire to get too close to Lucy.

Every time she'd stumbled against him, he'd wanted to keep her close. He'd wanted to inhale the clean, rosy scent of her skin, to touch his lips to her skin, right there, in front of the wedding guests.

Thank heavens he'd had the sense to stop dancing before things got out of hand.

But it didn't really make sense that he was feeling this way about Lucy now. Why would he want to play second fiddle to the memory of his brother?

If he'd wanted Lucy as his girlfriend, he should have grabbed the chance when they were at university, before she got to know Josh. Problem was, he'd been too distracted by the sheer numbers of girls at Sydney Uni and he'd wanted to play the field.

And, truth be told, when he thought about those days, he had to admit that whenever he'd made a move in Lucy's direction she'd adroitly held him at a distance. She'd insisted that she was his buddy, not his girlfriend.

And yet she'd fallen for Josh quite easily. Will knew that was exactly why he mustn't think twice about her crazy suggestion.

Lucy had loved his brother. She'd been

about to marry his brother and have his brother's baby.

Did he honestly think he could make amends by stepping in as a substitute?

The question teased him as he steered the truck over a single lane wooden bridge that crossed Willow Creek. He felt the familiar sickening slug of guilt he always felt when he thought about Josh and remembered the row they had on that last fateful morning before he'd died.

That was what he should have talked about tonight. He should have confessed his role in Josh's death.

Oh, God. The mere thought of telling Lucy the truth caused a sickening jolt in his chest. She would hate him.

He couldn't take that risk.

The next day, Sunday, dragged for Lucy. She wasn't on call so, apart from checking on her patients, including the python, who was recovering nicely, she couldn't distract herself with work.

She collected her car from the Careys' and spent a happy half hour discussing the wedding with Mattie's mum over a cup of tea. In the afternoon, she took her dogs for a lovely long walk along Willow Creek, but they weren't good conversationalists, so she was left with far too much time to brood over the huge gaffe she'd made during last night's conversation with Will.

She couldn't believe she'd actually asked her schoolgirl crush to help her to have a baby. Talk about a Freudian slip!

What must Will think of her?

Why in heaven's name had she blurted out such a suggestion when she'd once been engaged to Will's brother?

The question brought her to a halt, standing at the edge of the creek, staring down into the clear running water. She remembered the happy times she'd spent here with Will, panning for gold or sapphires. How excited they'd been over the tiniest speck of gold or the smallest dull chips of dark glass that signified sapphires.

She'd never once let Will see how much she loved him. She'd been too scared to risk losing him by telling him how she felt.

She was so totally lost in thought that she was startled when her dogs began to bark suddenly.

'Stop that, Harry,' she called. 'Seamus, what's the matter?'

Then she heard the snap of twigs and the crunch of gravel underfoot. Someone was coming along the track.

'Come here,' Lucy ordered but, to her dismay, the dogs ignored her. Their tails kept wagging and they yapped expectantly as a tall figure came around the bend.

It was Will.

A flare of shock burst inside her, as if someone had lit a match. Will looked surprised too, but he seemed to recover more quickly. He smiled, while Lucy's heart continued to thump fretfully.

'Fancy seeing you here,' he drawled.

'I brought the dogs for a walk.'

He grinned and bent down to give the boys a quick scruff around the ears. 'I needed to get out of the house.'

'Already? But you've just arrived home.'

'I know.' His grey eyes sparkled as he looked up at her. 'But I've had this crazy idea rattling around in my head and I needed to get away to think.'

'Oh,' Lucy said uncertainly.

The dogs, content with Will's greeting, went back to hunting for the delectable smells in a nearby lantana bush. Watching them, Will said, 'I've been thinking about your baby proposal.'

'Will, it wasn't a proposal. You know I didn't mean it.'

With a distinct lack of haste, he said, 'But is it such a bad idea?'

Lucy's mouth fell open. Surely he wasn't serious? 'Of course it's a bad idea. It's crazy.'

He looked about him, letting his gaze take in the silent trees and sky, the smooth stepping stones crossing the creek. 'You really want a baby,' he said quietly. 'You said so last night, and you're worried you're running out of time.'

Now it was Lucy who didn't answer. She couldn't. Her heart had risen to fill her throat. She'd never dreamed for a moment that Will would take her flippant comment even halfway seriously.

He stood, blocking her way on the narrow track, watching her carefully. 'I'm sure you'd prefer your baby's father to be someone you know.'

She still couldn't speak. Her hand lifted to the base of her throat as she tried to still the wild pulse that beat there.

Will pressed his point. 'I imagine a friend

must be a better option than an unknown donor in a sperm bank.'

'But friends don't normally have babies together.'

She couldn't see his expression. He'd turned to pluck at a long grass stalk and it made a soft snapping sound.

'People accept all kinds of convenient family arrangements these days,' he said. 'The locals in Willowbank have accepted the idea of Mattie's surrogacy very well.'

'Well, yes. That's true.'

But, despite her silly dreams, Lucy couldn't imagine having a baby with Will. He'd never fancied her. And, even if he did, he was Josh's brother.

'Look, Lucy, don't get me wrong. I'm not pushing this, but I'm happy to talk it through.'

'Why?'

A slow smile warmed his eyes. 'We haven't talked for years and we used to be really good at it.'

Lucy felt a blush spread upwards from her throat. Her mind was spinning, grasping desperately at the idea of Will as her baby's father and then slipping away again, as if the thoughts were made of ice. 'But what exactly are you saying? That you would be willing to…um…donate sperm for another round of IVF?'

Surprise flared in his face. He tossed the grass stalk into the water. 'If that's what you want.'

'I…I don't know.'

'Of course, there's always the natural alternative. If you've had trouble with IVF, that shouldn't be ruled out.'

Lucy bit her lip to cover her gasp of dismay. She watched the grass float away, disappearing behind a rock. The dogs began to bark again. 'They're tired of this spot and they want to move on,' she told Will.

'Let's walk, then,' he suggested.

There was just enough room on the track for them to walk side by side, and it should have been relaxing to walk with Will beside the creek—like in the old days. But today an unsettling awareness zapped through Lucy. She was too conscious of Will's tall, rangy body. So close. Touching close.

She couldn't think straight. She was so tantalised by the idea of a baby, but how could she even talk about having a baby with Will when she'd never admitted that she'd always had a crush on him?

She didn't want to frighten him away, not now when he'd made such an amazing suggestion.

Dragging in a deep breath, she said, 'OK. Just say we did…um…give this some thought. How do you actually feel about becoming a father?'

She glanced at Will and saw his quick smile. 'To be honest, fatherhood has been well down on my wish list. But I guess I'm seeing it in a new light lately. I've been hit by the feeling that I've been wasting my life.'

'Because of the little boy at the funeral?'

'Yes, that little guy really got to me. But there've been other things too—like Gina's twins. They knocked me for six. They're so damn cute.'

'I know. I'm eaten up with envy every time I see them. But you haven't answered me. Would you really want to be my baby's father?'

Will stopped walking. 'I can't promise I'd be a terrific help, Lucy. I don't even know where I'm going to be working yet, so there's not much chance I'd be a hands-on father. But, if you want to have a child, I'd certainly be ready to help.'

She was so surprised she found her thoughts

racing ahead. 'I don't mind managing on my own. It's what I'd planned anyway.'

Will smiled. 'So what does that mean? Do you want to give this some serious thought?'

'I…I don't know.' She was feeling so dazed. 'I know I was the one who started this, but I never dreamed you'd take me up on it.'

Even as she said this, Lucy wished she'd sounded more positive. This was her dream, to have Will's baby. OK, maybe the dream also involved Will falling madly and deeply in love with her, but surely half a dream was better than none?

'But I guess there's no harm in thinking about it,' she said.

His eyes were very bright, watching her closely. 'I wasn't even expecting to see you today. There's no pressure to make a decision now. We should sleep on it. If we decide to go ahead, we can fine-tune the details later.'

'Fine-tune?'

'IVF versus the alternative,' he said without smiling.

The alternative.

This time Lucy's skin began to burn from the inside out. She hadn't even been able to dance with Will last night without getting upset. How on earth could she possibly make love with him without a gigantic emotional meltdown?

The very thought of becoming intimate with Will sent flames shooting over her skin. She began to tremble.

'There's no rush,' he said. 'I could be around here for a while yet, and if I move to Armidale it's only a couple of hours away.'

Lucy frowned at him. 'Armidale?'

'The job I mentioned. At the university.'

Oh. She expelled air noisily.

'Look, we both need time to think about this, Lucy.' Will watched her dogs running impatiently back and forth, trying to urge her to get walking again. 'And I should head back now.'

'All right.'

'I'm glad I ran into you,' he said.

Lucy nodded.

'So you'll give this some thought?'

'Yes,' she said, but a shiver rushed over her skin and she wrapped her arms around her as she watched Will walk away.

At the bend in the track he turned back and lifted his hand to wave. Then he smiled. And kept walking.

* * *

He hadn't been totally crazy, Will told himself as he strode back along the track beside the creek. He hadn't committed to a full-on relationship with his brother's ex. He'd simply offered to help her to have a baby.

This was purely and simply about the baby.

The baby Lucy longed for.

But it meant he'd be a father and he really liked that idea.

He'd be able to watch the baby grow. He'd help out with finances—school fees, pony club, whatever the kid needed. And who knew? Maybe, some day in the future, the kid might take an interest in Tambaroora, if it still belonged to the Carruthers family.

But the big thing was, the lucky child would have Lucy as its mother.

If any woman deserved to be a mother, Lucy did.

Will had dated a lot of women, but he couldn't think of anyone who was more suitable than Lucy McKenty to be the mother of his child.

And it wasn't such a crazy situation. Being good friends with his baby's mother was a vast improvement on some of the unhappy broken family set-ups that he'd heard his workmates complain about.

But the details of the baby's conception caused a road bump.

Will came to a halt as he thought about that. He snagged another grass stalk and chewed at it thoughtfully.

Any way he looked at this situation, leaping into bed with Lucy McKenty was stretching the boundaries of friendship.

But it was highly unlikely that she would agree to sex. Apart from the fact that Will was the brother of the man she'd planned to marry, and setting their friendship issues aside, Lucy was a vet. She used IVF all the time in her practice and she was bound to look on it as the straightforward and practical solution.

Except that she'd tried the clinical route once and it hadn't worked.

Which brought him back to the alternative. With Lucy.

Damn. He could still remember their long ago kiss on the veranda.

He should have forgotten it by now. He'd tried so hard to forget, but he could remember every detail of those few sweet minutes—the way Lucy had felt so alive and warm in his arms, the way she'd smelled of summer and tasted of every temptation known to man.

Hell. There was no contest, was there?

IVF was most definitely their sanest, safest option.

Lucy was in a daze as she walked back to her ute. She couldn't believe Will had given her suggestion serious thought. It was astonishing that he was actually prepared to help her to have her baby.

She couldn't deny she was tempted.

Tempted? Heavens, she was completely sold on the whole idea of having a dear little baby fathered by Will.

It was the means to this end that had her in a dither.

Sex with Will was so totally not a good idea. The very thought of it filled her with foolish longings and multiple anxieties.

She'd loved Will for so long now, it was like a chronic illness that she'd learned to adjust to. But to sleep with him would be like dancing on the edge of a cliff. She would be terrified of falling.

If only IVF was simpler.

She'd hated the process last time. All the tests and injections and clinical procedures and then the huge disappointment of failure. Not to mention the expense and the fact that, if she wanted to try again, she'd have to go back on that long waiting list.

Oh, man. Her thoughts went round and round, like dairy cows on a milking rotator. One minute she rejected the whole idea of having Will's baby, the next she was desperately trying to find a way to make it happen.

Could it work?

Could it possibly work?

Lucy remembered again how she'd felt when she'd seen Will at the wedding rehearsal, standing at the front of the church with tiny Mia in his arms. Just thinking about it made her teary. He would be such a fabulous father.

She drove home, but when she was supposed to be preparing dinner she was still lost in reverie, going over and over the same well worn thoughts.

She found herself standing at her kitchen sink, thinking about Will again. Still. She caught sight of her reflection in the window and was shocked to see that she was cradling a tea towel as if it were a baby. And her face was wet with tears.

The picture cut her to the core and, in that moment, she knew she had no choice. She wanted Will's baby more than anything she'd ever wanted in her life.

That precious baby's existence was a hundred times more important than the method of its conception.

Tomorrow, she should tell Will she'd made a decision.

Early next morning, however, there was a telephone call.

'Is that the young lady vet?'

'Yes,' Lucy replied, crossing her fingers. Calls this early on a Monday morning usually meant trouble.

'This is Barney May,' the caller said. 'I need someone to come and look at my sheep. Four of them have gone lame on me.'

Lucy suppressed a sigh. Lame sheep usually meant foot abscesses or, worse still, footrot, which was highly contagious. There'd been plenty of rain this spring so the conditions were ripe for an outbreak. *Darn it.*

'Could you come straight away?' Barney asked. 'I don't want a problem spreading through my whole herd.'

'Hang on. I'll have to check my schedule.'

She scanned through the surgery's diary for the day's appointments. It was the usual assortment—small animals with sore ears or eyes or skin conditions; a few vaccinations and general health checks for new puppies and kittens— nothing that her assistant couldn't handle.

'I'll be there in about an hour,' she told Barney.

'Good, lass. You know where I live—about ten kilometres out of town, past the sale yards on the White Sands Road.'

An hour later Lucy knew the worst. The sheep indeed had footrot and it had spread from the neighbouring property via a broken fence.

After paring the hooves of the unlucky sheep and prescribing footbaths, she had to continue her inspection and, all too soon, she discovered more evidence that the disease was spreading beyond the Mays' property, thanks to another farmer who'd really let his fences go.

Which spelled potential disaster.

Without question, it would mean a full week of hard work for Lucy. Her assistant would have to man the surgery while she toured the district, visiting all the farms as she tried to gauge just how far the problem ranged.

Each night she was exhausted and when she arrived home she had to face the surgery work that her assistant couldn't handle. By the time she crawled into bed she was too tired to tackle a complicated phone call to Will.

And, because the Carruthers family farm was at the opposite end of the district from the initial footrot outbreak, it was Friday afternoon before she got to Tambaroora.

It was a beautiful property with wide open paddocks running down to the creek and a grand old sandstone homestead, bang in the centre, surrounded by a green oasis of gardens. Lucy could never think about Tambaroora without seeing the garden filled with summer colour and smelling roses, jasmine, lavender and rosemary.

By the time she arrived, Will and his father had already completed a thorough inspection of their herd and they reported that their sheep were in good condition, but Lucy still needed to make spot sample checks.

Will hefted the heavy beasts she selected with obvious ease, and he kept them calm while she examined their hooves. She'd been dealing with farmers all week and she knew he made a difficult task look incredibly easy.

'For someone who doesn't think of himself as a farmer, you handle sheep well,' she said.

'Will's surprised us,' his father commented wryly. 'We didn't think he had it in him.'

A smile twisted Will's mouth as his father trudged off to attend to a ewe that had recently delivered twin lambs.

'I meant it,' Lucy told him. 'Not all farmers are good at handling stock. You're a natural.'

He looked amused. 'Maybe I was just trying to impress you.'

She rolled her eyes, but that was partly to cover the attack of nerves she felt at the thought of telling him she'd reached a decision about the baby. Her stomach was as jumpy as a grasshopper in a jar as he helped her to gather up her gear, then walked beside her to her ute.

'Do you have to hurry away?' he asked as she stowed her things. 'I was hoping we could talk.'

'About the baby idea?' She spoke as casually as she could.

There was no one around, but Will lowered his voice. 'Yes, I've been thinking it over.'

Her heart jumped like a skittish colt and she searched his face, trying to guess what he was going to tell her. If he'd decided to scrap the baby idea, she wasn't sure she could bear the disappointment. She'd become totally entranced by the thought of their adorable infant and she'd convinced herself that this time it would work.

With Will as her baby's father, she was confident of success.

She could be a mother. At last.

She forced a smile and willed herself to speak calmly. 'So, what have you decided?'

CHAPTER SIX

WILL'S eyes were almost silver in the outdoor light, so beautiful they stole Lucy's breath. 'I'd like to go ahead,' he said. 'I think you should try for a baby.'

'Wow.'

'So, are you keen too?'

'I am, yes.'

He smiled. 'Why don't we go for a walk?' He nodded towards the dark line of trees at the far end of a long, shimmering paddock of grain.

'Down by the creek again?' she asked, smiling.

'Why not?'

Why not, indeed? It had always been *their* place.

As Lucy walked beside Will, they chatted about her busy week and she tried to stay calm, to take in the special beauty of the late afternoon.

Cicadas were humming in the grass and the sinking sun cast a pretty bronzed glow over the wheat fields.

She tried to take in the details—the tracks that ants had made in an old weathered fence post, the angle of the shadows that stretched like velvet ribbons across the paddocks.

She really needed to stay calm.

It was ridiculous to be so churned up just talking to Will, but now that they'd agreed to go ahead with this baby plan they had to discuss the more delicate details, like the method of conception.

How exactly did a girl tell a truly gorgeous man she'd fancied for years that she'd carefully weighed up the pros and cons and had decided, on balance, to have sex with him?

As they neared the creek she saw two wedge-tailed eagles hovering over a stick nest that they'd woven in the fork of a dead tree.

'I hope they don't plan to dine on our lambs,' Will said, watching them.

She might have replied, but they'd reached the shelter of the trees and her stomach was playing leapfrog with her heart.

It was so quiet down here. Too quiet. This

part of the creek formed a still and silent pool and now, in the late afternoon, the birds had stopped calling and twittering. It seemed as if the whole world had stopped and was waiting to listen in to Lucy and Will's conversation.

'We need rain,' Will said as they came to a halt on the creek bank. 'The water level's dropping.'

Rain? How could he talk about rain? 'Now you're talking like a farmer.'

He pulled a comical face. 'Heaven forbid.'

Lucy drew a tense breath. 'Will, about the fine-tuning—'

'Lucy, I think you're probably right—'

They had both started talking at the same moment and now they stopped. Their gazes met and they laughed self-consciously.

'You first,' Will said.

'No, you tell me what you were going to say. What am I right about?'

'IVF. I know it's what you'd prefer and I think we should go that route.'

'Really?'

Oh, heavens. She hadn't sounded disappointed, had she?

Will's blue shirt strained at the shoulder seams as he shrugged. 'I can understand that it makes total sense to you and I'm prepared to do whatever's necessary.'

Lucy gulped as she took this in.

He watched her with a puzzled smile. 'I thought you'd be pleased.'

'Oh, I…I am. Yes, I'm really happy.' In truth, she couldn't believe the piercing sense of anti-climax she felt. 'I'm just surprised,' she said, working hard to cover her ridiculous disap-pointment. 'I spent the whole week worrying that you were going to back out altogether.'

Dropping her gaze to the ground, she hooked her thumbs into the back pockets of her jeans and kicked at a loose stone.

'So what were you going to say about the fine-tuning?' Will asked.

Lucy's face flamed. Now that Will had agreed to IVF, there was no point in telling him her decision. He'd never fancied her in that way, so it would be a huge challenge to become intimate.

'Lucy?'

'It doesn't matter now.'

'Why not?' Will swallowed abruptly and his eyes burned her.

'Honestly, Will, it's really great that you'd

like to help with IVF. I'm very grateful. I couldn't be more pleased.'

His grey eyes were searching her, studying her. Suddenly they narrowed thoughtfully and then widened with surprise. 'Don't tell me you'd come around to…to the other option?'

'No, no. If you want to use IVF, that's good,' she said.

'I didn't exactly say it's what I *want*.' A nervous smile flickered in his face, then vanished. 'I was trying to look at this from your point of view. I thought it's what you'd prefer.'

'Thanks, Will. I appreciate that.' Lucy bit her lip to stop herself from saying more.

He stood very still, his hands hanging loosely at his sides, and she knew he was watching her while she continued to avoid his gaze.

'Or are you actually worried about IVF?' he asked cautiously. 'I know it didn't work for you last time.'

Lucy drew a sharp breath, and let it out slowly. Without meeting his gaze, she said, 'I can't say I'm in love with the idea of going through all those clinical procedures again.'

'The alternative is much simpler.'

'In some ways.' She knew her face must be turning bright pink.

To her surprise, Will looked as worried as she felt. He pointed to a smooth shelf of shady rock hanging over the water. 'Look, why don't we sit down for a bit?'

'Very well,' she agreed rather primly.

Despite the shade from overhead trees, the rock still held some of the day's warmth and they sat with their feet dangling over the edge, looking down into the green, still water. They'd sat like this many times, years ago, when they were school friends.

How innocent those days seemed now.

A childish chant from Lucy's schooldays taunted her. *First comes love, then comes marriage, then comes Lucy with a baby carriage.*

Now she and Will were putting an entirely new spin on that old refrain.

She picked up a fallen leaf and rolled it against her thigh, making a little green cylinder. 'Are we mad, Will? Is it crazy for us to be trying for a baby without love or marriage?'

She sensed a sudden vibrating tension in him, saw his Adam's apple slide up and down in his throat. He picked up a small stone and lobbed it into the water. 'I don't think it's a crazy idea. Not if you're quite sure it's what you want.'

She let the leaf uncurl. 'I definitely want to have a baby, and I really like the idea of having you as the father.' She rolled the leaf again into a tight little cylinder.

'But sex is a problem,' Will suggested and his voice was rough and gravelly, so that the statement fell between them like the stone he'd dropped in the water.

'It could be.' Lucy concentrated on the leaf in her hand.

'I know I'm not Josh,' Will said quietly.

Her head jerked up. With a stab of guilt, she realised she hadn't been thinking about Josh at all. Poor Will. Did he think he had to live up to some romantic ideal set by his brother?

If only he knew the truth.

But if she told him how she really felt about him, he might be more worried than ever.

No, this rather unconventional baby plan would actually work best if they approached it as friends.

Lucy looked down at Will's hand as it rested against the rock. It was a strong workmanlike hand, with fine sun-bleached hairs on the back. She placed her hand on top of his. 'I don't want you to be like Josh,' she said.

His throat worked.

'But this might be too hard,' she said. 'Friends don't usually jump into bed together.'

'But they might,' he said gently, 'if it was a means to an end. The best means to a good end.'

She sucked in a breath, looked up at the sky.

The best means to a good end.

A baby.

'That's a nice way of putting it,' she said, already picturing the sweet little baby in her arms. Oh, heavens, she could almost feel the warm weight of it, feel its head nestled in the crook of her arm, see its tiny hands. Would they be shaped like Will's?

'So what do you think?' he asked.

Lucy nodded thoughtfully. 'You're right. It's a means to an end.' After a bit, she said, 'It would probably be best if we took a strictly medical approach.'

Will frowned. 'Medical?'

'I can get ovulation predictors.' She was gaining confidence now. 'I'll need to let you know exactly when I'm ovulating.'

His eyes widened in surprise.

'You do know there are only a very few days each month when a woman is fertile, don't you?'

'Ah, yes, of course,' he said, recovering quickly. He sent her a puzzled smile. 'So what happens when it's all systems go? Will you send me a text message?' His smile deepened. 'Or fly a green flag above your door?'

Lucy saw his smile and she felt a massive chunk of tension flow out of her. To her surprise, she found herself smiling too. 'Oh, why don't I just go the whole hog and place a notice in the Post Office window?'

Now Will was chuckling. 'Better still, you could take out a full page ad in the *Willowbank Chronicle*.'

Suddenly, it was just like old times. Laughter had always been a hallmark of their friendship.

'What about hiring Frank Pope, the crop duster?' Lucy suggested. 'He's a dab hand at sky-writing. Can't you just see it written in the sky? Will Carruthers, tonight's the night.'

Laughing with her, Will scratched at his jaw. 'That's a bit too personal. What about a subtle message in code?'

'All right…let me see…something like…the hen is broody?'

'In your case it would have to be the Goose.'

Lucy snorted. 'Oh, yes. A broody goose.'

She collapsed back onto the rock, laughing.

Their conversation was ridiculous, but it was so therapeutic to be able to joke about such a scary subject.

Her anxiety was still there, just under the surface, but she felt much better as she lay on the warm rock, still chuckling as she looked up at the sky through a lacework of green branches.

She and Will would have to stay relaxed if this plan was to have any chance of working. Perhaps everything would be all right if they could both keep their sense of humour.

Will's mobile phone rang a week later, when he was sitting at the breakfast table with his parents. Quickly, he checked the caller ID, saw Lucy's name and felt a jolting thud in the centre of his chest.

'Excuse me,' he mumbled, standing quickly. 'I'll take this outside.'

His heart thumped harder than a jackhammer as he went out onto the back porch, letting the flyscreen door swing shut behind him.

'Good morning.' His voice was as rough as sandpaper.

'Will, it's Lucy.'

'Hi. How are you?'

'Fine, thanks.'

There was an awkward pause—a stilted silence broken only by a kookaburra's laughter and the whistle from the kettle in the kitchen as it came to the boil. Will's heartbeats drummed in his ears.

Lucy said, 'I was wondering if you were free to come to dinner tonight.'

'Tonight?'

'Yes, would that be OK?'

Will was shaking, which was crazy. This entire past week had been crazy. He'd been on tenterhooks the whole time, waiting for Lucy's call. He'd actually lent a hand with drenching the sheep, much to his father's amazement. He'd enjoyed the work, even though he'd originally made the offer simply to keep himself busy, to take his mind off Lucy.

'Sure,' he said now, walking further from the house, out of his parents' earshot. 'Dinner would be great. I'll bring a bottle of wine. What would you prefer? White or red?'

'Well, I'm making lasagne, so perhaps red?'

'Lasagne? Wow.' As far as he could remember, cooking had never been Lucy's forte. Perhaps she'd taken a course? 'Red it is, then.'

'See you around seven?'

'I'll be there.' And then, because he couldn't help it, 'Goose?'

'Yes?'

'Is this—?'

'Yes,' she said quickly before he could find the right words.

Will swallowed. 'OK, then. See you at seven.'

He strolled back into the kitchen, body on fire, affecting a nonchalance he was far from feeling.

'I won't be home for dinner this evening,' he told his parents.

His mother smiled. 'So you're going out? That's nice, dear. It's good to see you catching up with your old friends.' She was always happy when she thought he was seeing someone. She'd never given up hope of more grandchildren.

Will's father looked more puzzled than pleased. This was the longest stretch his son had spent at home since he'd left all those years ago. Will knew they were both surprised, and expecting that he would take off again at a moment's notice.

But Gina and Tom's babies were to be chris-tened as soon as Mattie and Jake returned from their honeymoon, so it was an excellent excuse for him to stay on.

As he tackled the remainder of his bacon and eggs he wondered what his parents would think if they knew he planned to help Lucy McKenty to become pregnant before he headed away again.

Half an hour before Will's expected arrival, Lucy's kitchen looked like a crime site, splattered from end to end with tomato purée and spilt milk, eggshells and flour.

She wanted everything to be so perfect for tonight and she'd actually had a brand-new whizz-bang stove installed. She'd even taken a whole afternoon off work to get this dinner ready for Will.

So far, however, the only part of the meal that looked edible was the pineapple poached in rum syrup, which was precisely one half of the dessert.

How on earth had she thought she could manage stewed fruit and a baked custard as well as lasagne? She'd never been much of a cook and these dishes were so fiddly.

But now—*thank heavens*—everything was finally in the oven, although she still had to clean up the unholy mess and have a shower and change her clothes and put on make-up and set the table. She'd meant to hunt in the garden for flowers for the table as well, but the dinner preparations had taken her far too long.

She was never going to be ready in time.

Guys never noticed flowers anyway.

In a hectic whirl she dashed about the kitchen, throwing rubbish into plastic bags, wiping bench tops and spills on the floor, hurling everything else pell-mell into the dishwasher to be stacked again properly later.

Later.

Oh, heavens, she mustn't think about that.

The only good thing about being so frantically busy was that it had helped her not to dwell too deeply on the actual reason for this dinner. The merest thought of what was supposed to happen *after* the meal set off explosions inside her, making her feel like a string of firecrackers at Chinese New Year.

Hastily Lucy showered, slathering her skin with her favourite jasmine-scented gel and checking that her waxed legs were still silky and smooth.

Her hair was short so she simply towelled it dry, threw in a little styling product and let it do its own thing.

She put on a dress. She spent her working life in khaki jeans and she didn't wear dresses very often, but this one was pretty—a green and white floral slip with shoestring straps and tiny frills around the low V neckline. It suited her. She felt good in it.

A couple of squirts of scent, a dab of lip gloss, a flourish with the mascara brush…

A truck rumbled to a growling halt outside. Lucy froze.

Her reflection in the bedroom mirror blushed and her skin flashed hot and cold. Frenzied butterflies beat frantic wings in her stomach.

Firm footsteps sounded on the front path and her legs became distinctly wobbly. This was crazy.

It's only Will, not Jack the Ripper.

Unfortunately, this thought wasn't as calming as it should have been.

Concentrate on the meal. First things first. One step at a time.

It was no good. She was still shaking as she opened the door.

Will was dressed casually, in blue jeans and an open-necked white shirt with the sleeves rolled up to just below the elbow. Behind him, the twilight shadows were the deepest blue. He was smiling. He looked gorgeous—with the kind of masculine fabulousness that smacked a girl between the eyes.

'Nice dress,' he said, smiling his appreciation.

'Thanks.'

With a pang Lucy allowed herself a rash moment of fantasy in which Will was her boyfriend and madly in love with her, planning to share a future with her and the baby they hoped to make.

Just as quickly she wiped the vision from her thoughts. Over the past ten years she'd had plenty of practice at erasing that particular dream.

Reality, her reality, was a convenient and practical parenting agreement. There was simply no point in hoping for more. She was incredibly grateful for Will's offer. It was her best, quite possibly her only prospect for motherhood.

'Something smells fantastic,' he said.

'Thanks.' Her voice was two levels above a whisper. 'I hope it tastes OK. Come on in.'

She'd planned to eat in the kitchen, hoping that the room's rustic simplicity and familiar cosiness would help her to stay calm.

Already, that plan had flown out of the window. She was almost sick with nerves.

'Take any seat, Will.' She gestured towards chairs gathered around the oval pine table. 'You can open the wine if you like. I'd better check the dinner.'

She opened the oven door. *Concentrate on the food.*

Her heart sank.

No, no, no!

The baked custard, which was supposed to be smooth as silk, was speckled and lumpy. Like badly scrambled eggs.

The lasagne was worse.

How could this have happened?

The lasagne had been a work of art when it went into the oven—a symphony of layers—creamy yellow cheese sauce and pasta, with red tomatoes and herb infused meat.

Now the cheese sauce had mysteriously disappeared and the beautiful layers were dried out and brown, like shrivelled, knobbly cardboard splattered with dubious blobs of desiccated meat.

It was a total, unmitigated disaster.

'I can't believe it,' she whispered, crestfallen. She'd spent hours and hours preparing these dishes—beating, stirring, spicing, testing, reading and rereading the recipes over and over.

'What's happened?' Will's question was tentative, careful.

Fighting tears, Lucy shook her head. 'I don't know. I followed the instructions to the letter.' Snatching up oven gloves, she took out the heavy lasagne pan.

Stupidly, she'd been picturing Will's admiration. 'It's disgusting,' she wailed.

'It'll probably taste fine,' he said gallantly as she dumped the hot dish onto a table mat.

Lucy wanted to howl. 'I'm sorry, Will.' Unwilling to meet his gaze, she retrieved the dreadful looking custard and set it out of sight on the bench, beneath a tea towel. 'They've opened a pizza place in town. I think I'd better run in there.'

'This food will be fine,' he insisted again.

Hands on hips, she shook her head and glared at the stove. 'I can't believe I spent so much money on a brand-new oven and I still made a hash of the meal.'

'It might be a matter of getting used to the

settings.' He bent closer to look at the stove's knobs.

Lucy followed his gaze and squinted at the little symbols. Now that she took a closer look, she saw that a tiny wriggly line on one knob differentiated it from its neighbour.

She swore softly. 'I think I turned the wrong knob. Damn! I've been trying to grill the food instead of baking it.'

She'd been too distracted. That was her problem. She'd kept thinking about the *reason* for this dinner and a moment's loss of concentration was all it had taken to ruin her efforts.

Will's grey eyes twinkled, however, and he looked as if he was trying very hard not to laugh.

To Lucy's surprise, she began to giggle. She'd been so tense about this evening, so desperate for everything to be perfect and now, when she had to try to cover her disappointment, she could only giggle.

It was that or cry, and she wasn't going to cry.

Will flung his arm around her shoulders in a friendly cheer-up hug, and her giggling stopped as if he'd turned off a switch.

'Right,' she said breathlessly as she struggled

for composure. 'If we're going to try to eat this, I'd better set the table.'

Will opened a long-necked bottle with a fancy label and poured dark ruby-red wine into their glasses. Lucy took the salad she'd prepared from the fridge. At least it still looked fresh and crisp. She removed the plastic film, added dressing and tossed it. She found a large knife and cut the lasagne and was surprised that it cut easily, neatly keeping its shape. That was something, at any rate.

'I told you this would taste good,' Will said after his first mouthful.

To Lucy's surprise, he was right. The lasagne's texture might have been a bit too dry, but it hadn't actually burned and the herbs and meat had blended into a tasty combination. She sipped the deep rich wine and ate a little more and she began to relax. Just a little.

'Have you rescued any more pythons?'

She shook her head. 'The only wildlife I've cared for this week is a galah with a broken wing. But I discovered who dropped the python off. It was one of the schoolteachers. Apparently, he accidentally clipped him with his ride-on mower. He's going to care for him for another week or so, then let him go again in the trees down near the creek.'

They talked a little more about Lucy's work, including the good news that the footrot hadn't spread to any more sheep farms.

'What have you been up to?' she asked. 'I hear you've been lending a hand with drenching.'

He sent her a wry smile. 'News travels fast.'

'I saw your father in town the other day and he was so excited. He said you haven't lost the knack.'

Will shrugged.

'I told you you're a natural with animals.'

'Are you trying to turn me into a farmer, too?'

She didn't want to upset him, so she tried another topic. 'Have you started job-hunting?'

Over the rim of his wine glass his eyes regarded her steadily, almost with a challenge. 'I'm going for an interview at Armidale University next Thursday.'

Lucy could feel her smile straining at the edges, which was ridiculous. She knew Will would never settle back in the Willow Creek district. 'That's great. Good luck.'

'Thanks.'

He helped himself to seconds, but Lucy was

too tense to eat any more and she wasn't sure if she should offer Will the dessert. However, he insisted on trying her lumpy custard and rum-poached pineapple and he assured her it was fabulous.

'Very courteous of you to say so.' She took a small spoonful of the custard. 'Actually, this does have a scrumptious flavour, doesn't it?' She smiled ruefully. 'At least I had all the right ingredients.'

'And that's what counts.'

Something about the way Will said this made Lucy wonder if he was talking about more than the food. With a rush of heat, she remembered again what this night was all about.

The butterflies in her stomach went crazy as she stared at the mouthful of wine in the bottom of her glass. In a perfect world, people created babies out of love, but tonight she and Will were supposed to make a baby by having 'friendly' sex.

Leave your emotions at the door, please.

She wasn't sure this was possible for her. But, if she wanted a baby, she was going to have to pretend that she was OK about the 'only friends' part of their arrangement.

Cicadas started their deafening chorus outside in the trees and in the soft pink-plumed grasses, as they did every evening in spring and summer, calling to each other in the last of the daylight.

Lucy cocked her ear to the almost deafening choir outside. 'Those cicadas are just like us.'

Will's eyebrows lifted. 'They are?'

'Sure. Listen to them. They wait till the last ten or fifteen minutes of daylight, till it's almost too late to find partners, and then they go into a mad panic and start yelling out—*Hey, I need to pass on my DNA. I need a mate. Who's out there?*'

Will laughed and topped up their wine glasses.

A startling image jumped into her head of his white shirt slipping from his broad brown shoulders, of the fastener on his jeans sliding down.

Consumed by flames, she gulped too much wine. 'This would be so much easier if we were aliens.'

Will almost choked on his drink. 'I beg your pardon?'

'Oh, you've seen the movies.' She held out her hand to him, fingers splayed. 'If aliens want to have a baby, they just let their fingertips touch. Or they hook up by mental telepathy and *voila*! One cute triangular baby.'

Shaking his head, Will stood. He wasn't smiling any more as he collected their plates and took them to the sink.

Slightly dazed by this abrupt change, Lucy watched him with a mixture of nervousness and longing. His long legs and wide shoulders—*everything*, really—made him so hunky and desirable.

'Shall I put the leftovers in the fridge?' he asked.

Goodness. He was hunky and desirable and unafraid to help in the kitchen. Lucy was so busy admiring Will she almost forgot that this was her kitchen and she should be helping him.

She jumped to her feet. 'My dogs will adore that custard in the morning.'

They made short work of clearing the food away, then Will snagged the wine bottle and their glasses. 'Why don't we make ourselves more comfortable?'

'C-comfortable?'

He smiled at her. 'If you stay here chattering about mating cicadas and alien sex you're going to talk yourself out of this, Goose.'

Well, yes, she was aware of that distinct possibility.

'Where do you want to go, then?'

Amusement shimmered in his eyes. 'I thought we might try your bedroom.'

Lucy gasped. 'Already?'

'Come on.' Will was smiling again as he took her hand. 'We can do this.' He pulled her gently but purposefully across the room. 'Which way?'

'My room's the first on the right.' Lucy was super-aware of their linked hands as she walked beside him on unsteady legs.

Think about the baby. Don't fall in love.

Will stopped just inside her bedroom doorway. 'Very nice,' he said, admiring the brandnew claret duvet with silvery-grey pillows. She'd chosen the pillow slips because they were the colour of Will's eyes.

She was glad she'd turned on the bed lamps and drawn the new curtains. The room looked welcoming. Not too girly. Smart. Attractive.

Will put the bottle and glasses down on one of the bedside tables, then came and stood beside her. He took her hands.

Lucy's mouth was drier than the Sahara. How could he be so calm?

She felt a riff of panic, found herself staring at his shoes, thinking about them coming off and then the rest of him becoming bare. She could picture his shoulders, his chest, his tapering torso…

He was so gorgeous, but he was only doing this because he wanted to help her. He only thought of her as a friend. He couldn't possibly fancy her. She'd always known that.

If she'd ever doubted it, she only had to remember the way Will had kissed her on the night of his farewell party, and then left for overseas as if it hadn't meant a thing. Now he would be so much more experienced with women.

Oh, help. It was ages since she'd had a boyfriend. Why had she agreed to this? How had she ever thought this could be OK?

'Will, I don't think—'

'That's good.'

'Pardon?'

'Don't think,' he murmured and he smiled as he drew her closer.

Nervously, she looked down at their linked hands and watched his thumb gently rub her knuckles. She wondered if she should warn him she was scared—scared of not living up to his expectations. Scared of falling in love.

But no. He was so confident and calm about this, he probably wouldn't understand. She could frighten him off and she would end up without a baby.

'I want our baby to be like you,' Will said softly.

Lucy gulped. 'Do you? Why?'

'You're so sweet, so clever and kind.'

'You're all of those things too.'

She saw the stirring of something dark and dangerous in his eyes.

He touched her collarbone and she held her breath as his fingers traced its straight line. Her pulses leapt as he reached the base of her throat.

'Any baby who scores you as his mum will be born lucky.' His voice was a deep, warm rumble running over her skin like a fiery caress.

She could see Will's mouth in the lamplight. So incredibly near. She remembered that one time he'd kissed her and how she'd marvelled that his lips were surprisingly soft and sensuous compared with the rough and grainy texture of his jaw.

He trailed his fingers up the line of her throat to her chin and, for a hushed moment, his thumb rode the rounded nub, then continued along the delicate edge of her jaw.

She held her breath as he lowered his head, letting his lips follow where his fingers had led.

Despite her tension, a soft sigh floated from her and she closed her eyes as his breath feathered over her skin and she felt the warm, intimate pressure of his mouth on the hollow at the base of her throat.

He was unbelievably good at this. Her tension began to melt beneath the sweet, intoxicating journey of his lips over her throat.

He whispered her name.

'Lucy.'

His lips caressed her jaw with whisper-soft kisses. He kissed her cheek, giving the corner of her mouth the tiniest lick, and she began to tremble.

Please, Will, please…

At last his lips settled over hers and Lucy forgot to be frightened.

Her lips parted beneath him and he immediately took the kiss deeper, tasting her fully, and she decided it was too late to worry about what Will thought of her. About having babies or not having them. She just wanted to enjoy this moment.

This, now.

Will framed her face with his hands and he kissed her eagerly, ardently, hungrily and Lucy returned his kisses, shyly at first but with growing enthusiasm, eager to relearn the wonderful texture and taste of him.

His voice was ragged and breathless as he fingered the straps of her dress. 'How do I get you out of this?'

'Oh, gosh, I forgot. Sorry.' The spell was broken as Lucy remembered that her dress had a side zipper. She had to lift one arm as she reached for it.

'I've got it,' Will said, his fingers beating hers to the task.

She heard the zip sliding south, felt his hands tweak her shoulder straps and suddenly her dress was drifting soundlessly to her feet. She wasn't wearing a bra and she felt vulnerable and shy, but Will drew her close, enfolding her into a comforting embrace.

With his arms around her, with his forehead pressed to hers, he whispered, 'Your turn, Goose.'

'My turn?'

'Take off my shirt.'

'Oh, yes. Right.'

Her eyes were riveted on his chest as she

undid the buttons to reveal smooth masculine muscles that she longed to touch. She felt breathless and dizzy as she slid the fabric from his shoulders.

Her breath caught at the sight of him. She'd known he was beautiful, but she'd forgotten he was *this* beautiful.

Will kissed her again, letting his lips roam over hers in slow, lazy caresses that made her dreamy and warm so that again she gave up being scared. Still kissing her, he drew her down to the edge of the bed and then he took her with him until they were lying together, their limbs and bodies touching, meshing, already finding the perfect fit.

Bravely, she allowed her fingers to trail over his chest and felt his heart pounding beneath her touch. She smelled the long remembered midnight scent of his skin and she closed her eyes and gave in to sensation as he kissed her ears, her throat, her shoulder.

Every touch, every brush of his lips on her skin, every touch felt right and perfect and necessary.

She wasn't sure when she first felt the hot tears on her face, but she smiled, knowing they were tears of happiness.

How could they be anything else? This was her man, her passionate, hunky Will, and she was finally awake in her dream.

CHAPTER SEVEN

THEY sat in a pool of soft golden lamplight.

Will moved to the edge of the bed, shaken by what had happened.

He'd known that making love to Lucy would be a sweet pleasure, but he hadn't expected to be sent flying to the outer limits of the universe.

He felt an urge to ask her: *Does this change… everything*?

But that was lovers' talk and she expected friendship from him. Nothing more.

His thoughts churned while Lucy lay very still, with her knees bent and her shoulders propped against the pillows. She looked deceptively angelic with her short golden curls and a white sheet pulled demurely up to her chin.

'I mustn't move,' she said.

'Why can't you move?'

'I want to give your swimmers their very best chance of reaching my egg.'

He smiled at the hopeful light in her blue eyes, but his smile felt frayed around the edges.

It was hard to believe that this folly had been his idea. His foolish idea.

Lucy had been joking when she'd first suggested this, but he'd turned it into something real. He'd thought he was so damned clever. But he hadn't known, had he? Hadn't dreamed that making love to Lucy would turn his world upside down.

Was this how it had been for Josh?

He forced himself to remember why they'd done this. 'So I guess it's now a matter of wait and see?' he asked.

Lucy nodded. 'My period's due in about two weeks.'

So matter of fact.

Two weeks felt like a lifetime. 'I'll wait for another phone call then,' he said. 'And I'll hope for good news.'

Her eyes shimmered damply. Shyly, she said, 'Thank you, Will.'

His abrupt laugh was closer to a cough.

A tear sparkled and fell onto Lucy's flushed cheek, making him think of a raindrop on a rose. Reaching out, he gently blotted the shining moisture with the pad of his thumb. 'You OK, Goose?'

'Sure.'

She smiled to prove it and he launched to his feet and dragged on jeans. 'Can I make you a cup of tea or something?'

Lucy looked startled.

'I just thought…' He scratched at his bare chest. 'If you're planning to lie there for a bit, I thought you might like a cuppa.'

'Oh…um…well, yes, that would be lovely. Thank you.'

He went through to her kitchen, filled the kettle, set it on the stove and, as he rattled about searching for teabags and mugs, he saw a familiar piece of framed glass hanging in the window.

It was dark outside so he couldn't see the jewel-bright colours of the stained glass, but he knew the dominant colour was deep blue.

Memories unravelled. He'd given this to Lucy as a graduation gift, to remind her of the times they'd spent as schoolkids fossicking for sapphires.

She'd always been fascinated by the change in the chips of dark sapphire when they were held up to the light and transformed from dull black into sparkling, brilliant blue.

The same thing happened when sun lit the stained glass.

But he hadn't expected her to keep this gift for so long, or to display it so prominently, as if it was important.

Now, Will looked around, trying to guess which piece among Lucy's knick-knacks had been a present to her from his brother.

Lucy managed not to cry until after Will had left. She heard the front door open and close, heard his footsteps on the front path, the rusty squeak of the front gate, the even rustier squeak of the truck's door and then, at last, the throaty grumble of the motor.

As the truck rattled away from her house, she couldn't hold back any longer.

The mug of tea Will had made for her sat untouched on the bedside table, and the tears streamed down her face.

She should have known.

She should have known this was a terrible mistake. Should have known Will Carruthers would break her heart.

Her sobs grew louder and she pulled a pillow against her mouth to muffle them, but nothing could diminish the storm inside her.

She loved Will. Loved him, loved him, loved him, loved him.

She'd always loved Will, and she'd wrecked her whole life by getting involved with his brother in a bid to make him jealous. She felt so guilty about that. And even now her memories of her mistakes cast a shadow over what had happened tonight.

Almost two weeks later, Lucy bought a packet of liquorice allsorts.

It was an impulse purchase in the middle of her weekly shopping. She saw the sweets, felt the urge to buy them and tossed them into her supermarket trolley. It wasn't until she was unpacking her groceries at home that she realised what she'd done and what it meant.

She only ever had the urge to eat sweets on the day before her period was due.

Which meant…

No.

No, no, no.

This didn't mean she wasn't pregnant, surely?

She'd been tense all week, alert to the tiniest signs in her body. But she hadn't noticed any of the well-known symptoms. No unusual tiredness. No breast tenderness. And now—she was having pre-menstrual cravings!

She couldn't bear it if her period came. She so wanted to be pregnant.

Just this week she'd delivered five Dachshund puppies and two purebred Persian kittens and each time she'd handled a gorgeous newborn she'd imagined her own little baby already forming inside her.

Heavens, she'd imagined her entire pregnancy in vivid detail. She'd even pictured the baby's birth and Will's excitement. She'd pictured bringing the little one home, watching it grow until it was old enough to play with Gina and Tom's twins. She'd almost gone into Willowbank's one and only baby store and bought a tiny set of clothes.

She *had* to be pregnant.

But now, on a rainy Friday night, she sat curled

in a lounge chair with the bag of liquorice in her lap, aware of a telltale ache in her lower abdomen.

She was trying to stay positive. And failing miserably.

She'd had so much hope pinned on this one chance. She couldn't risk another night in bed with Will, couldn't go through another round of heartache. She really, really needed that one night to have been successful.

Time dragged for Will.

November, however, was a hectic month on a New South Wales sheep farm so, even though he couldn't stop thinking about Lucy, he found plenty of ways to keep busy.

Now that the shearing was over, all the sheep had to be dipped and drenched, prior to the long, hot summer. It was time to wean lambs and to purchase rams for next year's joining. To top it off, it was also haymaking time.

Will found himself slipping back into the world of his childhood with surprising ease.

In his wide-ranging travels, he'd seen breathtaking natural beauty and sights that were truly stranger than fiction, but it was only here at home that he felt a soul-deep connection to the land.

He supposed it flowed in his blood as certainly as his DNA. He'd always been secretly proud of the fact that his great great-grandfather, another William Carruthers, had bought this land in the nineteenth century.

William had camped here at first and then lived in the shearers' quarters, before finally acquiring sufficient funds to build a substantial homestead for his bride.

Will found himself thinking more and more often about Josh, too. His brother had been the family member everyone had expected to work this land as their father's right hand man. The man who had won Lucy's heart.

He remembered the fateful morning Josh had woken him early, proclaiming that this was the day he was going to fly the plane he'd worked on for so long.

It had been too soon. Will had known that the final checks hadn't been made by the inspector from the aero club, but Josh had been insistent.

'I'm not waiting around for that old codger. I've put in all the work on this girl. I know she's fine. This is the day, Will. It's a perfect morning for a first flight. I can *feel* it.'

Will had gone with great reluctance, mainly

to make sure Josh didn't do anything really stupid. As they drove through the creamy dawn towards the Willowbank airfield, he'd conscientiously reread all the flying manuals, anxious to understand all the necessary safety checks.

'I still don't think you should be doing this,' he'd said again when they'd arrived at the hangar.

'Give it a miss, little brother,' Josh had responded angrily. 'Just accept that we're different. I'm my own man. I go after what I want and I make sure that I get it.'

'Is that how you scored Lucy McKenty?' Will hadn't been able to hold back the question that had plagued him ever since he'd arrived home.

Josh laughed. 'Of course. What did you expect? In case you haven't noticed, Lucy's the best looking girl in the district. I wasn't going to leave her sitting on the shelf.'

'She's not another of your damn trophies.'

'For God's sake, Will, you're not going to be precious, are you?'

An unreasonable anger had swirled through Will. His hands had fisted, wanting to smash the annoying smirk on his brother's handsome face. 'You'd better make bloody sure you look after her.'

'Don't worry.' Josh laughed. 'I've already done that.' He was still laughing as he climbed into the pilot's seat. 'Now, you sit over there and stay quiet, little brother, while I take this little beauty for her test flight.'

Once more, Will had tried to stop him. 'You shouldn't be doing this. You only have to wait for one more inspection.'

Josh had ignored him and turned on the engine.

'I'm not going to sit around here like your fan club,' Will shouted above the engine's roar. 'If you're going to break your bloody neck, you can do it by yourself.'

From the cockpit, Josh had yelled his last order. 'Don't you dare take the car.'

'Don't worry. I'll bloody walk back.'

They had been his parting words.

The plane had barely made it into the air before it had shuddered and begun to fall. Will had seen everything from the road.

So many times in the years that followed, he'd regretted his actions that morning.

He'd washed his hands of his brother, turned

his back on him, but he should have stood up to Josh, should have found a way to stop him.

But then again, no one, not even their father had been able to stop Josh when he'd set his mind on a goal.

Lucy wouldn't have stood a chance either.

The next morning, Lucy knew the worst.

She sent Will a text message.

Thanks for your help, but sorry, no luck. We're not going to be parents. L x

She felt guilty about texting him rather than speaking to him, but she was afraid she'd start blubbing if she'd tried explain over the phone.

If Will's parents were nearby when he took the call, it would be really awkward for him to have to deal with a crying female who wasn't actually his girlfriend.

But it was a Saturday morning and she wasn't working, so she wasn't totally surprised when Will turned up on her doorstep within twenty minutes.

She hadn't seen him in two weeks and when she opened her door and saw him standing there with his heart-throb smile and blue jeans sexiness she felt a sweet, shivery ache from her breastbone to her toes.

'I guess you got my text,' she said.

Will nodded. 'I'm really sorry about your news, Lucy. It's rotten luck.'

She quickly bit her lower lip to stop it from trembling and, somehow, she refrained from flinging her arms around Will and sobbing all over him, even though it was exactly what she needed to do.

Instead she took two hasty steps back, tried for an offhand shrug. 'I guess it wasn't meant to happen.'

Will shook his head. 'I can't believe that.'

Her attempt to smile felt exceptionally shaky.

As they went through to the kitchen, she couldn't help remembering the last time they had been here together on *that* night.

'I should warn you, Will, I'm rather fragile this morning.' Her hands fluttered in a gesture of helplessness. 'Hormones and disappointment can be a messy combination.'

'Maybe we were expecting too much, hoping it would all happen the first time.'

'I don't know. Maybe I should have more tests. I'm so scared that my eggs aren't up to scratch.'

Before she knew quite what was happening, Will closed the gap between them. His arms were around her and she was clinging to him, snuffling against his clean cotton T-shirt and inhaling the scents of the outdoors that clung to his skin. Trying very, very hard not to cry.

His fingers gently played with her hair. 'I'm sure your eggs are perfect. I bet they're the healthiest, cutest little goose eggs ever.'

She muffled a sob against his chest.

'We might have to be patient,' he said.

'Patient?' She pulled away. 'What do you mean?'

His eyes reflected bemusement. 'In a couple of weeks we can try again, can't we?'

No. No, they couldn't. She couldn't do this again. It had been a mistake.

'No, Will.' Lucy swallowed. 'I'm afraid we can't try again.'

Unhappily she slipped from the haven of his arms and turned away from the puzzled look in his eyes.

'But surely you're not ready to give up after just one try?'

'Yes, I am. Perhaps nature knows best.'

'What are you talking about?'

'Perhaps friends shouldn't try to be parents.'

'Lucy, that's not rational.'

'I'm sorry if you're disappointed, but I couldn't go through this again.'

Not with Will. It would be a huge mistake to sleep with him again. It was too painful, knowing that he was only being a friend to her, that he didn't love her.

In the agonising stretch of silence he stood with his arms folded, frowning at a spot on the floor. Eventually, he said, 'You're disappointed right now. That's understandable. But you're sure to feel differently in another week or so.'

Lucy shook her head. 'No, Will. I'm sorry. This isn't a snap decision I made this morning. I'd already made up my mind last week. I decided I should give up on the whole idea of a baby if there was no pregnancy this month.'

'But that doesn't make sense.'

Tears threatened, but she kept her expression carefully calm. 'It makes sense to me.'

If only she could explain her decision without confessing that she had always been in love with him. But that meant talking about Josh and she felt too fragile this morning to go there.

Perhaps it was better to never talk about it. If they stopped the friendship plan now, they could leave the past in the past, where it belonged.

Somehow she kept her voice steady. 'It was a great idea in theory, but I'm afraid it's not going to work, Will. I might take months to fall pregnant. *Friends* don't keep having sex month after month, or possibly several times a month, trying to becoming parents.'

'But I thought you really wanted to have a baby.'

'Well, yes, I did want a baby. But—' Oh, help. What could she tell him? 'Maybe sex is different for guys,' she finished lamely.

'I wouldn't be so sure about that.'

Lucy's heart stuttered as she watched a dark stain ride up Will's neck. Knotted veins stood out on the backs of his hands as he gripped the back of a kitchen chair.

Lucy knew she mustn't cave in now. She should have recognised from the start that this convenient baby idea could never work. She should have known that her emotions would never survive the strain of making love to him when he'd only ever offered her friendship and a fly in, fly out version of fatherhood.

She should have heard the warning bells then. She'd been foolish to agree.

Even so, a huge part of her wanted to remain

foolish. She longed to rush into Will's arms again. She longed for him to kiss her, longed for a future where Will Carruthers figured in her life, no matter how remotely.

'So,' he said tightly, 'you're quite certain you want to ditch our arrangement?'

'Yes, that's what I want.'

His jaw clenched tightly and a muscle jerked just below his right cheekbone. For a moment he looked as if he wanted to say more, but then he frowned and shook his head.

'Will, I do appreciate your—'

He silenced her with a raised hand. 'Please, spare me your thanks. I know what this is all about. It's OK.' Already he was heading back down the hallway to her front door.

Puzzled by his sudden acceptance, but aching with regret, Lucy followed. On the doorstep, she said, 'Gina's invited me to the twins' christening. I guess I'll…see you there?'

'Of course.' He smiled wryly. 'We're the star godparents.'

It occurred to Lucy that this christening would be like the wedding—another gathering of their friends and families. Another ceremonial rite of passage. Another occasion when she and Will would be in close proximity. But she wondered if either of them could look forward to it.

The heaviness inside her plunged deeper as she watched Will swing into the truck. It was only as the driver's door slammed shut that she remembered she hadn't asked him about his job interview.

She ran down the path, calling to him, 'Will, how was the interview in Armidale?'

His face was stony. 'I didn't end up going.'

Shocked, she clung to her rickety front gate. 'Why not?'

'When I really thought about working there, shut up in a building all day, preparing lectures, marking papers, talking to academics, I knew I wasn't cut out for it.'

Before she could respond, he gunned the truck's motor and sent it rattling and roaring to life. Without smiling, he raised his hand in a grim salute. Dust rose as he took off.

Miserably, Lucy watched him go.

Soon he would probably disappear completely, off to another remote outpost. Now, too late, she realised that she'd been secretly hoping he'd get that job in Armidale and stay close.

At least Will had been honest with himself. He

was right—unfortunately—Armidale wouldn't have suited him. Alaska or Africa were more his style. Anywhere—as long as it was a long, long way from Willowbank.

The christening was perfect—sweet babies in white baptismal gowns, white candles, a kindly vicar, photos and happy onlookers.

But it was an ordeal for Will.

Lucy was a constant distraction in a floaty dress of the palest dove grey, and Gina and Tom's obvious pride in their beyond cute, well behaved babies was a poignant reminder of her recent disappointment.

Spring was at its best with clear blue skies and gentle sunshine, but Will felt like a man on a knife edge. He so regretted not being able to help Lucy to achieve her goal of motherhood.

He was deeply disappointed that she wasn't prepared to have a second try. In fact, the depth of his disappointment surprised him. It was disturbing to know that she'd found the whole process too stressful.

Will reasoned that his relationship to Josh was the problem. He was too strong a reminder of the man she'd loved and lost. Why else had she looked so miserable when he'd tried to convince her to keep trying?

After the church service, the Carruthers family held a celebratory luncheon at Tambaroora. Long tables were covered in white cloths and set beneath pergolas heavy with fragrant wisteria. Everyone helped to carry the food from the kitchen—platters of seafood and roast meat, four different kinds of salads, mountains of crispy, homemade bread rolls.

Two white christening cakes were given pride of place and crystal flutes were filled with French champagne to wet the babies' heads.

Will chatted with guests and helped with handing the drinks around and Lucy did the same but, apart from exchanging polite greetings, they managed to avoid conversing with each other.

It seemed necessary given the circumstances, as if they both feared that a conversation might give their strained relationship away.

Fortunately, no one else seemed to notice their tension. Everyone was too taken with the babies, or too eager to hear about Mattie and Jake's honeymoon travels in Italy.

Gina's father-in-law, Fred Hutchins, broke

off an animated conversation with Lucy to catch Will as he passed.

'Great to see you again,' Fred said, shaking Will's hand. 'We old-timers have been following your exploits in Alaska and Africa and Mongolia. It all sounds so exciting.'

'It's been interesting,' Will agreed, without meeting Lucy's gaze.

'Good for you. Why not enjoy an adventurous life while you can? I should have headed off myself when I was younger, but it just didn't happen. I'm pleased you didn't get bogged down here, Will. I suppose, in some ways, we look on you as the one who got away.' Fred chuckled. 'When are you heading off again?'

'Pretty soon.'

Fred clapped Will on the shoulder. 'Good for you, son. Don't hang around here. It's too easy to grow roots in a place like this.'

Will caught Lucy's eye and saw the sad set of her mouth and the thinness of her smile. He wondered, as the laughter and chatter floated about them, if he was the only one who noticed the shadowy wistfulness in her eyes whenever she glanced in the direction of the babies.

Unlike the other women, Lucy hadn't begged

for a chance to cuddle little Mia or Jasper and Will's heart ached for her.

When it was time for dessert, silver platters piled with dainty lemon meringue tarts appeared.

'Lucy, these are divine!' Gina exclaimed with her mouth full.

For the first time that day, Lucy looked happy. 'They turned out well, didn't they?'

'Did you make these?' Will was unable to disguise his surprise, which he immediately regretted.

Lucy's smile faltered. 'Yes.' She tilted her chin defensively. 'As a matter of fact, I made them entirely from scratch—even the pastry.'

'What's got into you, Will?' Gina challenged. 'Are you trying to suggest that Lucy can't cook?'

The eyes of almost every guest at the table suddenly fixed on Will and he felt the back of his neck grow uncomfortably hot. He smiled, tried to mumble an apology. 'No, no, sorry. I…I…'

To his surprise, Lucy came to his rescue. 'Back when Will and I were at uni, I used to be an atrocious cook.'

This was greeted by indulgent smiles and

nods and comments along the lines that Lucy was an accomplished cook now. As general conversation resumed, Lucy's eyes met Will's down the length of the table. She sent him a smile, nothing more than a brief flash, but its sweet intimacy almost undid him.

Shortly afterwards, the babies woke from their naps and the christening cakes were cut and glasses were raised once again. Tom made a short but touching speech of thanks to Mattie for her wonderful gift of the surrogate pregnancy and, just as he finished, baby Mia let out a loud bellow of protest.

'Oh, who's a grizzly grump?' Gina gave a theatrical groan. 'She probably needs changing.'

To Will's surprise, Lucy jumped to her feet and held out her arms. 'Let me look after her,' she said.

'Oh, thanks, I won't say no,' Gina replied with a laugh.

Lucy was smiling as she scooped the baby from Gina's lap.

Will watched her walk back across the smooth lawn to the house and thought how beautiful she looked in her elegant dress with its floaty grey skirt, the colour of an early morning sky. Her pale blonde hair was shining in the sunlight, and the baby was a delicate pink and white bundle in her arms.

Without quite realising what he'd done or why, he found himself standing. 'I'll fetch more champagne,' he offered, grasping for an excuse to follow her.

'No need, Will,' called his father, pointing to a tub filled with ice. 'We still have plenty of champers here.'

'I…er…remembered that I left a couple of bottles in the freezer,' Will said. 'I don't want them to ice up. I'd better rescue them.'

As he entered the house he heard Lucy's voice drifting down the hallway from the room that used to be Gina's. Her voice rippled with laughter and she was talking in the lilting sing-song that adults always used with babies. For Will, the sound was as seriously seductive as a siren's song and he couldn't resist heading down the passage.

In the doorway he paused, unwilling to intrude. The baby was on the bed, little arms waving, legs pumping as she laughed and giggled and Lucy was leaning over her.

Will couldn't see Lucy's face, but he could hear her soft, playful chatter. It was such a touching and intimate exchange. A painful brick lodged in his throat.

Lucy was laughing. 'Who's the cutest little baby girl in the whole wide world?'

Mia responded with loud chuckles and coos.

'Who's the loveliest roly-poly girl? Who's so chubby and sweet I could gobble her up?'

Will felt a twist in his heart as he watched Lucy kiss the waving pink toes, watched her gently and deftly apply lotion to the petal soft skin, then refasten a clean nappy.

Aware that he was spying, he stepped back, preparing to make a discreet departure, but just at that moment, a choked cry broke from Lucy and she seemed to fold in the middle like a sapling lashed by a storm.

She sank to her knees beside the bed.

'Lucy.'

He didn't want to startle her, but her name burst from him.

Her head jerked up and she turned and her face was white and wet with tears. She looked at Will with haunted eyes and then she looked at the baby and she tried to swipe at her tears, but her emotions were too raw. Her mouth crumpled and she sent Will a look of hopeless despair.

In a heartbeat he was in the room, dropping to his knees beside her. He pulled her into his arms and he held her as she trembled and clung to him, burying her face, warm and wet with tears, against his neck.

It was then that he knew.

He knew how deeply she longed for a child.

He knew how very much he wanted to help her.

Most of all, he knew that Lucy's need was greater than her fear.

'We can try again if you like,' he whispered close to her ear. 'Lucy, why don't you try again?'

'Yes,' she sobbed against his shoulder. 'I think I have to. Please, yes.'

His arms tightened around her.

In a few minutes Lucy was calmer. She stood and went to the bathroom to wash her face while Will held Mia.

It was quite something the way his little niece snuggled into him, with her head tucked against his chest and one chubby starfish hand clutching at the fabric of his shirt.

Will tried to imagine a son or daughter of his

own. A tiny person like this. Mia smelled amazing. She smelled…pink.

Yes, if pale pink was a fragrance, he was sure it would smell like this baby. Warm and fuzzy and incredibly appealing.

The baby was wearing the gold bracelet he'd bought for her christening—a little chain with a heart shaped locket—and it almost disappeared into the roly-poly folds of her wrist. Her skin was so soft. Peach soft.

No, softer than a peach.

Wow. No wonder fathers wanted to protect their daughters.

'Oh, gosh, Will, that baby really suits you,' Lucy said, almost smiling as she came back into the room.

'Not as well as she suits you.'

He handed the tiny bundle back to Lucy and she buried her nose in Mia's hair. 'I'd bottle this smell if I could.'

Turning, she checked her appearance in the mirror above the dressing table. 'I just need a minute to compose myself. It's a pity I don't have my make-up with me.'

To Will, Lucy looked absolutely fine just as she was, but he offered to fetch her handbag.

'No, it's OK,' she said. 'You'd better go back to the party. Gina will be wondering why we're taking so long.'

CHAPTER EIGHT

LUCY'S words were prophetic. Will had barely left before Gina appeared at the bedroom door.

'Oh, there you are,' she said. 'I was wondering—' She stopped and frowned. 'Is everything OK, Lucy?'

'Yes.' Lucy dropped a swift kiss on the baby's head. 'Mia's fine.'

But gosh, she couldn't quite believe that she'd actually agreed to try again for a baby with Will.

'But what about you?' Gina asked. 'You look upset.'

Lucy tried to shrug this aside.

'You've been crying.' Gina came closer, her dark eyes warm with concern.

It was too hard to pretend. Lucy tried to smile but her mouth twisted out of shape.

'Lucy, you poor thing. What's the matter?'

'I'm just emerald green with jealousy, that's all.' She looked down at Mia, curled in her arms and this time she managed a rueful smile. 'I would so love to have a little one like this for myself.'

'Oh.' Gina made a soft sound of sympathy. 'I know how awful that longing can be. It just eats you up, doesn't it?'

That was the great thing about Gina. She wasn't just a good friend. She really understood. She'd been through years of painful endometriosis before her doctor had finally told her that she needed a hysterectomy. The news that she could never have children had broken her heart, but then Mattie had stepped in with her wonderful surrogacy offer.

Now, just as she had when they'd been school friends, Gina plopped down on her old bed and patted a space for Lucy, who obeyed without question. She was so totally in need of a girly heart-to-heart and where better than Gina's bedroom, still painted the terrible lavender and hot pink she'd chosen when she was fourteen?

'Are you thinking about tackling another round of IVF?' Gina asked.

Lucy shook her head and hastily weighed up the pros and cons of confiding in Will's sister.

Quite quickly she decided it was necessary. Out of any of the women in her circle of friends, Gina would most understand her longing for a baby. And she also understood her history with Will.

'I'm trying for a baby, but not with IVF,' she said.

To Gina's credit, she didn't look too shocked, although she was understandably puzzled. 'So how's that work? You have a secret boyfriend?'

'Not exactly.' Lucy settled Mia's sleepy head more comfortably into the crook of her arm. 'Actually, Will's offered to help me out.'

This time, Gina did look shocked.

Momentarily.

'Will's helping you to have a baby?'

'Yes.'

'Wow!' Gina gasped. 'That's…that's…far out. You and Will.' She gave an excited little squeal. 'Gosh, Lucy, that's wonderful.'

'Unconventional is probably the word most people would use.'

Gina frowned. 'Excuse me? I'm lost.'

'Friends don't usually plan to have a baby together.'

'Friends?'

'Yes. Will and I are still only friends. But

he's quite keen to be a dad and he knows how I feel, so he wants to help me to have a baby. It's actually rather convenient.'

'Right.' Gina frowned as she digested this. Then she smiled. 'But friends often fall in love.'

Lucy felt bad, knowing she was about to watch Gina's happy smile disintegrate.

'Not this time,' she said. 'There's no chance.'

For a moment Gina seemed lost for words. She traced the pattern of pink and lavender patchwork squares on the bed quilt. 'I guess it must be awkward,' she mused, 'because you were engaged to Josh.'

Unwilling to dwell on that subject, Lucy tried to steer Gina's thoughts in a different direction. 'The thing is, Will's not a settling down kind of guy. You and I both know that. We've always known it.'

Gina pulled a face. 'Will's annoying like that, isn't he? I really love my brother but, I have to admit, he's always been a bit of an outsider in our family. Middle child syndrome, I guess.'

'I wouldn't know. I was an only child.'

'In our family, it was always about Josh, as the eldest son. He was the heir apparent. And I was the spoiled baby girl. Poor old Will was caught in the middle, neither one thing nor the other.'

Gina lowered her voice importantly. 'Even though I was the youngest, I could see how it was. Dad spoiled me rotten. Gosh, when I was little, he used to take me out on the tractor every night just to get me to sleep. I'd sit up there with my security blanket and my head in his lap, while he went round and round the paddock.'

'Lucky you,' Lucy said.

'And then Josh was always trailing after Dad like a faithful sheepdog and the old man adored it. They were always together, working with the sheep, tinkering with machinery. They had a special bond and I'm sure Will felt left out. I think that's why he drifted towards books and study, rather than helping out on the farm. And then he started taking off on his own to fossick for rocks.'

'Which he's still doing, more or less,' Lucy suggested.

'I guess.' Gina let out a loud sigh. 'It's not fair on you, though.' She pulled at a loose thread in the quilt. 'Will might still feel as if he's living in Josh's shadow.'

Bright heat flared in Lucy's face. 'I hope he doesn't,' she said quietly.

'What is it with my brothers? Why do they both have to mess up your life?'

'Because I let them?'

Gina's face softened and she reached out to touch her daughter's hair as she slept in Lucy's arms. 'Well…for what it's worth, I think this baby idea is fabulous. OK, maybe it's a tad unconventional, but it's still fabulous. I do wish you luck.'

'Thanks.' Lucy smiled. It was good to know she had someone on her side. 'You won't say anything to Will?'

'Heavens, no.' Gina threw a reassuring arm around Lucy's shoulders. 'A little sister's advice would be the kiss of death, and I really want this to work.'

After the last of the guests had left, Will helped with the dismantling of the trestle tables and the stacking away of the chairs in a storage room below the hayloft. As he worked, his thoughts were focused front, back and centre on Lucy.

It wasn't possible to think about anything else. His heart had cracked in two today when he'd seen her weeping beside little Mia.

Mattie had achieved the impossible for Gina and Tom and no doubt that made Lucy's situation all the more distressing. But what upset Will was the fact that she'd told him last week she wanted to call off their plan, when it was so obvious that she still wanted a baby.

There could only be one reason, of course. She wasn't happy about having to sleep with him again. He'd created a problem for her.

For possibly the thousandth time Will thought about that night. He'd been a lost man the minute he'd touched Lucy McKenty. That was his problem. One caress of her skin, one brush of his lips against her soft, sweet mouth and he'd forgotten his plan to have simple, 'friendly' sex with a focus on procreation. Damn it. He'd been so carried away, he'd practically forgotten his own name.

Problem was, he'd put their kiss of ten years ago out of his mind. He'd gone into this without thinking about how Lucy might taste, or how she'd react. He certainly hadn't expected such a passionate response from her.

Was that how she'd been with Josh?

Hell.

Will was shocked by the violent force of his

feelings when he thought about Josh and Lucy together.

He tried to stop thinking about them but, with the last chair stacked, he strode to the end of the home paddock. He looked out across the valley to where the distant hills were blue smudges on the horizon and he drew a deep breath and caught the sharp tang of eucalyptus and the dusty scent of the earth.

He looked up at the wide faded blue of the sky, searching for answers to the turmoil inside him.

Some answers were easy. He knew exactly why Lucy loved this land, and he knew that he wanted his child to live here with her.

It felt right that Lucy should be the mother of his child.

It felt good.

But was he fooling himself? Was it madness to think he could replace his brother?

No, he decided. It was actually a greater madness to dwell on the Josh-Lucy scenario, to keep letting the past haunt him.

For more than twenty years he'd lived in Josh's shadow, but it was time to get over that. His task now was to concentrate on the living. To do the right thing by Lucy.

Heaven knew she deserved to be treated well. She was a wonderful girl. Gutsy and clever. Sweet and fun.

She was his friend.

And she needed his help.

And he needed—

Hell, he wasn't sure what he needed from Lucy. He had the feeling though, that he couldn't stop wanting to help her.

But, if that was so, if they were going to keep trying until Lucy was pregnant, he had to make this baby plan easier for her. Which meant he had to make sure that their next rendezvous was as friendly and functional as possible.

Will let out a sigh—which he smartly decided was a sigh of relief. He felt marginally better now that he had his thoughts straight.

All he had to remember was that he was Lucy's friend, not her lover.

Friendship gave them clear boundaries and boundaries were good. Breaking the boundaries could completely mess up her life.

In line with that thinking, he should start making plans to get a job outside this district. That way Lucy would know he wasn't going to crowd her once their goal of pregnancy was achieved. He'd heard of jobs in Papua New Guinea that he could apply for.

PNG wasn't too far away, so he could come back to Willowbank from time to time to play whatever role in their baby's life that Lucy wanted.

Good. Will was glad he had that sorted.

It always helped to have a plan.

Three days later he received a text message from Lucy:

Can you come over tonight? I have evening surgery, so can't offer dinner. Is 9.30 too late? L x

He sent a hasty reply:

I'll be there.

I'll be there…

All day Will's message drummed inside Lucy with a pulsing, electrifying beat.

She knew she was weak. She was supposed to be giving up on this baby idea and protecting her emotions, but she'd only spent five minutes with little Mia and her brave plans to abandon the project had toppled like bowling pins.

She shouldn't have jumped at Will's offer to

try again for a baby, but heavens, if he hadn't offered, she might have begged him.

Now, she couldn't stop thinking about him arriving on her doorstep tonight, coming into her house, into her bed.

For the first time in her professional life she found it hard to concentrate on her work. She was excessively grateful that the tasks were routine, so she could more or less function on autopilot.

But, by the time the hands of the clock eventually crawled to nine-thirty in the evening, she was jangling with tension and expectation.

And she was falling apart with insecurity.

She wished she knew how Will really felt about this second night, but it was such a difficult question to broach. And she might not like his answer.

She told herself that she should be grateful he was willing to help, and she should be pleased that he hadn't pressed her to talk about Josh. If she started down that track, she might reveal too much about her feelings for Will. She could complicate the delicate balance of their friendship. Spoil everything.

Perhaps Will was nervous too, because he arrived two minutes and thirty-five seconds early, but Lucy opened the door even before he knocked.

'Evening, Lucy.' His smile was shy, yet so charming, she was sure it was designed to make her heart do back-flips.

She ran her damp hands down the side seams of her jeans. 'Come on in.'

Will came through the doorway but then he stopped abruptly. 'I've brought you a little something,' he said, holding out a slim box tied with curling purple ribbons.

'Oh.' Lucy gulped with surprise. 'Thank you.'

'I know rocks don't really have special powers, but see what you think.'

Her hands were shaking and she fumbled as she tried to undo the ribbon, pulling the knot tighter, instead of undoing it.

'Hey, I'll get that.'

The brush of Will's hands against hers sent rivers of heat up her arms. Her heart thumped as she watched the concentration in his face, the patience of his fingers as he deftly prised the knot free. Finally, he lifted the lid and showed her a neat little pendant on a pretty silver chain.

'Will, it's gorgeous. Is it an amethyst?'

'Yes.' He sent her another shy smile. 'Apparently, amethysts have traditionally been linked to fertility.'

'Oh, wow. That's so thoughtful. Thank you. It's beautiful. I love it.'

He smiled gorgeously. 'Let me do up the clasp for you.'

Lucy decided it was quite possible to melt just from being touched. She was burning up as Will fastened the pendant. She turned to him.

'It suits you,' he said. 'It brings out the deep blue in your eyes.'

To Lucy's surprise he looked suddenly nervous. Bravely, she stepped forward and kissed him. On the mouth.

Gosh. When had she become so brave?

Will returned her kiss carefully, almost chastely, and she felt a cold little swoop of disappointment.

She lifted her hands to his shoulders and felt him tense all over. 'Will,' she whispered, 'what's wrong?'

CHAPTER NINE

WILL knew he could do this.

All day, he'd rehearsed in his mind how he would make love to Lucy as her friend. He'd thought about nothing else as he'd driven the tractor up and down the paddocks at Tambaroora and the whole idea had seemed solid and plausible.

Now, however, Lucy was close—kissing close—and his certainty evaporated.

Or, rather, his certainty shifted focus. And the focus was *not* on friendship. Far from it.

He wanted nothing more than to gather Lucy in to him, to kiss her with the reckless frenzy of a lover, to kiss her slowly, all night long, to lose himself in her fragrant softness.

He wanted to forget *why* they were doing this. He wanted to forget her past history with

his brother. He wanted to think of nothing
but…

Lucy.

He wanted *her*.

Tonight.

She was simply dressed in jeans and a tomboyish grey T-shirt. No pretty floral dress. No
sexy high heels.

It didn't matter. She was Lucy. And he
wanted her.

Too much.

Her disappointment was clear as she stepped
away from him and nervously fingered the
amethyst, feeling the smooth facets beneath her
fingertips. Her blue eyes were cloudy. Understandably perplexed. 'Will, there's something
wrong, isn't there?'

'No,' he muttered and he forced his thoughts
to focus on restraint.

'You don't want to…' she began, but she
couldn't finish the sentence.

'I don't want to hurt you, Lucy.'

Cringe. Had he really said that? The only
way he could hurt Lucy was by walking away
and denying her the chance to become a mother.

Or perhaps that was the only way he could

save himself from eternal damnation? Why the hell hadn't they stuck to the IVF option?

His throat worked.

Lucy looked away. They were still standing in her hallway, for heaven's sake.

'Would you like a drink?' she asked.

'A drink?' he repeated like a fool.

'To…er…relax.'

He shook his head. He would need a whole bottle of alcohol to douse the fire inside him.

Lucy looked as if she wanted to weep and he knew that, at any minute now, she would thank him for the gift and send him home. It was exactly what he deserved.

She dropped her gaze to the empty box in her hands. 'I thought a drink might help with… um…getting in the mood.'

With a choked sound that was halfway between a groan and a sick laugh, Will fought back the urge to haul her against his hard, aroused body. 'There's nothing wrong with my mood, Lucy.'

'Right,' she whispered hoarsely, but she looked upset, a little shocked. And maybe just a tad angry. Her chin lifted and her unsmiling eyes confronted him.

His heart slammed inside his chest. He couldn't believe he'd been so cool about this last time. What a poor naïve fool he'd been. Back then, he hadn't known what it was like to take Lucy into his arms. He'd forgotten how dangerous it could be to get close to her, to know that the slim curves pressed so deliciously against him were Lucy's.

Until then, he'd innocently assumed that their kiss on the veranda all those years ago had been an aberration.

Now, Will knew better.

Now, he knew that kissing Lucy, making love to Lucy could all too easily become a dangerous addiction.

With a soft sigh, she set the box and purple ribbon on the hallstand, and when she looked at him again, she set her hands on her hips and her eyes were an unsettling blue challenge. 'What do you want to do, then?'

'Kiss you.'

The answer jumped from Will's lips before he could gather his wits. He saw the flare of confusion in Lucy's eyes, the soft surprised O of her mouth. But his hands were already reaching out for her and then he kissed her as if this were his last minute on this earth.

He kissed her as if at any moment he might lose her.

For ever.

Lucy couldn't quite believe this.

She hadn't dared to hope that Will could possibly want her with such intensity.

One minute he'd looked as if he wanted to bolt out her front door, the next his mouth was locked with hers. His hands cupped her bottom and he pulled her against him and suddenly she stopped worrying.

All the fantasies she'd lived through that day—actually, all the romantic fantasies she'd dreamed about her entire adult life—rolled into one sensational here and now.

Never had she experienced such a hot kiss. Flashpoints exploded all over her skin. Recklessly, she pushed even closer to Will, winding her arms around his neck, seeking the closest possible contact. To her relief, he most definitely didn't seem to mind.

Gosh, no.

His fever matched hers, kiss for kiss, and a kind of wonderful madness overcame them.

Together they made it down the hall, bumping against the walls in a frenzy of kissing and touching, until they reached the first doorway.

It led to the lounge room, and it seemed that would have to do.

They stumbled to the sofa, sinking needfully into its velvety cushions.

Bliss.

Bliss to help and be helped out of clothing. Bliss to lie together at last with Will, to run her hands over the satin of his skin as it stretched tightly over hard bands of muscle.

Even greater bliss when Will took charge and deliberately held back the pace, stilling her seeking hands and kissing her with unhurried, leisurely reverence.

It was sweet, so sweet. He kissed her slowly and deeply, drawing her gradually but relentlessly down into an intimate dark cave where only the two of them existed.

And everything was fine. It was perfect. Because this time she knew that Will Carruthers was the one man in the world she could trust to fulfil her innermost secret longings.

Will woke as the pale buttery light of dawn filtered though the curtains in Lucy's bedroom.

He didn't move because she was still asleep with one arm flung across his chest and her soft, warm body nestled against him, her breath a sweet hush on his skin.

Staying with her till morning had not been part of his plan. Hell, practically none of last night had been part of his plan, although he had rationalised that he should make the most of this one night.

Tomorrow he was flying out to Papua New Guinea to check out job prospects.

At that thought Will suppressed a sigh, but perhaps Lucy felt it for she stirred against him and her blue eyes opened.

'Morning, Goose.' He thought about kissing her, but decided against it. This morning was all about seriously backing off.

Lucy looked at her bedside clock and groaned. 'I've slept in.'

He thought guiltily about the amount of time he'd kept her awake.

'I'm going to have to hurry,' she grumbled, reaching for a towelling robe draped over a nearby chair.

Will swung his legs over the edge of the bed. Lucy tightened the knot at her waist and stood. She ran a hand through her tumbled curls and sent him an uncertain smile. She let her gaze travel over him, and it seemed to settle rather sadly on his bare feet.

He looked down. 'Yeah... I worry about that too.'

'What?'

'Whether the baby will inherit my freakishly long second toes.'

'Oh.' She laughed. 'It might end up with my freakishly tiny ears.'

He fought back an urge to pull her to him, to nibble and taste those neat little ears. 'Cutest ears in the southern hemisphere,' he said.

'But they might not look too flash on a boy.'

She bit her lower lip and touched the pendant at her throat. 'I wonder if it's happening, Will. I wonder if I'm pregnant.'

'You're sure to be,' he said and he did the only thing that was right.

He reached for his clothes.

Lucy held back her tears until after Will left, but she'd never felt so desolate. To watch him walk away was like cutting off a lifeline and she felt like an astronaut, adrift in endless emptiness.

But there was no point in letting him see how much she'd hated to let him go. He was heading off to Papua New Guinea tomorrow and he was sure to get a job there. She'd always known he was never going to be tamed and kept in one place.

He was a catch and release kind of man, like the wild bush creatures she cared for and then set free.

Will telephoned when he got back a week later. 'Have you started tucking into the liquorice allsorts?'

Lucy was relieved to report; 'Not yet.'

'Any symptoms?' he asked hopefully.

'Hard to say. It's still too soon, but I've been rather tired and I need to go to the bathroom in the middle of the night.'

'They're promising signs, aren't they?'

'Could be.'

Problem was, Lucy had become hyper-aware of her body, anxious to discover the slightest hint of change. She was sure she felt different this month, but she couldn't be certain that the differences were real and not simply the result of her overactive imagination.

Just in time she bit back an impulse to tell

Will she'd missed him. But it was true, of course. She'd missed Will terribly. Desperately. The longer he'd stayed away the more she was certain that making love to him on a second night had been even more dangerous than she'd feared. She loved him.

Still.

Always.

With all her heart.

She could no longer hide from the truth and she had no idea how she could go on pretending anything else.

But she had to accept that Will was never going to change, never going to settle down. He might be attracted to her, but he'd always been restless and he would always need to keep travelling, seeking new sights and challenges.

When she was younger, she'd known this, and she'd tried to protect herself by simply being his friend. Now she'd thrown caution to the wind and she had to accept that her love for him was a weakness she'd have to learn to adjust to and live with—the way other people adjusted to a disability.

'How was your trip to Papua New Guinea?' she asked, keeping her voice carefully light.

'Oh, there's plenty of work up there. I've had a couple of offers, so it's a matter of deciding which job to take.'

'That's great.' Good grief, she hoped she didn't sound as unhappy as she felt. 'A very fortunate position to be in.'

'No doubt about that,' Will agreed. 'So… about you. This week is the week of the big countdown, right?'

'Yes.' Lucy let out a sigh. 'I wish I didn't have to wait. I'm afraid I've become mildly obsessive. I've taken to reading my stars in every magazine I can find. I've even thought about going to see Sylvie.'

'Who's Sylvie?'

'The hairdresser in the main street. She tells fortunes as well as cutting hair, but I'm not quite desperate enough to trust her talents. I'm actually trying very hard to be sensible and philosophical.'

'Will you use a home pregnancy test?'

'Oh, yes. Definitely. I've a carton of tests ready and waiting, but I'm holding off till next Friday. If I try too soon, I might get a false reading and I don't think I could bear the disappointment.'

'Lucy, I want to be there.'

The sudden urgency in his voice made her heart jump.

'You want to be here when I do the test?'

'Yes. Is that OK?'

She pressed a hand against her thudding heart. She shouldn't be surprised. The baby would be as much Will's as it was hers, but somehow she hadn't expected this level of interest from him.

'It doesn't seem right that you should be all alone when you find out,' he said.

She couldn't deny it would be wonderful to share her news with Will. If it was good news they could celebrate, and if she was disappointed again he would be there to comfort her.

'You'd better come over first thing on Friday morning,' she said and her voice was decidedly shaky.

Friday morning produced an idyllic country dawn. As Will drove to Lucy's place, the paddocks, the trees and the sky looked as if they'd been spring cleaned for a special occasion, and the landscape had a gentle and dreamy quality as if he was viewing the scene through a soft focus lens. The air was balmy and light.

A pretty white fog filled the bowl of Willow Creek and he watched it drift from the dark cluster of trees like magician's smoke. He felt keyed up, excited, anxious, hopeful.

Torn.

He longed for good news, but in many ways he dreaded it. If Lucy was pregnant, he would have no choice but to take a back seat in her life.

He found that prospect unexpectedly depressing so he tried, instead, to enjoy the picture perfect scenery.

It shouldn't have been difficult. The road from Tambaroora wound past a small forest of pines, then over a low hill before it dipped to a rustic bridge where another arm of Willow Creek was bordered by yellow and purple wildflowers.

But he was still feeling edgy when he reached Lucy's place, even though her dogs rushed to the front gate to greet him with excited barks and madly wagging tails.

Lucy was dressed for work in a khaki shirt and trousers, but he could see the amethyst pendant sitting above the open V of her shirt collar.

Valiantly, he ignored the urge to pull her in for a kiss.

'How are you feeling?' he asked her.

'Totally nervous,' she admitted. 'I didn't sleep very well.'

'Neither did I.'

She looked surprised. 'I…I'm assuming you'll stay for breakfast? I've started sausages and tomatoes.'

'Thanks. They smell great.'

'And I've made a pot of tea. Why don't you help yourself while I…er…get this done? I can't stand the suspense.'

'Off you go,' he said, but as she turned to leave he snagged her hand. 'Hey, Goose.'

Her blue eyes shimmered. 'Yes?'

'Good luck.'

To his surprise she stepped closer and gave him a swift, sweet kiss on the jaw. The room seemed intolerably empty when she left.

Will poured tea into a blue pottery mug and walked with it to the window, saw the stained glass feature winking bright blue in the morning light and felt shocked by the tension that filled him.

For Lucy's sake he really wanted this test to be positive.

He wondered about that other time, eight years ago, when she'd discovered she was pregnant. Had she been ecstatically happy? Just as quickly he dismissed the question. There was little to be achieved now by reminding himself that he could only ever be a second best option after Josh.

It was time to be positive, to look forward to the future. A new generation, perhaps.

When he heard Lucy's footsteps he set his mug down, unhappily aware that she wasn't hurrying. She hadn't called out in excitement.

He turned, arms ready to comfort her, and his heart stood still in his chest as he prepared himself for disappointment.

He didn't want to put extra pressure on her, so he summoned a smile and tried to look calm, as if the result really didn't matter either way.

Lucy came into the kitchen and he saw two bright spots of colour in her cheeks. Her eyes were huge and shiny with emotion.

She waved a plastic stick. 'There are two lines.'

'What does that mean?'

'It means—'

She looked as if she was going to cry. Will's throat tightened.

'We did it, Will.'

She didn't look happy.

'You mean—' He hardly dared to ask. 'You're pregnant?'

'Yes!'

He wasn't sure if she was going to laugh or cry.

'Congratulations,' he said and his voice was choked. 'You clever girl.'

Tears glistened in her eyes but at last she was smiling.

And then she was grinning.

'Can you believe it, Will? I'm pregnant!' With a happy little cry she stumbled towards him and he opened his arms.

'Thank you,' she cried as she hugged him.

'Congratulations,' he said again.

'Congratulations to you, too. You're going to be a father.'

He grinned shakily.

A soft look of wonder came over her face as she touched the amethyst pendant, then pressed her hands to her stomach. 'I'm going to be a mother.'

'The best mother ever.'

'I don't give a hoot if it's a boy or a girl.'

'Not at all,' Will agreed, although he realised with something of a shock that he would love to have a son.

Happiness shone in Lucy's eyes as she

looked around her kitchen, as if she was suddenly seeing it with new eyes. She grinned at the table that she'd set for breakfast, at the dogs' bowls on the floor near the door. 'Oh, gosh, Will, I'm pregnant!'

He laughed, but it felt inadequate.

'Thank you,' she said again, and her smile was so sweet he wanted to sweep her into his arms, to hold her and kiss her and murmur endearments, all of which were completely inappropriate now that they were reverting to friendship.

Lucy's mind, however, was on a more practical plane. She looked over at the stove. 'I've probably burned the sausages.'

'They're OK. I turned them down low.'

'Well done. Thanks.' She glanced at the clock and sighed. 'We'd better eat. I still have a day's work ahead of me.'

'That's something we need to talk about,' Will said. 'You need to look after yourself now.'

She frowned at him, then shrugged. 'We can talk while we eat.'

It felt strangely intimate to be having breakfast with Lucy—pottering about in the kitchen, buttering toast, finding Vegemite and marmalade.

When they were settled at the table Lucy

looked at him across the seersucker tablecloth, her blue eyes wide and innocent. 'Now, what were you saying about my work?'

'You're going to need some kind of support now you're pregnant. You can't manage such a big workload on your own.'

'I have an assistant.'

'But she can't take on the tough jobs like delivering difficult calves. And she's not qualified to operate. I don't like the thought of you standing for long hours over difficult surgery.'

'Are you going to get bossy already?'

'You had a miscarriage once before,' he reminded her gently. 'And you're quite a bit older now.'

'Thanks for bringing that to my attention.' Lucy's mouth was tight as she spread Vegemite on her toast. 'Isn't it a bit hypocritical of you to be worrying about my age and personal safety?'

'Hypocritical?'

Her eyes blazed. 'You're not exactly taking care of yourself.'

'How do you mean?'

'You're about to become a father. You barely escaped with your life from your last job and you told me you'd learned a big lesson. But now you're heading off to Papua New Guinea, where a mudslide wiped out an entire village last summer. And everyone knows how often planes crash in the highlands. The airstrips are the size of postage stamps and they're perched on the edge of massive deep ravines.'

'I'm not going to the highlands.' Will rearranged the salt and pepper shakers like pieces on a chessboard. 'And I'm not the one who's pregnant. Your safety is more important than mine.'

Lucy opened her mouth as if she was going to say something more, but apparently changed her mind. She shrugged. 'Actually, I'd already been planning to cut back on work if I became pregnant. I can use locums. I have quite a few city vet friends who love it out here.'

'What kind of friends?' Will felt foolish asking, but he'd been attacked by an unreasonable fit of jealousy. 'Married couples?'

'Chris is a bachelor,' she said in a matter of fact tone. Her eyes were defiant as she looked at him. 'Leanne and Tim are married. If I have time later today I'll phone around and send out a few feelers.'

'I think that's wise.'

Lucy concentrated on piling tomatoes onto her fork. She looked upset and they finished their breakfast in uncomfortable silence.

Will felt upset too, but he wasn't sure why. He and Lucy had achieved their goal and now they were moving onto the next stage of their plan. She was going to be a single mum and he was going to visit their child from time to time.

That was what he wanted, wasn't it? Fatherhood without strings. He should have been on top of the world.

From the start he'd said that he would remain an outsider in their child's life. The silent scream inside him didn't make sense.

He heard the sound of a car pulling up and a door slamming.

'That's Jane, my assistant, ready to start work,' Lucy said pointedly.

Will got to his feet. 'I'd better get out of your way.' He indicated the breakfast dishes. 'Can I help with these?'

'No, don't worry.'

She walked with him to the front door and waved to her assistant, who was using a side gate to reach the surgery. 'I'll be there in a minute, Jane,' she called.

'Don't hurry,' Jane called back, smiling broadly when she saw Will.

Lucy looked unhappy. 'Make sure you come and see me before you go,' she told him.

'Yes, of course.'

Her mouth trembled and she blinked.

He said inadequately, 'Thanks for breakfast.' And then he dipped his head and kissed her cheek.

Lucy mumbled something about a very busy day, gave him a brief wave and shut the door.

After Will left, her day proved to be even busier than she'd expected but, every so often as she worked, she would remember.

I'm pregnant.

Excitement fizzed inside her and she hugged herself in secret glee. She'd been waiting for this for so long. She couldn't help thinking about all those busy little cells inside her, forming their baby.

Their baby.

Wow.

There was no time to celebrate, however. As well as her usual line-up of patients, she had to perform emergency surgery on an elderly dog and she found the work unusually stressful. She was very fond of this sweet black and white cocker spaniel. He'd been one of her first patients when she'd started working in Willowbank.

She would do what she could for him now, but she feared he was nearing the end of his days. His owner would be distraught when his time was up.

If that wasn't enough to dampen Lucy's spirits, she was upset about Will. She couldn't stop thinking about him, felt utterly miserable about him going away.

Again.

How could she bear it?

The threat of his impending departure had made her snappy with him this morning and she felt bad about that, after he'd been so excited. But how could she not be upset by the thought of saying goodbye?

She loved Will.

Letting him go felt like cutting out a vital organ. Whenever she pictured him leaving, she grew angry again. How could Will pretend to be terribly concerned about her and then take off to the wilds of a New Guinea jungle?

How could he leave her so soon? So easily?

All day, her mind churned with things she

wished she'd asked him, as well as things she wished she'd told him. But the crux of her message was hard to admit—their friendship plan was a farce.

It was rubbish.

Sharing responsibility for a child required a commitment that went way beyond friendship.

And she and Will had already shared a beautiful intimacy that she could never classify as friendship.

Maybe it was easier for guys to be interested in sex without actually being in love, but she'd never been brave enough to be honest with Will about her feelings, so wasn't it possible that he'd hidden some of his feelings, too?

Should she try to find out?

It was crazy that she was still afraid to admit the truth about her feelings. She'd always been so worried that her disclosure might shock him, that she might alienate him completely. But today she felt different.

Determined.

She'd been hiding behind fear for too long. She was going to be a mother now and that required courage.

For her baby's sake, she should tell Will how she really felt and then face the consequences bravely.

Her confession might not make any difference. There was a chance it could make everything worse but, as the day wore on, Lucy became surer and surer that it was time to take the risk she'd shied away from for too long.

At lunch time Gina popped her head around the surgery door, her dark eyes brimming with curiosity. 'Mum's minding the twins while I do my shopping, so I thought I'd duck in quickly to see how you're going.'

'You must have a sixth sense about these things,' Lucy said, smiling.

Gina's eyes widened.

'Come and have a cuppa.' Lucy took her through to the kitchen.

'Do you have some news?' Gina asked as soon as the door that linked back to Lucy's office was firmly shut.

'I only found out this morning.'

'That you're pregnant?'

Lucy couldn't hold back her grin. 'Yes.'

Gina squealed and knocked over a kitchen

chair in her rush to hug her friend. 'Oh, Lucy, I'm so excited for you.'

'I know. It's fantastic, isn't it? I have to keep pinching myself.'

'Our babies are going to be cousins,' Gina gushed.

Lucy smiled again, but this time there wasn't much joy behind it.

'I'm assuming that Will is the father,' Gina said less certainly.

'Yes, he is, and he knows about the baby. But I haven't told anyone else yet, so keep it under your hat.'

'Of course.'

The kettle came to the boil and Lucy was aware of Gina's thoughtful gaze as she poured hot water over the teabags.

'So how are things between you and Will?' she cautiously asked as Lucy handed her a mug.

'Hunky-dory.'

'Oh. That doesn't sound too promising.' Gina took a sip of tea. 'I suppose Will hasn't admitted that he loves you.'

Lucy felt the colour rush from her face. 'Don't talk nonsense, Gina. He doesn't love me.'

'Do you really believe that?'

'Yes. He can't love me. If he did, he wouldn't be taking off for PNG.'

Gina sighed. 'Is he really going away again?'

'Yes.'

'Sometimes I could wring his neck.'

'He's the man he is,' Lucy said, surprised that she could sound philosophical about a sad fact that was breaking her heart. 'Everyone in Willowbank knows Will doesn't belong here.'

'I'm not so sure about that, actually. But, anyway, he could always take you with him when he goes away.'

'I can't take off for some remote mining site when I'm pregnant. I certainly couldn't live there with a tiny baby.'

'Well…no. I don't suppose you could.' Gina gritted her teeth. 'So, do you need me to wring my brother's neck or try to hammer some sense into him?'

'No,' said Lucy, crossing her fingers behind her back. 'Leave it to me.'

By mid-afternoon the pace in the surgery wasn't quite so hectic and Lucy sent her father a text message:

Are you busy? Can I phone you?

The two of them had always been good mates and she wanted him to know her news.

Almost immediately, he called her back. 'Darling, I have five minutes. What can I do for you?'

'I just wanted to share some good news, Dad. I'm pregnant.'

She waited for his shocked gasp, but he surprised her. 'That's wonderful news. Congratulations.'

'Really, Dad? You don't mind?'

'Do *you* mind, Lucy?'

'No. I'm actually very, very happy.'

'Then so am I. I'm delighted. Couldn't be happier.'

Lucy was amazed that he didn't immediately bombard her with predictable questions about the baby's father, or when she was planning to be married.

Her dad simply asked, 'Are you keeping well?'

She grinned. First and last, Alistair McKenty was a doctor. 'It's very early days, but I'm feeling fine. I have good vibes about this pregnancy.'

'You'll see Ken Harper?'

'Yes, Dad.' Ken Harper was Willowbank Hospital's only obstetrician. 'And, as you know, Ken will give me top antenatal care.'

She heard a chuckle on the other end of the line and she waited for more questions. When there was silence, she said, 'In case you were wondering, Will Carruthers is the baby's father.'

'Ah.'

'Ah? What does that mean?'

'I noticed that Will's been home for rather longer than usual.'

Heat suffused Lucy. 'Is that all you can say?'

'No. I'm actually very pleased. I like Will. I always expected you two to get together.'

'You did?'

'You used to be such terrific friends, but then you took up with that older brother.'

'Yes.'

'I never understood that, Lucy. Josh Carruthers had girlfriends all over the district.'

'Dad, I don't really want to go back over that now.'

'I'm sorry. You're right. It's all in the past.'

'Actually, there is one thing about that time I've been meaning to ask you.'

'What's that, dear?'

'Why didn't you tell me that Will telephoned and tried to visit me after Josh died?'

A sigh shuddered down the phone line. 'You were so distressed, Lucy, and I was upset too. Your mother wasn't around to advise, and I suppose I went into over-protective mode.'

'But Will was my friend.'

'I know, dear. I'm sorry, but I did what I thought was right. Mattie was there almost every day, and she was a huge help. And, to be honest, Will wasn't his normal self at the time. He was acting quite strangely. Extremely tense. Distraught, actually. I didn't see how he could do you any good.'

Lucy pressed two fingers to the bridge of her nose to hold back the threat of tears. She knew there was no point in getting upset about this. It wasn't her father's fault that Will had taken off again, without leaving her any hint that he'd wanted to keep in touch.

It wasn't her father's fault that her own feelings of guilt had driven her to silence, adding more strain to an already tense friendship.

'Well, things are still complicated between Will and me,' she admitted.

'Is he planning to continue working overseas?'

'Yes.'

'How do you feel about that?'

'OK.' Lucy forced a smile into her voice. 'It's what we planned.'

'So this baby was planned?'

'Yes. Will and I decided we'd like to have a baby together, but we'll just remain friends.'

There was a significant pause. 'Are you really happy with that arrangement, Lucy?'

She couldn't give a direct answer. 'Dad, I knew what Will was like when we started talking about this.'

There was another sigh on the other end of the line. Another pause. 'My big concern is that you must look after yourself.'

'I will, Dad. I promise.'

'I'm afraid I have to go now. Come and see me soon. Come for dinner.'

'I will. Thanks. Love you, Dad.'

Lucy was about to disconnect when her father spoke again. 'Lucy.'

The tone of his voice made her grip the phone more tightly. 'Yes?'

'I've always thought that if two very good friends fall in love, they should grab their good luck with both hands.'

Lucy couldn't think of anything to say.

'It's the greatest happiness this life can offer,' her father said.

And then he hung up.

CHAPTER TEN

IT HAD been a long hot day and a summer storm broke late in the afternoon. By the time Lucy closed up the surgery, it was raining and thunder rumbled in the distance.

It was still raining heavily half an hour later when she set out for Tambaroora. She was nervous, but she was determined to see Will this evening before she chickened out again.

It wasn't yet six but the sky was already dark and her windscreen wipers had to work overtime. The winding, unsealed country roads had quickly turned to slippery mud so, despite her impatience, she had to drive very slowly and carefully.

She could see wet sheep clustered beneath the inadequate shelter of skinny gum trees. Thunder rolled all around the valley and white flashes of sheet lightning lit the entire sky. She was relieved when she finally saw the lights of Tambaroora homestead.

As soon as she pulled up at the bottom of the front steps she made a dash for the veranda.

Will's mother, wearing an apron, greeted Lucy warmly and she could smell the tempting aroma of dinner cooking. 'You were brave to come out in this terrible storm,' she said.

'I know it's not a good time to be calling, but I was hoping to see Will.'

Jessie Carruthers smiled. 'He's told us your news.'

'Are you pleased?' Lucy asked.

'Very,' Jessie said. 'Especially when Will told us that you were so happy about it.'

Lucy held her breath, wondering if Jessie would make a reference to her previous pregnancy with her elder son. But she said simply, 'Will and his father have spent the whole afternoon out in the shed, working on the tractor.' She smiled. 'You know what boys are like with their toys.'

'You must be pleased that Will's taking an interest.'

'Well, yes, I am, actually, and he's still at

it. Robert came back a few minutes ago and he's in the shower. But Will's still out there, tinkering away.'

'I'll drive over and see if I can find him.'

'All right, love.' Jessie gave a wistful sigh. 'I suppose you're as disappointed as I am that Will's going away again so soon.'

'Well…I'm not surprised.'

'You might be able to talk him out of it, Lucy.'

Lucy stared at Will's mother, surprised. 'I could try, I guess. But I'm afraid it might be like trying to persuade a leopard to change his spots.'

Jessie frowned. 'I don't understand young people these days.'

'I'm not sure that we understand ourselves,' Lucy admitted.

Jessie accepted this with a resigned shrug. 'Anyway, it's lovely to see you, dear. And you must join us for dinner.'

Lucy thanked her and then drove her ute around to the back of the house, past garden beds filled with blue hydrangeas and a vegetable plot where tomatoes and fennel and silverbeet had been drenched by the heavy rain.

From there, she went through a gate, then followed muddy wheel tracks across a wet paddock till she reached the old galvanised iron structure that served as a machinery shed.

There was a light inside the shed and her heart was as fluttery as a bird's as she turned off her ute's motor. Consciously gathering her courage, she hurried to the lighted doorway.

The rain was making a dreadful racket on the iron roof so there was no point in knocking. She went inside and the smell of diesel oil seemed to close in around her. The shed was almost a museum of ageing tractors and the walls were hung with relics from the past—an ancient riding harness, the metal steps of a sulky, even a wagon wheel.

She saw the top of Will's head as he bent over a modern tractor engine, tapping at it with a spanner.

The storm battered against the iron walls and Lucy began to wonder why she'd thought it was so important to hurry over here. She'd never seen Will working at any kind of mechanical task and she felt like an intruder. He was probably trying to get the job finished by dinner time and he might not appreciate her interruption.

'Will,' she called.

He looked up and his eyebrows lifted with surprise. 'Lucy, what are you doing here?'

Setting down the spanner, he grabbed at a rag and wiped his hands as he hurried around the front of the tractor.

His shoulders stretched the seams of a faded blue cotton shirt. Weather-beaten jeans rode low on his hips and everything about him looked perfect to her.

He smiled and she felt a familiar ripple of yearning, but she felt something deeper too— the painful awareness of how very deeply she loved this man.

That love hurt.

'Is everything all right?' he asked.

'I'm fine, Will. Still pregnant.'

His face relaxed visibly.

'I needed to talk to you, but it's been a busy day. I came as soon as I could get away.'

'You should be sitting down.' He frowned as he looked about the untidy shed. 'We used to have a chair out here somewhere. Oh, there it is.'

He freed a metal chair from a tangle of tools in the corner and wiped cobwebs and dust from it with a rag. Then he carefully tested the chair's legs and, finally satisfied, he set it on the concrete floor.

Lucy thanked him and sat with necessary dignity.

She thought, for a moment, that Will would remain standing, towering over her and making her more nervous than ever, but he found a perch on the tractor's running board.

'So you've had a busy day,' he said, still wiping the last of the grease from his hands. 'Have you had time to tell anyone your good news?'

'Gina called in at lunch time and I told her about the baby. She's over the moon, of course. I rang my dad, and I spoke to your mother just now. Everyone seems really pleased.'

She dropped her gaze to her hands, clenched white-knuckled in her lap. 'But they're all a little mystified when they realise you're still going away, Will. Somehow we're going to have to explain our arrangement to them. They need to understand we won't be living together as traditional parents.'

She wished she didn't feel so sick and nervous. Outside, a gust of wind caught a metal door, slamming it against the shed wall.

'Actually, I've changed my mind about going away.'

Lucy's head snapped up and she stared at him. Her heart hammered and she wasn't sure she could trust what she'd heard.

'I've rung the PNG mining company,' he said. 'It's all arranged. I'm not going.'

'But I've just spoken to your mother and she—'

'Mum doesn't know about it yet. My father should be telling her right now.'

'Oh? I...I see.'

She felt faint. Dizzy.

'I've spent most of the afternoon talking about it with my father,' Will said, 'and it's all planned. I'm going to take care of this place, while Dad takes Mum on the trip of a lifetime to Europe.'

Oh...so his reason for staying had nothing to do with her or the baby.

Lucy tried to swallow her disappointment. 'Your mother will love that,' she said. 'I heard her plying Mattie with questions about Italy at the christening. She's dying to go overseas.'

The faintest of smiles glimmered in his eyes. 'And I don't want to be too far away from you.'

Lucy's heart leapt like an over-eager puppy, bouncing with too much excitement.

'I need to keep an eye on you now,' he said.

'I see.' She twisted her hands in her lap, hating the realisation that at any minute now she might burst into tears from tension.

'I want to court you.'

'Court me?'

Lucy was sure she'd misheard Will, but then she saw a flush creeping upwards from his shirt collar.

'I thought that perhaps we should go out on dates like other couples,' he said. 'To find out—'

He stopped, as if he was searching for the right words.

'To find out if we can fall in love?' Lucy supplied in a cold little voice she hardly recognised.

'Yes,' he said, clearly grateful that she understood.

Lucy was devastated. She was fighting to breathe. Will had been her friend since high school. For heaven's sake, he'd slept with her on two occasions. He was the father of her baby, and yet he still needed to take her out on dates to find out if he loved her.

A cruel icy hand squeezed around her heart.

'I really don't think dating would work,' she said, miserably aware that her life and her silly dreams were falling to pieces. 'If you were ever going to fall in love with me, it would have happened by now.'

'But, Lucy, I—'

'No!' she cried and the word sounded as if it had been ripped from her.

She held up her hands to stop him. 'I'm an expert when it comes to falling in love, Will.' Despair launched her to her feet.

Will's face was as pained as it was puzzled. He stood too.

Tears clogged Lucy's throat and she gulped to force them down. 'I know all about trying to manipulate love.'

'What do you mean?'

She saw the colour flee from Will's face and for a moment she almost retreated. Why should she force Will to hear her confession?

He wasn't going to PNG any more. Perhaps that was enough. She should be grateful for small mercies.

But no, she'd promised herself that she wouldn't be a coward. Will was, after all, her baby's father. Her confession wouldn't change that.

She took a deep breath and dived in. 'I tried to make you fall in love with me once before, Will, but it didn't work.'

Dismayed, he shook his head. 'I don't understand.'

'I'm telling you something rather terrible, actually.' She fixed her gaze on a huge muddy tractor tyre. 'I started going out with Josh because I was hoping you'd hear about it and be jealous.'

She heard the shocked sound Will made, but she couldn't look at him.

'My plan backfired,' she said. 'Josh was more than I'd bargained for.' Her cheeks flamed. 'Then I discovered I was pregnant.'

Shyly, she lifted her gaze.

Will's eyes were wild, but he held himself very still, hands fisted. 'Please tell me that Josh didn't force you.'

'No, he didn't use force, but I was young and he was very persuasive.'

A harsh sound escaped him. He began to pace, but then he whirled around to face her. 'Is that why you became engaged to Josh? Because you found out you were pregnant?'

'Yes.' Tears spilled suddenly.

Tears of shame.

And relief.

It was so good to have her confession out in the open at last.

'I was such an idiot, Will, and I ended up being trapped by my mistakes.'

'Goose.' With a choked cry, Will closed the gap between them, pulling her roughly into his arms. 'I thought you were in love with Josh.'

She shook her head and pressed her damp face into the curve of his neck.

A groan broke from him. He enfolded her against the wonderful warmth and strength of his chest and she could feel his heart knocking against hers.

'I was so angry with Josh,' he said. 'I was scared he wouldn't love you enough. Scared he wouldn't try hard enough to make you happy and keep you happy.'

'Oh, Will.'

'We had a terrible row just before he took off in the plane.'

Lucy leaned back and looked up at him, saw horror and tenderness warring in his eyes. 'How awful.'

'I still feel sick every time I think of it.'

'That's a terrible burden to have carried all these years.'

'Yes. I've blamed myself for a long time.'

She wanted to ease the pain in his eyes. 'But it wasn't your fault. Josh always made his own decisions.'

He nodded sadly. 'Short of holding a gun to his head, I couldn't have stopped him.'

Lucy shivered and took a step out of the comforting circle of Will's arms. She thought about the way that one event had shaped their lives. Wished that her confession had brought her a sense of peace.

It would be too much to expect a similar avowal of love from Will.

'It was nice of you to offer to court me,' she said and she pressed a fist against her aching heart, as if somehow she could stop it from bleeding. 'But if you don't mind, I think I'd rather not go on those dates.'

'But—' Will began.

Lucy hurried on. 'I think it would be better if we stick to friendship.'

'Why?'

Why? How could he ask that? After everything he'd had to say on the subject of friendship.

Lucy gave a shrug of annoyance. 'We've managed very well as friends for a long time now.'

'But you said you loved me.'

Oh, God.

Her heart stopped.

Will sent her a bewildered little smile. 'You don't have a monopoly on mistakes, Lucy.'

She felt rooted to the floor and her body flashed hot and cold. 'What do you mean? Have you made mistakes?'

His smile tilted with faint irony. 'Self delusion tops my list.'

Tears burned her eyes but she dashed them away because she wanted to see the raw emotion in Will's face. She'd never seen anything more beautiful.

'I've always cared about you, Lucy. I've always wanted to make you happy, but somehow—' He gave a sad shake of his head. 'Some *crazy* how— I couldn't see what that caring really meant.'

His eyes shimmered brightly. 'I made my first terrible mistake when you kissed me goodbye.' He reached for her hand. 'That was the kiss to end all kisses. I should have bound you to my side and never let you out of my sight. Instead, I was a fool, and I took off overseas.'

'I didn't know you liked that kiss,' she whispered.

He gave an abrupt laugh. 'I tried to tell myself I'd read it wrongly. That maybe you were a particularly talented kisser, and that you kissed everyone that fabulously.'

'Not a chance, Will.'

'I spent far too much time on that first trip trying to forget you.' He tucked a curl behind her ear. 'I think that was about mistake number thirty-three.'

Lucy could hear the frantic beating of her heart and she realised the rain and the wind had stopped. 'Were there any more mistakes?'

'Dozens,' he admitted with a rueful smile. 'Every time I talked to you about friendship I was being an idiot.'

She felt the warmth of his fingers stroking her cheek. He touched her chin, lifted her face so that she was lost in the silver of his eyes. 'We should have been talking about love, Lucy.'

She couldn't speak.

'I love you,' he said again, and she tried to smile but she sobbed instead.

'I love you, Goose.'

Will kissed her damp eyelashes. 'You're the most important person in the world to me. That's got to be love, hasn't it?'

She could feel a smile growing inside her. 'It does sound promising.'

His eyes shone. 'I want to protect you and your baby.'

'Our baby,' Lucy corrected, and yes, she was definitely smiling on the outside now.

'I want to make you happy every day. I want to sleep with you every night and have break-fast with you every morning.'

'That definitely sounds like more than friend-ship, Will.' Smiling widely, she reached up and touched the grainy skin of his jaw. 'And I should know. I've loved you for so long I don't know any other way to be.'

His hands framed her face and his eyes were shining. With love. 'Do you think you could marry me, Lucy?'

She smiled as a fleeting memory from a time long ago flitted through her mind—pages of a school book filled with her handwriting: *Lucy Carruthers. Mrs Lucy Carruthers.*

'I'd love to marry you, Will.'

He punched the air and let out a war whoop. 'Sorry,' he said, 'but I couldn't help it. I just feel so damn happy.'

And then Will kissed her.

He poured his happiness and his love and his soul into the kiss and Lucy discovered that an old shed with a leaky roof was the most romantic place in the world.

CHAPTER ELEVEN

THEIR baby chose to be born on a crisp clear winter's day in July.

Will rose early when it was still dark. He built up the fire in the living room so it could heat the whole house and, with that task completed, he returned briefly to his bedroom doorway. He smiled at the sight of Lucy still sleeping, the tips of her blonde curls just showing above the warm duvet.

He continued on to the back door, donned a thick, fleecy lined coat and heavy boots and went out into the frosty dawn to the first of his daily tasks—checking the condition of the pregnant ewes and any lambs born during the night.

The sun was a pale glimmer on the distant horizon and the sky was grey and bleak, his breath a white cloud. Grass underfoot was crisp with frost. Last week he'd started spreading hay and feeding their flock with winter grain stored in their silos.

Farming was constant work, but Will loved his new life. Loved being in the outdoors, loved working with the animals and the land, planning the seasonal calendar of tasks required to keep the business running smoothly.

Best of all, he loved sharing every aspect of farm life with Lucy.

His wife was a walking encyclopaedia when it came to sheep and there'd been plenty of times when he'd had to humbly ask for her advice. But lately Lucy had been endearingly absent-minded, her attention turning more and more frequently inward to their baby.

And that was the other grand thing about Will's life these days—the pregnancy.

Of all the adventures he'd enjoyed, this surely had to be the greatest. Will never tired of watching the happy light in Lucy's eyes, or the proud way she carried herself as their baby grew and grew. Never tired of seeing the baby's movements ripple across her belly, or feeling stronger and stronger kicks beneath his hand.

Together Will and Lucy had converted his

old bedroom into a sunny nursery, with yellow walls and bright curtains and a farmyard frieze.

'The kid will only have to look out the window to see a farmyard,' Will had teased.

But Lucy wanted farm animals so that was what they had, along with a wicker rocking chair and a fitted carpet, a handmade quilt lovingly pieced by his mother, as well as a white cot with a soft lamb's wool rug.

And any day their baby would arrive and they'd be a family.

At last.

This morning, Will refilled the water troughs and pulled down extra bales of hay which he spread for the pregnant ewes, and he checked the three healthy lambs that had been born overnight.

Satisfied that all was well, he returned to the warm kitchen, ready for breakfast, and found Lucy already up and busy at the stove. His heart lifted as it always did when he saw her.

She was wearing one of his baggy old football jerseys—blue and yellow stripes—over blue maternity jeans and her feet were encased in fluffy slippers.

'Hey there,' she said, turning to smile as he entered.

He came up behind her, slipped his arms around her and kissed her just below the ear. 'How's my favourite farmer's wife?'

'Fat, pregnant and in the kitchen.' Lucy laughed as she leaned back against him and lifted her lips to kiss the underside of his jaw.

'That's exactly how I want her,' Will growled softly, dipping his lips to trap hers for a longer, deeper kiss.

When they sat down to eat, he was surprised to see that Lucy had nothing besides a mug of tea.

'Aren't you hungry?' he asked, feeling guilty that he'd already started on his mushrooms and toast.

She smiled and shook her head.

'That's not like you.'

'It's just a precaution.'

He felt a stab of alarm. 'A precaution?'

'I've been having contractions.'

Will almost choked on his food. 'Lucy. My God, what are you doing, sitting here watching me eat breakfast? I've got to get you to hospital.'

'It's OK, Will. There's no rush.' She smiled at his dismay. 'The contractions are still twenty minutes apart.'

'Twenty minutes?' He couldn't have been

gone much longer than twenty minutes. 'How many have you had? When did they start?'

'They began around four this morning.' She must have seen the panic in his face and she laughed. 'Don't worry. With a first baby it might take ages. I could go on like this all day.'

'But you might not. And it's a good hour's drive to the hospital.' How could she sit there looking so calm? Was she crazy? 'Shouldn't you ring the doctor?'

Lucy nodded. 'I'll ring him when I'm certain that it's not a false—'

She didn't finish the sentence. Without warning, her entire manner changed. She sat very still, her face concentrated. Inward. Breathing steadily but deeply. In, out. In, out.

Nervously, Will watched his wife. If Lucy was in labour he wanted her safely in hospital, surrounded by a team of medical experts.

'Phew,' she said at last. 'That was stronger.'

'What about the timing? How far was it from the last one?'

She looked at the clock. 'Gosh, it was only ten minutes.'

'That's it then.' Will lurched to his feet. 'Come on, we've got to leave *now*.'

Lucy caught his hand. 'Are you sure you don't want your breakfast?'

'Not now.'

Lucy's suitcase had been packed and ready for some weeks. 'I'll put your bag in the car,' he said, grateful that they'd bought a comfortable all wheel drive station wagon some months back.

'OK. I'd better get the rest of my things.'

He gave her a tremulous smile, but there was nothing tremulous about Lucy's grin. Her face was alight with exhilaration. 'Isn't this exciting, Will? Our baby's coming.'

A tidal wave of emotions flooded him. Glorious love for her. Chilling fear and a desperate need to protect her. Closing the gap between them, Will took her in his arms. 'I love you so much.'

'I know, my darling.' She touched a gentle hand to his cheek.

He clasped her to him, his precious, precious girl. 'I'm going to get you there safely, Lucy. I promise.'

Will drove with his heart in his mouth. Despite Lucy's calm assertion that all was well, he knew her contractions were getting stronger and he suspected they seemed to be coming closer. He could tell by her bouts of deep breathing and the way she massaged her stomach and he knew she needed all her concentration just to get through the pain.

Now he cursed himself for not making better contingency plans. He'd tried to suggest that Lucy stay in town with her father for these final weeks, but she'd insisted she'd be fine. He'd read the books on childbirth. He knew every case was different. Hell, he shouldn't have listened to her.

'Sorry, this is going to be bumpy,' he said as they came to the old wooden bridge crossing Willow Creek.

'It's OK,' she said, smiling bravely. 'I'm between contractions.'

But they had only just made it to the other side of the bridge when Lucy gave a loud gasp.

'What's happening?' Will sent her a frantic sideways glance.

She couldn't answer. She was too busy panting.

Panting? Didn't that mean—?

'Lucy!' he cried, aghast. 'You're not in transition already, are you?'

'I think I might be,' she said when she'd recovered her breath. For the first time she looked frightened. 'First babies shouldn't come this fast.'

She no longer sounded calm. All too soon, her eyes were closed, her face twisted with pain, one fist clutched low, beneath the bump of the baby.

Oh, God. They were still thirty minutes from the hospital. Will felt helpless and distraught as he pressed his foot down on the accelerator. His heart began to shred into tiny pieces.

As they rounded the next curve, Lucy cried out and the guttural animal force of the sound horrified Will. Seizing the first possible chance to pull off the road, he brought the car to a halt.

'I'll ring for an ambulance,' he said, already reaching for his mobile phone.

Lucy nodded and managed a weak smile. 'Good idea. I…I think the baby's coming.'

Will choked back a cry of dismay.

The voice on the other end of the emergency hotline was amazingly calm as he explained their situation and gave the necessary details, including their location.

'The ambulance is on its way,' he said, wishing he felt more relieved.

Lucy nodded and fumbled with her door handle.

'What are you doing?' he cried as her door swung open. Had she gone mad?

Leaping out of his seat, he hurried around the car and found his wife slumped against its side, panting furiously.

Helplessly, he tried to stroke her arm, to soothe her, but she pushed him away and shook her head. He stood beside her, scared she might collapse, arms at the ready.

When the panting was over she opened her eyes. She looked exhausted. Sweat beaded her upper lip. 'It's too painful sitting in that front seat. I think I need to get into the back.'

'Right,' he said, biting back his fear. 'Let me help you.'

He hated to see Lucy's pain as he struggled to help her with the unwieldy transfer. Her contractions were fast and furious now and there seemed to be no spaces between them. He found a cushion for her head and helped her to lie along the back seat.

In a tiny lull, she sent him a wan smile. 'I'm sorry. I didn't dream it would be this fast.'

'Our baby can't wait to get here,' he said, doing his best to sound calm. 'He knows what a great mother he's getting.'

After the next contraction Lucy said quite calmly, 'Do we have any towels? Can you get the baby blanket out of the suitcase, Will?'

The baby blanket? He must have looked shocked.

'In case we beat the ambulance,' she said.

No, no. That couldn't happen, surely?

But by the time he'd found a beach towel—freshly washed, thank God—and retrieved the baby blanket from the hospital suitcase, Lucy was panting so hard she was in danger of hyperventilating.

'It's coming!' she cried. 'Will, help me!'

With frantic hands, she was trying to push her clothing away in preparation for the baby's imminent birth.

Oh, God it was actually happening. This was it. The birth of their child. On the side of the road beneath a river red gum.

Over the past nine months Will had imagined this birth, but he'd always pictured himself watching from the sidelines while medical experts did the honours. Mostly he'd seen himself emerging from a delivery room wearing a green hospital gown and a beaming smile as he shared the good news with their waiting families.

But, to his surprise, as soon as he accepted that he had no choice about where their baby might be born, an unexpected sense of calm settled over him. The terror was still there like a savage claw in the pit of his stomach, but Lucy needed him and he had to pull himself together.

Before they'd left home, he'd promised to protect her. He'd never dreamed what that might involve, but this was the moment of reckoning. She needed him to be calm and competent.

He could do this. For her. For their baby.

'OK, Goose, you're doing really well,' he said as he settled the folded towel beneath her.

Lucy merely grunted and went red in the face. Her right hand was braced against the back of the front seat. With the other she clung to an overhead strap.

She held her breath and grimaced, and Will couldn't bear to think how much this was hurting her.

Then he saw the crown of their baby's head.

Lucy finished pushing and let out an enormous gasp as she wilted back against the cushion.

'Good girl,' he said. 'Our baby has dark hair.'

She tried to smile. 'I'm going to have to push, Will. I can't hold back any longer. If you can see the baby's head, that means I can push without doing any harm.'

'Tell me what to do,' he said, ashamed of the hint of fear that trembled in his voice.

'Just be ready to catch. Support the head.' Lucy sent him an encouraging smile before her belly constricted and she was overtaken by the force of another contraction.

Inch by inch, their baby emerged.

'You're brilliant, darling,' he told her. 'I can see the eyebrows, eyes, nose.' Excitement bubbled through him now. 'I can see the mouth. It's kinda scrunched but cute.' He held his hands at the ready. 'OK, the head's out.'

Somehow he managed to sound calm. 'It's turning.'

With the next of Lucy's grunts, he gently but firmly held his child's warm damp head. He saw a slippery shoulder emerge and then another. In the space of three heartbeats, he was steadying his baby as it slipped from its safe maternal cocoon.

He and Lucy had chosen not to know the baby's sex, but now his heart leapt with incredible joy.

'Lucy, it's a boy.'

'A boy?' Her eyes opened and a radiant smile lit up her face. 'Oh, the little darling. I had a feeling he was a boy.'

Will's throat was too choked to speak as he lifted his son onto Lucy's tummy. Their son had thick dark hair, and his little arms were out-stretched, tiny fingers uncurled, as if he was reaching out for life, or bursting through the winner's tape at the end of a race.

'Oh, Will!' Lucy whispered, looking pale but happy. 'Isn't he handsome? Isn't he gorgeous?'

'He looks like a champion,' Will agreed, but then he frowned as a new fear worried him. 'Should I do anything? Is he breathing OK?'

'I think he's fine.' Lucy spoke calmly as she rubbed the baby's back and, as if to answer her, the little fellow began to cry, with a small bleat at first, then with a loud gusty wail.

She grinned. 'He's got a terrific set of lungs.'

'He's got a terrific mum,' Will said as he helped her to wrap their son in the soft white blanket dotted with yellow ducklings.

The whine of a siren sounded in the distance and Will felt a weight lift from his shoulders.

'Help is on its way,' he said.

Lucy smiled. 'I've already had all the help I

needed.' With a wondrous, soft expression she touched the top of their son's head. 'Thank you, Will. Thank you.'

By midday Lucy was happily ensconced in a private room in Willowbank Hospital in a lovely big white bed, with her darling baby boy, wrapped in a blue bunny rug, beside her.

Surrounded by flowers.

Surrounded by so many flowers, in fact, that she felt like a celebrity.

'You *are* a celebrity,' Gina told her. 'Think how many puppies and kittens and ponies and sheep you've looked after in this district. Every household in Willowbank is thrilled that you now have your own dear little boy.'

'And he's such a beauty,' said Mattie, gazing fondly at the sleeping little cherub in the crib.

Lucy watched the soft glow in Mattie's eyes, watched the reverent way Mattie stared at little Nathan, at the way she gently touched his cheek, and she felt a tiny current of excitement inside her.

The excitement grew as Lucy saw the meaningful glance Mattie sent to her husband, and a thrilled shiver ran through her as she witnessed the warm intimacy of Jake's answering smile.

They had important news. Baby news. Lucy could feel it in her bones.

'Mattie…' she said, but then she stopped, not sure how to continue.

Mattie smiled, almost as if she was encouraging Lucy to question her.

'You're not?' Lucy began and then she stopped again.

'Yes!' Mattie exclaimed and she was smiling broadly now. She reached for Jake's hand and their fingers twined. Her eyes glowed. 'I'm three months pregnant.'

'And we couldn't be happier,' said Jake, backing up his words with a huge grin.

The room suddenly erupted with excited questions and congratulations.

'That's the most perfect news,' Lucy said and she knew she was beaming with joy as she looked around the room, filled with the people who were so important to her—Gina and Tom, Mattie and Jake—and Will, her darling Will. And now, dear little Nathan William Carruthers.

'There's going to be a whole new generation of the Willow Creek gang,' Tom said, grinning.

Everyone laughed and, from his vantage point near the door, Will sent his wife a conspiratorial wink. He thought Lucy had never looked more beautiful.

He looked around the room at their friends and he marvelled at the sense of completion he felt. He thought about the long and roundabout journey he'd taken to reach this satisfying moment.

And he knew at last that he was finally home.

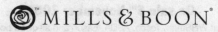

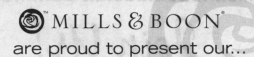

MILLS & BOON®

are proud to present our...

Book of the Month

The Wicked Baron
by Sarah Mallory
from Mills & Boon® Historical

The *ton* can talk of nothing but Luke Ainslowe's
return from Paris – and his reputation as an
expert seducer of women. Innocent Carlotta
Durini refuses to become the Baron's next
conquest, but what if the Wicked Baron
refuses to take no for an answer'?

Available 2nd October 2009

Something to say about our
Book of the Month?
Tell us what you think!
millsandboon.co.uk/community

millsandboon.co.uk Community

Join Us!

The Community is the perfect place to meet and chat to kindred spirits who love books and reading as much as you do, but it's also the place to:

- Get the inside scoop from authors about their latest books
- Learn how to write a romance book with advice from our editors
- Help us to continue publishing the best in women's fiction
- Share your thoughts on the books we publish
- Befriend other users

Forums: Interact with each other as well as authors, editors and a whole host of other users worldwide.

Blogs: Every registered community member has their own blog to tell the world what they're up to and what's on their mind.

Book Challenge: We're aiming to read 5,000 books and have joined forces with The Reading Agency in our inaugural Book Challenge.

Profile Page: Showcase yourself and keep a record of your recent community activity.

Social Networking: We've added buttons at the end of every post to share via digg, Facebook, Google, Yahoo, technorati and de.licio.us.

www.millsandboon.co.uk

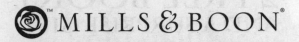

2 FREE BOOKS
AND A SURPRISE GIFT

We would like to take this opportunity to thank you for reading this Mills & Boon® book by offering you the chance to take TWO more specially selected books from the Romance series absolutely FREE! We're also making this offer to introduce you to the benefits of the Mills & Boon® Book Club™—

- **FREE home delivery**
- **FREE gifts and competitions**
- **FREE monthly Newsletter**
- **Exclusive Mills & Boon Book Club offers**
- **Books available before they're in the shops**

Accepting these FREE books and gift places you under no obligation to buy, you may cancel at any time, even after receiving your free shipment. Simply complete your details below and return the entire page to the address below. You don't even need a stamp!

YES Please send me 2 free Romance books and a surprise gift. I understand that unless you hear from me, I will receive 5 superb new stories every month including two 2-in-1 books priced at £4.99 each and a single book priced at £3.19, postage and packing free. I am under no obligation to purchase any books and may cancel my subscription at any time. The free books and gift will be mine to keep in any case.

Ms/Mrs/Miss/Mr_____ Initials _____

Surname _____

Address _____

_____

_____ Postcode _____

Send this whole page to: Mills & Boon Book Club, Free Book Offer, FREEPOST NAT 10298, Richmond, TW9 1BR

Offer valid in UK only and is not available to current Mills & Boon Book Club subscribers to this series. Overseas and Eire please write for details.. We reserve the right to refuse an application and applicants must be aged 18 years or over. Only one application per household. Terms and prices subject to change without notice. Offer expires 31st December 2009. As a result of this application, you may receive offers from Harlequin Mills & Boon and other carefully selected companies. If you would prefer not to share in this opportunity please write to The Data Manager, PO Box 676, Richmond, TW9 1WU.

Mills & Boon® is a registered trademark owned by Harlequin Mills & Boon Limited.
The Mills & Boon® Book Club™ is being used as a trademark.